the Other Brother

A
RED DOOR
NOVEL

DYAN LAYNE

ISBN: 978-1-7364765-1-2
ASIN: B098M4LCPC

Cover photography: Michelle Lancaster,
@lanefotograf, michellelancaster.com
Cover model: Tommy Pearce
Cover designer: Lori Jackson, Lori Jackson Design
Editing: Michelle Morgan, FictionEdit.com
Formatting: Stacey Blake, Champagne Book Design

This book contains subject matter which may be sensitive or triggering to some and is intended for mature audiences.

Things happen as they're meant to.

There's no avoiding your destiny...

Dillon Byrne always believed in fate.

He would meet someone. Fall in love. Be a family.

All in that order.

Sometimes fate has other plans...

Life changes in an instant. Love is lost.

But how do you let go of the life you once had?

To appreciate the magic of a brand new beginning, you have to make peace with the ending first.

Endings are never easy, but a beautiful beginning is destined to follow, isn't it?

And just maybe out of sorrow, joy can grow...

Playlist

Absofacto | *Dissolve - acoustic*

Limp Bizkit | *Eat You Alive*

Pearl Jam | *Once*

FINNEAS | *Life Moves On*

Two Feet | *Love Is a Bitch*

Two Feet | *You?*

Hanson | *MMMBop*

Meat Puppets | *Lake of Fire*

Harry Styles | *Sign of the Times*

Hozier | *The Parting Glass*

Chase Holfelder | *Danny Boy - Minor Key Version*

Brian Boru Irish Pipe Band | *Amazing Grace - Bagpipes*

BYU Vocal Point | *Danny Boy*

Mad Season | *All Alone*

Lindsey Stirling | *My Immortal*

Our Last Night | *Sunrise*

Mourning Ritual (feat. Peter Dreimanis) | *Bad Moon Rising*

Bexley | *Run Rabbit Run*

Nothing But Thieves | *Your Blood*

Bring Me The Horizon | *Can You Feel My Heart*

ZABO | *Breathe*

Sixx:A.M. | *Life is Beautiful*
A Perfect Circle | *The Outsider*
Bring Me The Horizon | *One Day The Only Butterflies Left Will
Be In Your Chest*
Architects | *Dead Butterflies*
HELLYEAH | *Welcome Home*
Ciara | *Paint It, Black*
Alter Bridge | *Watch Over You*
A Perfect Circle | *Weak And Powerless*
John Legend (feat. Gary Clark Jr.) | *Wild*
Stabbing Westward | *Shame*
Matt Maeson | *The Hearse*
Tommee Profitt feat. Fleurie | *In The End - Mellen Gi Remix*
Bien | *Last Man Standing*
Gotye | *Hearts A Mess*
Alice In Chains | *Down In A Hole*
Hozier | *Talk*
Matt Maeson | *Dancing After Death*
Shawn Mendes | *Wonder*
Tommee Profitt feat. Brooke | *Can't Help Falling In Love - Dark*
Linkin Park | *One More Light*
1920's Wurlitzer Carousel Organ | *Who Made Me Love You*
Harry Styles | *Watermelon Sugar*
Måneskin | *FOR YOUR LOVE*
FINNEAS | *Die Alone*
Fuel | *Hemorrhage (In My Hands)*
Saint Claire | *Haunted*
Two Feet | *Fire In My Head*

PALESKIN | *Joy Is Temporary*
Dropkick Murphys | *I'm Shipping Up To Boston*
Nine Inch Nails | *In This Twilight*
Dropkick Murphys | *Cadence To Arms*
Stabbing Westward | *Waking Up Beside You*
Lewis Capaldi | *Someone You Loved*
Two Feet | *Call Me, I Still Love You*
Our Last Night | *Astronaut In The Ocean*
Puddle of Mudd | *Blurry*
Alice In Chains | *Rain When I Die*
Bruno Mars | *Talking to the Moon*
Ewan J Phillips | *I Wish I Was the Moon*
U2 | *With Or Without You*
Dropkick Murphys | *I Wish You Were Here*
Dropkick Murphys | *Kiss Me I'm #!@'faced*
Ruelle | *The Other Side*
Dropkick Murphys | *Rose Tattoo*
Billie Eilish | *Six Feet Under*
Velvet Revolver | *Fall to Pieces*
Alice In Chains | *Black Gives Way To Blue*
Dave Matthew Band | Crash Into Me
Staind | *Tangled up in You*
Disturbed | *Hold on to Memories*
Of Monsters and Men | *Lakehouse*
Meghan Trainor (feat. John Legend) | *Like I'm Gonna Lose You*

Author's Note

This book contains subject matter which may be sensitive or triggering to some readers and is intended for mature audiences.

While you don't need to read the previous books in the series, as this is a standalone novel featuring a unique romance, it is *highly* recommended. *Red Door* is a series of interconnected standalone novels. All of the main characters reappear and some storylines connect throughout each book. For the best experience, the series should be read in order.

If you are following the series, **The Other Brother** begins shortly after the epilogue in **Maelstrom**.

For Melissa Rain, and she knows why.
I love you.

the Other Brother

Prologue

Kyan, where the fuck are you, man?

How many more of these never-ending interviews did they have on the schedule today anyway? He was hungover from partying at the club opening last night. The pounding hammers and buzzing saws pummeled into his already-throbbing brain. The smell of paint and varnish was making him gag. Dillon reached for some ibuprofen and a bottle of water to wash it down with.

He glanced around the restaurant, still under construction, that would bear his father's name and took a seat at a table made from two sawhorses and a sheet of plywood. It was hard to believe this place would be ready to open in just a few short weeks. His brother said everything was right on schedule, though.

She tentatively pulled the door open and stuck her head inside, looking right and then left, as if she wasn't sure she was at the right place. Straight dark-blonde hair fell past her breasts, the ends curled into waves. Young. Fresh-faced. No makeup. She wasn't short, but she wasn't tall either, maybe five-four, and slender. Black pants, white shirt, black flats.

This girl was an unspoiled natural beauty.

Fucking gorgeous.

Dillon glanced at the schedule of interviews in front of him and pulled her application off the top of the stack, quickly scanning it before she reached the table. There wasn't much on it. Recent high school grad enrolled at the university. One previous job at the Dairy Queen in Crossfield. He'd never heard of the place.

The girl carefully maneuvered her way into the bar area. Dillon stood and extended his hand. "Linnea? I hope I'm pronouncing that right." He shook her hand. It was so tiny compared to his. Soft and warm. "Dillon Byrne."

She tucked her hair behind her ear and shyly smiled. Her eyes were a stunning shade of light green. "Hi, and yes, you said it right."

They sat across from each other. Dillon loosened his tie. It was hot in here and the damn thing was strangling him. "So, Linnea, did you move to the city for school?"

"No, but I am starting online classes in the fall." Her eyes flicked up to his. "I bought a little place over on Oak Street. Near Eighth. By the park. So, this is home now."

He was impressed. How does an eighteen-year-old have the wherewithal, not to mention the smarts, to purchase real estate in an up-and-coming neighborhood in the city? This girl intrigued him.

"Family?"

"Uh, no. My grandmother passed away, so it's just me."

That explained the how. The neighborhood she lived in, while just eight blocks away, leaned toward the seedier side. Gentrification was creeping in her direction, though, so she'd actually made a very wise investment. It worried him that she was on her own in a big city with no one to look out for her. Dillon decided right then and there he was giving her a job here at Charley's, and he'd keep an eye on her. Be her friend—like an older brother.

Maybe one day he could be more. But she was only eighteen and he was twenty-six. So, maybe one day was far away. She screamed virginal innocence and purity. He was anything but. Besides, it probably wasn't a good idea to get involved with the staff and he had no intention of settling down with one girl anytime in the near future—not before he was thirty anyway.

The door opened and Kyan walked in.

She took one look at him from beneath her lashes and blushing, she smiled.

Of course, she did. That's how every female on the planet reacted to his brother. He had a way with the ladies.

Kyan smiled back.

He shook his head with a chuckle.

Dillon blinked his eyes open. He looked across the bed to long brown hair splayed out on the pillow beside him, wondering why his subconscious chose to replay that day six years ago. He loved Linnea then. God, he'd been so in love with her he didn't think he'd survive it when she chose his brother.

It was his own fault. He made her a friend when he really wanted to make her more. He waited too long.

Admittedly, Dillon went a bit off the deep end after they got engaged. He must have fucked every available pussy from here to Milwaukee in an effort to forget her, which considering they lived next door wasn't exactly easy. They'd been married a couple years now, and were finally expecting their first baby in January. Took fertility treatments to make that happen too. He was genuinely happy for them.

Dillon would always love her, though. He just tucked those feelings away and locked them deep inside his heart, because Linnea was Kyan's, and he was hers.

He ran his fingers through the long brown hair beside him on the pillow. Kelsey was a good girl. They'd been seeing each other a couple months now. Longest he'd ever dated anybody. Dillon liked her a helluva lot, so maybe he could love her too. He wanted to fall in love with her, and get married and start a family of his own one day. He was thirty-two years old, for fuck's sake, with a big house that he lived in all alone.

New Year's.

Dillon would give it until his birthday. If he and Kelsey were still happy and together then, he'd marry her. Besides, she wasn't that bad in bed and gave a halfway decent blowjob. He could do worse, right?

He yanked on the long brown hair and nuzzled into her neck, kissing up the column of her throat. She rolled over toward him and smiled.

"Mm, good morning, handsome."

He took her mouth and pulled her warm naked body into his.

Yeah, he could do a helluva lot worse.

PART I

"Everything you love, you will eventually lose; but in the end love will return in a different form."
—Franz Kafka (1883-1924)

One

I t was a glorious August day. The skies were blue. Not too hot with a gentle breeze coming in off the lake. Dillon closed the door to Kelsey's apartment and filled his lungs with sweet city air. He walked almost a block to get to his car. That's the one thing he hated about coming here. There was never any goddamn parking.

Dillon hit the button on the key fob to unlock his Porsche. He smoothed his hand over the leather steering wheel and rubbed the bulge between his legs with the other, like he hadn't come three times already this morning. He should be tapped, but he knew he'd go again in the shower when he got home.

And he did.

He walked out his front door, past Kyan and Linnea's house, to the office. At least he didn't have any outside appointments today. They'd just closed a deal on a new property. Another old warehouse. Kyan was drawing up prelims to convert it to a shopping mall of sorts. It wasn't quite as big or ambitious of a project as First Avenue had been six years ago, but they'd done more than a few of these conversions since then. It would be a boon to the neighborhood it was located in.

Brendan sat in the club chair he favored like a king on his throne, sipping on coffee as he peered at the phone resting on his thigh. Dillon peeked over his shoulder. He was watching a live feed of his kid. At home. Asleep in his crib.

Who is this imposter and what the fuck happened to my cousin?

Is this what married life and fatherhood did to you? Sometimes Dillon wished they could go back to the days when they were all single, hanging out at the club every night. He missed the four of them sharing some laughs, a bottle of whiskey…amongst other entertainment. Nothing lasts forever, though, does it? It was bound to happen. One by one his brother and cousins got married. Started making babies and all that stuff. He was the only one left now. So he had to put all his effort into this thing he had going with Kelsey. No more fucking around.

"Morning, Dill." Brendan was still watching his sleeping son.

"Morning." He went over to the coffee machine and popped a pod in to brew. "Where's Ky?"

"Upstairs at his drafting table, I think."

"And Jess?"

Brendan finally set down his phone. "He's coming. Probably helping Chloe. The girls are taking the kids to the zoo today."

"Dec doesn't look like he wants to go." Dillon snorted. The baby had his thumb in his mouth and his legs tucked up beneath him.

"Yeah, he had a rough night." Brendan's gaze returned to his phone. "Teething."

Chrissakes.

He absently nodded. Every day, it became more and more obvious to Dillon that he had less and less in common with his cousins and his brother. And he hated it. He didn't have a wife or a kid, so he was excluded from contributing to just about every conversation they had. There was no more just shooting the shit. Unless they were discussing a project, it was playdates and terrible twos and birthday parties. It was like a bunch of big-ass men on *The View*, or whatever the fuck that show was housewives watched on TV in the morning, every damn day around here.

The outsider. That's what he was now.

Thank fuck Kodiak and the Venery boys were in his camp. Even though Bo was dealing with some shit of his own and Sloan had turned into a fucking hermit, locking himself inside his house for days on end. He could still count on them to hang out at the club, watch a game, or whatever.

The front door opened, and as if to drive the point home, Jesse walked into the room carrying his five-month-old daughter, Ireland. "Fuck, I need coffee bad."

Need more than that, I think.

Jesse thrust the baby at him and went to the coffee machine. Holding the infant, Dillon took a seat on the sofa. "That's my coffee there, Jess. Can you bring it over?"

"Yeah," Jesse replied.

Ireland stared up at him with her big baby-blue eyes. The same eyes they all had. Dillon couldn't help but smile at her. The baby smiled back, waving her little fists. It occurred to him then. Kelsey's eyes were brown, so it was unlikely any of their children would inherit the Byrne family trademark. That's how it worked, right? Brown beats out blue.

Not that he and Kelsey had come even remotely close to talking about the future yet. Dillon was only just starting to consider the possibility of one himself. And since he wasn't sure yet, he didn't want to be giving her any ideas.

Jesse brought the coffee over and sat next to him. Ireland remained in his arms, though. She smelled like baby shampoo and seemed fascinated with the thick, silver chain-link bracelet on his wrist. Dillon chuckled and glanced over at his cousin. Looked like he could use a break anyway.

"Tired, Jess?"

"Yeah, man." He gulped his coffee and rested his head on the back of the couch. "I can't wait for this damn tour to be over with and Tay to be back home."

Venery was on a short six-week tour, their first since Chandan was born two years ago, so the boys wouldn't be back until right after Labor Day. Probably wasn't the most convenient time for them to be away, but you never know what the future holds, right? Besides, they'd booked the tour over a year ago.

"That boy is a hellion. He never stops." Jesse picked his head back up. "I took Ireland so Chloe could get him ready to go to the zoo."

Here it comes.

Dillon raised his brow and shook his head with a grin, focusing on the baby. He held her in his hands and lifted her up to blow raspberries on her tummy. He'd much rather listen to her sweet laugh than another dissertation on the trials and tribulations of the terrible twos. He got it. Chandan was a handful, but what two-year-old boy isn't?

He tuned his cousin out. This was the kind of shit he had to listen to now. In five months, when his little human arrived, he had no doubt Kyan would be just like them. Probably worse. Dillon would lose his fucking mind then, for sure.

Ireland got another raspberry.

He got another sweet giggle.

"Dillon." Jesse tapped his shoulder. "Weren't you listening, Dill?"

Not really, no.

"Yeah, Chandan is a hellion." He rubbed noses with Ireland for Eskimo kisses.

"He didn't hear a fucking word." Brendan's booming laugh filled the room. "Party on the twenty-fourth at my house."

A string of baby drool landed on his face. "Party?"

Jesse gave him a burp cloth in exchange for his daughter.

"It's Dec's first birthday, Dill." Brendan cocked his head with a look that dared him to admit he'd forgotten the significance of the date.

"Mine too," Jesse reminded them.

"We'll grill some steaks. Have a few beers. Eat some cake."

Sounds like a swell time. Can't wait.

Family parties weren't quite the same anymore. Just another occasion where he'd get to be the odd man out. An empty lap for Chand, Dec, or Ireland to sit on for a few moments to give their parents a break. But they were his family, and he loved them. Their celebrations belonged to him too.

"Yeah, course I'll be there."

"Bring Kelsey," Brendan commanded.

Did he have to? Would it make them more comfortable or something if he wasn't the lone bachelor at the party?

"It's a work night for her. We'll see."

Kelsey was a paralegal—or was it a legal assistant? Legal secretary? Dillon couldn't remember exactly what her title was, but she worked at one of the big, fancy law firms downtown. That's how he met her. He'd gone there to sign documents on a business deal with one of their clients.

"You never bring her around, Dill. How are we supposed to get to know your girl?"

Because maybe he wasn't ready for that. Not yet. Bring a girl around your family and she starts planning a wedding in her head. And between Linnea and Chloe, she'd get a lot of encouragement.

"I said, we'll see."

Fifteen minutes later, said encouragement walked into the room. Chloe balanced Chandan, dressed and ready for the zoo, on her hip. He noticed the starting swell of a baby bump, a gentle curve to Linnea's abdomen, beneath the fabric of her tank sundress. It made him smile to see her so radiant and happy. That's all he ever wanted her to be. Happy. And she was.

"Hey, gorgeous." Dillon stood to hug her and breathed in her sweet almond scent. "How's my favorite sister-in-law?"

Linnea pecked his cheek. "I'm the only one you got."

"So? You're still my favorite." He let her go and gave Chloe a squeeze as he ruffled the hair on Chandan's head. "Hey, Chlo."

Kyan must have heard them come in. He came down from his office and tossed his drawings on the table, taking his wife in his arms. "You're so beautiful, baby." With his hands cupping her face, he soundly kissed her. One hand dropped to rub the burgeoning swell where their baby grew.

Too intimate of a moment for him to witness, Dillon shifted his sights to Jesse, the expression on his face akin to pity. The guy was a living, breathing empath. He wished he'd never admitted his feelings to his cousin all those years ago. Even then it was already too late.

They didn't stay. Linnea retrieved Ireland from Jesse and kissed her husband on the cheek as she went out the door. Chloe kissed her husband and followed. Then it was quiet.

Dillon looked to Brendan. "Shall we take a look at these prelims or are Katie and Dec coming to kiss you goodbye too?"

Brendan's lazy smirk turned into a grin. "Already taken care of." And he winked.

Shaking his head, Dillon snorted out a laugh. It was good to know some things didn't change.

Kyan took a seat in the unoccupied club chair beside Brendan and spread out his drawings. "C'mon, Dillon wants to work."

Kelsey had to stay late at the office, even though it was Friday, so Dillon offered to take her to dinner somewhere downtown when she finished. He figured she'd be too tired to do more than that, and they could find something to watch on Netflix when they got back to her apartment. He sat in the lobby of the high-rise office building waiting for her to come off the elevator.

Thirty minutes later he was still waiting. He called the restaurant to see if they could change his reservation, but they were booked solid the rest of the evening.

"Fucking bullshit," he complained to no one at all. The only other person in the lobby was a security guard at the desk.

Dillon was scrolling through his phone, trying to find another restaurant, when the elevator doors finally opened. Kelsey got out with two attorneys from her firm—at least he assumed that's who they were. She surveyed the empty lobby and when she spotted him sitting there, still waiting on her like some pussy-whipped asshole, she shrugged with a sheepish smile.

Yeah, he was peeved.

After saying goodbye to the suits, Kelsey strolled toward him. Her long brown hair was up in a high ponytail, pant suit, silk blouse, Louboutin pumps. She was a pretty girl, but dressed like that she looked older than twenty-eight. Too…conservative? Severe? Serious? Boring? Dillon couldn't put a word to it. He knew it was because he wasn't happy with her at the moment, so he quickly dismissed the thought.

Dillon stood as she approached. Kelsey kissed him on the cheek. "I'm so sorry."

"We missed our reservation."

"I said I was sorry, Dillon." Her face fell. "We can go to the burger bar. No reservations required."

He'd waited an hour. At the very least, she could have texted him. Didn't she think of that? This kind of shit wasn't going to fly with him, but he didn't say anything.

Effort.

"Yeah, sure." He grabbed her hand. "Let's go. I'm starving."

The burger bar was exactly what it sounded like. It was a loud, bustling bar that served craft beer, custom burgers, and fries. No tables. It was not the kind of place to hold a conversation with a date and enjoy a nice dinner together. Dillon couldn't even hear himself think in here.

Two seats at the bar opened up and he grabbed them. Dillon pulled out the stool for her and Kelsey took a seat. She must come here a lot, because she didn't even bother looking at the menu.

He had to shout over the din to be heard, "What are you getting?"

"My usual." She tipped her chin at the bartender.

Dillon ordered a beer and a burger with the works. At this point his objective was to eat and get the hell out of here, hoping the evening would get better once they went to Kelsey's place.

He didn't bother trying to make further conversation. It was impossible. He dug into his food while she picked at her avocado burger. After he swallowed the last of his beer, Kelsey was still picking.

Dillon leaned right into her ear. "Is your food okay?"

She nodded. "It's fine."

Fine never means fine.

She pushed her plate away and caught the attention of the bartender, handing him her credit card. Before Dillon could protest, the guy behind the bar swiped her card and closed out their check. Kelsey got up from her seat.

"Finished?"

At least he thought that's what she said.

"Yeah." He took her hand and led her outside. Kelsey began walking at a brisk pace down the sidewalk. "Whoa. Stop." She did. "Want to tell me what's wrong?"

"Nothing."

"Sure seems like something to me, babe."

Kelsey released a loud exhale. "You didn't even talk to me at dinner."

"Are you serious?" He shook his head. "Would you have been able to hear me if I had? It's loud as fuck in there."

"Right." She resumed walking.

His patience was wearing thin. He grabbed her hand and slowed her pace. "You've had a long day. Let's just go watch a movie and relax, okay?"

"I don't think so." She let go of his hand. "I'm tired. I think I'm just going to go to bed." She waved down a taxi. "Thanks for the burger."

He stood there and watched as the taxi, with Kelsey in it, disappeared from view.

Bitch move.

Dillon tapped out a text and waved down a taxi of his own. "Where to?"

"The Red Door." He smirked. "First and Ash."

Here's my dick move, baby.

Two

Kodiak was already in their booth by the bar when Dillon got there. He was surprised to see Brendan sitting there with him, a familiar bottle of Glenlivet in front of them. His cousin only made an occasional evening appearance at the club these days, and even then he didn't stay very long. Not that Dillon blamed him. If he had someone…well, except that now he didn't. She'd left him standing on a sidewalk downtown.

I'm done.

Nope. That shit didn't fly with him.

Dillon slid into the semicircular booth that could easily hold ten people if you wanted it to. The three of them were swallowed up in it, but it was always ready and waiting for them when they came in. Hans and Brigitta insisted upon it. No one else was permitted to occupy it except for them or the Venery boys, and so it sat empty more often than not.

"What you doing here, Bren?"

"I could ask you the same question." His cousin raised his brow, taking a sip of whiskey. "Didn't you have plans with Kelsey?"

"I did." He sniggered, pouring a finger of Glenlivet into a glass. "And now I don't."

He downed it in one swallow and poured himself another.

"I see." Brendan smirked. "Have a little tiff?"

"Heh." Dillon nodded. "Yeah, if you want to call being left standing on a downtown sidewalk a tiff. I call it over and done." He swirled the amber liquid in his glass and peered at his cousin. "So why are you here?"

"Katelyn and Dec fell asleep early." Brendan smiled. "Long day at the zoo. Figured it was as good a time as any to come by and check on things. I'm not staying long."

"You never do."

Brendan angled his head and looked at him. "You all right, Dill? Besides Kelsey, I mean."

"Yeah, man." He rubbed the back of his neck. "Just fucking pissed. I'll get over it."

Pissed that he wasted two months of effort on someone who didn't deserve his attention—or his affection. Pissed that he never could get it quite right. He was the golden boy, wasn't he? That's what they always told him anyway. Charming. Enigmatic. A keen mind for business and a body built for pleasure. Dillon was the guy who convinced the prom queen to fuck him in the bathroom during lunch. Fucking he was good at. Really good. Relationships not so much.

It seemed like he always caught the eye of the wrong girl or his timing was off with the right one. Too much effort. Not enough. Too soon…too late. The miserable state of his love life was his own doing. And he knew it.

So he was pissed at himself more than anything. He could have what his brother and cousins did, too, if just for once he could get it right. He'd fallen in love once, so he knew it was possible. Dillon knew what loving someone felt like. He just needed to find it again. And that was exactly what he feared would be next to impossible.

Holding his glass of whiskey, Dillon looked past his cousin to Kodiak. "Glad you came out, man." He took a sip. "Hope I didn't take you away from anything."

"Nah," he drawled out with a smirk. "I was at Beanie's getting a matcha tea when I got your text."

"Oh yeah?" He tittered. "How's the ice queen?"

Brendan rumbled with laughter. He tolerated Kelly for Katie's sake, and she him, but there was no love lost between them. Made holiday dinners and family get-togethers a heck of a lot of fun, though.

"Icy?" Kodiak shrugged. "She barely acknowledges my existence when I go in there."

Dillon chuckled. At least it wasn't just him then. "Don't take it personal, brother. You own a dick."

"So? Not like I want to stick it in her either." Kodiak swept his gaze toward Brendan. "Sorry. She's rude."

"Kelly has her moments." Brendan nodded, checking his phone. "You don't have to tell me."

"Chicks, man." Dillon drained his glass and shook his head. "I'll never figure them out."

As if reading the actual intent behind his statement, Brendan clasped his shoulder in a sympathetic gesture. Lazy smirk on his face, he audibly inhaled. "That's the thing, brother. There's nothing to figure out, so stop fucking thinking that way. You're not a mind reader and neither is she, so you have to be able to share what's going on in here." He pointed to his head. "Scary as fuck, isn't it?"

He didn't respond.

"But worth it." Brendan squeezed his shoulder. "If you believe Kelsey's the one for you." He pocketed his phone and stood. "I've got to get going."

Dillon watched as Brendan stopped to speak with Hans and Axel on his way out. His gaze drifted over to the bar. A girl with silver hair, the ends dipped bright pink, sipping on a martini caught his eye. She looked to be in her twenties. Her head turned toward him and her gaze locked with his, the corners of her mouth lifting slightly. With her eyes still on his, she slipped the strap of her companion's dress down her arm, exposing the swell of her breast. She brushed a manicured thumb over her nipple as she leaned in and kissed her.

He looked away.

Kodiak smirked with a shrug. "If they want to put on a show for us, I don't mind watching."

"Is that what they're doing?"

"Fuck, yeah." Kodiak poured some whiskey in both their glasses. "And if they want to play, I won't mind that either."

That's not what he came here for. He wasn't looking to fuck.

Dillon just wanted to share a few drinks and some laughs. Forget about Kelsey and salvage the end of this night somehow before he went home alone to his big house and his empty bed. He could have done that a million other places, though, couldn't he? Instead, his first choice had been to come here.

Maybe he was kidding himself.

Maybe that's exactly what he was looking for.

Licking his wounds inside a random pussy or two is what he did best after all, wasn't it? It's just that it didn't work like it used to. Hadn't in a long time. Nothing more than a temporary balm at best. As soon as the cum left his cock and the endorphins faded from his bloodstream, the ache of his festering wounds would return.

"What's goin' on with you, Dillon?" Kodiak drawled in that laid-back voice of his. "Thought you had a good thing going with Kelsey. What happened?"

Dillon recounted the events that led him to get inside the taxi that brought him here to the Red Door. Pissed him off all over again. He'd always been good to Kelsey. Thoughtful. Respectful. At least he tried his best to be. After the shit she pulled tonight, he decided she probably wasn't worth his effort after all.

"Okay, I see your point." Kodiak slowly nodded and sipped his whiskey. "Maybe she was just having a bad day."

Dillon cocked his head and raised his brow.

He snickered. "Or maybe she's just a bitch."

Sweet floral perfume hit heavy out of nowhere, then Dillon spotted the girl with silver hair sliding into the booth beside him. Her companion entered on the opposite side, scooting in next to Kodiak. Linnea's brother drained his glass and winked.

She turned her head toward him and looking into his eyes, rested her chin on his shoulder. "Hi."

"Hi."

"This is the owner's booth, you know." She rubbed her hand slowly up and down his thigh. "You shouldn't be sitting here."

"Oh, yeah?"

"Yeah." Her hand crept closer and closer to his dick. "Axel said it's reserved for them."

"You don't say." Dillon dipped his fingers inside the hem of her skirt. "You're new here, aren't you?"

"Why do you ask?"

He didn't answer, instead pushing her tiny panties to the side. She opened her thighs to give him access and finding her wet, he slid a finger inside her. Then two. With his thumb pressing into her clit, he pumped his fingers in and out of her. She closed her eyes, bit her lip, and tipped her head back against the booth. Seeing she was close to coming, Dillon removed his fingers from her pussy and sucked them into his mouth.

She opened her eyes. "Why'd you stop?"

Taking her hand, he answered her with a smirk. He stood and tipped his chin to Kodiak as he pulled her from the booth, walking her past the platform to the private alcoves. Dillon pulled her inside one, with Kodiak and her companion coming in behind them. He punched the button on the wall and closed the velvet drape.

As temporary as the balm would be, he'd take it.

Dillon took a seat. "Ladies."

That's all he said. They took it upon themselves to undress each other. Kiss each other. Silver hair sucked on her friend's nipple, rubbing a finger back and forth between her folds. Kodiak stood to the side, casually leaning against the wall with his arms crossed over his chest, watching.

Silver pushed two fingers inside her friend, fucking her until her back bowed. Kodiak stepped in behind her, supporting her head with his chest. Pinching her nipples he leaned over and sucked the skin at the curve of her neck. He murmured in her ear, but Dillon couldn't make out what he said.

Whatever it was, she agreed to it, because Kodiak pulled her away from silver hair and carried her to the opposite end of the plush velvet sofa-like bed he sat on. Then she set her sights on him.

Silver hair prowled over to him. Naked. Her nipples were pierced. She shoved her fingers, wet from fucking her friend's pussy, into his mouth. Dillon sucked as, one-handed, she unbuckled his belt and unfastened his pants. He let go of her fingers so she could free his dick. She smiled and licked her bottom lip at the sight of it.

"Suck it."

She easily took him to the back of her throat. He closed his eyes and just savored the feeling, thrusting inside her hot, wet mouth. Listening to her gag on his dick. He fucking loved that sound.

Thrusting faster, Dillon fisted the pink and silver hair at her nape. Holding her head to his cock. Saliva spilled from the corners of her lips. She held onto his thighs, long fingernails digging into his flesh. He kept going until she swallowed every drop of cum he gave her.

She sat beside him, wiping her mouth with a grin, like she was proud of herself for making him come. Dillon glanced to Kodiak and the other girl, who were still fucking, as he zipped up his pants.

He stood and tucked in his shirt. Silver hair looked up at him confused until Kodiak pulled her over to join him and her friend. Then Dillon exited the alcove, giving Axel a brief wave as he walked through the red doors to the real world outside.

His phone vibrated in his pocket.

"I'm sorry."

Too late.

Too fucking late.

Three

"Linn, why are you crying?"

She was curled up in a chair, Kindle balanced on her lap, swiping at the tears that leaked from her pretty green eyes. Dark-blonde hair piled on top of her head. Oversized T-shirt slipping down her shoulder. In his eyes, Linnea was the epitome of beautiful.

She glanced up. "It's one of my favorite books and it's sad." A tear rolled down her cheek and she quickly brushed it away. "Makes me cry every time."

Dillon angled his head, the corners of his mouth pulling up as he peered over her shoulder at the e-reader and made note of the title. "What's it about?"

Linnea looked down at her lap, her cheeks tinged pink. "A girl and the two men she loves. They both love her too." She shrugged. "That's not saying much because there's so much more to it than that."

"I see." He smiled. "Aren't they happy?"

"Very happy until…" She paused with a sigh, fresh tears building. "…until shit goes down and the three of them are ripped apart."

He cupped one side of her face, catching a fallen teardrop with his thumb. "No happily ever after?"

"Yes, just not the one I imagined."

"Why do you read it if it makes you cry?" Crying was foreign to him. He genuinely wanted to know.

"Because it's just so fucking good." She sniffled. "And I'd much rather cry over fiction than real life. A good ugly cry can be cathartic, not that you'd know anything about that."

"You're right." He chuckled. "I wouldn't."

She rolled her eyes at him. "It's got to come out sometime, Dillon."

"What does?" Kyan entered the room with a smirk.

"Your wife is reading one of those romance novels," Dillon informed his brother. "And apparently ugly crying over fictional characters is therapeutic. Who knew?"

Kyan chuckled and leaned down to kiss his wife. "We shouldn't be too long. We're going to meet with the project manager over at the warehouse."

"Do you have plans tonight, Dill?"

It was Friday. He should, but he didn't. He never replied to Kelsey's text that night, and a week had gone by, so that was the end of that.

Dillon shook his head. "Nope."

Linnea looked at them both and smiled. "Why don't you two grab my brother on your way back? The four of us can have dinner together."

"Sounds good." Dillon pecked her cheek.

Kyan gave Linnea one last kiss and followed him out the door.

His brother was a lucky man and he couldn't begrudge him for it. Kyan manned up. He made his move and in one fell swoop he got the girl. The girl Dillon had stupidly made his friend. The girl he'd secretly loved from the sidelines. Linnea never picked up on his subtle cues and he hadn't been sure how to get her out of the friend zone—or if he even should. And then it was too late. He couldn't deny that she and his brother were good together. Things happen as they're meant to.

There's no avoiding your destiny.

That's what he always told himself anyway. For a long time, years in fact, he believed that one day he and Linnea would be together. When the time was right. But the universe had other plans and Linnea's destiny was with Kyan. Not him. He'd accepted that in his heart. Made peace with it. One day he'd have his own destiny to fulfill, right?

After they met with Jenkins at the warehouse and picked up Kodiak, Dillon found himself sipping on a cold beer in a plush-cushioned lounger on his brother's patio. Kyan was grilling shrimp and New York strips that Linnea topped with her homemade chimichurri. Watching them, he was reminded of that first get-together at her old place on Oak Street. At Chloe's invitation he, Kyan, and Jesse had crashed their girls' night. A lot had changed in the three years since that night, but looking back he'd been the odd man out even then.

"Let's eat," Linnea announced.

They all moved over to the outdoor table, passing around platters of food. Kyan tipped the neck of his beer bottle toward him and then Kodiak. "Cheers, my brothers."

"I haven't heard from you all week, Seth. What have you been up to?" Linnea was the only one who called Kodiak by his given name.

He tipped his head and cut into his steak with a smirk. "A little of this. A little of that."

The guy was an odd motherfucker. Eerily soft-spoken. Resourceful. Very private, he was often evasive. Kodiak was a good man who'd endured a helluva lot. Dillon liked him and from the time he'd come back from Cali they'd been buds.

His phone vibrated in his pocket. A spoonful of Spanish potato salad in his mouth, he ignored it. The intrusion irritated him. Whatever it was could wait until after dinner. Dillon wanted to enjoy this relaxed evening with his family. Delicious food al fresco. Cold beer. Laughter. Smiles. The baseball game on the outdoor TV in the background. He'd missed this.

Minutes later he ignored the annoying jiggle once again. Dillon ignored a succession of them until Kyan placed a fresh beer in his hand and they kicked back on the patio to watch the end of the game. Only then did he look at his phone.

Kelsey.

"I said I was sorry. It was a shit day."

"Don't ignore me."

"I miss you."

But did he miss her? Dillon wasn't sure, so he didn't respond right away. He didn't know what to say to her or if opening up a dialogue between them was even wise at this point. They'd only been two months into their relationship so maybe it was best to keep the cut clean and not reply. Silence itself was a response, right?

He set his phone down on his thigh just as it began to vibrate again.

"Will you come over tonight so we can talk? Please…"

Kelsey was nothing if not persistent, he'd give her that much. Maybe he should at least talk to her. Not that he'd make it easy. He tapped out a reply.

Dillon: Can't see you tonight. Sorry.

Kelsey: Why not?

Dillon: I'm at dinner and I made other plans

Kelsey: Change them

Dillon: Not happening

Kelsey: Meet for coffee tomorrow then?

That seemed harmless enough. Neutral territory. He anticipated an argument not a reconciliation. It couldn't get too heated if they were in public. She was going to have to come to him, though. He was done going out of his way for her.

Dillon: Beanie's Coffee Roasters. Three o'clock.

Kelsey: I'll be there…

Dots danced on his screen. He turned off his phone.

She was standing outside the door to the coffee bar waiting for him when he reached First Avenue. Pale-pink sundress. Flat sandals. Her long brown hair caught in the mild summer breeze. She fought to keep it off her face. Kelsey looked more like herself, more like the girl he'd been thinking about wanting 'more' with. And now Dillon wasn't sure if he wanted her at all, but he was willing to listen to what she had to say.

Kelsey offered up a small smile when she spotted him on the sidewalk. "Hey, handsome."

"C'mon." He took her hand and opened the door. "Pick a table. What do you want?"

"Just a latte with an extra shot, please."

Dillon let her hand go and went to the counter, thankful it was Katie and Leo behind it. The last person he wanted to spar with today was the ice queen. He didn't have the energy for it.

Katie came out from behind the counter and hugged him like he didn't live two doors down and across the street. "Dillon!"

"Hey, beautiful." He hugged her back and kissed her cheek.

"You hardly ever come in here," she said with a pout.

"I try to stay out of your aunt's way." He chuckled. "She doesn't like me. I have a dick, you know."

"I did try to warn you, didn't I?" Katie glanced over to where Kelsey sat at a table by the window. "That her?"

"Yeah."

She pursed her lips, surveying her, then returned her attention to him. "What can I make for you?"

Dillon handed Kelsey her latte. He noticed Katie topped it with a flower instead of her signature heart. Glancing back at her, she winked with a smirk. He took a seat across from Kelsey and sipped on his americano.

She just looked at him. Mute.

"You're the one who wanted to talk. Floor is yours."

Kelsey took a sip of her latte and cleared her throat. "I wanted to apologize in person."

He raised his brow.

"Look, I know you're mad and you have every right to be, but I'm sorry."

He didn't say anything.

"I have no excuse for my behavior except it was a really shitty day and I guess I took it out on you. I'm really sorry, Dillon…I don't want to lose you." She swallowed, blinking back tears. "Have I?"

Jesus, don't fucking cry.

"I don't know," he answered honestly, looking into her brown eyes. "I appreciate the apology, though."

"I really fucked up, didn't I?"

"Yeah, you kinda did. See, I've always gone out of my way to do what I know makes you happy. To be thoughtful. Respectful. Because I cared about you." He looked down at his coffee, shaking his head. "I should at least get the same consideration from you. Instead, I sat in a lobby waiting on you for more than an hour without even a thought from you only to be left standing there on the sidewalk like an asshole because you had a shitty day?"

"I couldn't help it."

"You could have at least texted me."

She nodded. "You're right. I'm sorry. Can you give me another chance?"

Should he? Did he even want to?

"What happens the next time you have a shitty day? Because I have to tell you, that shit will never fly with me. We all have days that turn to crap. I get it. You can pout, complain—whatever you have to do to vent. But do unto others, baby…get me?"

"I do." She worried her lip.

He still wasn't sure he should.

Fuck it.

"Make no mistake, I have feelings for you." He reached for her hand across the table and laced his fingers with hers. "But I won't do this again."

"So, we're good?" Hope written in her eyes, she meekly smiled.

He glanced at Katie, who was shaking her head behind the counter, and returned his focus to the brown eyes in front of him. "We're good."

Kelsey followed his gaze. "Who the fuck is she?"

"She's family. That's Brendan's wife, Katie." He smirked, already regretting his decision.

"Oh."

"Jealous or something, Kels?"

She wouldn't look at him.

"You think that little of me?"

"No," she whispered, shaking her head. "It's just that she looks barely out of high school and Brendan is older than you."

"So, now you're judging?" He swallowed down the rest of his coffee. "Let me tell you something. In my family, we don't judge anyone for who or how they choose to love. Ever. And if you're not on board with that, it's a dealbreaker for me."

Was he being a dick? Yeah, maybe. But his sexual ideology was strong and deeply rooted. Besides, the last thing he wanted to do was bring someone around his family who would think less of them for who they loved.

"Let's continue this conversation somewhere else, okay?" He waved to Katie and Leo, then escorted Kelsey out to First Avenue. They walked in the direction of Coventry Park, and when they reached it he spoke again.

"You know my cousins and me own the club together."

"Yeah." She nodded. "The Red Door."

"It was Brendan's baby, but we opened it because we believe in its purpose. People should have the freedom to love who they want to, to fuck how they want to, to express their sexuality in whatever way they want to." He stopped walking and placed his hands on her shoulders. "You never have to step a foot inside those red doors and I'll never ask you to participate in anything you don't want to be a part of, but I can't be with you, or anyone, who doesn't believe the same."

He dropped his hands and waited for her to walk away, but she didn't. With a smile, Kelsey took his hand and resumed walking. "Can we go now?"

"Where?"

"Your house."

"Why?"

"Make-up sex." She grinned. "That's the best part."

Dillon was on board with that. He hadn't touched a pussy in eight days, not since…silver hair at the club.

It's not like he fucked her. And he and Kelsey had just split so he didn't actually cheat on her, right?

Right.

So why did he feel guilty about it?

He shouldn't.

It was a dick move, asshole.

He was just going to have to come clean and tell her.

Four

He'd barely gotten the door closed behind them when she pounced on him.

Kelsey slid her tongue in his mouth and her hand down his pants, squeezing his dick in her fingers. Her other hand moved slowly up his body, over his abs and chest, to rest at his throat. She peeled her lips from his and breathlessly whispered, "Fuck me."

Reaching for the hem that rested at mid-thigh, she pulled the pale-pink sundress up her body and lifted it over her head. Tossing it to the floor, she kicked off her sandals and stood there, in nothing but her bra and panties, in the foyer. She grazed her bottom lip with her teeth. "Right here."

Dillon took a step closer. "You want me to fuck you here on the floor?"

"Yeah."

She reached for him and popped the button on his jeans. He firmly grasped her wrist to stop her. "We're not done talking."

If Kelsey still wanted him to fuck her after he finished saying what he had to say, Dillon would be more than happy to oblige her. He'd fuck her on the floor, on the stairs, on top of the washer during the spin cycle. He'd fuck her six ways from Sunday if she wanted him to. That wasn't her style, though.

She didn't like being on top and doggie was as adventurous as she got.

He picked up her dress and shoes from the hardwood floor and grabbed her by the hand, leading her into the family room at the back of the house. Sitting on the chaise end of the suede sofa,

Dillon pulled Kelsey onto his lap so she straddled him. He combed the long brown hair away from her face with his fingers and licking his lips, released a slow breath.

"I think it's important that we're totally honest with one another." His thumbs brushed over her nipples, visible beneath ivory lace. "No bullshit. No games."

Her lips parted slightly, but she didn't speak.

He cupped the creamy swells of flesh in his palms and squeezed. Flicking his eyes to hers, he brought his hands to her shoulders and held them. "When you left me and took off in that taxi, I was done." His fingers traced along her collarbone. "As far as I was concerned we were over and I got in a taxi of my own."

"Oh." Kelsey lowered her lids. "Where'd you go?"

Dillon tipped her chin up with his finger, forcing her to look at him. "The Red Door."

She nodded. "You were with someone else."

He nodded. "But I didn't fuck her."

Clasping his neck, she smiled. "What are you waiting for then?"

Leaning in, she brushed her lips across his. Dillon fisted her hair in one hand and pushed his tongue inside her mouth. He should be glad that she wasn't pissed off at him, but a thought niggled in the back of his brain.

She doesn't care.

He just admitted he was with someone and she didn't give a fuck, but she almost lost her shit when he just looked at Katie? It didn't make sense. Why'd that bother him? She slithered off his lap, and dropping to her knees in front of him, Kelsey unzipped him. She pulled off his jeans and ran her tongue along his dick, sucking the head into her mouth. And he stopped trying to figure it out.

With his hand fisted in her hair, Dillon watched her head bob up and down as she sucked on his cock. Kelsey kept her eyes closed and as soon as she started to gag even the tiniest bit she'd pull back. Not one to just allow herself to feel and let go, she held everything in. She rarely made noises of pleasure. No whimpers or moans. She did everything she could to stifle her screams. They were there. She was just too self-conscious to let them be heard.

That was going to change. Starting right the fuck now.

It's not her pretty face, her perky tits, or her nice ass in tight jeans that makes a woman sexy. At least Dillon didn't think so. He'd known and been with plenty of women with all those assets and then some. It was her confidence. Spontaneity. Taking pleasure and giving it with uninhibited joy. Owning her sensuality. That's what made a woman sexy to him.

He lifted her off his dick and pushed her down onto the sofa. Pulling the shirt over his head, naked, he straddled her thighs. With a flick of his fingers he opened the front clasp on her bra, freeing her tits from the ivory lace. Dillon drove forward and grasping her wrists tightly he held them above her head. He sucked her breast into his mouth and bit down on her nipple, eliciting a cry.

"Yeah, that's it." He kissed her nipple, soothing the sting with his tongue.

Pinned beneath his body, she tried to squirm as he moved on to the other breast. He licked and kissed the puckered flesh, waiting for her to relax, before the areola disappeared inside his mouth. He suckled until her breaths were reduced to jagged pants, then he slowly released her swollen nipple, grazing it with his teeth.

Dillon let go of her wrists, but she didn't move them. Her arms remained at her head. He sat up and looked at her. Eyes shut tight as her chest rapidly rose and fell. He grasped the ivory lace panties with his fingers.

"Look at me," he rasped.

Kelsey opened her brown doe eyes and with one swift tug he tore the delicate lace from her body. Before she could protest, he pushed her thighs apart and his mouth was at her cunt. Her hands flew to his head, tugging on his hair. Dillon tugged on her nipples and lapped at her clit, soft thighs squeezing his ears. He didn't plan on stopping until she screamed out her orgasm.

No mercy.

Only then would he relent and fuck her.

Her teeth dug into her bottom lip. She held her breath to keep from making a sound, but he could tell she was close and Dillon knew just what would push Kelsey over the edge. With his mouth on her clit, he pushed two fingers inside her and hooked them to graze along her wall, stimulating her g-spot.

He sucked on her clit and she screamed his name.

Not wanting Kelsey to come down from her orgasm, Dillon sheathed himself and pushing her knees back to her shoulders, he entered her. She'd finally let go a little and he wanted her to stay in that headspace. He fucked her hard and fast, flesh slapping flesh. Hand at her throat, he kissed her fervently so she could taste herself on his tongue.

He kept to his frenzied pace, thrusting into her again and again and again, until the fireball burned at the base of his spine. Reaching between their slick bodies, he sought her clit and pinched it between his fingers. She cried out once more. Then he let himself come.

He knew she wouldn't go. Dillon didn't know why he'd even bothered asking her, but he did, and just like he presumed she would, Kelsey used work as the reason why she couldn't. He figured it was just an excuse, and a pretty lame one at that.

Not that he cared much.

Dropping off the load of presents he brought for baby Declan in Brendan's family room, Dillon followed the delicious smell and the sound of feminine laughter coming from the kitchen. Katie, Chloe, and Linnea were huddled together at the island, taking turns tossing peanuts in the air. He watched them for a moment, heads tipped back, mouths open, as they each missed the catch more often than not.

With a shake of his head, he chuckled and grabbed some peanuts out of the bowl. "Ladies, let me show you how it's done." Then one by one, he launched the nuts into the air in rapid succession, catching each and every one.

Eyes wide, Linnea gaped at him. "How'd you do that?"

Dillon chewed and swallowed the mouthful of peanuts with a wink. "Years of practice, gorgeous."

"Just don't let him near the mashed potatoes," Katie deadpanned.

"I was eight." He grinned. "I'll have you know, I've gotten a lot better at it since then." He popped another peanut in his mouth. "You'll see."

Turning the crystal knob, Dillon opened the French door and stepped out onto the patio. Brendan was helping his son, who had only recently taken his first steps, toddle in the grass. Chandan and Elliott were running laps around a lounger, chasing each other, as Monica, Jesse, and even baby Ireland watched them like they were racing the Indy 500. He plucked a beer out of the cooler and popping off the cap, stationed himself next to his brother at the grill.

Kyan flipped the burgers and glanced over at him. "Hey, bro." He nodded toward the cooler. "Can you grab me one?"

"Here." He gave his brother the bottle and got another for himself.

"Isn't Kelsey here?"

Dillon drained half the bottle before he answered, "Nope."

Kyan's brow rose. "I thought you two kissed and made up."

"We did." He shrugged and took another swig of beer. "It's a work thing. She couldn't make it."

"You guys are coming up to the lake house for Labor Day weekend, aren't you?"

"Haven't asked her yet," he admitted and emptied the rest of the bottle.

He should ask her. Dillon was still debating, though. It seemed they had worked everything out. Kelsey spent the night and most of the next day with him. But the thought was still niggling at the back of his brain that she really didn't care, at least not enough.

Maybe he didn't either.

He'd have to give it some more thought.

Dillon dug another beer out of the ice. Kodiak stepped out onto the patio and he waved. "Looks like we're just waiting on Kelly and Kevin, I guess," he informed Kyan.

"You're going to invite her, right?"

Fuck's sake. Back to that, are we?

He shrugged. "Maybe. Haven't decided yet."

Narrowing his brows, Kyan gave him the side-eye.

"Look, we made up but I'm not sure we're back to the same place we were before, if that makes sense." Dillon ran his fingers through the hair on top of his head. "I was just starting to think maybe we had something, you know?" He sniggered. "I actually had this crazy idea of asking Kelsey to marry me on New Year's Eve..."

"Here's the steaks, Ky." Linnea put a container of raw meat on the table next to the grill, got on her tiptoes to kiss her husband, and went back inside the house.

Kyan took the burgers off the grill. "And now?"

"That's not happening, but we'll see how it goes."

Later that evening, after they watched Declan smash his cake and paint himself with blue frosting, after three little boys finally wore themselves out and one baby girl slept on her father's chest, Brendan broke out a bottle of Redbreast.

Chloe got up from where she sat beside her husband and softly murmured, "Here, sweetie." She gently lifted their daughter into her arms. "Let me take her."

She went inside the house, returning a moment later. "I laid her down. The boys are out."

Not that she needed to tell anybody that, Katie had the live feed pulled up on her phone.

Brendan poured shots of the Irish whiskey into ten glasses and passed them out to everyone except Linnea, who got sparkling water instead. He raised his glass and looked to Jesse. "You didn't think I forgot it's your birthday, too, did you?"

Chloe smiled up at her husband from beneath his arm.

"*Lá breithe shona duit. Sláinte!*" Brendan toasted and swallowed the whiskey. "Happy birthday, brother!"

"He only reminded us every day," Dillon said, grinning. He reached behind the lounger for the gift he'd brought for Jesse and handed him the large, oblong box he'd actually wrapped himself. "Happy birthday."

His cousin tore off the paper and lifted the lid, pulling the custom-framed enlargement from the nest of tissue that protected it. Jesse glanced up at him, and Dillon could have sworn his eyes were flooding. Understanding, he smiled. Because what do you get for the sentimental cousin that has everything he could ever possibly want?

Jesse turned his gift around so everyone could see the black-and-white photo of four young boys. A moment in time captured twenty-four years ago based on the date written on the back of the original photograph. A piece of their childhood he'd found digging through a box of his father's things. They sat together on the steps of the three-flat building where they'd grown up, more brothers than cousins even then.

"Ohhhh," Chloe crooned. "You guys were so cute! Not that you aren't cute now, but…" She giggled. "Well, you know what I mean."

He caught Jesse swipe beneath his eye. Caught up in the nostalgia of the long-forgotten image, even Brendan appeared misty-eyed. "I remember Uncle Charley taking that."

"Lots of happy memories there," Kyan wistfully added. "Still makes me angry they tore the place down."

He and his brother were both in college when it happened.

Over several years, developers bought up every building on the block and razed them to make way for ostentatious new townhomes. Hideous monstrosities that didn't fit in with the neighborhood that surrounded it, that ignored the history and architectural style of the city. They didn't realize it then, but that event was the catalyst for the company the four of them created and built. Restoring these old buildings was a passion they all shared.

"How old were you there?" Linnea asked her husband.

Dillon answered for him. "When that photo was taken Kyan was six, Jesse was seven, Brendan was ten, and I was eight." He smiled. "And before you ask, I got a copy made for all of you."

"Even back then your hair was long, Jesse," Chloe exclaimed, shaking her head with a grin. "You looked like that kid from Hanson."

Jesse chuckled. "I think I was trying to look like him."

Chloe started singing "MMMBop" and it didn't take long for everyone to join in and sing it with her. Everyone except for Katie. She looked lost, her lips pursed as her eyes flitted from person to person as if they'd all lost their minds.

"What the hell song is that and who's Hanson?" Katie asked.

Kevin snickered at his sister. "C'mon, Katie, you know it."

The singing stopped and Kelly smirked at Katie. "You weren't even born yet."

"And your point is?" Chloe smirked back at her. "I wasn't born yet when this song came out either, and how old were you, Kelly? Five?"

The ice queen didn't respond and Chloe pulled out her phone to google Hanson for Katie.

Kelly whispered it softly, Dillon assumed so no one would hear her, but he heard it. "I guess it runs in the family."

He pivoted on the lounger toward where she sat. "What's that, Kelly?"

Not that he needed to ask. He knew she was making a crack

about the age difference between her niece and Brendan. Dillon wanted to make sure she knew that he heard her.

He cocked his head with a smirk. "Anyone ever tell you that you're a fucking miserable bitch?"

"No." She smirked back. Kevin sniggered behind his hand.

"Consider yourself told," he sneered as he stood.

"Dillon, man." Kodiak stood with him, his hand clasping him on the shoulder.

"I'm sick of her snide little comments." He took a step back and turning away from Kodiak and the ice queen he went inside the house before he caused a scene.

Dillon wasn't kidding when he told Kelsey he couldn't abide anyone who judged other people like that, especially the people he loved.

"Dillon," Brendan called after him.

He held up his hand in a wave and kept going.

Out the front door and across the street to his big empty house.

Five

His eyes opened at the first sign of light coming in through the bedroom window. Dillon blinked away the last vestiges of sleep, irritated that he'd woken so early on a Saturday. He and Kelsey were out late last night and he was looking forward to sleeping in. That wasn't happening now. He envied those people who could just close their eyes and drift back to dreamland, because once his opened he was awake for the day.

Through the glass he stared at nothing in his backyard as the fog cleared from his brain. Dillon still hadn't asked Kelsey to go to the lake house with him next weekend, and he was still undecided about it. The way he saw it, bringing her was tantamount to committing to this relationship, and that's what he was really unsure of. But if he was going to ask her, he'd have to do it soon. Like today.

There was movement behind him on the bed. Kelsey's arm came around his waist, her hand resting on his chest, as she cuddled her warm body up against his back. Dillon placed his hand on top of hers and held it there, resisting the innate urge to push it in the direction of the erection he woke up with. Fucking her would require more than he had in him at the moment.

"Good morning," her sleepy voice whispered in his ear.

"Morning," he murmured softly on an exhale.

Kelsey moved her hand down his chest and over his abs until her fingers wrapped around his dick. She stroked him, squeezing from base to tip. Dillon gripped her wrist and rolled over so he faced her, placing the hand he held on her pussy.

"Go on," he urged her.

"What?"

She went to move her hand away, but he kept it there. "Show me how you play with that pussy."

He could see blush stain her cheeks in the muted light.

"Dillon," she protested and bit into her lip.

With his hand guiding hers, he pushed her fingers until they disappeared between her legs. "Are you wet?"

She squeaked.

He moved her fingers back and forth. "Show me."

She drew up her top leg so her foot rested at her knee, putting her pussy on display so he could see the wetness glistening on her fingers. Determined to push Kelsey out of her comfort zone, Dillon nudged them to her opening. She hesitated.

"Keep going," he crooned, brushing the hair away from her face. "Fuck that pussy with your fingers."

Closing her eyes she whispered, "Why?"

"Because I want you to. Because it gets me off." Her eyes opened. "I like watching, so fuck yourself real good and come hard for me, doll. And after you do, I'll make you come again even harder."

Kelsey gasped as she slid a single finger inside her pussy. Dillon gazed at her intently as she timidly worked herself and she went from biting her lip to softly parting them. He could hear how wet she was with every thrust of her finger. She was getting off on it too.

"Put in another one. Fuck that pussy for me, Kels." Dillon lifted her leg over his shoulder, opening her cunt wider, watching her do as he asked. "That's a good girl. So fucking hot."

He tweaked her nipple and she let out a small whimper, pumping her fingers a little faster. She began rubbing her clit. He watched as she allowed herself to simply feel. To let herself go. And it was a beautiful thing to see.

Bright sunlight streamed in through the window as they laid there after they finished fucking. He leisurely stroked her arm while she caught her breath, then he rolled onto his side. "Do you have any plans for next weekend?"

"Um…" She audibly exhaled. "No."

Fuck it.

"My family is spending Labor Day weekend up at the lake house." He stopped his movement on her arm. "Would you like to go with me?"

Kelsey turned onto her side. "Yeah." She smiled at him. "I'd like that a lot."

It was a hectic day at the office on Park Place. Three of them trying to get everything tied up before the start of a long holiday weekend. Kyan was out at an appointment and construction had begun on the warehouse restoration project, so that only added to it.

Dillon looked forward to getting out of the city. He loved being at the lake house, the memories, the solace to be had there. It was a special place. Their lives and their love for each other were woven inside its walls, embedded in its foundation. For Dillon, it was even more than that. The lake house was the one place on Earth he could recharge and gain clarity. He always left with a fresh outlook on his life, a new perspective. A better one.

Maybe his relationship with Kelsey would fare better after being there together too.

Or not.

He wasn't convinced he'd made the right decision by inviting her. Was he sending her the wrong signal by doing so? His family? Because that was the last thing Dillon wanted to do. He didn't want to dwell on it, but the shit Kelsey pulled that night still bothered him, and it forced him to look at all the other little things that weren't quite right between them. She was trying to be more accommodating, though, in bed and out of it. She even asked for tomorrow off so they could leave for the lake house with everyone else.

Effort.

You get what you give.

He might not be committed to their relationship yet, but he *was* committed to trying to have one. Dillon wanted a wife. Children.

There was hope for them maybe. The only thing he knew for sure was he wasn't quite ready to give up on her.

Kelsey was finally beginning to bloom, to awaken sensually and own her sexuality. That meant something to him. While Dillon understood there was a lot more to a relationship than sex, it was a big deal to him. He needed his partner to allow him to worship her body freely, without reservation, as she deserved to be. As she was made to be.

Dillon was also aware few people, Kelsey included, were as comfortable with sex as he was. He was so fucking grateful to have been enlightened by Brendan, Monica, and the sex-positive community. He and his brother and his cousins, Linnea, Chloe, Venery—they'd all embraced it. Human sexuality was beautiful and wondrous. And if he and Kelsey were to have any chance at all, she'd have to embrace it too.

How could he welcome her into his family if she didn't?

He couldn't. Not ever.

So he was determined to enlighten her just as he had been. To push her boundaries to their limits. To show her the magic of her sensuality, her body, and everything she was capable of. To release her from the inhibitions society had taught her. To love freely. Fuck freely. Jesus, it was so beautiful to be free and let go. He wanted Kelsey to feel that.

Because Dillon needed that and he hadn't been able to achieve it with her. Not yet. To fuck her without reservation. To fully let himself go with her. They made some progress on Saturday. She allowed him to watch her get herself off. Knew now he enjoyed it, though she didn't know yet just how much. They'd stayed in bed all day, fucking like rabbits, only stopping for food. She even got on top and rubbed her clit while bouncing on his dick. So, yeah. Progress.

And this weekend he hoped to kick it up a notch.

This weekend could make them.

Or break them.

Jesse was smiling and tapping away on his phone, which meant he was texting with either Chloe or Taylor. Since his wife was across the street with their children, Dillon's money was on Taylor. It was their first separation in a long time and he imagined Jesse missed him a lot—Chloe too. Dillon had to admit Park Place felt empty with Venery gone on the road. It wasn't the same without them around.

His cousin put the phone down on the table and returned to the document he was reviewing. "How's Tay?"

"He's good considering." Jesse nodded. "They left Pittsburgh. Columbus tomorrow, Louisville on Sunday, Indy on Monday, be home on Tuesday." He grinned then. "And I cannot fucking wait."

"Tuesday will be a happy day around here for sure," Brendan agreed.

Dillon clasped Jesse on the shoulder. Kyan and Linnea came in the front door holding hands as they always seemed to do. Both of them had wide smiles on their beaming faces. They stood there like they were ready to burst at the seams. Something was up.

"Tell them, princess."

Linnea was doing the bouncy thing that Chloe often did. "You should be the one."

He kissed her and turned to the three of them, his face lit up like Dillon had never seen before. Not on Christmas, his birthday, or even his wedding day. "We're having a little girl."

A daughter.

That explained it, and he couldn't be happier for his brother—and for Linnea. They'd wanted this baby so badly. Afraid it might never happen. Kyan was going to be the most amazing dad.

He and his cousins jumped up to congratulate them. Lots of hugs. Linnea was crying happy tears and his brother was misty-eyed, overcome by what must have been an emotional afternoon.

"Our girls will be less than a year apart," Jesse exclaimed. "They're going to be so close, just like their moms."

"I thought you wanted it to be a surprise." Brendan chuckled, patting Kyan on the back and kissing Linnea's cheek.

Dillon knew they'd opted not to take the blood test early in Linnea's pregnancy because if she happened to miscarry she didn't want to know. Maybe she wasn't worried about that so much now.

"We did, but the doctor was doing an ultrasound today," Kyan happily explained. "And Linn's almost five months. The baby is healthy."

"Doctor Torres asked if we wanted to know and we decided we did," Linnea added, handing him photos of their unborn daughter. "Look, Uncle Dill. Here's your niece."

"Oh, wow!" He was in awe. "You can see her face and everything!"

"I know," she sighed dreamily.

He passed the photos to Jesse and put his arm around his brother. "I love you, man. I'm so fucking thrilled for you."

"I love you too. Couldn't have asked for a better brother. I got the best one ever." Kyan swiped beneath his eye and chuckled. "Charlotte's a lucky little girl. I know you, and you're going to spoil her rotten. I can see it already. You'll be her favorite."

"Charlotte?"

"Yeah, we want to name her Charlotte Grace." He said it so proudly. "After Dad and Linn's mom." He paused with a smile. "And you."

Charles.

Dillon and his father shared the same first name, though he rarely used it. Charles was on his driver's license and credit cards— legal stuff. That's it. His dad went by Charley and his mom hated the nickname 'Chuck', so he'd been called by his middle name all of his life. Most people, those outside of the family anyway, didn't even know Dillon wasn't actually his first name.

He didn't know what to say and hugged his brother a little bit tighter.

Kyan was right. He *was* going to spoil that little girl and he would be her favorite. And while he'd never admit it to Jesse or Brendan or anyone, because he loved their kids to the moon and back and you're not supposed to have a favorite, she would be his.

Charlotte was his namesake, after all.

And she came from the two people in the world he loved most.

Six

"**M**oomy, juice. Moomy, juice."

Chandan waved his sippy cup, tugging at the hem of Chloe's shirt, as she, Linnea, and Katie unloaded the groceries for the weekend that were being brought in.

"In a minute, sweetie." Chloe patted him on the head.

Apparently not happy with that answer, he threw his cup on the floor. That's what started it. The sound of the cup bouncing across the tile startled Ireland, who'd been asleep in her baby swing, and she began to cry. Upon hearing his cousin's piercing wail, Declan woke up from his nap and joined her.

It was at that precise moment Brendan, Jesse, and Kyan came in with the last of the bags and boxes the girls had packed for the trip. Jesse dropped his load and rushed to his daughter. Katie and Brendan reached their son at the same time, his father scooping him up to soothe him. Chloe wrangled an unhappy Chandan from the floor. His brother and his wife stood there watching it all unfold with eyes wide and dopey grins on their faces, Linnea rubbing her little baby bump.

Dillon couldn't hide his chuckle.

Yeah, you're next, brother.

Kelsey was at his side, mouth hanging open, slowly shaking her head from side to side, like she'd never seen a two-year-old in action or heard babies cry before. "Good God, I don't ever want any kids."

She's kidding, right?

She had better be kidding. They'd never talked about it but Dillon wanted a family of his own one day in the not-too-distant future. If she wasn't on board with that he was definitely wasting his time. And hers. Are you supposed to have a checklist of questions, tick off all the boxes, before you date someone? Maybe not, because that seemed a bit absurd to him, but then again perhaps he needed those answers before this thing between them went much further.

His cousin brought the baby over to his wife and she put their daughter to her breast. Ireland immediately quieted, eagerly suckling. Chloe stroked the wispy strawberry-blonde hair on her little head and Jesse, sitting on the arm of the chair beside his wife, combed his fingers through her long auburn locks and leaned in to kiss her cheek. Seeing them like that brought a smile to Dillon's face. Two kids later and they appeared to be more in love than ever.

Seeming uncomfortable, Kelsey averted her gaze and murmured under her breath, "She could be discreet at least."

What the fuck?

Maybe they weren't a family of Puritans, but there was nothing wrong with nursing your baby out in the open, for chrissakes. They'd all seen Chloe and Katie do it countless times. It was natural and beautiful, not something that needed to be hidden. Was she really that offended by it? Didn't women stop feeding their babies in toilet stalls and back bedrooms a long time ago?

"Better now, Irie?" Chloe cooed.

Jesse put his arm around his wife's shoulders. "No one calls her that. Give it up, babe." He kissed her temple and smirked. "She's Ireland."

Chloe blew out a breath with a pout, then she giggled. "I know."

He smiled. "I love her name."

"Me too." Her smile widened to match his.

"And I love you," Jesse said as he leaned in to kiss her.

After everyone had unpacked, dinner was eaten, and the little ones had been tucked snug in their beds, Dillon took Kelsey by the hand. "Let's go for a walk."

"In the dark?"

"Moonlight, Kels."

Three quarters full, the light of the waxing moon reflected over the placid water. Scents of summer hung in the fresh, mild air with a faint hint of the fall soon to come. Crickets chirped. A lone lightning bug flitted across the lawn, bioluminescence marking its flight. They'd all be gone soon.

He thought she'd like a moonlit stroll around the lake. Just the two of them. Most women would think it was romantic, right? Kelsey was quiet, though, as they walked hand in hand toward the water.

"What are you thinking?"

She shrugged. "Nothing really."

"You looked overwhelmed back there." He gave her hand a gentle squeeze.

"Your family is…um…different." Kelsey stopped walking to peer up at him. "It's a lot to take in."

"How so?" Dillon asked, giving her a half smile.

"I'm not sure how to explain it." She worried her lip in thought for a moment and shrugged. "You just seem a lot closer…more familiar than I know most families to be."

And you have a problem with that?

If they were going to be together, Kelsey was going to have to get used to it. Admittedly, they were all freely affectionate with one another, and public displays were the norm rather than the exception. No one batted an eyelash if Brendan playfully swatted Chloe on the ass or if she called him 'baby'. Hell, nobody looked side-eyed at anything. Kisses, hugs, and warmhearted touches amongst them were commonplace—and there was nothing sexual about it. Well, most of the time. People would probably describe them as a lovey-dovey bunch. And they'd be right.

Because they were.

Always had been.

Always would be.

All of them were comfortable together and their love for one another was limitless.

They came around a bend to a small cove hidden by tall grass and rock. Dillon heard sounds coming from it. Splashes of water. Murmurs. Moans.

He pulled them off the path that circled the lake and backed into a large weeping willow. Holding his index finger to his lips, he signaled for Kelsey to remain silent and positioned her in front of him. His brother and Linnea were naked together, illuminated in moonlight, kissing in the water. From this vantage point he could see them clearly, yet he and Kelsey were safely camouflaged under the tree's graceful hanging branches.

Kelsey half turned in his embrace and whispered, "We shouldn't be here."

"But we are."

Dillon supposed he could have turned Kelsey around when he spotted them in the water, but he didn't want to. Kyan wouldn't mind him watching. It's not like he hadn't seen them together like this before. Three years ago, before Park Place, he lived with them for close to eight months. More often than not, they all slept together in the same bed while Linnea healed from the aftermath of Crossfield. Holding her. Soothing her. One or both of them always had to be near. And those days were some of the best, and some of the worst of his life.

Kyan cradled Linnea, her breasts skimming the surface of the water, nipples peaked. Dillon closed his eyes and he was in another place, a different time. As beautiful and cherished as those memories were, he couldn't afford to go there again. It hurt too much to think of them.

He turned Kelsey around in his arms, and taking her face in his palms he softly brushed her lips with his. Then fueled by his memories, he kissed her. Devoured her. Demanding. Rough and raw. She was breathless, gasping for air, when he finally pulled away.

What the fuck am I doing here?

This wasn't right. It was all sorts of wrong. Kelsey gazed at him with something he'd never seen in her eyes before. It looked a lot like...*nah*. He exhaled, tracing his teeth with his tongue. It could have been different, maybe. If only she had looked at him like that a month ago.

They silently slipped out from beneath the willow's weeping

branches and went back the way they came. Neither one spoke. Dillon held Kelsey's hand as he waved to his cousins, their wives cuddled against them, sitting on the back deck. Then he led her inside the house and up the stairs to their room.

Kelsey ducked inside the en suite to shower. Dillon could join her, he supposed. Push her up against the wet tile and fuck her senseless. He stripped off his clothes, leaving them on the floor, and got into bed instead.

With his hand cupping the back of his head, Dillon stared up at the ceiling, but he didn't see it. He saw Jesse with his arm around Chloe as she nursed their daughter. Katie and Brendan reaching together for their son. Kyan kissing Linnea as he tenderly caressed the life growing inside her. The depth of their love for each other was undeniable. Enviable.

It was that kind of all-encompassing love he wanted for himself.

He left Kelsey on the deck with the girls to toss a football out on the lawn with Jesse. Kyan and Brendan peeled off their shirts and joined them. The four of them hadn't done this in years. Dillon was pretty sure his brother was still in high school the last time they scrimmaged two against two. Feeling like a kid again, he paired off with Jesse and grinned.

It wasn't fair really. Even with his superior stature, Brendan, and his brother, were no match against him and the former pro wide receiver. Football was in Jesse's blood. He could still catch any throw and run like the devil was chasing him. Shame he gave it all up. Dillon understood, though. He traded one dream for an even better one.

They played hard, grunting in the September sun, covered in sweat. Dirt and grass clung to his skin. Dillon observed all their faces. Smiling. Laughing. Whoops and whistles. Pumped muscles. Back slaps and high fives. He was reminded of his youth, here in this place where they learned to run and play. Where they'd learned what love was, what family was, and forged a bond that even death could never separate. In that moment, he remembered the feeling of happiness. Kyan caught his gaze, and as if his brother knew what he was thinking, and he usually did, he winked.

Wiping the dirt and the sweat off his skin with a towel, Dillon failed to notice the girls had come down to the grass until Kelsey was smiling at his side, holding out a bottle of water for him.

"Thanks." He took it and gulped it down in one go.

Dillon glanced around the lawn. Jesse had returned to Chloe and Brendan to Katie, but Linnea was ascending the deck stairs and Kyan was crossing the lawn toward him, two bottles of beer in hand.

His brother clapped his shoulder. "That was fun."

"Yeah, almost forgot how much," he replied, dusting off his chest.

Kyan turned to Kelsey then and flipped on a smile that didn't reach his eyes. "I need to ask a favor. Can you hang with Linnea and keep her company while I take a walk with my brother? I promise we won't be too long."

She seemed a bit startled by his request. Her lips parted, head angled, but she nodded. "Yeah, sure."

Dillon kissed her cheek and she turned away to join his sister-in-law up on the deck. He looked over at his brother. "Everything okay, Ky?"

"Yeah, man." Kyan put his arm around his shoulders and they walked toward the dock that jutted out on the lake. "Just wanted some time to shoot the shit with my brother—that okay with you? We don't get the chance too often anymore."

"We don't," he agreed. They sat down at the end of the dock, feet dangling in the water. Kyan handed him a beer. "And I miss it."

"Me too," his brother admitted, twisting the cap off his bottle and taking a swig. "You're right next door…I see you every day, but we don't talk enough."

"Yeah, well…" Dillon tipped some beer in his mouth and shrugged.

"What's going on with you, Dill?" Kyan tugged on his arm. "You seem so disconnected from us lately."

"Maybe I am." He blew out a breath with a slight shake of his head. "Being I'm the only single one now."

A sudden awareness came over his brother's face. Kyan angled his head, seeing right through him, but then he always could. There wasn't a thing they could keep from each other even if they tried. From the time they were little, they'd been inside each other's heads, knew the other's mind, had their own unspoken language, often finishing the other's sentences. Used to freak their mother out.

"What are you doing with her, brother?"

Dillon looked out at the lake and shrugged.

"Kelsey seems like a nice girl, but she's not the girl for you." Kyan clasped his shoulder.

He kept staring at the water. "Why do you say that?"

"I know you don't love her, Dillon."

Truth.

He turned his head toward Kyan then. "How do you know I don't?"

The corners of his lips turned up in a sympathetic smile. Kyan didn't have to give voice to the answer and they both knew it. Because Dillon had been in love once.

"Love will come back to you, brother. You'll see." He sounded so sure. "Wait for the girl you can't live without. I promise you, she's worth it."

Dillon only nodded.

"I want you to be happy." The hand on his shoulder squeezed. "I love you, Dill."

"I love you too, Ky."

He returned his gaze to the peaceful lake and they finished their beer together in silence.

As he always did, Dillon found the clarity he needed, here with his brother at his side.

A fresh outlook.

A new perspective.

He knew what he had to do.

And then he would wait.

Seven

Going back to work after a long holiday weekend always sucked, didn't it? Especially when the sun was shining, not a cloud to be seen anywhere, and the sky was the loveliest shade of blue. If he'd woken to a shit day of rain and dismal gray, he might not have minded being stuck inside the office all day. But it was a fucking perfect day and he wanted out.

As luck would have it, he got his wish.

Jenkins needed one of them to come down to the warehouse—something to do with the permits. He jumped at the chance to go, and now he was walking through the park to First Avenue, breathing the unique flavor of the city deep into his lungs. Glorious. Nothing else quite like it.

He opened the door to Beanie's and went inside to grab a coffee for his walk. Katie, Kelly, and Leo were behind the counter. Kevin was wiping off a table. Katie's aunt rubbed a lot of people the wrong way. Brendan. Dillon, especially. He got it. She *was* a bitch, but he couldn't help but think it was some kind of defense mechanism on her part. Maybe someone in the past had hurt her, because there had to be a reason she treated people the way that she did.

"Hey, Kyan," Katie greeted him with her usual sweet smile and he leaned over the counter to plant a kiss on her cheek.

"Hey yourself, coffee girl." He winked. "Long time, no see."

"You just saw me yesterday." She looked up to the ceiling, shaking her head with a grin on her face.

He smirked. "Yeah, and yesterday was a long time ago."

Katie burst out laughing.

Kelly rolled her eyes. He ignored it.

Whatever.

"I'll love you forever if you make me a large quad-shot latte to-go."

"You'll love me forever even if I don't." She winked as she grabbed a cup.

He would. Katie was family. He couldn't imagine ever not loving any of them—even the ice queen.

Kyan glanced over at her while Katie made his drink. "How's it going, Kelly?"

"Uh, okay, I guess." She seemed surprised that he spoke to her.

He tipped his chin and winked. "Sometimes okay is okay, you know?"

Kelly arched a brow, her lips curved up the tiniest bit. She was trying so hard not to smile, but he could see it. This woman just needed someone to pull them out of her.

Katie snapped the lid onto his coffee and handed it to him. "You and Linn are coming for dinner tomorrow, right?"

"Wouldn't miss it." He smacked another kiss to her cheek. "And you're right."

"About what?"

Kyan just smiled. "Thanks for the coffee, Katie." And heading toward the door he held up his hand in a wave.

He could have driven, grabbed an Uber, or taken the train, but then what was the point of leaving the office if not to take advantage of this gorgeous late summer day? Winter would be here soon enough, bringing the cold and the snow and the slush along with it. And his daughter.

Charlotte.

She would be here in January and Kyan couldn't wait to meet her. To be able to hold her. He'd memorized every feature of her precious little face from the ultrasound pictures. Linnea said she looked like him, but he saw his wife in their baby girl. She was perfect and she was beautiful.

And he felt like he was the luckiest fucking man alive.

But then why shouldn't he? He had more than he'd ever imagined or hoped to have. A wife he adored and a baby on the way. A thriving family business doing what he loved. Park Place—he got to live with his brother and cousins close to him, and that's just how he wanted it. How it had always been. Charlotte would grow up knowing the same abundant love he had as a child, and to Kyan that was everything. *Family* was everything. What more could he ask for?

His phone vibrated in his shirt pocket. Holding onto his coffee with one hand, he cursed at himself for leaving his AirPods behind and reached for it with the other. Her name blinked on the screen. Just seeing it brought a smile to his face.

Linnea.

"Hey, beautiful."

The absolute love of his life. His heartbeat. Sometimes Kyan wished he could thank Kodiak for the part he played, unbeknownst to him, in bringing them together. He couldn't, though. Even after three years, Crossfield was still too painful to think of. For all of them.

Yet, if Linnea hadn't choked into her napkin that afternoon at Charley's, as Chloe animatedly regaled them with the mystery of Fuckboy, Kyan might not have taken her hand in his from behind the bar. It was at that moment he realized he'd held off long enough, and if he waited even one more day to make his interest known to her, he'd be one day too late.

As it turned out, he was right on time.

Linnea was at Beanie's having coffee with Chloe before they took the kids to the park on their way home from shopping. He must have just missed her. She only called to tell him that.

"I've got salmon marinating for you to grill. We can have dinner outside, okay?"

"Okay." Kyan grinned because she didn't have to ask.

"And hurry home." He heard the hint of what awaited him when he got there in her voice. "I love you."

"I love you too."

Kyan quickened his pace. The sooner he got to the warehouse, the sooner he'd be home with Linnea. No one ever told him that a pregnant woman's sex drive can go into overdrive, and it was a delightful surprise. He'd expected the opposite. But that hadn't been the case at all, for which he considered himself extremely fortunate. Her gentle curves, the swell of her belly, her lush breasts with their extra-sensitive nipples were such an incredible turn-on and her insatiable desire for him was the ultimate boost to his ego.

He pocketed his phone, sipping on his now-lukewarm coffee as he walked the last couple of blocks. Was it the sound of creaking metal that made him look up? Kyan couldn't say for sure, but it amplified in his ears like the loud groan of a rusty hinge. Unexpected and out of place. Just ahead, at the corner, a section of the scaffolding that surrounded the warehouse looked precariously unstable, its diagonal brace loose, the topmost deck at an uneven slant.

It couldn't hold up like that. Kyan was an architect, not a structural engineer, but even he knew it was going to collapse. Two kids wearing Catholic school uniforms stood at the corner waiting for the light to change. The girl, in her plaid pleated skirt, held tight to the younger boy's hand. He heard it again. The groaning screech of metal. And he didn't allow himself even a second to think about it.

Kyan threw his coffee to the sidewalk as he sprinted to the corner. His only thought was he had to get those kids out of harm's way before the whole thing came crashing down on top of them. Before the warehouse became the site of some horrific tragedy. Before it was too late.

He got to them just in time.

The ringing in his ears was so fucking loud and the sun in his eyes was so bright it was blinding. Kyan blinked, looking up into the afternoon sky from where he lay on metal-littered concrete.

He wasn't in any pain, so apparently nothing was broken. The girl scrambled away from the curb to comfort the boy who was crying.

I'm okay. Good. Everyone's okay.

At the moment, that was all that mattered. He breathed a sigh of relief.

The girl hobbled to his side then. She couldn't be older than thirteen, with blonde hair in a ponytail and a scraped-up knee. Her eyes were blue and they widened as she surveyed him. She sat down beside him on the sidewalk and took his hand in both of hers, squeezing it tight.

"Does it hurt?" she asked. "You're bleeding."

He looked at her knee. "So are you."

"It's nothing." She smiled a little. "What's your name?"

"Kyan." His throat tickled and he coughed. "What's yours?"

"Hailey."

"That's a pretty name." The tickle was still there and he coughed again. "Is that your brother?"

"Yeah." The girl shrugged a shoulder. "He's eight."

"Is he okay?"

"Not a scratch on him."

"Good." Kyan managed a smile. He licked his lips. They felt dry. "I have a brother too. Dillon."

The ringing in his ears wasn't quite so loud now. Through the clamor, someone shouted to call 911. The light was just so fucking bright. He closed his eyes.

"Don't do that," she implored. "Tell me about him. Your brother, Dillon, is he a pain like mine is?"

He blinked them open. "No, that would have been me. I'm the younger one."

Tickle.

Tickle.

Tickle.

The sensation lodged at the back of his throat. Once more he coughed, attempting to clear it. Warm liquid bathed his tongue, its metallic taste triggered his awareness. Blood. Kyan swallowed it.

It's nothing.

I'm okay.

Kyan reasoned he must have some kind of internal injury, but he wasn't in any pain. If it didn't hurt it couldn't be that bad, right? Maybe he ruptured his spleen or something stupid like that. That's what the diagnosis usually was on *Grey's Anatomy.* Linnea loved to watch that show. What does a spleen do anyway? It must not be a necessary organ considering doctors cut them out of people every day—on TV anyway. He wasn't too worried.

"How much younger?" Hailey prompted him, squeezing his hand again.

He swallowed the blood that steadily crept into his mouth before he answered. "Two years."

"That's not such a big difference."

He huffed out a snicker. "It is when you're eight and he's ten."

The light was too bright. The girl glowed in the middle of it, as if the sun were a stage light illuminating her face. Kyan flicked his eyes right and left, taking in the scene that surrounded him. Nothing seemed right. Like overexposed film, what he saw was lighter than he thought it should be. Strange. He closed his eyes to it.

"Don't you do that!" the girl, Hailey, yelled at him before softening her voice. "Please keep them open and talk to me. I'm scared."

She gripped his hand harder and opening his eyes, he nodded. "You're okay. Don't be afraid."

"Do you like having a brother?" She lowered her voice. "Sometimes I don't."

"I do. I'm so lucky. I got the best one." Kyan entwined their fingers, the words sputtering from his throat, "And so did you. Your brother is everything you'll always have. No matter what. Family first, Hailey. Never forget that."

"Kyan."

He blinked his eyes open, only he didn't remember closing them. The girl was there at his side still, yet it wasn't her voice that he'd heard.

"Mom?"

"It's me, baby."

She was so very beautiful, more beautiful than he remembered, but then it had been so long since he'd seen her. She smiled at him, her long blonde hair gently fluttering with the breeze. Her blue eyes sparkling in the light. He must be hallucinating or perhaps he was dreaming. His mother died when he was eight.

"I've missed you so much."

"I missed you too." Her fingers skimmed his cheek and brushed the hair back from his eyes. "Come on, we have to go now."

Go? Where?

The only place he had to go was home. Kyan supposed he'd have to go to the hospital first to get his spleen taken out, but then he was going home. Linnea was there waiting for him to grill the salmon. They were going to have dinner on the patio, and after he'd make love to her there too. Then again while cleaning up the kitchen. In the shower. Their bed.

"Can't go with you…Linn…I have a wife now, Mom…we're having a baby."

His mother tilted her head and gazed down at him, smiling. "I know, sweetheart, and she's beautiful."

She held out her hand for him to take it.

He shook his head. "I can't."

"It's too late, my beautiful boy. Take my hand. You have to come with me now."

"Wake me up from this fucking dream," he shouted. "I said I can't."

The faint shrill of sirens could be heard in the distance. They seemed so far away.

"Kyan." The girl tugged on his hand, their fingers still laced together. "Hold on. Hear that? Help is almost here."

But he could feel himself slipping.

He'd always heard your life replays before your eyes like a movie in fast-forward. They were wrong. It came in clips and still images. Precious moments. All the people he loved.

Who could love and care for Linnea and Charlotte like he would?

"Dillon," his mother answered.

She was right.

There was no one else in the world he felt safe leaving them with more than his brother. No one he trusted more. Dillon had always loved her, and Linnea loved him too. She'd just never been able to accept it in the way Chloe had with Jesse and Taylor. Kyan tried to make her see it wasn't wrong—Dillon too.

Without him they'd find their way to each other. They had to.

"Take my hand now, baby."

"Dillon. Take care of them, brother."

I love you.

And he reached for her.

Eight

Something prompted him to glance at the clock.

3:28 p.m.

It was an odd feeling, a whole-body shiver passing through him, that made him look. Dillon couldn't explain it. He had no reason to check the time at that particular moment. He didn't have anything on the schedule for the rest of the day. In fact, he considered knocking off early and going home. Kelsey was coming over later and he planned to tell her it was probably best if they ended things. Gently. There was no reason to continue a relationship when they didn't have a chance in hell for a future.

And they sure as hell didn't.

He'd come to that conclusion at the lake house, even before he and his brother talked about it. Kelsey was a nice girl, but she wasn't the girl for him. He knew it. Kyan knew it. Everyone else probably knew it too. They didn't fit together, and as much as he'd tried he couldn't force it, so why prolong the inevitable?

Brendan stretched his arms and got up from his throne where he'd been playing with numbers for the past hour. "I need coffee. Actually, whiskey would be better." Crossing the room, he asked, "Anyone want anything?"

"Whiskey sounds good." Dillon snickered. He was going to need it.

"You could have both, you know," Jesse absently added, tapping away on his phone. "Put a shot in your coffee, Bren." Then he glanced up. "Bus pulled out of Indy. They'll be home in a few hours."

They being Taylor and the Venery boys.

Brendan popped a pod in the coffee machine just as his phone buzzed. He answered it, but Dillon didn't hear what he was saying. Then his cousin looked at them, his face blank, and said, "It's Jenkins. There's been an accident at the warehouse. We've got to go."

The coffee cup was left behind empty. Brendan never got to push the brew button.

It was the longest twenty minutes ever. At four o'clock in the afternoon the city streets were already clogged with traffic, rush hour well underway. And the closer they got, the worse it became.

"Didn't Jenkins tell you anything?" Jesse asked from behind the wheel of his Rover, honking the horn. "Fucking side streets would have been faster."

"I told you." Brendan tugged his fingers through his hair. "He only said some scaffolding fell and to hurry."

Jesse glanced at him in the rearview mirror, then back at Brendan. "He didn't mention if Ky was still there?"

"No."

Odd.

Dillon texted his brother. He called him. No answer. He told himself Kyan was too busy dealing with the chaos over there.

They saw the barricades and flashing lights of emergency vehicles from more than a block away. That shiver ran through him again. Jesse turned down a side street and parked. They'd have to walk from here.

Only they didn't walk. They ran.

Jesse reached the barricade first, the street and sidewalk closed. A police officer stood sentry to ensure no one got past it. Even them.

"That's our warehouse," his cousin attempted to explain.

The cop wouldn't budge. "Don't care if you own the whole damn block. Can't let you through."

Brendan started making phone calls. Probably to Jenkins. Maybe Murphy.

It seemed like an eternity later, though in reality it was

probably a couple of minutes at most, another police officer with a distraught-looking Jenkins appeared.

"Let them in," the officer instructed.

"I'm so fucking sorry," Jenkins choked out, his eyes red and glassy.

Brendan clasped his shoulder. "What happened?"

"A section of scaffolding collapsed," he answered, rubbing the back of his neck.

His cousin cocked his head. "How?"

"I don't know. I was inside when it came down."

A crowd of police officers and rescue workers blocked their view of what lie ahead. Right then Dillon didn't care about how it happened. The why and the how of it could come later. He just hoped no one was badly hurt. Or worse.

Judging by the ambulance on standby, it didn't look like they'd be that lucky.

"Is my brother here?"

Jenkins paused on the sidewalk. He just stood there, his mouth gaping like a fish out of water, then he tipped his chin with a slight nod. "Yeah."

"Where is he?"

The cop looked down the sidewalk and bowed his head. Jenkins wouldn't look at him at all. At once, tingles zipped up his spine and his breath caught in his throat. Through the emergency workers moving about the debris, he glimpsed a sheet-covered form perhaps twenty feet from where they stood. Dillon took a step forward, his heart pounding in his chest, but the officer grasped his forearm to stop him from going any farther.

"Trust me, you don't want to go over there."

Dillon wrenched his arm free.

No, no, no, no, no... It's not Kyan.

Not my brother.

It's not him.

It can't be him.

But even before he reached him, Dillon knew that it was.

The officers gave him room, backing away, as he approached the white, crimson-stained sheet. He didn't want to see. He didn't want to lift that sheet, because then it would be real. In his mind, until he saw his brother lying there beneath it, he wasn't dead. He sucked in a lungful of air, the tainted smell of blood and debris assaulting him, as he slowly sank to his knees, holding onto these last precious seconds before reality slapped him in the face.

His fingers trembled as he gripped the edge of the sheet. Strangled sounds came from Jesse behind him. He could hear the sobbing of a girl. She sat watching him from the passenger seat of an open squad car with a young boy. He felt Brendan's hand squeeze his shoulder as he lifted the sheet away and saw his brother's face.

Frozen. He just sat there, staring at him.

Jesse emitted a bellowing, anguished scream, "Noooo! Fuck! God, no!"

Dillon heard him, but it didn't register. He sensed Brendan had a hard grip on both of his shoulders, but he didn't feel it. This wasn't real. It couldn't be happening. He pulled the offending cloth all the way back.

Kyan.

My God, Kyan...what happened to you?

His beautiful brother.

Because if any man could be described as beautiful, it was him. He looked as if he were simply asleep, except blood coated his lips and he was unnaturally still. Dillon took his brother's hand and held it in his own. He kissed his knuckles and held Kyan's palm against his cheek. He was still warm.

Blood formed into a puddle by his body. The white button-down he wore stained with the same ghastly crimson as the sheet that covered him. A piece of rebar impaled his abdomen. Dillon closed his eyes, but the image of Kyan, bleeding out until he lay dead on a sidewalk was still there. Rocking on his knees, he gasped for air but couldn't get any into his lungs.

Brendan tried to pull him away, but Dillon refused to budge

from his place beside his brother. He opened his eyes to see Jesse next to him, tears streaming down his face in torrents as he gently combed his fingers through Kyan's hair, his strangled sobs breaking free. Numbly, he rocked with his brother's hand on his face, memorizing the feel of it while he still could.

Jesse leaned over and choking on tears, he kissed his cousin's forehead. Brendan got down on his haunches opposite him and did the same. With watery eyes, he glanced at him and tipped his chin in a nod. Dillon kissed Kyan's hand once more and placed it back on his chest. Then his cousin pulled the sheet back up over his brother's face.

"He saved us."

The girl studied him with vacant eyes from the open patrol car. She blinked. Tears rolled down her cheeks.

Dillon rose from the sidewalk and went to her. "What?"

"He pushed us out of the way just as it fell down," she said, softly. The girl stared ahead at the torn metal as if seeing it happen all over again. "You're Dillon, aren't you?"

He turned his head abruptly to Brendan and Jesse who stood with him, stunned that she seemed to know who he was. "I am, but how did you know that?"

Her teary gaze returned to him then. "Kyan. He told me about you before he…" She squeezed her eyelids together tight. "…before he died."

Blinking, Dillon looked up to the sky and inhaled deeply through his nose. His throat closed up and he couldn't speak. He just nodded. Fortunately, Brendan was able to.

He got down on his haunches and took the girl's trembling hand. "I'm Kyan's cousin, Brendan."

"I'm Hailey."

Brendan offered the sniffling girl a sympathetic smile. "Can you tell us what happened, Hailey? Everything he said?"

"I can," she spoke softly, nodding, and handed Brendan a folded-up piece of notebook paper. "I thought I should write it all down while we waited for my mom to get here. I didn't want to forget anything."

He slid the paper into his pocket. "Thank you, Hailey."

The girl took a stuttering breath. "We were waiting to cross the street—me and my little brother. I was holding his hand when Kyan pushed us off the sidewalk. The noise was..." She paused as if trying to think of a word to describe it. "...I can still hear it."

Her brother, a sandy-haired young boy, winced as he sat beside her, looking down at his lap.

"We were all right, but he was lying there on the sidewalk. I went over to him to see if he was okay, but as soon as I saw...*that*, I knew that he wasn't." A sob escaped her. "He didn't seem to realize how badly he was hurt, and I didn't want him to freak out, you know?"

"He wasn't in any pain?"

"I don't think so." She shook her head. "I thought if I could just keep him talking 'til the ambulance got here everything would be okay. He told me he had a brother, just like me..."

Dillon pressed his lips together to keep the scream inside. Determined to escape, it sputtered out through the flare of his nostrils. He almost didn't want to hear this because he was so close to losing it. Every cell in his body wanted to lie down with Kyan; to hold him and howl, to cradle him and cry, to plead with a God, who couldn't possibly fucking exist, to give his brother back to him.

He had to hear it, though. Kyan's words. He would never get to hear his brother speak to him again.

Her voice cracking, Hailey spoke through her tears, "...and that he was so lucky because he got the best one." She locked her sad blue eyes on his. "He said I was too, that your brother is everything. That I'll always have him. No matter what. And to never, ever forget family first."

It was me, Kyan. I got the best one. I got you.

"He closed his eyes. It was only for a second or two, but

when he opened them again it was like he didn't see me anymore." She shrugged with a shake of her blonde ponytail. "He was talking to someone, but it wasn't to me."

"Who then?" Brendan asked her.

"I heard him say, 'Mom.'"

Jesse let out a strangled sob and clutched onto his shoulder. Dillon looked to the sky. Shouldn't he be comforted by that? He wasn't. It was too much. He had to get away from here.

"God, I can't hear any more." He spotted the coroner's van pulling up to the curb. "And I can't watch that. I'll be over there."

"Wait," Hailey beseeched him, gently clasping his forearm. "The last thing he said was, 'Dillon...take care of them, brother.'" Chewing on her lip, she released a pent-up breath. "I'm sorry. I tried."

He squatted down so his eyes were level with hers and took Hailey's hand. "I'm so sorry you had to go through that, but I'm so glad you were with him. That he wasn't alone." He gently squeezed her fingers in his palm. "I want to thank you for that, Hailey."

Then he stood, and with one last parting glance to where his brother lay, Dillon walked away.

He stopped, just inside the barricade, and leaned against the brick where he wouldn't have to look at the bloodstained sheet on the sidewalk. Where he wouldn't have to see them pick Kyan's body up off the concrete and carry him onto a stretcher. Instead he stared at nothing in front of him, too numb to process the immense tragedy of his reality.

Take care of them, brother.

In his mind he could hear his brother's voice so clearly. He didn't have to ask. He would always take care of Linnea...*fucking Christ!* How in the hell was he going to tell her that Kyan was never coming home? That the person they both loved most in the world was gone?

Pushing all thoughts of his own pain aside, Dillon took in a deep breath. He had to think of her. Be strong for her. Linnea was pregnant. He had to be present for her and the baby in every way. Family first, and they were his.

I will, Kyan. I promise you.

He needed to call Kodiak so he could be there to support his sister. Hell, they were all going to need each other, to lean on each other, for a long time to come. But Linnea was foremost in his thoughts. She was his priority and what she needed came before anything else.

My brother died.

It was the first time he said the words out loud, and saying them somehow made it so horribly real. He knew it was just the first time of many he'd have to say it. Kodiak was going to meet them at the office. They'd tell his sister together.

The sound of a paper cup skittering along the curb with the evening breeze caught his attention and he looked in the direction that it came from. Dillon knew that blue cup, recognized the Beanie's logo even before he bent over to pick it up. Kyan was written on it in Katie's even script. Seeing that almost made him smile. Silly, wasn't it? He straightened, the cup in his hand, just as the coroner's van drove past. He just stood there, watching the van drive away with his brother inside, until it turned the corner and was gone.

They walked back to the Rover in silence. Dillon held onto that paper cup. He couldn't let it go. It wasn't until they got inside the SUV that he spoke. "We'll talk to Linnea together. I already called Kodiak."

Jesse solemnly nodded. "I called Tay. They're almost home. He'll stay with Chloe until…until we call for them. My mom will be on the next flight here."

"Monica will come if we need her." Brendan turned to face him from the passenger seat. Already he looked weary, and their ordeal had only just begun. He stared at the paper cup in his hand, and though Dillon saw his eyes fill, his cousin did not allow a single tear to spill. "Katelyn just saw him."

Dillon turned the cup to show Brendan her writing was on it.

"I made sure Hailey and her brother are okay. Their mother came and I gave her our card in case they need anything." He patted his pocket. "And I'll hold onto this for whenever you're ready to read it."

Dillon glanced at the clock.

6:28 p.m.

Had it really only been three hours since the last time he'd looked at it? Brendan's cup remained empty, the coffee he'd wanted long since forgotten.

"She's probably already worried that he isn't home yet." Kodiak paced.

"Yeah," Jesse agreed. "Taylor's telling Chloe now. We can't put it off any longer."

Brendan glanced to him and he nodded, Kyan's voice in his head.

Take care of them, brother.

Nine

Devastation.

The dictionary defines it as great destruction. Severe and overwhelming grief. And while the noun was an apt one, as Dillon surveyed the faces gathered in Linnea's family room, he couldn't help but think the word was sorely lacking.

What comes after? What happens after the shock dissipates and the numbness wears off? What's left then? What word defines that?

He should know. He'd been through this before, and more times than he cared to remember. His mother. His father. Every aunt and uncle, save for one. But this was Kyan, this was his brother, and it was different. It cut deeper. A fresh, hemorrhaging wound to add to the scars he already carried on his heart.

The front door opened. Chloe and Taylor came in, Katie right behind them, arms laden with containers wrapped in plastic and tin foil. Brendan and Jesse automatically got up from the sofa to relieve their wives of the load they carried. Katie stayed back while Chloe rushed to fling her arms around him. She held him tight, but didn't say anything, but then what could she say? There were no words. None at all. And all of them were grieving.

"I love you, Dill." Her voice trembled and she kissed his cheek. "How is she?"

Brendan was the one who gently delivered the words that forever altered her future. The words that made Linnea a twenty-four-year-old widow with a baby on the way. A daughter his brother would never get to see or hold or know. Dillon held her hands in his as he did, helplessly watching her world shatter in her eyes. It ripped him apart to see it. Then he held her as she cried.

"She's...Monica is with her."

Chloe let out a breath and nodded. "Ava's got all the kids at my house. Me and Katie needed to do something while we waited to come over. I know you probably don't feel like eating, but there's plenty."

Katie came up and hugged him then. She'd been the last one of them to see Kyan alive and he envied her for that. "I kept the cup."

She lifted her head from his shoulder with a puzzled look, blue-green eyes shining with unshed tears. "Cup?"

"I found it by the warehouse. You wrote his name on it."

"Oh, God." Hugging him again, she began to cry. "What're the chances of that?"

Slim to none, coffee girl.

He took it as a sign. Of what he wasn't sure. But he wanted to believe it was Kyan's way of showing him he was there with him. Crazy, right?

They were all here now, gathered together in Kyan's house to be there for Linnea, to be there for each other. His cousins. The girls. Venery. Kodiak. Monica and Danielle. He was surprised then, to hear the doorbell ring.

Who in the hell is that already?

Now was not the time for outsiders. Linnea was in no condition to see anyone besides the people that were already here. Her family. Those closest to Kyan needed this time alone together to begin to process their immeasurable loss. To grieve in private. They'd have to go through the public spectacle of a wake and funeral soon enough. Couldn't they be left alone until then?

Fuck.

Dillon opened the door to look into the face of a very pissed-off Kelsey staring back at him. He'd forgotten all about her. She pushed past him into the foyer, not even giving him the chance to explain.

"You told me to come over at seven," she yelled, waving her phone back and forth in front of his face. "It's after eight. I've been waiting at your front door for more than an hour. Texting. Calling. Worried out of my fucking mind. For. Nothing!"

Kelsey held up her hands, her phone clutched in one, and peeked around the corner to see everyone assembled there. "Having a little party, I see. Forget about me?"

She should have looked a little closer. She might have noted the somber faces then, gauged the temperature of the room. Kelsey was about to feel like an ass, and Dillon didn't feel the least bit sorry about it.

"Yeah, I did actually," he admitted.

Moving her hands to her hips, she huffed, "What?"

"My brother died."

Her face fell and her voice softened to almost a whisper, "What?"

"Kyan." He nodded, choking up.

"Oh, my God," she gasped, hugging him. "Baby, I'm so sorry. When? How?"

Kelsey *was* an outsider, and this was exactly the shit he wasn't ready to deal with. Endless questions he didn't want to answer and condolences he didn't want to hear. Not now. Not yet. And considering he'd been planning to end their relationship tonight, not from her.

Dillon pulled away from her and put some space between them. It wasn't her fault, but right now everything about her just annoyed him. "There was an accident at the warehouse this afternoon."

"Accident?" She shook her head. "What happened?"

Nope. Not doing this.

She could read it online or in the paper. Hell, it might even be on the news. But right now he needed to get back in there and Kelsey needed to go home.

"Look, I'll try to call you tomorrow or the day after," he said and nudged her toward the door. "But I've got a lot going on right now."

"I want to stay here with you," she insisted. "Can't I help?"

"Yeah, by going home." He pushed a strand of hair off her face, his hand settling on her shoulder. "I need to be with my family, okay?"

Kelsey pursed her lips to the side, nodding. "Okay."

Dillon opened the door for her and she kissed him. "Call me."

He tipped his chin and quietly closed the red-painted door.

Was that rude of him? Maybe. He didn't really care, though. While he was sorry he'd forgotten about her, and wished he'd thought of texting her to cancel, Dillon reasoned it was more than understandable why he didn't. She might think he was being a dick, and while that wasn't his intention, in all honesty, Kelsey Miller and her feelings were no longer his priority.

He heaved a sigh, glancing around the foyer before he rejoined the others. Linnea loved her books. Kyan had built-in shelves and custom bookcases put in every nook and cranny of the house for her. Like a library, white-painted wooden shelving lined one wall of the wide hallway that led to the living room. He even installed a rolling library ladder so she could reach the upper shelves. Framed photographs and original works of local artisans hung on the other.

Dillon paused in front of an old photo of him with Kyan and their mother. Linnea or his brother must have hung it just recently, because he didn't recall seeing it here before, but he vividly remembered when the photo was taken. It was New Year's Day. His eighth birthday. Kyan was five going on six. All three of them wore silly paper party hats on their heads.

Their mother was stunningly beautiful. To Dillon, as a child, she looked like a model or a movie star. Funny, how he got his mother's blonde hair, but resembled their father, while Kyan got his dark hair and their mother's beautiful features. Both of them inherited those Byrne baby blues, though.

He reverently stroked the frame with his fingertips. His mother was only thirty in this photo. Less than three years later she'd be dead.

"I heard him say, 'Mom.'"

Did Kyan call out for her, or did he see her as he lay there dying? Were they together now in the afterlife? Was there an afterlife? Dillon wasn't sure, but he liked to think so. The earthly body might rot away in the ground to dust, but not the soul. And the energy of a person had to go somewhere, releasing into the atmosphere upon death—conservation of matter and all that. He placed a kiss on the photo with his fingertips and continued down the hallway.

Dillon reclaimed his seat on the turquoise suede sofa. It wasn't the same one she'd had in her old place on Oak Street, but Linnea was fond of the color and wouldn't settle for any other. A dozen weary faces sat around the coffee table, the usual knickknacks replaced by bottles of whiskey and platters of food to nosh on. It looked good, but Chloe was right. He didn't feel like eating.

"Mom made the flight. I'm picking her up at O'Hare in the morning." Jesse cleared his throat. "She'll, um, help with the arrangements."

They'd need it. Fuck if his aunt didn't have enough practice at it. She'd already buried a sister, a husband, and a brother.

"Good." He nodded.

The sound of footsteps could be heard padding down the hallway. They all turned their attention toward it, hoping to see Linnea, but it was Monica who entered the room. She looked drained, her usual smile missing from her face. Kissing her wife, she laced their fingers together and perched herself on the arm of the chair Danielle sat in.

"How is she?" Chloe asked what they all wanted to know.

"Doing as well as can be expected," Monica answered with a sigh. "I got her to rest for a bit, but I'm sure that won't last long."

Fresh tears rolled down Chloe's face. "I don't know what to do."

"Be there when she needs you, and anticipate what that is because she won't ask. Don't be afraid to talk about Kyan with her, to reminisce—she'll want to. We're all grieving here, so we'll support her, and each other, while we grieve right along with her."

Monica got up then and crossed the room to where he sat next to Kodiak. She got down in front of him and took his hands in hers. "How are you, Dillon?"

"I don't know how to answer that." He shrugged.

She squeezed his hands. "I'm here for you too."

"I know." He squeezed back. "Thank you."

"I'm going to go and get Elliott home, but I'm just a phone call away." Her hands settled on his knees as she stood. "It would be good if someone could stay here with her."

"Yeah." He nodded. "Of course."

One by one, everyone went home after that. Katie and Chloe the last to go after they set everything back to rights and put all the food away, leaving him, Kodiak, and a bottle of Glenlivet alone together at the kitchen island.

Kodiak poured himself a shot and downed it. "You know I can't spend the night here, but I'll be back first thing in the morning."

Dillon understood. "I know."

"You okay, man?" he asked as he stood to leave.

No.

Dillon stood with him. "I will be."

He found her still asleep in one of the guest bedrooms. Dillon tiptoed inside and gazed down at Linnea atop the still-made bed, a throw blanket covering her, and was reminded of all the nights he'd lain with her to keep the nightmares away. He couldn't do that for her this time, though. This was one nightmare they'd both have to live through. He softly kissed her on the temple and headed for the door.

"Dillon?"

"I'm here, Linn." He returned to her side. "I'm right here."

She burst into tears. "Don't leave me."

"Not going anywhere," he soothed. Lying down beside her, he wrapped her in his arms.

I promise.

And he held her through the night while she cried.

Ten

He read the paper in his hand.

Time of death. 3:28 p.m.

And that now all-too-familiar chill passed through him.

Dillon shook his head in disbelief. It hadn't been quite forty-eight hours since he was compelled to glance at the clock in the office. The four of them sat in Jesse's kitchen. The coroner released Kyan's body this morning and they'd just come back from making the final arrangements for him. Wake tomorrow. Funeral on Saturday. And then what? What comes after that?

Sunday, asshole.

Right now he couldn't think even that far ahead.

"Is it too early to crack a bottle open?" Brendan wondered out loud.

"It's never too early," his aunt, Colleen, immediately replied. "And anyway, we're grieving."

Jesse went to the liquor cabinet, and returning with a bottle of Irish whiskey, poured a generous dose in a glass for each of them. Dillon drained his in one swallow. He'd gladly put himself in an alcohol-induced haze to get through the next few days if he could. But he couldn't. Not if he was going to be someone Linnea could depend on.

She slept on and off most of the day yesterday, which considering how emotionally drained and physically exhausted she must be, wasn't surprising. That first night had been a rough one. For both of them. Soothing Linnea gave him a sense of purpose, though, and

Dillon was grateful for it. As strange as it might seem, that he could do that for her, provided him with some measure of comfort too.

"Another?" Jesse went to refill his glass.

Dillon shook his head. "No, thanks. I should get going."

Not wanting to overwhelm her with the grim task, Chloe and Katie had been keeping Linnea company while they took care of arranging the funeral. Fortunately, Aunt Colleen knew what to do and saw to most of the details. If they were finished here, Dillon needed to get back over there.

Brendan glanced over at him. "Relax, Dill. She's okay."

I'm not.

He stood, and with a tip of his chin went to the door. Aunt Colleen followed, pulling him into an embrace as he reached for the knob. She cupped his cheek in her palm. "I love ya, Dillon."

"I love you too, *Aintín*," he murmured and pulled her in for another hug. Then he walked across the street.

Chloe and Katie left them with a casserole warming in the oven. Linnea sat at the kitchen island, peeling the label off a bottle of water. "I don't know what to do with myself."

"You don't have to do anything."

"Yes, I do, or I'll go mad." She swallowed some water, staring vacantly through the glass doors to the backyard. "I think I'm going to sit outside."

Dillon figured Linnea needed a few minutes alone with her thoughts. He watched her curl up on the outdoor sofa from the open patio doorway. She tilted her face up at the late-afternoon sky. Leaves on swaying branches cast dancing shadows over her face. Her skin was splotchy, eyes puffy and swollen from two days of crying. Still, she was beautiful.

It surprised him when she spoke, "I miss him so much, Dillon. It hurts."

"I know, Linn." He sat down beside her and wrapped an arm around her shoulders. "I miss him too."

"I know." She laid her head on his shoulder. "How do we go on without him?"

"I don't know," he sighed, combing her hair with his fingers. "We just…we just do."

She curled into him then, wrapping her arm around his waist, holding him tight. Dillon squeezed her shoulders. He just kept stroking her hair. They stayed like that for a while. Neither one of them spoke.

"I love you, Dill."

"And I love you. I'm always going to be here for you, and for Charlotte. Anything you need." He kissed the top of her head. "Anything. You know that, right?"

Dillon felt the nod of her head on his shoulder. "Your girlfriend probably misses you."

But I don't miss her.

"You come first."

She hugged him tighter. "Just hold me a little while longer."

Always.

Seven years had passed since the last time he stood in this chapel. When his father died. He didn't want to think about all the times he'd been here before that. All the people he loved who had left him. And it was the same now as it had been then. The sickening stench of flowers hung heavy in the room. Cloyingly sweet. Lilies. Gladiolas. Roses. Carnations. It was getting to him. Dillon couldn't pinpoint which bloom was the offending culprit, but it was nauseating. He needed air.

They'd been standing here for nearly two hours already. People filing past them to shake their hands, or worse, hug them and whisper, "*I'm so sorry.*" Aunt Colleen was to his left, Linnea to his right, her trembling fingers held in the crook of his arm. He patted her hand. This part was almost over.

But the hardest part was still to come.

Leaving Kyan in the ground tomorrow.

Kelsey sat in the second row of chairs watching him, Linnea, and his aunt, as they stood just beyond the open casket, receiving condolences from those who had come to say their silent goodbyes to his brother. She seemed uncomfortable in her surroundings, fingers fidgeting in her lap, but then who here wasn't? Dillon told her she didn't have to come, and actually, he would have preferred it if she hadn't. He never did get the chance to have *'the talk'* with her, though, and now was not the time. So, of course, Kelsey was here to play her part as the dutiful, dedicated girlfriend.

Bo sat next to her with Sloan beside him. He didn't pay Kelsey the least bit of attention, though, or anybody else either. With his elbows on his knees, his hands clasped beneath his chin, he just gazed upon Kyan lying there in repose. Trance-like. Like he was waiting to see his chest rise and fall, like if he stared at him long enough he could will him to breathe again.

Kit and Matt were on the other side of her, directly behind Brendan and Katie. Matt patted Katie's shoulder as she wept into her husband's neck. Brendan sat solid and stoic, her hands grasped tightly in his, but he couldn't veil the profound sorrow in his bloodshot eyes. Dillon could read every tragic memory his cousin kept hidden in their depths, but then he held them in his too. How much fucking loss could this family endure? Hadn't they already been through enough?

The line filing past the casket dwindled until no one except them remained and the double doors to the chapel closed. Dillon guided Linnea to a chair next to Chloe. The two girls just held each other, swaying side to side in their seats, Jesse rubbing Linnea's back. It tore him apart to see her in so much pain, but as long as he focused on her, he didn't have to think of his own.

Brendan got up and went to Kyan. He knelt down on the kneeler in front of him and bowed his head. Katie followed, her hands resting upon his shoulders. They were shaking. Then he rose and stood with Aunt Colleen. Taylor got up next and did the same. One by one, the Venery boys followed. Monica and Danielle. Kelly and Kevin. Kodiak.

He stood from the kneeler and joined his sister. Jesse and Chloe got up to take Kodiak's place with Kyan. The others waited at the chapel doors. Close friends had been invited to join them at Charley's to 'wake' Kyan properly, as Aunt Colleen put it. The Irish way.

Kelsey came to stand beside him. Grabbing his hand, she laced their fingers together and looked up at him. "Are we going now?"

"In a minute." Dillon gave her hand a squeeze. "Go on and wait with the others."

It was his turn with his brother.

Jesse and Chloe rose and turned toward him, wrapping him up in their arms, tears streaming down both their faces. Chloe quietly wept. His cousin, unable to contain his grief, openly sobbed. Born less than a year apart, he and Kyan were the closest of the four cousins growing up, and very much alike. Thick as thieves. Kindred spirits. Both of them had always worn their tender hearts on their sleeve, while he and Brendan had taken great pains to keep theirs in check.

"Love you, Jess." Dillon hugged his cousin and Chloe a little tighter. "I need a minute."

He gazed down at his brother. Choking on the perfumed air. Choking back the tears he wouldn't allow to surface. *Big boys don't cry.* He wanted to touch him, but he knew better than to do that. Dillon had made that mistake with his mother when he was ten years old. He wouldn't feel warm flesh. Instead, he gently stroked Kyan's long dark hair and closed his eyes. He squeezed them tightly shut as he remembered the feeling of his brother's still-warm hand that he'd held to his face.

Fuck!

How do I do this? How do I say goodbye?

I can't.

I love you, Kyan.

A hand squeezed his shoulder. Inhaling a deep breath, Dillon recognized her familiar scent. Sweet almonds. It canceled out the noxious lilies and gladiolas surrounding them. He let go of his brother's hair and covered her hand with his, grasping her fingers and squeezing them tight.

They stayed like that for a moment, then Linnea pulled down on his shoulder and leaned into his ear. "I'd like to have a few minutes alone with him. Can you ask everyone to step out?"

Dillon turned to look at her. He took her in his arms and held her for a moment, then with a nod of his head he let go.

They waited for Linnea on the other side of the double doors. No sooner did they close when her anguished sobbing could be heard. The mournful sound had Dillon flinching with every cry. Kelsey held onto his hand, and ignoring her, Chloe came up from behind him and circled her arms around his waist. She understood. He'd always been the one who could comfort her, even when Kyan couldn't.

Minutes went by, but those minutes felt like forever, and still she cried. Dillon couldn't stand to hear her in pain like that anymore. It couldn't be good for her—or for the baby, right? Even Chloe sobbed into his back listening to Linnea suffering.

He didn't think even he could ease it for her this time.

But he had to try.

Dillon glanced to Brendan and reached for the crystal knob to open the double doors, but before he could turn it and step back inside, Monica put her hand on top of his to stop him. "Don't. She needs this time alone with Kyan—to grieve in private."

He cocked his head with a shake and furrowed his brow. "Do you hear that? She's hurting all by herself in there."

What the fuck?

Was he supposed to just stand there and listen to her falling apart? Do nothing. He *needed* to do something.

"Yes, she's hurting, and so are you. We all are." Monica's hand stroked up and down his arm. "I know you care for her, Dillon. But the pain can't be avoided, and trying to would only prevent the healing from happening. Pain is the agent of change that will eventually lead toward acceptance." With a tilt of her head she squeezed his arm. "Grief is a part of love. Allow Linnea this. Let her cry. She's going to be okay."

His hand fell away from the doorknob. He nodded. And when

he turned around Kelsey stood gaping at him, slack-jawed, a single tear rolling down her cheek.

Dillon poured another finger of Redbreast into his glass. Only Irish whiskey today. The bar area of Charley's was packed full with their family and friends. The glass to the sidewalk patio that his brother'd insisted on knocking out half a brick storefront for had been slidden wide open. He chuckled to himself. Originally he'd been against the idea, but Kyan was right. It was a good call. He could almost see his brother sitting there in his favorite stool, catching the breeze that wafted in through the open glass.

It was six years ago, almost to the very day, that they opened this place. So many memories here. Afternoon breaks with Kyan and the girls when they all worked here together. Jesse behind the bar. This is where it all began.

Marcus came over to their table with another bottle of whiskey and clasped Dillon's shoulder. He'd been here since day one and did a damn good job running Charley's for them. "You doing all right, Dill?" He choked up for a minute and regained his composure. "Is there anything I can do for you?"

"No, you've done more than we could've asked for. Thanks for taking care of all this for us."

The hand that clasped his shoulder squeezed and Marcus nodded. "The private dining room is all set for the luncheon tomorrow." Then he leaned over to the other side of the table and hugged Linnea.

Monica must've known what she was talking about. Linnea came out of that chapel with a tear-stained face, sniffling and trembling, her green eyes glassy and red-rimmed. She sat across from him, subdued and sad, flanked between Bo and her brother, but she was holding up okay. For now anyway.

The purpose of an Irish wake isn't to mourn. It's not a party like they depict in the movies. An Irish wake is a celebration of life, and that's why they were here—to celebrate his brother. To reminisce and share stories. Eat. Drink. Sing songs. Laugh and cry together.

So the whiskey flowed, and as platters of food were passed around the bar, with rapt attention, Kelsey quietly listened to their anecdotes of Kyan and the history they all shared. The bond. The love. With every story told, she held onto him a bit tighter, clingy and possessive. Did she sense she would never be a part of their stories? Dillon wasn't exactly sure what to do about her. No, actually, that wasn't true. He just wasn't equipped to deal with another ending right now.

"Is it almost time to go?" She squeezed his thigh and whined, "I'm tired and we still have tomorrow."

What the fuck did she just say?

His nostrils flared as he inhaled. Dillon could think of a million comebacks to her insensitivity if he cared to. Except that he didn't. He hadn't asked her to be here in the first place. Pushing her hand off his thigh, he turned toward Kelsey. "I'm going to be a while. I'll call a car to take you home."

"I thought I'd stay with you tonight." Her face fell. "I brought a bag."

You thought wrong, Kels.

He never got to say it out loud.

Over the din, a clamor erupted. The loud clinking of glasses with silverware, a signal for everyone to be quiet. Sloan, no doubt already fucked up, though he appeared sober, stood up at the bar. A glass of whiskey raised high in his hand. He cleared his throat. His voice cracked as he spoke, "This one's for you, Ky. I'm gonna fucking miss ya, little brother. So much. Love you."

He swallowed the contents of his glass and with clear resound began to sing "The Parting Glass". A chill ran through him. Fans often described Sloan's voice as hypnotic and haunting. Right then Dillon couldn't disagree with them. He'd never heard a rendition of the traditional song sung so beautifully.

Maybe it was the words or maybe it was the way Sloan sang them. Tears streamed down Linnea's face and she stood from the table, one hand on Bo's shoulder and the other on her brother, taking in tiny gulps of air between hiccups. She looked at Dillon with that look. It was one he remembered well. The look that told him she was about to break.

He stood too. "Are you okay, Linn?"

"Yeah." She shakily nodded. "I just can't do this anymore…"

"C'mon, baby girl." Bo motioned to Kodiak. "We'll get you home."

"No." Dillon reached for Linnea's hand from across the table. "Don't worry. I've got her."

"Dillon?" Kelsey looked up at him from where she still sat. Brow raised. Eyes wide.

"I'll get a car to take you home."

She bit her lip with a nod.

Sorry, Kels.

No, he wasn't.

And with his arm around her shoulders, he escorted Linnea outside.

Eleven

Fucking hell.

Dillon slowly cracked one eye open to rain splattering against the windowpanes. He felt like utter shit. With a groan he attempted to lift his head from the pillow. It felt like a lead brick. Fisting the gray linen sheet in his hands, he forced himself to sit upright and leaned back against the headboard.

He ran his fingers though the mop of hair on his pounding head and massaged his scalp. The room swam in and out of focus. Was he still fucked up? Maybe. And so what if he was? He put his brother in the ground yesterday. Was there a better reason than that to drink yourself into oblivion? Right then, Dillon couldn't think of one.

It was a beautiful day for a funeral. Sunny and warm, but not so warm that you'd roast in a suit standing under the September sun. The air smelled like the end of a golden summer with just a hint of fall to remind you it was coming. Everything has its season, doesn't it? Eventually, everything and everyone you love dies.

But it shouldn't have been Kyan. Not yet. Not for a long, long time.

There's no avoiding your destiny.

His head lolled to stare out the window. "Yeah, well…Fate, you're a cruel fucking bitch," he whispered to the rain beating on the glass.

Water turned on in the en suite. Dillon turned his head away from the window at the sound of the shower running. Who the fuck was here? There was a dent in the pillow beside him. Rumpled sheets. Condom wrappers on the nightstand. A black dress was draped over a chair. Kelsey's dress.

Jesus, fuck.

Dillon didn't remember sleeping with her. Hell, he couldn't even remember how he got home. Scratching his head, he swung his legs over the side of the bed and stood. He ambled into the bathroom and relieved himself while she showered. Then he swallowed some ibuprofen and took his sorry ass back to bed. His recollection of yesterday was quite clear and vivid in his mind. Until Charley's. That's where things got fuzzy.

Venery carried Kyan to his final resting place. Irish pipers played "Amazing Grace" as they walked in procession behind the casket. They were so fucking loud, their legato sound blaring in a never-changing volume. Dillon watched the shake of Linnea's shoulders in front of him, crying as she held onto her brother's arm. In much the same way Aunt Colleen held onto him. Brendan and Katie walked directly behind him, followed by Jesse and Chloe. The closer they got to the open grave beside his parents, and their reserved row of empty chairs, the more she trembled.

He wanted to comfort her. Wished that somehow he could. Dillon placed a hand on her shoulder in front of him. She grasped it.

Rain tapped against the glass. The sound of water running in the shower stopped. He closed his eyes in the hope that Kelsey would find him asleep when she stepped out of the en suite and go home. Dillon just wanted to wallow in his grief and he couldn't do it with her—or with anyone. He could only do it alone.

But when he closed his eyes that burned from the remnants of tears left unshed, sleep evaded him. Memories of the cemetery flashed through his mind. Kodiak patting Linnea's hand in the seat beside him. His father's name, so similar to his own, carved into granite. Floral tributes arranged in a miserable attempt to camouflage the mound of dirt that would fill Kyan's grave. The boys' choir from their old high school singing "Danny Boy" *a cappella*. That's when Linnea's trembling turned into tremors, and her silent tears, pain-filled sobs.

The hair dryer turned on in the bathroom. Dillon opened his eyes. He should just give it up. Get out of bed, make some coffee, and send Kelsey on her way.

She found him on a stool, hunkered over the breakfast bar on the end of his galley kitchen, clutching a mug in his hands. He didn't look at her. Dillon took a slow sip before he acknowledged he knew she was there.

He set his cup down and turned toward her. Wearing the same dress she had on at the funeral, Kelsey had her purse in her hand. "Morning," he muttered. "You leaving?"

She took a hesitant step forward and kissed him on the cheek. "Morning. Yeah, I, uh…I didn't bring clothes with me because I didn't think you'd want me to stay."

You thought right.

"Are you okay?" Kelsey ran her fingers through his hair. "I can come back later if you want."

Was he okay? No, he was not fucking okay. His brother was dead, Linnea was next door, and he had the hangover from hell. He was far from fucking okay.

And none of that was Kelsey's fault.

He took a breath. "No, it's okay. I'll be all right."

"Are you sure?"

Dillon reached up and stilled her fingers that combed through his hair. "Yeah." Then he brought her fingers to his lips and kissed them. "Go on home. I'm okay."

Once Kelsey was gone he stepped into the shower and leaned against the enclosure, bracing his hands on the glass. Hot water seeped into his skin, making him feel somewhat human again, easing the tension from his muscles, but it didn't ease the ache in his chest.

They started with the back row. One by one, those who came to mourn with them filed past to place a flower on Kyan's casket as the high school choir sang. Linnea squeezed one hand, his aunt the other. Dillon didn't pay attention to who walked by until he noticed young Hailey with her mother.

The weeping girl turned from the casket with a nosegay of flowers in her hand, the stems wrapped in ribbon. Instead of proceeding down the aisle between the rows of chairs to the line of cars parked on the cemetery drive, she nodded at him and walked over to Linnea.

"I'm so sorry," Hailey choked out, handing Linnea the little bouquet. "And I'll never forget him. Your husband will always be my hero."

He almost lost it then.

Linnea choked on a sob and hugged the girl.

And Brendan stood.

Theirs was the only row left.

He turned off the water, unsure what to do with himself next. He knew Chloe was with her, but he needed to check on Linnea. She'd left Charley's with Monica yesterday shortly after the luncheon ended—and the drinking started. At least she hadn't been there to watch him get shit-faced.

Everything felt wrong and Dillon didn't know how to make it feel right again. Maybe it never would. He couldn't recall a world without Kyan in it and he couldn't make sense of the one he found himself in. They'd done just about everything together. Always had each other. But he didn't have him anymore and that was his new reality. How was he supposed to exist now?

You just do.

He stood there in his family room. It looked as it always did. Nothing had changed, yet everything was different. His gaze fell to the framed photo hanging on the wall. A copy of the enlargement he'd given to Jesse for his birthday. Four young boys sat on the front steps of their old apartment building. If Dillon had known then what fate had in store could he have changed its course somehow?

If only Kyan had left the office just a minute later.

If he hadn't stopped at Beanie's for coffee.

If he hadn't gone at all.

He'd still be here.

There's no avoiding your destiny.

Funny, isn't it? How even the smallest things, inconsequential as they might seem at the time, can put the domino into motion. Set off a chain reaction. Irrevocably alter the course of a life. And there's no way of knowing that first domino just tipped over.

A soft tap sounded at the front door. He knew just by the cadence of it that it was Kodiak. "Hey, man." He clasped Dillon on the shoulder as he stepped inside. "You look hungover as fuck."

"Probably because I am."

At least the pounding in his head had lessened to a persistent dull ache. He still felt like shit though. Kodiak followed Dillon into the kitchen and grabbed two bottles of water out of the fridge, handing him one.

"Figured as much." He tipped his chin toward the bottle Dillon still held in his hand. "Drink up. You need to rehydrate."

"On your way to Linn's?" Dillon unscrewed the cap and took a swig.

"No, I just left there." He exhaled and took a seat at the banquette. "Thought I should check on you too."

"Why?"

"To make sure you weren't choking on your own vomit, for starters." He smirked.

Rubbing his temple, Dillon grimaced.

"It's okay, man." Kodiak patted his arm. "It was a rough one."

Absently, he nodded and swallowed some water. "How's Linnea doing? I was just about to go over there."

"She's, um…" He looked out the window and lifted his shoulder. "…sad. Angry. Told me she was fine and to go on home."

"Angry? At you?"

He turned his head from the window. "Nah, she's angry at God."

The knock came after the front door opened. "Dill?"

"In the kitchen, Chloe."

She wearily entered the room and plunked herself down in the seat beside him, blowing out a breath. A ribbon of auburn hair fluttered upward, then fell to rest on her face. Chloe tucked it behind her ear.

"She send you on your way too?" Kodiak asked her.

Chloe sighed. "Yeah." She leaned her head against his shoulder. "How are you, Dill?"

He answered with a shrug and patted her head.

"Have you eaten? I can fix you something," she offered.

Kodiak answered for him. "He hasn't."

"I don't want anything right now." Apparently Chloe didn't like that answer. She pursed her lips, her brow knitting in disapproval. "I will in a little bit, okay?"

"Promise?"

"Promise." He crossed his heart.

"Where's Kelsey?" she inquired. "Why isn't she here?"

"I sent her on home." He gave her shoulders a squeeze.

Chloe and Kodiak exchanged a glance, then he stood. "I'm going to get going, man. I'll swing back by later."

Dillon got up for the bro-hug. "Thanks."

"I love you, Dill." Chloe hugged him tight. "If you need anything..."

"I'll call you." He hugged her back. "Thank you for always being here...for taking care of us and our girl." Then he walked her to the door and pulled her in for one more hug. "I love you too."

Linnea went last. She lovingly placed a single red rose atop the casket. Different from the rest, it stood apart from the white blooms already resting there. The choir boys still sang. She kissed the lid and laid her head upon it, rubbing and caressing the polished wood. Aunt Colleen clutched his arm, trying to stifle her sobs. Dillon was just trying to breathe.

It was killing him to see her like that.

It was over and his brother was really gone.

They'd never see Kyan's beautiful face again.

Kodiak rubbed Linnea's back and she lifted her head. He gently pulled her from the casket. She crumpled at his feet.

Before anyone else could react, Dillon crouched down at her side and took her in his arms. She held onto him, sobbing so hard, no sound came out. Slowly, he rose, lifting her to her feet. She buried her face in his chest. He held her close against him, smoothing her hair down her back.

"I've got you, gorgeous."

The choir still sang as they walked away.

"I've got you."

Dillon knocked on her door and stepped inside. It had been a couple hours since Chloe and Kodiak left. He figured she'd had enough time by herself. Her hand on her belly, Linnea was curled up in a plush, oversized chair by the window, reading a book.

She lifted her gaze from the page. "Dillon, you look like shit."

"Thanks." He smirked, and with his arm across her shoulders, got in the chair with her. "Whatcha reading?"

"Jane Austen." The corners of her mouth rose the tiniest bit. "I was in the mood for some classic literature. Brontë is my favorite, but…" Her hand moved slowly back and forth across her baby bump.

"Charlotte?"

"Emily."

Ah, Wuthering Heights.

Too tragic. Yeah, the Bennet sisters were a much better choice.

"Why don't I make us some lunch, yeah?" He tightened his arm around her shoulder.

"Um, I already ate." Setting her book on the side table she turned toward him. "But there's plenty in the fridge if you're hungry. Chloe and Katie packed it with food."

"I'm good," he lied. "I'll get something later."

"It's almost two, Dill." She rubbed her tummy again. Her gaze followed his to her bump. "I'm waiting."

"For what?"

"Charlotte." She smiled a little then.

Damn.

"At the ultrasound Roberta said I should start feeling her move soon." She glanced down. "Now would be good."

He had no words. Dillon placed his hand on top of her hand that rested on her belly and laced their fingers together. She laid her head on his shoulder. They stayed like that for a while.

She squeezed his fingers. "I have to learn how to be alone, Dill."

"I'm here." He held her even tighter. "You don't ever have to be alone."

"I know that, and I love you." She pushed the hair out of his eyes. "I guess what I'm trying to say is I don't need a babysitter twenty-four-seven, okay?"

She's not that fragile girl anymore, is she?

He nodded. "Okay."

"I'm always going to need you, Dillon. Always, always, always," Linnea implored, her tiny hand squeezing his. "But I don't want to *have* to need you—or my brother or Chloe or anyone. Am I making sense?"

"We all need somebody sometimes."

"You're right. We do." She nodded. "But it's not just me anymore. I have to be able to depend on myself, so Charlotte can too."

He pressed his lips together and combed his fingers through her hair.

"And I don't want to be the needy one all the time." She closed her sad green eyes for a moment. "It goes both ways, Dillon. You need somebody sometimes too."

Thirty minutes later he was in his car. With no destination in mind, he just started it and drove. Rain fell onto the windshield in a fine drizzle. Dillon still wasn't hungry, but his stomach growled at him, demanding to be fed, so he pulled into a drive-thru and got a burger. He took one bite. It tasted like cardboard. He tossed it into the trash.

Somehow he ended up at the cemetery gate. He turned onto the drive and parked. Even from here, through the mist outside and the condensation fogging his window, he could see the flowers that decorated his brother's grave. Dillon got out of his car.

He just stood there in the rain.

He wasn't sure how long he stood there, but it was long enough for the soft, gentle drizzle to soak his hair and drip off his face. He blinked water from his lashes. It didn't seem real. His eyes flicked from one stone to the next as he read the names upon them. James Murray. Maureen Murray. Thomas Nolan. Charles Patrick Byrne. Margaret Byrne. And next to their mother, on a temporary metal placard staked into the ground, Kyan Patrick Byrne.

What the fuck? Why?

He gasped for air. Just a week ago they were playing football on the lake house lawn.

"*May the road rise up to meet you. May the wind be always at your back. May the sun shine warm upon your face…*"

Brendan's toast. That was the last thing he remembered from yesterday with any clarity at all.

Soaked to his skin, a cold shiver ran through him.

And he doubted that he'd ever feel warm again.

Twelve

Autumn was settling in quickly this year.

There'd been no Indian summer. The air was crisp, accelerating the turning of the leaves from their vibrant green to the fiery red hue that preceded their plummet to the ground. Woodsmoke billowing from chimneys, combined with the familiar scent of the city, reminded Dillon of winter. He wouldn't be surprised if they got snow before November.

Still, there were plenty of people in Coventry Park on this cold October day. Going for a run or a bike ride along the path. Kids chasing fallen leaves in the wind. Reading a book on a blanket in the sun.

Crazy fuckers.

Dillon didn't like the cold. Never had. Sure, he'd played hockey in the street, ice-skated, and all that other winter shit as a kid and had fun with it. These days, he preferred getting his workout in a hot, sweaty gym—or in bed. Reading in a chair by the fire—or in bed. Snow might be pretty, but shoveling it sure as hell sucked. At least he paid someone to do that now.

He had a feeling it was going to be a very long, Baltic as fuck winter.

Maybe the chick lying in the sun wasn't so crazy after all.

Turning his collar up, he quickened his pace through the park. Kodiak was meeting him at Beanie's. Couldn't he have picked Starbucks? The coffee wasn't as good, but he wouldn't have to encounter the ice queen there.

Cold-hearted bitch.

He didn't like her either. And it didn't matter that she'd been a tad less frosty lately. Too fucking late.

Katie looked up and waved from behind the counter with the jingle of the door. The complete opposite of her aunt, she had to be one of the sweetest girls in the world. Beautiful too. Brendan was a lucky bastard.

"Dillon!" She leaned across the counter to hug him, then cautiously peeked around his shoulder. "Kelsey with you?"

"No." He chuckled with a smirk. Those two did *not* like each other. At all. Hadn't from the get-go. "She went to Milwaukee for the weekend."

"Oh?" Katie tipped her head to the side with a lift of her brow.

"Yeah, her roommate from college lives there."

Rolling her eyes, she pursed her lips to the side. "Uh-huh."

"Where's Kelly?"

"Kev's football game." She winked.

Leo came out from the back carrying sleeves of their trademark blue paper cups and lids. His hair was different every time Dillon saw him. Today he had it in long, thin braids that reached his ass and were pulled back at the crown. Winged eyeliner. Lashes and lip gloss. But that was Leo.

"It might be chilly outside ta-day, but it's hella hot in here," he crooned in his exaggerated way. Leo set the cups on the counter and fanning himself with a grin, he leaned over Katie and smacked a glossy kiss to his cheek. "How you doin', *bebé*?"

Shaking his head, Dillon laughed. When was the last time he'd done that?

"Now that's what Leo wanted to hear." He winked and sauntered back the way he came.

Katie giggled. "Your usual, *bebé*?" She said it just like Leo.

"You're so bad." Grinning, he wiped the lip gloss off his cheek. "Yeah, my usual. Make it two. Kodiak's meeting me here."

"Two americanos coming right up."

Dillon took a seat at the table by the window and checked his phone. Kodiak was late, and that wasn't like him. His fingers thrummed the table as he stared out at First Avenue. For everyone else, life moved on as it always did. A gangly kid walked by balancing three pizza boxes on his shoulder. An old man, his hands curled around a newspaper, waited at the bus stop. He could see Mrs. Rossi wrapping string around a box of sweets in the bakery across the street. Linnea loved her cannolis. He'd bring some home for her. Maybe sweets would make her happy—for a moment at least.

Linnea had good days and bad that ebbed and flowed like the tide. Highs and lows that changed without warning. She'd smile one minute and burst into tears the next. Dillon understood, though. He got it. Any little thing could trigger a long-forgotten memory. While those memories made them sad now, because the pain of losing Kyan was so jarringly fresh, he knew from experience that one day they'd smile for having them.

Dillon also knew that *'one day'* was far away. Right now, he was at a loss on how to best help her through it. Maybe because he was going through it too. His inclination was to hover over her, but sometimes he sensed she needed her space. Time alone. He got that too. Knowing when to keep a respectful distance and when she needed him close was the tricky part. He, Kodiak, and Chloe—everyone—just continued to reach out, to be there for her, support her, and keep her connected to all of them.

He let her talk.

Held her when she cried.

Tried to make her smile.

So, yeah, if a box of cannolis brought her even one minute of happiness, he was getting them for her.

His phone vibrated against the wood table. "Hey, bro. Where you at?"

"Home. Sorry, man. Something came up—not going to make it." Kodiak sounded…distracted.

Did he just hear a grunt? He was pretty sure that's what he heard.

"It's cool." Dillon chuckled. "Keep it wrapped, my friend."

"Dick." Kodiak snickered.

He ended the call and went back to staring out the window.

Katie came over with the coffee. "Hey." She set the cups on the table and took the seat beside him. "Whatcha lookin' at?"

Dillon slowly turned his head toward her. "Nothing." He shrugged. "Just looking."

"Are you all right, Dill?"

"Yeah, I'm fine."

Stock response. That's what he was supposed to say, right? No one needed to hear that a month later his heart ached and bled as if he'd held Kyan's lifeless hand to his face just yesterday. Losing him left this huge, gaping hole in all of their lives that could never be filled. Dillon couldn't burden them with his grief when they were all going through their own. That would be selfish of him. Weak. And he was anything but selfish and weak.

"Fine never means fine. Right?" She winked. "So talk to me. How are you—really?"

He rubbed the back of his neck and exhaled. "The opposite of fine."

"That's what I thought." Katie took his hand and squeezed it. "Do you have any plans for dinner?"

He didn't. "No."

"Come over tonight." She smiled, batting her lashes, and sing-songed, "I'm going to make chicken pomodoro."

Did she think she had to convince him? He'd never turned down a home-cooked meal in his life. "Oh, you tell me when and I am so there."

"Yay!" She clapped her hands together.

"Hey, Kodiak's not coming. Can you make these to-go?"

He kissed her cheek and went out the door with a double americano in a blue paper cup, then he crossed the street to get some cannolis.

Brendan was in the basement. Katie sent him down there while she finished up with dinner. He made a slow three-sixty of the space, amazed by what he saw. "Holy shit! What have you been doing down here?"

"Taking out my shit on some two-by-fours." He grinned. "And building a playroom for my wife."

His cousin had erected a wall with a double door across one end of the basement. Like many of the rooms upstairs, the walls were painted black. Racks were nailed into the wall where implements would be hung. Scraps of lumber were strewn about the floor.

"Convinced her to come over to the dark side, did you?"

"I didn't have to." Brendan winked. "She came willingly."

"Lucky bastard," Dillon muttered under his breath.

"I know I am." Then he smiled. "Could you give me a hand with this?"

They hefted the saltire up against the wall. Dillon held the X-shaped cross in place while Brendan secured it to the studs. Once again his mind wandered to those nights at the club when there were four of them.

"You don't have to tell me. I know where your head's at, brother." Brendan got off his haunches and sat on the floor. "So, I'm going to tell you the same thing your dad told me not long after my parents were killed. He said, '*Sometimes, when your world is a dark place you think you've been buried, but you've actually been planted. Good things will grow.*' I didn't believe it at the time, but fuck if he wasn't right."

Dillon sat down across from his cousin. "How?"

"Living." Brendan winked. "Every. Fucking. Day."

"That's deep, Bren." Dillon rolled his eyes.

"She isn't the one for you." He said it out of the blue. "But I'm sure you already know that."

His tongue was in his cheek as he nodded. "I know."

"Let her go, Dill," Brendan advised. He stood and clasped his shoulder. "Trust me, time will take care of the rest."

What's that supposed to mean?

"Guys?" Katie called to them from the top of the stairs. "Dinner's ready."

Baby Declan was already in his highchair, bringing little fistfuls of food to his mouth, most of it winding up on his bib or on the floor. When he looked up at Dillon his face broke into a wide, happy grin, light-blue eyes beaming.

He felt it then, and he couldn't say why. It only lasted for a moment, but when that baby smiled up at him, he felt it.

Joy.

Ruffling Declan's ginger curls, Dillon smiled back, thankful he could feel something other than sorrow.

Katie had just sliced up the limoncello cake he'd brought from Rossi's when Brendan cleared his throat and spoke up. "The accident investigation reports are in."

Dillon set down his fork.

"They fucked it all up. Cut corners erecting the structure. Failed to inspect it as they agreed to." Brendan rubbed his forehead and pushed his fingers through his hair. "Phil advised that we file suit against the scaffolding company for negligence."

"Okay, then we will."

"I'll tell him to be at the courthouse on Monday." Brendan worried his lip. "We have to talk to Linn."

"What about?"

"Filing for wrongful death."

Fuck.

He went back to Rossi's first and got a torte with pears and mascarpone cream filling. Linnea had devoured the cannolis he brought her yesterday. Dillon knocked before he opened the door. She smiled when she saw the bakery box he carried, tied with red and white twine. The smile almost reached her eyes.

"Hey, gorgeous." He set the box on the counter to hug her. "How's my girl?"

She stiffened in his arms for the tiniest second before hugging him tighter.

He patted her back and let go.

"What's in the box?" Linnea bent over the counter to sniff the sweet confection hidden inside.

Pleased with himself, he smirked. "You'll find out after dinner." He rubbed his hands together. "What are we having?"

Cooking was her therapy and Linnea threw herself into it. Releasing her pent-up emotions while chopping up a poor, unsuspecting tomato or rolling out a crust for a pie. He and Kodiak benefited as much as she did. She cooked and they ate. He'd call that a win-win.

"Garlic butter steak bites with mushrooms, zucchini noodles, and grilled blooming onions." She swatted him on the arm and went to the fridge. "I already prepped. This will only take twenty minutes, so if you can start the grill that'd be great."

"Darn, I missed out on the chopping." He winked.

And he almost got her to laugh. Almost.

Armed with a box of matches, Dillon stepped out onto the patio. It was fucking freezing out here. He punched the ignitor button at least a dozen times and it still wouldn't catch. Kyan was the grill master.

Fuck.

And he froze. Dillon closed his eyes and inhaled a long, slow breath of cold air through his nose, then he reached inside his pocket for the matches. He relit the pilot, and once he was sure the grill was going, he turned around to go back in the house.

He could see her through the panes of glass. Standing there in the kitchen, leaning back against the island, hands cradling her belly, tears streaming down her face. Dillon went to her, and as he pulled her into his arms she laid her head on his shoulder.

"Salmon," she croaked out. "The last thing I said to him was to hurry home because I needed him to grill the salmon."

He smoothed her hair down her back, trying to soothe her.

"Did you tell him 'I love you' before you hung up the phone?"

"Yes, of course I did." She sniffled.

"And did he say it back?"

Her head nodded on his shoulder.

"Well, there you go."

Linnea lifted her head and swiped her eyes. "How do you always do that?"

"What?"

"Make me feel better."

Dillon didn't have an answer for her. He only hoped he could keep on doing it. Because he'd do just about anything to put the light back in her pretty green eyes.

After dinner, they sat in the family room on her sofa of turquoise suede, eating cake of pears and mascarpone cream, to watch a movie.

"Something funny," she said.

She wanted to laugh. That was something, wasn't it?

They settled on *Bridget Jones's Diary*. She settled against his shoulder. Fifteen minutes in, she softly spoke, "Tomorrow would have been our second wedding anniversary."

He knew that, of course. The date hadn't escaped him. Dillon turned her slightly and laid her head on his chest. "I know."

Linnea was quiet after that. He wasn't sure if she was watching the movie or lost in her thoughts. Then she grabbed his hand, brought it to her belly, and held it there.

"Linn, what are you—"

"Shh, just wait."

It felt like a gentle wave rippling beneath her skin, then a little thump right into his palm.

Hello, Charlotte.

"Did you feel that?"

He smiled. "I felt it."

Joy.

Thirteen

"I still think we should just fucking sell it," Jesse insisted. "Let someone else finish the reno. I never want to see that place again."

There was no talk of teething and playdates in the office very much anymore. Dillon never thought he'd miss it, but even here he couldn't get away from the bleeding. Especially here. The four of them were deep-rooted, enmeshed into every facet of each other's lives from work to play to home—for chrissakes, they turned Park Place into a family compound, didn't they?

So they could keep each other close, as they had been all their lives.

So one day their children would grow up together the same way they had.

Family first.

For the three cousins that remained, there was no place that Kyan's absence was more glaringly apparent than right here. No drawings were spread out on the table. His spot on the eggplant-colored sofa sat empty. They were at a standstill, directionless and floundering without him. So while someone else might get to go drown themselves in work at the office, and maybe for eight hours not think about their dead brother lying six feet below the ground, for Dillon the reminders were constant. And everywhere.

Putting his MacBook to the side, Brendan leaned forward in his chair. "I understand how you feel, Jess, but…"

"Can we afford to take the hit?" Truth be told, Dillon never wanted to go near that warehouse ever again either. He'd bet he could probably still make out the bloodstains on the sidewalk.

Brendan shrugged. "Probably, but I don't care about that." He tugged at his hair, cocking his head. "It was his last project. We should finish it. For him."

"He died there, Bren," Jesse, who rarely raised his voice, shouted in anguish.

"All the more reason to fucking do it." Brendan's deep roar was even louder. His voice gentled as he croaked, "It's Kyan's project. We can't just hand it over to someone else."

"Brendan's right."

They must not have heard her come in. Linnea stood there, juggling an armful of what looked to be rolled-up architectural drawings. Dillon jumped up to take them from her, but before he could she dropped them onto the sofa next to Jesse.

"You should finish it. He'd want you to."

She remained standing. "I went into Kyan's home office this morning, and there's a lot more of those. Racks of them." She looked to the ceiling for a moment, then took a breath. "He was always working on something."

Dillon got up from his chair. "Here, Linn. Sit down."

Shaking her head, she licked her dry lips and rubbed them together. "I'm not staying." Her gaze went to his cousin then. "Bren, can you come help me next door?"

"Of course, sweetheart." Kissing her crown, Brendan hugged her.

She turned to him and Jesse. "We'll be right back."

The front door closed with a gentle click. Dillon sat down and looked to Jesse, whose fingers reverently skimmed across one of the rolled-up bundles. With a reluctant sigh he pronounced, "We finish it."

Jesse responded with a slow nod.

Almost an hour went by before they returned. Brendan held another rolled-up drawing, and Linnea hid something framed in black wood against her chest. Her eyes flitted from wall to wall, and seeming to settle on a spot, she walked over to it and hung the picture up with care.

And his heart bled some more.

The four of them perched on steps of brick. Dillon almost wished he'd never found that fucking photo.

Linnea stepped back, appraising its placement on the wall, then she turned to face them. "When you look at that, I want you to remember why you started this in the first place." Tears sprang to her eyes.

Dillon reached for her, but she brushed him off.

"It's okay to cry. I'm fine."

And just this once, he hoped that fine meant exactly that.

"I've got to go." Linnea hugged him and kissed his cheek. "I'll see you later." She did the same with Brendan and Jesse, then she was gone.

"Where's she going?"

"To see Phil," Brendan supplied. "I talked to her. She's filing suit."

Jesus! Today's their wedding anniversary, Bren.

He meant to talk to her about it after dinner yesterday, but he couldn't bring himself to do it.

Brendan unrolled the tube he carried. Their old apartment building drawn in pencil. "Kyan drafted this for a project when he was in college—from memory."

With computer-aided design, manual drafting was almost a lost art, but Kyan preferred it. He claimed creative style, expression, depth, and weight were better conveyed when drawn by hand. He'd captured every exquisite and minute detail of the red brick three-flat they'd all grown up in.

Jesse's gaze flicked from the photo on the wall to the vellum paper in Brendan's hands. "We need to get that framed. Hang it up in here."

Brendan nodded. "I'm on it." He reached inside his pocket and placed an external hard drive on the table. "Kyan stored all of his CAD files on that. There's a ton of manual drawings in his home office that Linnea said we can bring over. I bet there's even more of them in his office upstairs."

He sat down and shaking his head, Brendan pushed his fingers through his hair. "He left plans for just about every conceivable design project behind for us—residential and commercial, from bungalows to six-flats." He glanced up to where they still stood. "We'll probably have to retain an architect to make any needed tweaks and adjustments, but we have Kyan's designs to keep him and his vision—our vision, our brand—alive."

Jesse returned his gaze to the photo on the wall. "It's almost like he knew."

Determined to put a bit of light on what had to be a tough day for Linnea, Dillon tapped out a text. He only hoped he was doing the right thing for her. It was difficult to be sure sometimes.

Dillon: Are you finished with Phil yet?

Incoming.

He snickered to himself. Maybe he should finally listen to Brendan and change the sound of his text notifications.

Nah.

Linn: I'm just leaving

Dillon: Good! Come here—I've got dinner for us

Linn: ok

At least she didn't say no. Dillon was afraid she'd insist on spending what was left of her anniversary alone in her house with nothing but memories to keep her company. So he ordered her favorite Thai food and queued up some funny movies—hell, he'd teach her to play poker if that's what it took. Anything so she wouldn't have to dwell on *'til death do us part* anymore today.

She slipped in through the patio door just as he unpacked their food. "Hey, gorgeous. Perfect timing."

Linnea was pretty quiet all through dinner, but she ate her share of steamed dumplings and spring rolls, every last noodle of her shrimp pad thai. So there was that at least. She got up from her seat at the banquette without a word, reaching for their dirty plates.

Dillon put his hand on hers to stop her. "I'll do it. You want dessert now? I got those Thai donuts you like and coconut ice cream to go with them."

"I'm so full." She rubbed her tummy. "Maybe in a little bit. Are we going to watch a movie?"

"Sure, if you want to." He winked. "I've got a couple funny ones already lined up."

And just like she did the night before, Linnea curled up against his shoulder. They watched the movie without laughing at the funny parts. He thought he saw her smile a time or two, though. Baby steps, right?

Incoming.

Her eyes flicked to his phone on the coffee table in front of them, Kelsey's name on the screen. Dillon made no attempt to reach for it, but Linnea did. She handed him his phone. "Here you go."

He didn't bother reading the text and set it on the table beside him, returning to the movie playing on the big flat screen mounted to the wall. It wasn't quite as large as Jesse's, but it was pretty darn close. It kept him company on those nights when he was here by himself.

Dillon watched Ferris Bueller lip-synch to *Danke Schoen* on the screen while his fingers absently combed through the dark-blonde strands that rested on his shoulder. They caught in a tangle. "Sorry."

Linnea glanced up at him from beneath her lashes. "Aren't you going to get that?"

"What?"

"That was Kelsey." She lifted her head off his shoulder.

"I know." He pushed her head back down to where it was. "It'll keep."

He hadn't heard one peep out of Kelsey the entire time she was in Milwaukee. Not one. Though, to be fair, he hadn't texted her either. Their relationship was nothing more than a farce. A placeholder. Dillon wasn't sure why the fuck he was still with her.

Except that he was.

Well, Kelsey thought he was.

Truth is, he'd checked out weeks ago.

"But Dill—"

"Shh. I'm watching a movie with you right now." His fingers were back in her hair. "I told you, it'll keep."

She was quiet until Ferris uttered the famous 'life moves pretty fast' line at the end. "Dill?"

"Yeah?" He peered down at her.

"I know what you're doing." She wasn't looking at him, though.

"And what's that?"

"Holding my head above water so I don't drown." Her eyes met his then. "There isn't a person in this world I love more than you, that I want to see happy more than you…" Closing her eyes, she paused. "…so please don't fuck things up for yourself with Kelsey, or put your life on hold because of me."

Jesus, fuck.

The heart inside his chest squeezed. Didn't Linnea know there wasn't anyone alive who he loved more than her? That he'd do anything to see her smile again? He didn't give a flying fuck about Kelsey. Linnea was his life.

He couldn't tell her that, though.

"Hey." He tilted her chin up.

"I would hate it if you did that."

"Did you ever think that maybe you're holding me up too?" She was, even if she didn't know it. He brushed the hair from her face. "There is no one more important to me than you…" he softy whispered, placing a kiss on her forehead. "…and Charlotte."

Sniffling, she nodded.

Dillon pulled back to look at her and give her a reassuring smile. "Donuts and ice cream?"

"Okay."

She smiled back.

Just a little bit.

But it was enough.

Fourteen

Dillon stood at the railing looking out at the tranquil, still water. There was no movement upon it. Not even a ripple. Brilliant foliage reflected off its glass-like surface. It was always stunning at the lake house in the fall. He hadn't wanted to come here. Not yet.

His gaze swept over the empty dock. If he squeezed his eyes closed and focused really hard, he could almost see Kyan sitting there beside him with a beer. Could almost hear him. Almost. His voice was already fading. Often, he listened to old phone messages just to hear it.

The lawn, littered with fallen leaves, had turned dry and brown. Brendan, Jesse, and Taylor carried wood to the firepit. They'd have a bonfire, roast hot dogs and marshmallows later, he supposed. Chloe, Katie, and Linnea were inside with the kids making breakfast. He should quit standing here and go help them.

He trudged down the wood steps, hands in the pockets of his jeans. Dillon paused at the bottom, inhaling a deep breath. The late October air was crisp, but at least it wasn't quite as cold as it had been. He grabbed some wood chairs from the storage area hidden beneath the stairs, and traversing across the grass where they'd tossed a football not quite two months ago, brought them to the firepit.

Brendan glanced up at him from where he was crouched on his haunches stacking wood in the circle of stone. "Thanks, Dill."

He grunted in response and began unfolding the low-to-the-ground Adirondack chairs, placing them around the pit.

Brendan slowly rose. "You okay, man?"

"Yeah. Gonna grab the rest of the chairs." He turned away. "Be right back."

A hand on his shoulder stopped him. "What is it, Dillon? Talk to me."

He shrugged and faced his cousin. "I'm not sure coming here was a good idea. It's too soon."

"Linnea wanted to come and Monica said…"

"For me, Bren." His throat constricted and he sputtered, "It's too soon for me."

His cousin followed him. "Sit," he ordered, pushing down on his shoulder.

He sat.

Brendan made room on the stair to sit beside Dillon. "I used to think this place was filled with ghosts. Our parents and grandparents. The boys we used to be. Maybe it is." He huffed out a breath, his gaze fixed out there on the water. "I feel it too, Dill. Hurts like a motherfucker. I remember the day your mom brought him home from the hospital." He turned his head toward Dillon and grinned. "You were so mad Ky was getting all the attention. Snatched a teddy bear from his crib and stuffed it in the trash."

"I was two."

"I know." Brendan softly chuckled and was silent for a moment. "It's always going to hurt, man. Can't avoid it—trust me, I've tried. But it's that hurt, that pain, that's going to change us. Reshape us. You, me, and Jess are more fortunate than most."

"How do you figure? Everyone's dead, Bren. We're the only ones left."

"We still have each other." He smiled. "Taylor—and the guys. Linnea and Katelyn. Chloe. Babies." Brendan chuckled, shaking his head. "I have a feeling there's going to be a bunch of those running around here." His cousin swung his arm around his shoulders. "See, it's the love and connection this family has, the support we provide each other, that will see us through this. That, my brother, is the key to rebuilding life." Brendan gave his shoulder a squeeze. "And we have that in abundance."

Not trusting himself to speak, Dillon nodded.

"Monica said there are three steps to overcoming this wretched sadness. Love and connection, acknowledging Kyan's loss, and exercise—grief is embodied as well as embrained. That's why Linnea wanted to come here. This place might be filled with ghosts, but it's filled with memories too. So, we're going to roast some marshmallows. Introduce the boys to s'mores. Taylor will whip out his guitar. We can hold hands around the fire and sing 'Kumbaya' or some shit." He snorted. "It doesn't matter what we do. Laugh. Cry. But we're doing it together."

Dillon glanced at Brendan, his gaze once again returning to the lake. A single teardrop emerged from the outer corner of his eye to roll down his face.

Big boys don't cry.

"We won't ever move on from our grief, but we will move forward with it." Brendan made no attempt to wipe the liquid trail from his skin. "Together."

It's awkward, navigating toward a new normal, more so probably for Linnea—and for himself. Like a mosaic with a missing piece, the tesserae can be reconfigured into a new pattern, but it won't ever be the same as it was before. While Kyan's death affected all of them, he and Linnea had to figure out where and how to make their pieces fit without Kyan. Brendan and Jesse went home to their spouses, same as always, their nuclear families intact. Linnea went home alone now, same as he did. Both of them missing their other half.

They had each other, though. Brendan was right about that.

He watched her throughout the day. Dillon was worried that being here would prove to be too overwhelming for her. Linnea and Kyan got married here after all. She seemed to be holding up okay, though. While she got teary a few times when an anecdote involving Kyan was told, as it surely would, as it always would—so many of their stories lived here—she smiled a little too.

After hot dogs and s'mores, when the little ones were worn out and tucked into bed, the seven of them sat around the fire. Katie sat curled up on Brendan's lap because that's right where he wanted her to be. Jesse gazed up at the clear night sky. Taylor lazily strummed his guitar, nursing a beer. Nobody was singing "Kumbaya" and the only ones holding hands were Chloe and Linnea, who sat side by side, each in their own chair, sharing a blanket.

Blonde hair up in a messy topknot, Linnea rolled her head to the side facing him. She reached for his hand with her free one. "I know you didn't want to, but I'm glad we came." She squeezed the hand she was holding.

Dillon squeezed back. "Me too."

A year of firsts. The first one is always the hardest and then it gets easier, right? They faced the first weekend at the lake house without Kyan, and all the heartache and memories that came along with it, together. But the holidays—more firsts—were quickly approaching. Halloween was next week. Thanksgiving and Christmas would follow soon after. Birthdays.

God, he hated this.

"You should go, Linnie," Chloe coaxed. "Think about it, anyway. Might be good to get out, yeah?"

"I wouldn't feel right being there—especially six and a half months pregnant." Pursing her lips to the side, Linnea shook her head. "Besides, I am getting out. I'll be at Monica's. We're going to carve pumpkins with all the little ones."

"I'm not into it this year." Jesse reached over Chloe to kiss Linnea's cheek. "I think I'd rather be carving pumpkins."

Taylor stopped his strumming and took a swig from his beer.

Stroking his fingers up and down Katie's arm, Brendan sighed. "None of us are *into it* this year." He glanced to Jesse, then he pointedly looked right at him. "But nevertheless it's our obligation to be there."

Dillon didn't want to go. Fucking masquerade ball. Couldn't he just skip it? He hadn't been to the club since...the night Kelsey left him on a sidewalk downtown.

"I thought I'd stay back. Hang with Linn."

She whipped her head in his direction. "Stop it! We've had this discussion. You're taking Kelsey and you're going. She hasn't been to the club yet, has she?"

Brendan was biting his lip to mask a mischievous smirk.

Fucker.

"Uh, no. I don't think it's her thing…"

"You're going."

"Well, that's settled." Katie scooted off Brendan's lap and he stood, taking her hand. "C'mon, sweet girl."

Clutching her phone, Chloe got up next. "Ireland looks like she's waking up. I'm going to head in too." She kissed Linnea on top of her head. "Night, sweetie."

Jesse and Taylor went with her, leaving just the two of them with the dwindling fire.

Dillon looked up to the night sky. Without the lights of the city to obscure them, a shimmering river of stars could be seen. He found himself doing that often now. Looking up. Why did he do that? It was the moon that looked back at him. Only the moon.

"You promised." Linnea broke the silence.

"What was that?"

"To live your life."

He glanced over to her, patting his lap. "C'mere."

Taking the blanket with her, she came over and curled up against his chest. Stroking her hair, Dillon kissed her crown and peered back up at the stars. "Didn't I tell you that there's no one more important than you and the baby—so what makes you think I'm not?"

"You know what I meant, Dillon."

His hands skimmed up and down her arms as they both stared up at the sky. "Family stays together, just like the moon and stars, we shine in the darkness and give each other light."

"Love," she whispered.

He wrapped his arms around her. "That too."

"I miss him."

"I know, baby." His nose skimmed her hair, inhaling sweet almonds, and he held her tighter. "I do too."

"Do you think he's up there watching over us?"

"I don't know."

"I like to think so."

"Maybe he is." She shivered in his arms. "C'mon, you're cold. Let's get you inside."

They went left at the top of the stairs, and pausing at his bedroom door that was right next to hers, he pulled her in for a hug. "Night, gorgeous."

"Night, Dill." She kissed his cheek.

He closed the door behind him and stripped off his clothes. The scent of woodsmoke and sweet almonds lingered on them. After a quick shower, Dillon threw on a pair of sweats and gazed out the window. He could see the glow of the embers from the fire that no longer burned. The chairs around it sat empty. Then he looked up. The moon was still watching, its light shining down upon the lake.

Dillon liked to think Kyan was up there somewhere too.

He smiled up at the sky.

"Night, brother."

Fifteen

This was not going to go well.

Even half hidden behind a mask, it was written all over Kelsey's face, and they'd only just gotten here. She sat stiffly beside him, legs tightly crossed, clutching a drink in her hand. And the party hadn't even really started yet.

Dillon patted her on the knee. "Relax, Kels."

She side-eyed him. "People are next to naked out there doing… the nasty, and you're telling me to relax?" she scoffed. "Is that what *you* do here?"

"Nah." He winked. "Told ya, I like to watch."

Her eyes bugged out and she gasped. "Strangers? I thought you meant me. That you like watching *me*."

"Kelsey, it's a sex club—what'd you expect?"

Chloe leaned over Jesse to correct him. "Sex positive."

Kelsey tilted her head and wrinkled her nose at Chloe. "I know, but I thought this was supposed to be a Halloween party."

"At a sex club," he reiterated. "You won't see anyone doing the 'Monster Mash' or bobbing for apples here."

"Bobbing for dick, maybe," Sloan murmured under his breath. "Heh."

"Shut it, Sloan," Dillon spoke through gritted teeth.

"Just makin' a joke, man." He killed off the whiskey in his glass and turned in his seat toward Kelsey. "Sorry."

Dillon took Kelsey's hand and gave it a reassuring squeeze. "Look, you're here with us and you're perfectly safe. Nobody's going to touch you, okay?"

"Okay."

"So, drink your drink and relax." Dillon let go of her hand and patted her knee again.

Jesse, seated on the other side of him, leaned into his ear. "Think of tonight as…an opportunity."

"An opportunity?"

"You can thank Chloe. Since Brendan won't allow the vamps to come play upstairs anymore…" Then he howled, "…ahoooo."

Chloe tipped her head forward and grinned. "Say hello to the wolf pack." She tugged on Jesse's hair and giggled. "Give me a growl, baby."

"Lions don't growl, babe." Kissing her neck, he tickled her. "We roar."

"Wolf pack?" Kelsey was making that face again.

"Uh-huh." Chloe giggled. "Are you Team Edward or Team Jacob? Normally, I'd pick the vampire, but vampires are not supposed to sparkle, ya know?"

"What?"

"Alcide Herveaux?" she prompted her. "Girl, didn't you ever watch *True Blood*?"

"No."

Chloe tilted her head. "How is that even possible?" She pointed to the unlit stage, which had been transformed to look like a scene out of *Into the Woods*. Apparently the haunted forest thing was the theme for the ball this year. The motif had been carried out in every nook and cranny of the club.

"Ohhh, I get it now." Kelsey slowly nodded. "Werewolves. Halloween."

No, Kelsey, you do not get it.

"Yeah…uh, well, kind of." Chloe nodded.

Jesse sniggered. "She's gonna run for the hills, cousin."

She just might. Dillon was well aware Kelsey did not belong here. If she wasn't comfortable in her own skin, then how could she be accepting of others? No, this was not going to go well.

"See, baby?" Smiling now, Kelsey tugged on his arm. "It *is* a Halloween party."

"At a sex club, Kels," he reminded her. Again. "Wolves mate."

"Ohhh."

Matt smirked at her with a wink. "They claw and they bite too."

Brendan, who'd apparently overheard the exchange, stood at the bar in their private VIP space with Katie and Taylor, looking rather amused. He sipped on his whiskey with one hand, and stroked his wife's hair with the other. Taylor left his cousin to rejoin them on the sofa. Hans, accompanied by his wife, Brigitta, came in and took his place.

And her eyes widening, Kelsey took it all in.

They looked like any other couple here. Except they didn't. Austrian, Hans stood tall and imposing, lean and muscular, but not the bulky kind. Platinum hair buzzed short. Black suit with a white shirt unbuttoned to the navel, exposing pierced nipples. Next to him, his wife, also blonde, was a tiny, delicate-looking thing.

After speaking with Brendan, Hans led Brigitta from the bar to where they sat. He did this movement that looked something like a bow, a quick tip of his head. "Dillon, it's so good to see you back." He quickly glanced at Kelsey seated beside him, and spoke, his accent thick, "We've missed you here, my friend. Do let Linnea know she remains in our thoughts."

Dillon stood and clasped his hand. He didn't miss the roll of Kelsey's eyes or the way she blatantly stared. "Thank you. I'll be sure to tell her."

His gaze briefly returned to Kelsey before coming back to him. "Enjoy your evening."

Brigitta dipped her head in acknowledgment, but didn't speak. Then he led her away.

"What was that?" Kelsey slowly shook her head, her mouth hanging open.

"*That* was rude," he sternly replied. "I saw you and I'm sure they did too."

"He has her on a leash!"

"And he isn't forcing her." Dillon exhaled and explained, "She consented to it. Brigitta is his wife, his submissive."

"That's ridiculous!" She rolled her eyes. "You can't just walk your wife around in public on a leash."

"No, out there you can't, but in here you can. I told you what the club is all about, remember?" He chewed on his lip. "It's their dynamic, and we respect that. We don't judge anyone. Ever."

And you told her then you couldn't be with anyone who did, so screw this shit.

He should take her home. It's not like he wanted to be here tonight anyway. Brendan and Jesse would manage just fine without him.

"Look, why don't I…"

Just then, the house lights began to slowly dim and Kodiak hurried in, out of breath like he ran eight city blocks to get here. Knowing him, he probably did. Dude actually enjoyed it.

Kodiak briefly spoke to Katie at the bar, and raised his hand in a quick salute to everyone else before nudging Sloan over to claim a seat on the other side of Kelsey. He cocked his head with a grin. "Lost track of time. Did I miss anything?"

"Nope." Chloe giggled. "Five minutes to showtime."

"Excellent," he drawled, reaching across the table for the bottle of Glenlivet.

Kelsey's sleek ponytail whipped back and forth with every turn of her head. "You were saying—why don't you what?"

"Nothing." Dillon pressed his lips together. "Never mind."

Darkness.

It took a moment for his eyes to adjust to it. Tiny flickers of light shimmered from tabletop candles. There was no background music. No chatter. Nothing but expectant silence until a single beam of murky light hit the fog-filled stage.

Chloe grabbed her husbands by their hands and went to the railing that looked out upon the club's main floor. They linked their arms together behind her as they always seemed to do, kissing her and each other. Kelsey stared. Kelly tiptoed in, sidling past them to get to her niece and Brendan at the bar.

Can this night get any worse?

Dillon leaned forward to address Kodiak. "Why the fuck is she here?"

He only shrugged.

Kelsey whipped her head in his direction, glaring at him, her long ponytail smacking Kodiak in the face. "Is she one of your exes?"

Oh, for fuck's sake.

"No." He snickered.

"Then why do you care?"

"Because she's a judgmental bitch." Dillon brought his face up against hers to whisper, "And I won't tolerate one. Understood?"

He got up and went to the railing. A lone girl stood beneath the hazy light in a small clearing of artificial trees in the center of the platform. She appeared to be young, in her early twenties, and waif-like with her long blonde hair parted down the middle. Wringing her hands in front of her, fog swirled about her bare feet.

Wrapping her arms around his waist, Kelsey came up behind him, pressing her body into his. Once, Dillon would have welcomed her affection. Past the point of even trying to feel anything for her, it was lost on him now.

A low, drawn-out snarl echoed throughout the club, making it difficult to determine the direction it came from. Up on the big screen, the girl's eyes darted about as she scrambled to find a place to hide.

Matt and Kit joined them at the railing. Kelsey moved to his side. "What's happening?"

"We get to watch the hunt." Kit grinned.

"Hunt?"

"I told you." Dillon glanced down at her. "Wolves mate."

"And they claw." Matt moved in a little bit closer. "And bite."

Kelsey pulled a face. He winked.

Matt leaned into her ear, curled his lip, and growled out, "Run, rabbit, run."

"Asshole," she spat and spun on her heels, returning to the sofa.

Kit began to laugh. Dillon turned around to see Brendan pressing his lips together to keep from doing the same. Katie hid a snicker behind her hand. Maybe he should be pissed at Matt for teasing Kelsey, but he really couldn't blame him. It was actually rather funny.

Dillon left the railing to sit with her. Kelsey had her legs tightly crossed again, her Jimmy Choo bouncing a mile a minute. He stilled the movement with his palm on her shin. "Matt was just goofing around with you."

"Yeah." Sloan smirked. "You're not afraid of the big, bad wolf, are ya?"

Kelsey didn't answer.

"He's all bark." Sloan swallowed the contents of his glass and winked. "No bite."

Loud, menacing growls reverberated, shattering the silence.

Three wolves sought their prey.

Only one claimed her. With his teeth, and his claws, and his cock. He howled as he entered her.

Everyone was riveted to the primal tableau in front of them. Even Kelsey. She squeezed his hand. "Wolves mate for life, don't they?"

"That's a myth, actually."

If a wolf dies, the widowed wolf may choose another.

Apparently, that wasn't the response Kelsey was looking for. "*This* is so fucked up." She let go of his hand. "*This* is what you like to watch?"

Her focus was still on the screen. Dillon shrugged. "You like it too, I guess."

"No, I do not," she exclaimed as the house lights came back up, ponytail swishing, and she wasn't being quiet about it.

Now everyone was looking at her.

Kodiak and Sloan from the other side of the sofa. Brendan, Katie, and Kelly from the bar. Brendan's friend, Lucifer, behind the devil mask he always wore. When did he get here? Dillon hadn't noticed.

Chloe, Jesse, and Taylor remained at the railing, but Matt and Kit came forward.

Like the waif in the clearing, Kelsey's gaze darted from one person to the next, ending with Matt. "That was so fucked up."

He cleared his throat and licked his lip. "If this is about the growly, I'm sorry." He flashed his teeth, offering her a boyish smile. "I got a little excited."

"No," she scoffed. "This is not about the *growly*."

Then in the haughtiest tone Dillon had ever heard, and he'd heard plenty, Kelsey kept going. "Real men, grown men, do not behave like *that*," she sneered, pointing to the stage. "Like fucking animals."

Matt tilted his head slightly to the side, that boyish smile he charmed all the ladies with, never leaving his face. "But that's what we all are, Kelsey. Fucking animals. Some of us are just better at freeing ourselves." He winked. "To allow the animal that's inside each one of us to come out to play."

"Some of us have evolved, Fido."

Brendan's jaw ticked. Taylor moved from the railing. Lucifer's eyes got big.

Oh, shit.

"Kelsey," Dillon spoke in a warning tone.

"It's okay, Dill." Matt grinned. "She's misguided, that's all."

Kelsey rolled her eyes.

"Real men are hunters…warriors…beasts. It's programmed into our fucking DNA." Matt pounded his chest and then softened his voice. "We're caregivers, protectors, and supporters too. Your view of a *real* man is toxic, because a real man, a good man, is all of those things for his woman."

"That some bullshit you got here at the BDSM club or something?"

Brendan pulled the mask off his face, then his six-foot, eight-inch cousin stood in front of Kelsey. "You surely don't know what BDSM even is. I'm not going to put you down for your ignorance, but I am going to tell you what it isn't." His eyes quickly scanned her over. "It's not Christian Grey or the Italian dude with a yacht." Then he grinned. "It's not the paperback novel you keep hidden with your vibrator in the drawer beside your bed."

She gasped.

"So don't you dare look down on others for a lifestyle you really don't know anything about. Don't you dare look down on others for their sexuality just because it's different from yours. Do you think we haven't come across people like you before?" He shook his head. "You're the reason this place was created, sweetheart—and for the record, the club is sex positive."

"What does that even mean?" Her voice rose an octave with every word.

And with one word Brendan answered her, "Freedom."

"I'm your girlfriend." Kelsey looked to him then. "Aren't you going to stand up for me?"

Dillon shook his head. He wasn't doing this in front of his family. "I'm going to take you home."

"Just a minute, my friend." Raising his index finger, Lucifer walked over to Kelsey. "Can I ask you something?"

"I guess so." She shrugged with a hand on her hip. "Who are you?"

Dillon could see the smirk behind his mask. "You can call me Lucifer."

"Really?"

"Yes, really." He chuckled. "Did you agree to come here tonight?"

"Yes, for a Halloween party."

"With full knowledge the Red Door is..." Lucifer turned to Brendan. "...a sex-positive club."

"Well, yes."

"Did anyone touch you without your consent?"

Kelsey shook her head. "No."

"And Dillon told you what you'd see here, didn't he?"

Wolves mate.

"Yes." Her voice was just above a whisper now.

"Well then, you can't expect him to defend you or your lack of manners, now can you?" He winked.

Kelsey was silent.

"Right." Lucifer bro-hugged Dillon. "I just wanted to come by and see how you guys were doing. Give Linnea my love—and good luck with this one." Then he said his goodbyes to his cousins and was gone.

Kelsey snatched her bag from the table. "Let's go."

"You just had to make everything all about you, didn't you?"

Katie had been quiet until now. "You narcissistic bitch, you know the hell he's been going through the past couple of months. He still is, but you couldn't let him have one night, could you?"

Shaking his head, it was Brendan who spoke next, disgust lacing his voice, "Why the fuck are you still with her, man?"

Neither one of them spoke on the drive to Kelsey's apartment. Dillon turned onto her street. "Never any fucking parking here," he muttered to himself. Pulling up alongside a Honda Civic, close to the door of her building, he shifted his Porsche into neutral.

"Aren't you going to come in?"

He didn't want to look at her, but he did. "No, Kels."

Her brown eyes welled with tears. "But I love you, Dillon."

Why do chicks pull that shit when they know it's over? He kissed her on the cheek, but he couldn't return the sentiment.

A tear escaped. "Aren't you going to say it back?"

"We don't fit, Kels." He gave her hand a squeeze. "I wanted us to, but we don't."

"We can, Dillon."

"We can't." And he let go. "My family matters more than anything to me, and the girl I'm going to call mine has to accept me, and them, for who we are. I told you that I'd never make you do something you didn't want to do, that you didn't have to go to the Red Door. I only asked that you accept the choices others made for themselves without judgment. You didn't. Instead, you disrespected me. My family. Insulted my friends."

"I'm sorry."

"I know."

She got out of the car and closed the door behind her.

He watched her until he knew she was safely inside.

Because that's what a real man does.

Not that she would ever know.

Sixteen

She waited two whole weeks this time.

Dillon was upstairs, painting the baby's room, when the text came through. He set down the brush and wiped *'Victorian Mauve'* paint from his fingers. Was it really mauve, though? Maybe he was colorblind, but after looking at what seemed like a thousand color samples with Linnea, he couldn't see the difference between mauve, or blush, or taupe anymore.

Picking up his phone from the wood floor, Dillon saw Kelsey's name on the screen. He really didn't have any interest in what she had to say, but opened it anyway, cursing himself when he remembered she would know that he read it. There was no reason for any further communication between them. It would only encourage her, and hadn't he already learned that lesson? Without bothering to reply, he hit delete and put her on ignore.

Scents of baking apples and cinnamon drifted into the room from the kitchen to mingle with the fumes of drying paint. Linnea was trying her hand at a French apple tart since she'd charmed the chef at *Chez Moi* into giving her the recipe when a kid-free Chloe got her out for lunch last week. She informed him *coq au vin* was on the dinner menu tonight too. Chopping up poor, unsuspecting tomatoes was still her therapy. Monica said it wasn't that so much, but rather the entire process itself, from planning a meal to serving it. Food was her love language. Maybe it was his too, because he sure loved eating it.

They fell into a comfortable routine. Every day, after he finished up at the office and did his time in the gym, Dillon rushed home to shower and go next door. He'd come in through the patio, sure to find her making magic in the kitchen. They'd have dinner together. More often than not, Kodiak showed up to eat with them. Afterward, they'd watch a movie or he'd help her out with whatever needed to be done—like painting Charlotte's room.

"Oh, Dillon," Linnea softly exclaimed, slipping through the door. "It's perfect."

"Keep the mauve to just these two walls then?" He'd already finished doing the others in a soft white.

Seven months pregnant, she sat beside him on the floor, and leaned back on her elbows. "Yeah, I think so."

Linnea admired the freshly painted wall, a smile Dillon could only describe as wistful on her face. She seemed lost in her thoughts and he wondered what she was thinking about. But then he figured he had a pretty good idea.

Kyan should be the one sitting here with paint on his hands. Not me.

Because what else would she be thinking?

"I'll put the crib together tomorrow if you want." He stood, and giving her his hand, helped her up from the floor.

"Yeah?" She smiled, and it was a real one.

He smiled back. "Yeah."

"I came up here to tell you dinner is almost ready."

"Let me clean up…" He kissed the top of her head. "…and I'll be right down."

After they ate up the *coq au vin*, that he teasingly referred to as chicken stew, because essentially that's what it is, but mostly because she made a cute face and laughed every time he said it, they took their plates of warm apple tart à la mode to the family room.

"As good as *Chez Moi?*" She looked at him expectantly.

Dillon flicked on the TV, French vanilla ice cream melting in his mouth. He swallowed with a grin and winked. "Better. I'm glad your brother isn't here. More for me."

"I'll make it again to take over to Kit's on Thanksgiving." The smile on her face slowly faded.

He didn't have to ask why. Here come all those firsts without Kyan they'd have to wade through. Dillon put his arm around her, drawing her closer to his side.

She laid her head on his shoulder. "Sometimes it feels like I'm just going through the motions, you know?"

"I know." He combed his fingers through her hair. "Me too."

"Thank you," she whispered.

"What for?"

"I can relax with you." She exhaled. "Pretending you're okay all the time gets exhausting."

"You don't have to pretend." He tipped her chin up to look at him. "You know that, right?"

"Not with you…" She shrugged. "…but with everyone else I feel like I have to. It's more than two months now—who wants to be around a pregnant chick who always gets sad?"

"Me." He squeezed her shoulder.

"You're different." Glancing away, she worried her lip. "I don't want to bring everybody down or have them walking on eggshells around me."

"Look at me." He took her face in his hands. "There's no time limit and you don't have to fucking pretend for anybody. No one expects you to, so don't put that on yourself." He kissed her forehead. "I love you—we all love you…" His hand went to her rounded belly. "…and you will know joy again, I promise you that."

"Can it co-exist with sorrow?"

Charlotte kicked beneath his palm.

"Yeah, gorgeous," he assured her. "It can."

Mother Nature can be such a fickle bitch, especially in November. Fall or winter? Rain or snow? Either way it was damp and fucking cold. Dillon toed off his shoes as soon as he stepped inside and saw Linnea bent over the kitchen island, pressing her fist into her back.

"Linn?" He sprinted over to her. "Are you okay? What's wrong?"

"You're early, and nothing." She straightened. "Been standing here slicing apples too long, I guess."

"Jesus, you fucking scared me."

He began kneading her shoulders. Dillon didn't think about what he was doing as he pressed his fingers into her spine and rubbed the skin on her lower back. Soft. Warm. Bare. Skin. And that's when he realized she was wearing only one of those little cropped bra tops and a pair of flannel pajama bottoms. He pulled his fingers away.

"Why'd you stop?" She turned around. Belly, breasts, and messy blonde hair. "It was helping."

Fucking beautiful.

Jesus.

"You were supposed to wait for me."

"I couldn't sleep." She lifted a shoulder and pursed her lips to the side. "So I went ahead and got started."

"Well, I'll finish."

"It's all done. Just have to clean up."

"I can do that." Dillon turned her around and nudged her in the direction of the stairs. "While you take a long, hot shower. It'll make you feel better."

With her hand on her back, he watched Linnea amble down the hallway. It was only eight in the morning, but he turned the TV on anyway—it wasn't Thanksgiving without the Macy's parade—and lit a fire in the hearth to take the chill out of the house. Even with the heat running and apple tarts in the oven he was cold.

More than an hour later, with the kitchen set back to rights and smelling of cinnamon, apple tarts cooling on the counter, Dillon was warm enough to shuck off the sweatshirt he had on over his Henley. Linnea was still upstairs. How long did it take a girl to shower? He'd known some that took a helluva long time in the bathroom, doing whatever it is women do in there, but Linnea wasn't one of them.

"Linn?" he called out to her as he went up the stairs. "Everything okay?"

She didn't answer.

He popped his head inside the nursery they'd finished putting together for the baby. Soft white and mauve, dreamy and sweet, with a dollhouse on the floor and a canopy draped over the crib. Ready and waiting for Charlotte.

Across the hall, the door to Linnea's room was ajar. "Linn?"

Silence answered him. No running water. No hair dryer. Nothing. With the tip of his index finger, Dillon widened the gap and peeked inside. The room was quiet and still. Bed made. He chuckled at that because he rarely made his. Why bother making it just to mess it up again, right?

The door to the en suite was closed.

He stood on the other side of it and softly tapped. "Linn, you in there?"

Still nothing.

Where is she?

His stomach clenched, and in that split second a hundred different scenarios, none of them good, flashed in his head. Steeling himself, Dillon turned the crystal knob and opened the door.

She slept.

Lying there in the clawfoot tub, her head cushioned on a towel, Linnea was sound asleep. The scented water did nothing to obscure her nakedness from him. Lush, enlarged breasts, nipples teasing the surface with every soft rise of her chest as she breathed. Her hands rested atop her rounded belly. Dillon inhaled, forcing sweet almond air into his lungs. He should look away, but he couldn't.

And God fucking help him, the scar on his heart—the one with her name on it—ripped wide open.

"Dillon," she murmured in a sleepy voice.

"I'm sorry." He closed his eyes. "I, uh, just came up to check on you."

Water sloshed in the tub.

He turned around and went back down the stairs.

On the TV, Macy's starflake balloons marched down 34th Street in New York. Dillon stared at the screen in an effort to get the image of Linnea, naked and beautiful, out of his head. But as much as he tried, it wouldn't leave him. And later that afternoon, he carried six French apple tarts and the vision of her still on his mind, across the street to Kit's, who was hosting the gathering for Thanksgiving this year.

With Kodiak scurrying to catch up behind them, Dillon paused on the porch and glanced at Linnea in her olive-green sweater dress. She favored that color. It matched her eyes. "You ready, gorgeous?"

She nodded.

One less place setting at the table. This wasn't going to be easy for her. Or for him. Not for any of them.

Every house on Park Place was different, showcasing the distinctive character of those who lived inside it. Of all the Venery boys, Kit was the quiet, reflective one. The quirky one. He was closest to Matt—had been since they were kids—and usually didn't say a whole helluva lot. Because he didn't have to. One look, just like his house with its walls of dark navy blue, hanging ferns, animal skin rugs, and kitschy, eclectic art, spoke volumes.

Bo pounced on her the very second they got through the door. He wrapped Linnea in a giant hug and squeezed her tight—well, as tight as he could with her baby bump in between them. "Baby girl," he crooned as he rocked her in his arms and kissed her on the lips. Then he bent over and kissed her tummy too.

Kit approached them then and elbowed Bo's side. "Move over, stud muffin."

Stud muffin?

There had to be a story behind that.

Dillon chuckled and winked at Linnea, trapped between Venery's drummer and bass player. "Now, there's a man candy sandwich for your bucket list."

She must have recalled that first Fourth of July at the lake house when she referred to him and Bo as exactly that, because she was laughing too.

It warmed his insides to see her laugh.

Sixteen adults sat around the dining room table. Same as always, since Kevin came with Kelly this year. Dillon was thankful they wouldn't have to look at an empty chair. The little ones were tucked between their parents in booster seats and highchairs. There'd be one more between him and Linnea next Thanksgiving. He grinned to himself. Sloan was going to need a bigger table.

In the seat beside him, Linnea and Chloe were talking all things baby, from swaddling to birth plans. Dillon didn't know what a birth plan was, and was pretty sure he didn't want to. His plan was to sit in the waiting room with Kodiak. Chloe was going to be with her when Charlotte was born.

"Don't worry. We'll be back from the UK in plenty of time," Chloe assured her. "And anyway, first babies are almost always late. Right, Katie?"

Dillon's gaze cut to his left. Katie was cleaning yams off her son's face. "Dec was four days late."

"Bren, pass the mashed, please?" A meat-and-potatoes kind of guy, made-from-scratch mashed potatoes was one of Dillon's favorite things. Katie made them, so he already knew how good they were.

She passed him the bowl with a smirk. "You can't play catch with those."

"Is that a challenge?" Dillon leaned forward. "What do you think, Bren? Sounds like one to me."

"Do it," Jesse chanted.

"Dillon." Linnea sank her fingers into his thigh as he formed a glob of creamy potato goodness into a ball with his spoon.

"It's okay, gorgeous." He winked at her. "I got this."

"You get that shit on my ceiling, I'm gonna kick your ass."

With that, Dillon catapulted the potato ball into the air. His aim was off just a little bit, but leaning to the right, with his head on Linnea, he caught it.

"And that is how it's done."

Brendan snorted.

Katie stared at him open-mouthed.

Dillon winked. "Years of practice."

After dinner, the assemblage moved to Kit's living room because besides turkey, parades, and pumpkin pie, Thanksgiving was

NFL game day—and football was in their blood. They grew up on it. Watching it on Sundays. Tossing a ball with each other. Hell, Jesse took it all the way and played pro. So, Dillon kicked back on Kit's velvet sofa of vivid plum with fringe and attempted to focus on the Bears game, but between the distractions all around him and the tryptophan coma that was calling his name, he was fighting a losing battle.

There had to be at least three distinct conversations going all at once, interspersed with the screech of a toddler or Jesse shouting at the players on the screen. Dillon's focus wandered from the TV to a disco ball sculpture propped against the wall. He threw his arm around Linnea and played with her hair as his eyes drifted closed.

He couldn't have dozed for long. The Bears game was still on. Fourth quarter. Dillon checked the score, and seeing there was no way they were going to salvage this game, decided he hadn't missed much. His fingers were still tangled in Linnea's hair, the soft feel of it so familiar, and at the same time not.

The image of her from this morning lingered. Dillon wasn't sure what to do with all of these feelings that were seeping out from that place hidden deep inside his chest where he'd stuffed them. He couldn't ignore them any longer, but he couldn't do anything with them either. Linnea was still Kyan's and he was still hers.

All he could do was to keep on loving her the way he always had.

He untangled his fingers from her hair. She turned her head and smiled at him with a smile that reached her pretty green eyes. And that was all he ever wanted for her.

"Have a nice nap?" She giggled, combing the hair away from his eyes with her fingers and slowly massaging his scalp.

He stretched his limbs. "Yeah, I guess so."

"You were snoring."

"I was?"

"Just a little bit." She held up her thumb and forefinger. "We're looking at Kit's old photo albums."

"Photo albums?" He raised his brow.

"You know, those things people used to put actual photographs in—back in ancient times, before we posted them on Instagram and stored them in the cloud?"

"Um, I know what a photo album is, silly girl." Dillon playfully tugged on her hair. "Photos of what?"

They'd made it through the holiday fairly well, so the last thing he wanted was for Kit to be dragging out old photos of them as kids. Dredging up old memories. The sadness of longing for yesterday.

"You guys back in high school—when the band started."

Kyan, being four years younger, wasn't in high school yet when Kit, Brendan, and the guys were there, so he probably wasn't in any of the photos.

Thank fuck.

Linnea pointed to a photo of sixteen-year-old Taylor. "You so do not look like you without the hair and the ink."

"Who do I look like then?"

"You were hot, baby." Chloe tugged on his beard and smacked a kiss to his lips. "Who's this girl here with you, Kit?"

He peeked over Chloe's shoulder. "Oh, that's Courtney," Kit answered, his expression impassive. "My wife."

"Your what?"

"Well, she was there." He shrugged. "Ex-wife now. Married at eighteen. Divorced at nineteen, so I don't think it even counts."

"Cunt," Taylor uttered beneath his breath.

"Yeah, as it turned out, she was." Kit smirked and gathered up the albums to put them away.

"I never knew he was married. Why didn't I know that?" Chloe looked to Taylor.

"Kit doesn't talk about it, Chloe. He didn't then and he doesn't now," Matt answered and worried his lip. "First time I've heard him even say her name in fifteen years."

"Because she hurt him?"

"Because even after all this time, it still hurts."

And he's still grieving the loss of a future that might have been, but is no longer possible.

Profound loss, whether death or divorce is the cause of it, probably feels the same, Dillon supposed. A perpetual hole that doesn't get bigger and it doesn't get smaller. It's just always there.

If a wolf dies, the widowed wolf may choose another.

And all these years later, Kit still chose to remain alone.

Dillon glanced at Linnea. Just the thought of that made him sad.

Seventeen

Dillon shook the snow from his boots and pushed the six-foot Fraser fir into the house through the patio door. There wasn't a shred of tinsel to indicate it was Christmastime here, unless the snowman cookie jar in the kitchen counted. Linnea told him there was no point in decorating or anything since none of the children were going to be here for the holidays. Chloe, Jesse, and Taylor took the kids to visit their grandmothers in the UK. Brendan and Katie were spending Christmas at Katie's parents.

He, Linnea, and Kodiak were on their own.

They had nothing special planned. Dillon was determined to change that. So, on this Eve of the Eve they were going to put up a tree. Maybe Christmas would never be like it was before, but that didn't mean it couldn't be magical. Just different.

He was surprised to find Linnea baking cookies in the kitchen. With a giggle, she shook her head as she watched him wrestle the tree into the family room. "Should I ask?"

Dillon propped the tree against the wall, and on his way back out the door he stopped in the kitchen. "Nope." And bent to kiss her cheek.

After giving it a lot of careful thought, he'd come up with a plan of his own. And she was going to like it. Dillon couldn't help but grin as he brought the rest of his haul into the house and started unpacking bags.

"Okay, now I'm asking." Linnea came up beside him. "What's all this?"

"First, I'm going to fix us some dinner and then we are going to decorate that tree."

"Oh, we are?"

"We are. I was lucky—got the last decent tree on the lot," he said over his shoulder as he put the groceries away. "And when your brother is here for Christmas Eve dinner tomorrow—prime rib, baby." Dillon closed the door to the fridge and turned around. "Have you ever made a gingerbread house?"

"Uh, no."

He held up the gingerbread house kits he got and winked. "Thought it might be fun."

Something different that they hadn't done before. He got new ornaments and stuff to trim the tree. New stockings to hang by the fireplace. Christmas could never be the same, so he was giving her a new one.

"You're doing it again."

"What's that?"

She hugged him. "Holding my head out of the water."

Linnea was hanging silver stars on the branches while he messed with a string of lights. Every now and then she'd take a step back to look at the tree. Dillon noticed she was wincing and rubbing her lower back.

"You okay?"

She nodded, bracing her back with both hands. "I can't get comfortable. My back's been kind of achy all day."

"C'mon, gorgeous." Dillon steered her toward the sofa. "Off your feet."

Linnea sat down and he picked up her feet. She was all belly on her tiny frame. It had to be uncomfortable carrying that around. How did women do it? He propped a pillow behind her back and covered her with a throw.

"That's it. Just relax." He kissed her temple. "You've been doing too much."

She snuggled under the blanket and he went to finish the tree.

After he'd fixed the lights and hung the last star, Dillon turned around. "How's it…Linn?"

Curled up on her side, almost writhing with her eyes scrunched closed, Linnea pressed a fist against her lower back.

Dillon got down on his haunches beside her, brushing the hair from her face. "What is it? What can I do?"

"I don't know." She opened her pretty green eyes. They were glassy. "Maybe a hot shower will help."

"Maybe you should call the doctor."

She shook her head on the pillow. "For a backache?"

"I see tears in your eyes, gorgeous." He took her hand off her back and replaced it with his own. "Call."

Dillon pressed the heel of his hand just above her tailbone. Linnea was fine. This was normal, right? He wished there was someone he could ask, but Chloe and Katie, and even Danielle, were away for the holiday.

"Doctor Torres wants me to go to the hospital to get checked." Linnea pushed against the sofa cushion to sit up.

"For what?"

Her eyes bore into his and she bit her lip. "Labor."

Fuck.

He'd never been so unprepared for anything in his entire fucking life. Dillon followed the nurse pushing Linnea in a wheelchair down the hall to her room, the antiseptic hospital smell invading his nostrils. Chloe was supposed to be here for this part, but she was on the other side of the Atlantic Ocean, and the baby was coming. Now.

'First babies are almost always late.'

Not Charlotte. She was arriving three weeks early.

Another nurse was waiting to greet them. They settled Linnea into the bed and plugged her into the monitor. Then the triage nurse waved and left with the empty wheelchair.

"My name is Gina, and I'm going to be your labor nurse." She smiled, tapping away on her keyboard.

"Linnea Byrne," she softly spoke from the bed.

"I know." The nurse looked at him then. "This birth plan has Chloe as the support person, but you don't look like a Chloe to me."

"New plan." He nervously chuckled. *And God help me.* "Dillon Byrne."

"I see." She grinned.

He stood at the head of the bed. Linnea glanced over at him and taking her hand in his, he bent over to kiss her forehead. "You doing okay, gorgeous?"

"Yeah." She nodded. "Can you call my brother?"

"Already did." He squeezed her hand. "He's on his way."

A baby-faced woman, all of five foot-nothing and dressed in scrubs, stepped inside the room. Dillon would have pegged her for one of the nurses, except she was dwarfed in a long, white coat and wore a funny-looking cap on her head. That, and she seemed to know Linnea.

What they were saying was lost on him until she said, "Let's see if we've made any progress."

He wasn't supposed to look, right? Linnea was covered with a sheet, but squeezing her hand Dillon diverted his gaze to the window. It was snowing.

The tiny woman, who was obviously the doctor, pulled a rolling stool over to the side of the bed. "Six centimeters. So, looks like we're going to have a Christmas Eve baby." She smiled. "Now, the baby is presenting occiput posterior or sunny-side up. So the back of her head is putting extra pressure on your sacrum, which explains why you've been feeling everything in your back."

Dillon flicked his gaze to the woman on the stool. "Is that bad?"

"It's common," she assured him. "And there are things we can try to coax her into turning around."

"What things?"

"Gina will show you." She just smirked. "Let's get you up, Linnea."

And that's how it came to be that they were slow dancing in a hospital room. Gina lowered the lights and turned on soft, relaxing music. Linnea hung onto his neck with her head on his chest, wrapped in his arms, gently swaying. Dillon rubbed her back as they danced, applying counter-pressure with every contraction.

He thought of all the other times he'd danced with her. At her wedding. In her kitchen. Dillon never imagined he'd be dancing with her like this, though. God, it should be Kyan here. It shouldn't be him. But sometimes fate has other plans, and nuzzling his nose in her hair as they swayed, he had the feeling he was right where he was supposed to be.

The door cracked slowly open. Kodiak quietly tiptoed into the room. Linnea lifted her head from his chest. "Seth?"

"I'm here, little one."

They both held her for a little while.

Every time a contraction gripped her, Linnea would hold still and quietly whimper into his chest, clutching him tighter. Kodiak whispered words of encouragement to her in his soft, easy cadence. Dillon's message was silent. Kissing her hair. Holding her. Massaging her skin. With every touch he told her how much he loved her without words.

She glanced up at him, her light green eyes wide and glassy. "I think I need to get back in the bed."

Dillon looked to Kodiak and he nodded. "I'll get the nurse."

Things seemed to move in a blur after that, so fast he couldn't take it all in. Kodiak kissed his sister's brow as Gina pushed a table draped in blue into the room. "I love you. I'm going to be right out there." He pointed to the door and tenderly caressed her belly. "Happy birthday, Charlotte."

Linnea took his hand and squeezed it, tears flowing.

Kodiak clasped a hand on his shoulder with a nod. "Take care of them, brother."

But it was Kyan's voice that he heard.

She clutched his shirt in one hand, the bed rail with the other. He held her right leg with one arm, wrapped her shoulders in the other. Gina did the same from the other side, instructing Linnea to push, counting, and reminding her to breathe with every contraction.

Breathe in.

Breathe out.
Breathe in.
Hold it.
And push. Push. Push.

There was no sheet to cover her now. The bottom half of the bed had disappeared where the baby-faced doctor now sat on a stool. Waiting. Mesmerized, he couldn't help but watch it all happen.

And just after midnight on Christmas Eve, Charlotte slid into the world. Looking up. He saw his mother's beautiful face in hers. His brother's face. Hair, dark and wet, covered her little head. The doctor cradled her tiny body in the crook of her arm and suctioned fluid from her mouth and nose. Then little arms and legs flailing, she cried. And for the first time in his life that Dillon could remember, he cried too.

The nurse unsnapped the hospital gown she had on, and still attached to the cord, the doctor laid the baby on her chest. Skin to skin. Linnea gazed at her daughter and then smiling, with tears running down her face, she glanced at him. He leaned into her, and tasting the salt on her cheek, he tentatively touched the baby's hand with a fingertip and felt her tiny fingers, sticky and wet, wrap around it.

And suddenly everything became so clear.

"Dillon." The doctor placed a pair of scissors in his hand and directed him to cut the cord.

Gina placed an identification bracelet on the baby and a matching one on Linnea. Then she reached for his wrist. "Congratulations, Dad. She's beautiful."

The doctor attempted to correct her. "He's—"

Linnea raised her hand to stop her. Gina fastened the band meant for the baby's father to his wrist. He gazed upon the blanket-covered newborn and squeezed his eyes closed, fresh tears falling down his face.

"What's her name?" he heard the nurse ask Linnea.

'We want to name her Charlotte Grace. After Dad and Linn's mom. And you.'

"Charlotte Kyann Byrne."

Hours later, just before dawn, Dillon stared out the window at the city streets below. Snow wrapped the city in a blanket, fresh and clean and white. It glowed blue beneath the lamplight. Cold. Why did he always feel so cold?

He was frozen. He never felt warm anymore.

A sound came from the bassinet. It wasn't a cry. Just a tiny squeak. He glanced at the bed behind him. Linnea was sleeping. Good. She needed to sleep.

He walked over to the little crib and picked up the tiny bundle inside. Rocking the baby, he sat in a chair by the window.

Tiny fists poked out of the warm bundle in his arms. He gazed at Charlotte's beautiful face and he couldn't breathe.

He was just so cold.

And he couldn't fucking breathe.

He tried.

He tried.

He tried again.

He finally inhaled a stuttering breath and cradled the baby against his chest.

"I'm so sorry," he whispered.

Take care of them, brother.

And he sobbed.

Dillon was just about to leave for the hospital when he heard the knock at his front door. It was Christmas morning. Linnea and Charlotte were coming home today. He'd hurried to the house to shower and install the car seat in the Beemer while Kodiak was there with them.

He opened the door to Kelsey standing on his porch, holding a box wrapped in shiny red paper. Sheepishly, she glanced up at him. "You haven't answered my texts."

And he didn't intend to. He put her on ignore two months ago, so what the fuck was she doing here?

"I wanted to wish you a Merry Christmas." She tried to give him the red-wrapped gift.

Refusing it, he pushed her hand away. "I was just leaving."

"But I wanted to talk to you."

"Kelsey." Exasperated, he took a breath. "We don't have anything to talk about. I'm sorry. Look, I've got to get back to the hospital."

"Hospital?"

"Yeah." He couldn't help but smile. "Linnea had the baby."

She spotted the band on his wrist. Her jaw going slack as her gaze traveled up to meet his. "You're in love with her."

"What?"

"I see it now. And here I thought everything was my fault." Kelsey cocked her head in anger. "But you've been in love with your dead brother's wife all along."

He couldn't deny it.

Kyan's death gave old memories new life.

"That's so fucked up."

"Merry Christmas, Kelsey." With that, he quietly closed the door.

Things happen as they're meant to.

There's no avoiding your destiny.

It was clear to him now, that Linnea and Charlotte were his.

PART II

"Grief is in two parts. The first is loss.
The second is the remaking of life."
—Anne Roiphe

Eighteen

She'd just put the baby down in the little portable bed she kept here downstairs for her. Only a week old, Charlotte was too brand new, and Linnea was too nervous, to leave her upstairs in her pretty mauve nursery all alone. Even if she could see her on the monitor. She liked to watch her as she slept and wonder what she was dreaming of.

Patting her tummy, Linnea kissed the wispy dark hair on her daughter's head and glanced down the hallway to see Dillon come in through the front door. Her knight in shining armor, her rock, and besides Kyan, the only other man she ever loved. But then, how could she not love him?

Everyone loved him.

Beautiful inside and out, good through and through, Dillon was probably the most selfless man she'd ever known. Linnea couldn't recall a single instance when he'd put himself first. Not one.

He became her first friend, and her best friend along with Chloe, when she came here to the city fresh out of high school. All alone, with no family to speak of then, she found one at Charley's. Linnea vividly recalled the day she went there for her interview and met him. Dillon looked like he belonged up on a Calvin Klein billboard or the cover of *GQ*—and he was so nice, so genuinely kind to her. That came as a surprise. She'd never known kindness. Or love. Not then.

Shy, meek, and so nervous, Linnea didn't know how she even managed to speak that day without stuttering. She could barely look at him and by the time Kyan walked in she was sweating beneath her blouse and surely blushing like a cherry tomato. She'd never told anyone, not even Chloe, but her eighteen-year-old self had the biggest crush on Dillon Byrne.

But he was older, and when you're eighteen and naïve, twenty-six seems otherworldly. He was her boss. And Dillon attracted gorgeous women to him like moths to a flame. Kyan did too, for that matter. So Linnea loved Dillon as her friend. Then she fell in love with his brother.

"Hey, gorgeous." He wrapped her up in a big bear hug and kissed the top of her head. "How are my girls?"

"I just put her down."

Dillon reached inside the little bed and carefully lifted Charlotte out of it, cradling her against his chest. He inhaled her sweet baby smell, and kissing her head, took a seat on the sofa. To say he was smitten would be a huge understatement.

Linnea took a seat beside him. "Careful, you're going to get spit-up on your thousand-dollar suit."

"It's just a suit." He glanced at her with a smile on his face. Charlotte's presence somehow made it easier to do that now. "That's what dry cleaners are for."

"Still, it's a nice suit." She smirked. "And you look rather handsome in it, by the way."

He grinned. "You think I'm handsome?"

Linnea tsked with a shake of her head. "Like I haven't said that before."

She had. In fact, over the years, she'd told him that numerous times. Especially when he wore a suit, and he wore them often.

"You might have mentioned it a time or two." He winked.

"When are you meeting up with Brendan and Katie?"

Glancing at his watch, he huffed out a breath. "Fifteen minutes, but I'd rather watch the ball drop on TV."

She frowned. "Dillon."

"It's true." He rubbed his nose against the baby's down-covered head. "I don't want to go to the club and leave you here."

"Stop it." Linnea placed her hand on his forearm. "It's okay. I told you I'm going to Chloe's."

She wasn't, but Dillon didn't need to know that. He needed to get out and have a little fun. She already felt guilty enough.

"It's your night, Dillon." She mustered up a convincing smile. "Everyone has to kiss you at twelve—it's a rule."

"Not this year."

"We'll have a nice dinner for your birthday tomorrow." She leaned over and kissed him on the cheek. "I'll even bake you a cake."

"Red velvet?"

"It's your favorite, isn't it?" She winked. "Now put Charlotte back. You need to go and I need to get changed."

Ten minutes later Linnea watched the white Mercedes SUV drive out of the gate through the window.

She flicked on the TV and scrolled through the channels. Appropriately enough, the movie *New Year's Eve* was on, but she passed on it. *Me Before You* was a definite no—way too sad. Linnea wanted to watch something funny and settled on *Leap Year*. That one always made her laugh. Except this time it didn't. It only reminded her that she was alone with a brand-new baby. Uncoupled. She didn't have anyone to kiss her at midnight anymore.

"I've got you," she whispered to her daughter, tracing the baby's hand with a fingertip.

She closed her eyes then, trying to remember what it felt like to have Kyan's lips on hers. Linnea could see it in her mind, but the memory of what he felt like, what he tasted like, and the way he smelled, was just out of reach. He seemed to fade away a little bit more each day.

Grabbing the remote, Linnea changed the channel to *Dick Clark's New Year's Rockin' Eve*, and laid back on the sofa, staring at nothing on the ceiling. It couldn't have been more than a few moments later when she heard a gentle tap on the door and then it opened.

Not now, Chloe.

Except it wasn't Chloe.

She stood up. Bo walked softly into the room, wearing nothing but a pullover sweater and those tattered jeans of his. No coat, and it couldn't be more than twenty degrees outside. He was the last person she expected to see tonight.

Bo opened his arms. "Baby girl."

"Hey, drummer boy." She stepped into them.

His arms came around her and Linnea's mind instantly flooded with a million memories. Strolling through the park with Kyan on that hot summer night during the festival—their first date, her first ride on a Ferris wheel, and her first Venery concert. Tears sprang into her eyes out of nowhere. She remembered how weirded out she'd been that first time she hugged Bo, only because he wasn't wearing a shirt, which meant she had to touch his skin. It seemed as if three and a half years was a lifetime ago and she giggled through her tears. She was such a different girl then.

They pulled apart and she swiped beneath her eyes. "You okay?"

"Yeah." She managed a tiny smile. "What are you doing here?"

"Well…" Bo pulled her down to sit with him on the sofa. "…Dillon came by Tay's and mentioned you were getting ready to come over." He scanned her with a quick up-down. No makeup, hair gathered in a heap on top of her head, dressed in a pair of leggings and an old oversized shirt that hung off her shoulder, it was apparent she didn't plan on going anywhere. "Chloe seemed confused by that because you told her you were staying home," he said, angling his head. He tucked an errant strand of hair behind her ear. "So, I thought I'd come see if you'd changed your mind."

"I haven't." She twiddled her thumbs in her lap.

"I see that."

Linnea glanced up at him. "He wouldn't have gone to the party if he thought I was going to be here alone."

He chuckled. "So? What's so wrong about that?"

"It's his birthday, Bo," she informed him, as if he didn't already know that. "I want him to enjoy it. He's sacrificed way too much because of me."

"Baby girl…" He hesitated. "…ah, never mind."

Bo surveyed the room. The Christmas tree in the corner. The photos hanging on the walls. Linnea had a thing for photos, snapshots of life frozen in time, and she displayed them everywhere. His eyes lingered on a shot of the two of them that Kyan had taken before the concert on that long-ago summer night in the middle of a heat wave. His arm casually draped across her shoulders like they'd been friends forever, when they'd only just met. They were family now.

A squeak came from the baby's bed. Bo peered at Charlotte and he grinned. "Can I hold her?"

"Of course." Linnea smiled as she reached for the baby and placed her into Bo's arms.

His deep blue eyes misty, he gazed down at Charlotte, enthralled. "I missed out on this part." Then he kissed the baby's head.

He held her for a while, and when Linnea put Charlotte back in her bed, Bo stood up to leave. "Are you sure you'd rather stay here?"

She nodded. "Yeah, I'm sure."

Bo tipped her chin up with his finger. "I've always loved you, you know."

"I know." Those pesky tears sprang to her eyes again. "I love you, too."

"Dry your eyes, baby girl." Smirking, Bo swiped at her tears with his thumbs. "I want my kiss now."

He leaned in, his hands still holding her face, and softly, gently, touched his lips to hers. "Happy New Year, Linnea."

"Happy New Year, Bo."

Dillon stood at the bar in the private VIP space with Brendan, Katie, Kodiak, and the ice queen, Kelly. He poured himself another shot of whiskey and downed it, savoring the sting of it going down his throat. If he had to remain in the presence of that woman much longer he was going to need a lot more of it.

Thinking to join the Venery boys, he glanced behind him to the sofa. Matt, Kit, and Sloan had a girl stretched out across their laps. With his cock in her mouth, Sloan pulled on her long auburn hair, while Kit fingered her and Matt tugged on her nipples.

Jesus.

Last year, he would have strolled on over and sunk his dick in her ass. That thought no longer held any appeal for him and he hadn't felt anything, except his own hand, on his cock in months. Dillon didn't see the sorry state of his self-imposed celibacy changing anytime soon.

He didn't want to be here.

He didn't want to be anyplace she wasn't.

But he especially didn't want to be here in *this* place, assaulted by the heady scent of sex. Here in this place where he'd first touched her skin. Tasted her mouth. Told her he loved her.

Dillon poured himself another shot. "Easy, man," Kodiak warned him. "The night is young. Keep going at that rate and you'll pass out before midnight."

The night might be young, but he wasn't. He'd be thirty-three in a matter of hours, but right now Dillon felt like he was sixty years old.

"You wouldn't want to miss out on all your birthday kisses, would you?"

Raising his brow, he looked at Kelly. There was only one person Dillon wanted a kiss from. "No kisses."

"Isn't it a rule?" she mocked.

"Not this year."

Brendan came between them and facing Dillon, he settled his palms on his shoulders. "The people we love, this family, is our strength—and our weakness. Through them we rise, and only for them do we fall, brother." His hands squeezed. "Go to her."

Dillon went to Chloe's first, but she wasn't there.

He came in through the front door and found Linnea asleep on the turquoise suede sofa. Times Square rocking on the TV. Charlotte slept in her little bed beside her. *His* girls. They were his strength as much as they were his weakness.

Maybe she sensed he was there, because her pretty green eyes fluttered open and she sat up. "Dillon, what are you doing here?"

He shrugged out of his coat and jacket, peeled off his tie that was strangling him, and sat down beside her. Hooking his arm around her shoulders, Dillon drew her against him. "Told you, I'd rather watch the ball drop on TV."

"Oh, Dillon," she sighed, settling her head on his shoulder.

He watched the TV without really watching it, fingers running through the tangle of her blonde hair. Dillon glanced to the tree, silver stars dangling from its branches, to the photos on the wall, to the open window. And he looked up. The man in the moon smiled down at him.

He held her tight.

"You were supposed to get engaged tonight," Linnea whispered out of the blue.

"What?" Dillon turned to look at her. "Whatever gave you that idea?"

"You." She peered up at him. "I heard you tell Kyan you were going to ask Kelsey to marry you on New Year's Eve."

Declan's birthday party.

He threw his head back against the sofa and laughed. "Well, gorgeous, I guess you missed the part where I told him it wasn't happening." Dillon took her face in his hands. "Kelsey was never the girl for me."

You are.

"Oh."

They counted down to midnight on the TV. A brand-new year. His birthday. He skimmed his thumbs across her cheeks and when the clock struck twelve, he kissed her. Not the way he wanted to, but for now it was enough.

"Happy New Year, gorgeous."

"Happy birthday, handsome."

Nineteen

"It's Baltic as fuck out there," Dillon muttered, hurriedly closing the door behind him. "Fucking bullshit."

He only had to walk a hundred feet to get to the office, but that's all it took. It was below zero and he was frozen to the bone. Just as he'd predicted, winter had wielded itself with a vengeance. Polar vortexes. Thundersnow. Everyone in the city was holed up inside waiting for spring.

"February's almost over." Jesse chuckled. "Maybe we'll see the sun tomorrow."

After he unbundled and hung up his coat, Dillon headed straight for the coffee machine. He needed something warm to heat up his insides. "Where's Brendan?"

"He said he had to meet Phil this morning." Jesse looked at him and shrugged.

"Huh, he didn't mention it to me," Dillon muttered under his breath. Clutching the mug of coffee in his hands, he took a seat in the club chair across from his cousin.

Dillon could only think of one reason why Brendan would be meeting up with Phil. Their lawsuit, and Linnea's, against the scaffolding company. Hard to fathom almost six months had already gone by. Construction on the warehouse project had been halted pending litigation. He just wanted to finish it, for Kyan, and so he'd never have to set foot near the place where he died ever again.

Jesse glanced to the photo of the four of them on the wall. Dillon surmised he was probably thinking the same. "How's things with Linn?"

"She's good." He smiled, pushing his fingers through his hair. "Definitely more highs than lows since Charlotte was born."

"My wife said that too, but that isn't what I was asking." Jesse leaned forward with his elbows on his knees, hands folded beneath his chin. "How are things with Linn and *you?*"

Dillon wasn't sure how to answer that, or if he even should. "What do you mean?"

"C'mon, Dill. You know exactly what I mean."

"*Things* are as they've always been." Rubbing the back of his neck, he gestured with a quick shrug of his shoulders. "I'm not going there, Jess. It's too soon."

"Maybe." Jesse tilted his head. "Maybe not."

"I don't know…"

His head was a fucking mess where Linnea was concerned because how do you take your brother's widow out of the friend zone? When is it okay? And for that matter, will it ever be? Plagued by guilt that he was here and Kyan wasn't, he still wasn't sure what to do with his feelings. The only thing he did know for certain was that he loved Linnea and that baby with every breath, every beat of his heart, and every fiber of his being.

"Kyan would want both of you to be happy." Jesse nodded, grasping Dillon's shoulder. "We all do. I know how much you love her, Dill. It's just a matter of time."

And timing was the one thing he was never very good at.

That evening, sitting in Linnea's kitchen eating dinner, for no particular reason except they were still there, his gaze was drawn to the flowers he'd gotten her for Valentine's Day. To think he'd agonized over such a simple thing as that. Dillon didn't want to do anything that would remind her of Kyan—like getting her the same flowers. He didn't want to make her sad, and he wanted her to see him for *him*, separate and distinct from his brother. In the end, he went with burgundy roses. The florist had told him that like the red rose, they convey love and affection, desire and longing, but the deeper burgundy shade shows your feelings have yet to be revealed—and wasn't that the God's honest truth?

After dinner, they sat down to watch a movie. Charlotte rested in her baby bed next to the sofa and Linnea rested her head against his shoulder as she often did. Dillon inhaled the sweet almond scent of her hair, combing his fingers through it as if it were the most natural thing in the world. Because it was. God, he just wanted to touch her. Kiss her. Hold her. But did Linnea want that? Was she ready for that? He wasn't sure and it had to be right. He could wait. Loving her was worth it.

The baby stirred and made that squeak that said if she wasn't picked up in the next thirty seconds she would wail. Dillon kissed Linnea on the top of her head. "I'll get her."

As he brought Charlotte over, Linnea pulled her arm out of the sleeve of the long-sleeved shirt she wore, exposing her lush breast. Dillon watched as Charlotte latched onto her mother's nipple and greedily suckled. He sat back down beside her, kissed the baby's downy hair, and rested his head on Linnea's shoulder, massaging her neck.

Dillon closed his eyes and felt when Linnea moved the baby to the other breast. She ran her fingers through his hair, massaging his scalp, as Charlotte nursed. He opened his eyes. The blanket had slipped from her breast. He stared at her wet, swollen nipple.

Milk beaded at the tip. He swallowed, wishing that nipple was in his mouth, wondering what it tasted like. Then he wondered if he was a freak for wondering. Dillon knew of men who had that fetish, but he'd never counted himself among them.

He watched the bead of milk grow bigger until it trickled down her breast and another bead took its place. An overwhelming desire came over him to lick it off her nipple. Unaware of his thoughts, Linnea just kept on playing with his hair. He wouldn't dare act on his urges, but he leaned down and softly kissed the swell of her breast. Tugging on the strands of hair in her fingers, she emitted a soft sound. He kissed her skin again.

What the fuck am I doing?

Dillon stood. He had to stop himself before he did something he'd regret. Before he went way too far and much too fast. "I'm gonna call it a night, gorgeous."

She glanced up at him, green eyes questioning. "You okay?"

"Yeah." He bent over to kiss the top of her head, and then Charlotte's. "I just have some things I need to take care of before bed."

Like the raging hard-on in my pants.

Dillon lay across his bed, her milk and honey-almond scent still invading his nostrils. Was he fucked up for having these thoughts? Maybe. But he couldn't help wanting her. He wrapped his fingers around his engorged cock and closed his eyes, thinking of her as he stroked himself.

She came into the room after putting the baby to bed, naked beneath transparent silk.

"C'mere, gorgeous."

Linnea straddled his thighs, the robe falling open, revealing her delectable breasts. Milk still dribbled from the tips of her nipples. He squeezed the globes of supple flesh in his palms. She bit her lip.

"Daddy's turn." He pushed the robe off her shoulders.

She squeezed the puckered areolae to elicit milk from her nipples for him. He licked it off her and pinched them. She moaned. "Fuck, Dillon, you know that makes me come."

Fuck, yeah. I remember.

He growled, pushing two fingers inside her, and latched onto her nipple. Sweet, warm milk flooded his mouth as he sucked. "Good fucking girl," he rasped, moving to the other nipple. "You take such good care of me."

"Because I love you," she panted.

"I love you too, gorgeous."

"Always?"

"Forever."

"You won't ever leave me?"

"Never."

"Promise?"

"Cross my heart and hope to die."

"Please don't."

"Don't what?"

"Die."

Dillon sat up in his empty bed.

What the fuck?

Linnea watched Dillon leave through the patio door, holding his hand up in a wave as he crossed the yard. She brought Charlotte up to her shoulder and rubbed her back. "What's up with him?"

The baby answered her with a small burp.

"Guess we're on our own tonight, huh?"

That was unusual. He'd become a fixture in her house. In her life. And she liked him there. Unless he was at the office, Dillon was always here. After Kyan died, it only made sense for them to lean on each other. Then Charlotte came. Now she couldn't imagine a day without him in it. Did that make her selfish? Was she keeping him from living his own life? Linnea worried about that. A lot.

She was changing the baby when she heard a soft knock on her door, followed by her brother's soft voice. "Linnea?"

"In here, Seth."

"You really should lock your doors, you know," he scolded her, and pulling the knit beanie off his head, he glanced around the room. "Where's Dillon?"

"You just missed him." She smirked up at him. "And if you're here to eat, you missed dinner too."

"I didn't come by for you to feed me." He unwound his scarf and threw his coat over the back of the sofa. "I came for my Charlotte fix…" He took the baby from her and sat down. "…and to see you."

Still smirking, she shook her head. "There's leftovers I could heat up for you."

"No, really, I just wanted to stop by for a bit." He gazed at the baby in his arms, who was wide awake and looking right back at him. "And how is Uncle Kodiak's little darlin' today?"

Kodiak like the city in Alaska or the bear.

He still looked every bit the part of hippie biker Jesus, but to Linnea he'd always just be Seth. The fairy tale prince of her childhood. She'd idolized him then. He didn't talk about it much, but Linnea knew he'd endured hell on Earth at the hands of their father. He was her blood and her pillar of strength. She loved him even more now.

Linnea stood, giggling, and headed into the kitchen. "Are you expecting her to answer you, brother?"

"Yes." He rolled his eyes and his gaze followed her. "It's about time you toss those flowers, don't you think? They're half dead, Linnea."

"No, I do not think," she responded, aghast that he'd suggest such a thing. "Dillon gave them to me."

"Oh, I know he did." He winked. "So, is it official now?"

"What are you talking about, Seth?"

"C'mon now, Linnea." He raised his brow with a smirk. "You two are playing house without the sleepovers."

She shook her head emphatically. "It's not like that."

"You sure about that, little sister?" he asked in his slow, soft voice.

She nodded. "Yes, I'm sure."

"But you want it to be, don't you?" He kissed Charlotte, who had drifted off to sleep, and put her in her little bed. "And just so you know, you have my blessing."

"I didn't know I needed it, but thanks." Linnea pursed her lips and sighed. "I haven't even thought about being with anyone…like that."

"No, I suppose not, but you will." He nodded, pressing his lips together.

"How do you get over it?"

"You don't." Seth took her hands in his. "I've only truly loved two people in my life. Jonathan…and you."

Love had given her brother nothing but pain. She burst into tears.

"Sh, sh, sh. You know I hate to see you cry." He hugged her as if she were a child, smoothing her hair down her back. "I'm probably the last person to give you advice on this..." He pulled back, swiping at her tears. "...but ready or not, when someone makes you feel alive again, I'd say they're worth the risk."

She angled her head. "Have you met someone?"

"We're talking about you," he replied, conveniently evading her question. "Let me ask you this. Can you imagine yourself with anyone else?"

"I can't see myself with anyone."

There is no one more important to me than you...and Charlotte.

Maybe she was selfish, but if one day she could ever picture anyone at all, it would be Dillon.

Twenty

Fresh out of the shower, Linnea came down the stairs, combing the tangles from her damp hair. She could hear the Hawks game on in the family room. Dillon talking hockey to an eleven-week-old was pretty comical.

Stopping in the hallway to listen, Linnea held her hand over her mouth to keep from giggling. "We suck this season, Char." The baby just looked at him and smiled. "You might as well get used to that, though. We went forty-nine years without a Cup win, but we're loyal anyway." Still smiling, Charlotte's fist tried to find its way inside her mouth. "No one does hockey like our city. When you're old enough, I'll take you and Mommy to a game. Would you like that?"

Watching them made her heart melt, they were so darn cute together. Linnea couldn't help but see Kyan when she looked at her daughter. She knew Dillon saw it too. Sometimes, she'd catch him gazing at her and he'd tear up. Charlotte looked more like Kyan—actually more like their mother, who he took after, every day.

"We would," she answered, coming into the room. Linnea sat down next to Dillon. "I heard hockey games are fun."

"Nothing else quite like it. Better than football." His blue eyes lit up with a grin. "We can go to the Billy Goat before the game and get a cheezborger."

She laughed, working the tangle from her hair. "Pepsi, no Coke?"

"That's it." He winked.

Charlotte had fallen asleep in his arms. Dillon laid her in her little bed by the sofa. "Here." He took the comb from her hand and pointed to the space between his legs on the floor. "Let me do it."

Linnea scooted off the sofa and sat between his feet. He gently ran the comb through her long, thick hair, one section at a time. She tipped her head back, her eyes closed, as his fingers slid between the strands.

Tugging.

Pulling.

Twisting.

It shouldn't feel this good.

"What are you doing?"

She could feel the smile in his voice. "Braiding your hair."

"Do I want to know how you know how to do that?"

He chuckled. "Probably not."

Did he braid Kelsey's hair? Someone else? The thought sparked a twinge of jealousy, even though it shouldn't. A flood of guilt followed. She *was* being selfish.

Dillon secured the end of the braid with a hair tie and she opened her eyes to look down at the floor. "You should get out more. Go to the club. Hang out with my brother, go on a date, something."

Turning her around, he scooped her up from the floor so she was straddling his lap. His blue eyes flared and his forehead lowered until it touched hers. "Is that what you really want, Linn?"

No.

Unable to say it, she swallowed.

"For me to date?" he sneered, pulling his head back.

With no choice but to gaze into those familiar blue eyes, she opened her mouth, closed it, opened it again. Then she shook her head. "No."

"Good." Dillon pulled the tie off the end of her hair, slowly loosening the braid, combing through it with his fingers. Clutching the strands at her nape, he dipped his head to her ear. Warm breath bathed her skin as he spoke, "Because you better believe I'm right where I want to be, gorgeous."

Kodiak, pushing a jogging stroller with a huge pink bow on top of it, barreled through the front door on the morning of her birthday. Linnea would bet he'd jogged it all the way over here too—not that six blocks was anything to him.

"Happy birthday, little sister." He bent to kiss her cheek. "The weather is going to get nice soon. You can take Charlotte and run in the park with me."

"Thank you, Seth." She hugged him. "I've missed it."

Linnea wasn't as dedicated as her brother was, but she still liked to get out there a few times a week. She hadn't gone for a run since…well, since before Labor Day. Monica had told her exercise was good for her mind as well as her body, and now she had no excuse, did she?

"I can't believe you're twenty-five," he said, almost dumbfounded, his head moving slowly from side to side. "That means I'm…"

"Old?" She arched her brow with a smirk.

"Yeah, well, I remember when you were born, so…"

Was he thinking of her sixth birthday that she hardly remembered at all? Her eighteenth? If she was, he had to be too.

Fuck you, Jarrid Black.

Linnea reached up on her tiptoes to kiss him. "I love you, Seth."

"I love you too." He wrapped an arm around her. "So, what are you doing today?"

"Um, Dillon is going to watch the baby while I go to lunch with Chloe," she told him as she took him by the hand and led him to the family room.

He chuckled.

"What?" Soft and low, his laugh came off as devious, but then he did always sound like he was up to something.

"It's supposed to be a whopping fifty-three degrees tomorrow." He was good at evasion too.

"And sunny for a change. I almost don't remember what it looks like." She sighed. "Hello, spring."

"I'll come by in the morning. We can take that stroller out for a test run. Grab a coffee." He winked. "How's that sound?"

Yeah, he's up to something.

Linnea smiled. "Sounds great."

Charlotte kicked her little feet while Dillon wrestled with the snaps on the outfit he was trying to dress her in. "C'mon, sweet pea, work with me here."

Her blue eyes locked on his and she smiled.

"It's Mommy's birthday and she's going to be back any minute." He picked the baby up and began rummaging through dresser drawers. "Now, where does she keep the bows? Mommy always puts a bow on your pretty little head, doesn't she?"

He was coming down the stairs carrying Charlotte, bow in hand, just as Linnea came through the front door. "Hey, birthday girl." Dillon kissed her cheek. How was lunch?"

Her eyes darted between the baby and himself. "Good."

"Don't bother hanging up your coat," he said over his shoulder, proceeding down the hall. "We're going out."

They went south on Lake Shore Drive. "Where are we going?" Linnea asked as the downtown skyscrapers passed by the window.

"To look at the stars."

Dillon hadn't been to the planetarium since he was a kid, when he went for a class field trip in the sixth grade. On Northerly Island at the shore of Lake Michigan, not only did it boast one of the largest public aperture telescopes, but a jaw-dropping view of the city.

They pushed Charlotte along in her stroller together, stopping to admire the sculptures and see the exhibits until shadows lengthened and daylight faded into dusk. Then he steered them in the direction of the observatory.

"In a dark sky, you can see thousands of stars with the naked eye, but here in the city, because of all the light pollution, we can only see about thirty-five," Dillon informed her, guiding her toward the big telescope. "Sad, isn't it?"

He didn't tell her that the night sky was a graveyard, studded with the remains of a thousand dead stars, black holes, and dim white dwarfs, remnants of stars that had once been much like the sun. Instead he helped her find celestial bodies, the constellations and planets. Orion. Jupiter. Saturn. "Keep looking up."

"Oh, wow," she exclaimed. "Dillon, it's so beautiful."

You're so beautiful.

"We're like the moon and the stars, remember?"

Lighting up the darkness...

Kodiak came through for him and picked up everything he'd ordered while they'd been gone. Dinner and a cannoli birthday cake from Rossi's awaited them. Flowers—Dillon stuck with the burgundy roses—sat on the table.

He'd been thinking about it since the night he braided her hair, and he decided that unless he made his feelings known and his intentions clear, he was being unfair to both of them. Not that Dillon expected them to jump right into the deep end—there were still more firsts to wade through—but he hoped they could get their toes wet at least, and ease themselves in gradually, a little bit at a time.

He was cleaning up from dinner when Linnea came into the kitchen after putting Charlotte to bed. Dillon turned around and leaned back against the counter. "C'mere."

She stepped up to him and he pulled the box from his pocket. "Happy birthday."

A simple platinum chain-link bracelet, adorned with a diamond-encrusted moon and a dangling silver star, lay nestled inside. Linnea gasped and glanced up at him. Tears swam in her pretty green eyes.

"Family stays together," she whispered.

"That's right." Fastening the bracelet to her wrist, he smiled, because she remembered.

She wrapped her arms around his waist and squeezed him tight. "Thank you, Dillon."

"You and Charlotte are my family, Linnea." He held her to him, stroking her hair down her back. "Always."

"Of course we are."

Dillon pulled back a little so he could see her face. "Not because we share the same last name." He held her cheeks in his palms. "Because I love you."

The tears in her eyes spilled over to roll down her skin. Closing her eyes, she licked her lips and whispered, "Dillon."

He took her in his arms and laid her head on his shoulder, then even though no music played, they slow-danced in the kitchen. "Perhaps not today, and maybe not tomorrow either, but one day, when you're ready…" He stopped moving. "…I'm going to make you mine."

The nod of her head was so subtle, it was almost imperceptible, but he saw it, felt it against his shoulder. She lifted her head and gazed up at him. Her full, soft lips were right there.

Just a kiss.

And with one hand holding her against him, Dillon stroked her cheek with the other, wiping the tears from her face as he lowered his lips to hers.

Softly. Gently. Slowly. That's how he kissed her, her mouth melting into his like ice cream. Sweet and delicious. Her hands slid up his back. His slid into her hair. She parted her lips to take a breath. He slipped his tongue inside.

She tasted like birthday cake. Love and longing. Hope and desire. She tasted like his future. Like home.

Linnea kissed him back, holding him tighter, pressing him closer. So close that the beat of her heart radiated through his shirt to his skin. He'd been waiting his entire life for this moment, the moment when passion feeds the body and love fills the soul. It was as if Fate had preordained it all. They were meant to be.

She was his destiny.

He was hers.

But then somehow he'd always known that, hadn't he?

Twenty-One

Dillon held her close against him. "You and Charlotte are my family, Linnea." He made her feel safe and protected. Cherished. "Always."

"Of course we are."

And family stays together…

For a girl who'd grown up as she had, Linnea would never take love and family for granted. She knew more than most what a precious gift it was, and she'd be forever grateful that Dillon was hers.

"Not because we share the same last name." Her vision blurred as she gazed up at him. "Because I love you."

Linnea closed her eyes to the tears that escaped and trailed down her face. "Dillon."

She knew that, of course. And she'd always loved him. But she *fell* in love with Kyan, and that felt different. Swift and unexpected, their love was like a luminous stellar explosion. A powerful supernova, it burned so hot and so bright, that a dense black hole was left behind with its tragic demise.

Dillon was the steady pilot light, burning at a constant simmer. He'd always been there. She must've fallen for him too, but the fall was so soft, so sweet, and so gentle, she hadn't even noticed when he caught her.

He held her now, dancing in the kitchen to a silent song that no one else could hear. "Perhaps not today, and maybe not tomorrow either, but one day, when you're ready…" He stilled. "…I'm going to make you mine."

I am yours.

But she wasn't ready to say it.

Hell, she could barely acknowledge it to herself. Because as much as she knew in her heart that she was in love with Dillon, she was still very much in love with a ghost.

Linnea lifted her head from his shoulder to find his bluer than blue eyes, warm and alive, gazing into hers, opening up her soul to see inside of it. Dillon came closer, a cool inhalation of oxygen that warmed her inside as she breathed in his distinctive, earthy scent. Crisp spearmint, thyme, and tarragon, layered with heady notes of sandalwood and oak moss engulfed her senses.

She held her breath when his lips touched hers, so soft and sensual. Dillon was a sweet aphrodisiac. A Pandora's box she couldn't help but open. What she was feeling could not be put into words, for there hadn't been a figure of speech yet invented to describe it. And for that one beautiful moment, nothing else existed. Just them.

But then it all came flooding back.

Was she crying?

Oh, fuck.

She was.

As their kiss ended, overcome by a multitude of conflicting emotions, tears streamed down her cheeks. She held onto him, burying her face in his neck, not wanting him to see what her eyes would surely reveal. Love. Desire. Longing. Sorrow.

She should have known better. Dillon didn't have to see her face to see inside her head. "Shh, baby, it's okay." He kissed her temple. "Look at me."

Linnea took a deep breath of spearmint and sandalwood before she unburied her face from his neck. Looking into her eyes, Dillon cupped her cheek. "It's okay."

Not trusting herself to speak, she nodded.

He dried her tears and taking her by the hand, led her to the sofa. She curled up on his lap, her head against his chest. "I'm sorry. I didn't mean to cry like that. It's just all these feelings came flooding in and…"

"I understand." He smoothed her hair, kissing her crown. "We both loved him, Linnea. We miss him. You and I are feeling a lot of the same things, I imagine." He exhaled. "It's going to take time for us, but I know one day we'll get there."

He sounded so sure, but she wasn't. "How?"

"Doing exactly what we're doing right now, gorgeous." He tipped her chin up. "Telling each other what we're feeling."

"I feel so many mixed-up things right now."

"Me too." His thumb skimmed her jaw. "But more than anything else, I love you."

Linnea took his face in her palms and brought his lips to hers. Then she kissed him. And love filled her soul again.

They were taking things slow. Very, very slow. Dillon was following the cues Linnea gave him. He didn't want to rush her, and there was no reason to. They had their entire lives, didn't they? But then, he knew all too well just how short life can be.

March rolled into April. They'd reached a settlement agreement on both suits against the scaffolding company. Brendan signed the papers this morning. Construction on the warehouse project could finally move forward. Linnea was meeting with Phil at his downtown office tomorrow, and he was going to take her. He'd already made reservations for the two of them to go to lunch after.

"Of course, Hailey. We'd be so honored," Brendan said into the phone. At the mention of the girl's name, Dillon's ears pricked up. "Yes, it sounds perfect. I'll send you the measurements and anything else you need. Thank you so much."

Brendan quickly swiped beneath his eye and ended the call. He looked up at Dillon and Jesse. "That was Hailey. She has an art project to do over the summer, and she wants to do it at the warehouse—as a tribute to Kyan."

"What a thoughtful thing to do," Jesse softly said.

"Yeah." Dillon nodded. "Linnea will love that."

He hadn't spared a thought for the young girl since the funeral. This girl who lived through that horrific day. This girl who heard his brother's last words, who held his hand as he bled out on a city sidewalk, who saw him take his last breath.

And he still couldn't bring himself to read what Hailey wrote down on a piece of notebook paper that Brendan kept.

The sun decided to show itself the next morning. Cotton-ball clouds softly floated in a bright cerulean sky. Dillon could hear the chirping of birds as he traipsed across the yard. A mild day for early spring, he hadn't even bothered to wear a coat.

He came in through the patio as he often did. She took his fucking breath away. Linnea stood there in a slim, knee-length, black pencil skirt and a taupe pullover sweater. Her black high-heeled boots reached past her ankles and revealed perfectly polished toes. Dillon licked his lips and found himself wondering what she wore underneath. Black lace? Nude satin?

She turned around and quickly glanced him over with a smile. "Morning, handsome."

"Morning, gorgeous." He leaned in and kissed the tender spot beneath her ear, breathing in the delicious scent of her. "You look beautiful."

"Thank you," she whispered, lashes fluttering as she glanced up at him. "Ava should be here any minute. She's watching Charlotte while we're gone."

The baby napped contentedly in her swing.

"I thought we were taking her to Chloe's."

"Ireland came down with a tummy bug," she explained, just as there was a knock at the front door. "That would be Ava. Can you get that? She still hasn't learned to let herself in like everybody else does around here."

Dillon opened the door for the babysitter, a college classmate and friend of Katie's. She carried a backpack of books on her shoulder. It looked heavy on her petite frame. Blonde hair up in a messy bun. Glasses. She reminded him of his third-grade English teacher. He'd seen her around, but he didn't know her very well.

While Linnea rattled off Charlotte's routine and showed Ava around the house, Dillon gently lifted the sleeping baby out of the swing. Kissing her wispy, dark curls, he snuggled her against his chest. "I promise me and Mommy won't be too long, Char," he told her, carefully returning her to her swing. He placed a kiss on his fingers and brought them to her head. "I love you."

He turned around to see Linnea leaning against the doorframe, a smile on her face, pretty green eyes watching him.

He smiled back. "Ready?"

"I'm ready."

They sat at a conference table in Phil Beecham's high-rise office on LaSalle Street, looking out at the sun reflecting off the Chicago River through its floor-to-ceiling windows. Fidgeting in her seat, Linnea twirled her diamond wedding ring around and around on her finger. She just wanted to get this unpleasant business over with. He did too.

Phil came in clutching a thick manilla file folder. After exchanging pleasantries and inquiring about the baby, he pulled the stack of documents out of the folder.

He handed Linnea a pen. Without a word, he pointed. She signed.

"It's a significant amount," he assured her when she finished.

"Is it?" She lifted her brow, a look of scorn twisting her beautiful face. "Is that what a life is worth?"

"Of course not, Linnea." Phil patted her hand. "No amount of money in the world can make up for that, and I apologize if I made it sound that way. Fact is, we bankrupted them. They had to sell the company off to settle the suits against them."

"Good. I guess that means they won't be killing anybody else."

Dillon took her hand in his and squeezed it.

"I set up the trust for your daughter and the scholarship fund in Kyan's name just as you requested. I'll be wiring the remainder directly to your account." Phil looked to Dillon and then gently smiled at Linnea. "The university asked me to extend their deepest condolences as well as their sincere gratitude to you for your generosity."

"Brendan told you our company's matching it, right?"

They were starting a memorial scholarship for architecture students at his brother's alma mater. Kyan would have liked that.

"Yes, Dillon. It's already taken care of."

Swiping beneath her eye, Linnea looked up from her lap. "Is that it then?"

"Yes, we're finished here," Phil said, patting her hand again.

Dillon rose, and shaking Phil's hand, assisted Linnea from her seat.

They stood there on LaSalle, holding hands, as he hailed a taxi. "Are you okay?"

"Yeah." She nodded, squeezing his fingers. "I'm fine." He looked at her and she laughed. "Really. I promise."

Dillon could have taken her to the steakhouse right there on the river in Phil's office building, but that place was filled with power suits and business deals in the making. He had a much better place in mind. Bavette's, with its speakeasy atmosphere, was his favorite steakhouse in the city—not to mention they had the best steaks too. And he wanted to take her someplace nice, where she'd be comfortable, and they could enjoy each other's company.

Jazz music from the 1920s softly played as they took their seats in a cozy booth for two. The waiter handed them menus, but too busy taking in the ambiance around her, Linnea didn't look at it.

"Have you ever been here before?"

"No." She smiled. "I love it."

He was hoping she'd say that.

"I love *you*."

She reached across the table and took his hand in hers. "I love you too, you know."

I know.

Then the waiter returned to take their order. Linnea quickly glanced over the menu. "I'll have the baked goat cheese, your petite filet with béarnaise sauce—medium rare, and a side of creamed spinach, please."

His girl knew her food.

"I'll have the same, but make mine the bone-in filet, and I'll have the buttery mashed potatoes too." They were his favorite, after all. He grinned at Linnea. "They should come with a defibrillator."

They talked about everything and nothing over their lunch. The flowers Linnea wanted to plant in the backyard. The events she'd booked. Properties he was considering for future projects. Baseball. Charlotte. Life.

He could see the sparkle in her eyes again.

And nothing else could have made him happier.

"How about some dessert, gorgeous?"

"I wish I had room." She bit her lip. "If I eat another bite I might bust right out of this skirt."

I'd love to see that.

Dillon turned his head to the waiter and winked. "Can we have two of the chocolate cream pie to take with us, please?"

She said it without preamble. "Seth told me we're playing house without the sleepovers."

"Did he now?" Dillon wasn't sure if he wanted to kick her brother's ass or kiss it, but since Linnea brought it up, he wasn't about to back away from the subject. "I'm not gonna lie. I'm looking forward to the sleepovers—a lot."

She blushed and looked down at their joined hands. "Me too."

Kyan's ring glittered on her finger. That alone told him she wasn't ready.

"I can wait." He squeezed. "You're worth it. We're worth it."

The waiter brought out their pie wrapped and boxed and bagged. Dillon helped Linnea out of the booth, and just as he did, someone knocked into him from behind.

Kelsey stood there. Hand on her hip, jaw slack, looking severe as ever in a houndstooth suit and her hair slicked back in a high ponytail. The receptionist and a couple suits from her office were right behind her.

"Oh, excuse me." Her lip curled. "I didn't see you standing there."

Liar.

She glanced to Linnea then, and sneered, "Out of mourning already, I see. How've you been?"

You fucking bitch.

Twenty-Two

She didn't say a word the entire way home.

Linnea retreated into herself, that sparkle he'd glimpsed in her eyes was gone. While he saw to Ava and checked on Charlotte, she took herself up the stairs. Dillon swore to himself if he ever saw Kelsey again, he'd throttle her.

He found her in her bedroom. Stripped of the sweater and skirt, she stood there in her bra and panties. Nude lace. Fucking exquisite.

"Leave me alone, Dillon." She wouldn't even look at him.

Oh, hell no.

He marched right on in. "Sorry, gorgeous. Can't do that."

She turned away from him. Dillon came up behind her, and grasping her wrists, he wrapped his arms around her middle. He held her tight, his chin resting on top of her head, inhaling her hair.

"I still grieve for him, Dillon." Her chest expanded and she exhaled. "I think I always will."

"Both of us always will." He squeezed her a little tighter, rocking her in his arms. "Time just makes it easier to live with, that's all."

Nodding, Linnea turned in his arms, facing him. She cupped his face in her hands, tears shimmering in her pale-green eyes, and brought his lips to meet hers. He kissed her, the blood rushing to fill his cock as he slipped his tongue inside.

Nearly naked, her body was soft and warm in his hands. Pliant. Dillon took hold of her thighs and lifted her. Twining her arms around his neck, she gripped him with her legs, and pressing his erection against her, Linnea whimpered.

With one arm across her back, fingers splayed, he walked them toward the bed, kneading the flesh of her ass with the other as he went. Still kissing her, Dillon lay across the bed with Linnea on top of him. Not wanting to push too fast or too far, he'd let her lead for now.

They kissed voraciously. Feverishly. Deeply. Time and space disappeared tasting her soul inside his mouth. His fingertips traced over her bare skin, pressing into her flesh, memorizing it. Her back, her sides, her arms, her thighs. Every inch of her he could reach.

Linnea tugged at his hair, rubbing against him, seeking friction. God, he wanted to give it to her too. His hands fell to her ass. Kneading the fleshy globes, he pressed her firmly against his dick that throbbed for her. He didn't give a fuck if he ended up coming in his pants. Then his fingertips grazed along the edge of her nude lace thong.

Wet. So fucking wet.

She was soaked for him. Dillon slid his fingers beneath the fabric, pushing it to the side, slowly sweeping through the lips of her pussy. Testing the waters. Gauging her reaction. Savoring the slippery soft feel of her on his fingers. She mewled into his mouth at the contact.

He slipped a finger inside her.

For the briefest moment, Linnea stilled. Then opening her eyes, she whispered his name on his lips, pulling him in even deeper. With his thumb on her clit, he pushed a second finger inside.

Melting on a moan, she released a pent-up breath.

With his lips to her ear, he softly crooned, "That's it, baby. Let it all go."

Linnea held his fingers inside her with a grip so tight wetness flowed down his hand to drip off his wrist. He scissored his fingers as he withdrew and pushed them back in again as far as they could go. She shifted her hips to meet him, arching her back, sinking her teeth into her lip.

He watched her. So enthralled he couldn't take his gaze off her face. Head tipped back. Skin flushed. Lips slightly parted. Fucking beautiful.

How had he ever thought he could love anyone else? His fate was sealed the moment he saw her. He knew it then. And nothing on Earth could keep him from loving her now.

"Dillon," she breathed.

"I've got you, baby," he promised her, pressing his thumb into her clit. She fluttered on his fingers. "I've got you."

Always.

Linnea wasn't sure what got into her that day, but it had been weeks and Dillon hadn't touched her like that again. He was affectionate. He'd hold her and kiss her. But nothing like the afternoon he carried her to the bed in her underwear. Not even close.

Was it because she sobbed like a baby into his shoulder after her first orgasm in seven months? Did he think she was sad? She was. Felt guilty? She did. Was it too soon? Probably.

And what was he feeling? He hadn't said anything. It was almost as if it had never happened. Except it had.

Maybe she should just ask him?

Yeah.

She'd do that.

After a day that began with a five-mile run with Seth, and then spent on the phone with vendors for upcoming events she wished she'd never booked, feedings, diaper changes, and tummy time, Linnea fired up the grill and kicked back on a lounger. She just needed a minute to breathe the fresh air and let the sun soak into her skin.

Soft lips kissed her forehead and she opened her eyes. "Hey, sleeping beauty."

"Dillon," she responded, smiling, then immediately bolted up in a panic. "Shit! Charlotte…"

"Is asleep." He chuckled, his strong hand urging her back down onto the lounger. "Looks like both of my girls needed a nap."

"I've got to get dinner going."

His fingers skimmed her cheek. "Relax. I'll do it."

"I got skirt steak...for the grill." Dillon hadn't gone anywhere near it since the blooming onion.

"I'm pretty sure I can handle it, gorgeous." He winked. "Finish your nap. It's so nice out. Let's have dinner here on the patio, yeah?"

Two brothers, so different from each other, and at the same time so very much alike. Their parents, this family, must have raised them right, because Dillon and Kyan were both amazing men. How'd she get so lucky?

He handled the task with ease. Smoke coming off the grill tantalized her tastebuds, making her mouth water. She loved that smell. Like freshly mown grass and suntan oil, it reminded her of summer. It would be here soon. Memorial Day, and the kick-off to the season, was this weekend. And Kyan's birthday. Forever thirty. He would have turned thirty-one on Saturday. They were going up to the lake house.

Dillon held five-month-old Charlotte in one arm and shoveled potato salad in his mouth with the other. "God, I love your potato salad. I could eat the whole bowl."

"Looks like you're well on your way." Linnea giggled with a shrug. "It's Paula Deen's recipe, so the credit goes to her."

"Ah, but you add love to it, see?" He winked. "It's all you."

Linnea pressed her hand to her abdomen to keep her ovaries from exploding. They weren't really exploding, but sometimes the things that came out of his mouth turned her into a puddle of goo. Like now.

And she figured now was as good a time as any. "Remember when you said we need to tell each other how we're feeling?"

"Yeah." He set his fork down.

"Well..." She wasn't exactly sure how to say it. "...I've been feeling confused. Kind of."

"About?" Still chewing, he raised his brow.

Linnea felt her cheeks heat and looked down at her lap before pursing her lips to the side and gazing back at Dillon. "I was just, um, wondering..." God, she didn't want to sound accusatory or make it seem like she was looking to jump into bed or anything. "...um, you haven't touched me again and I was thinking about it and I was wondering if you thought about it and...that's it, I guess."

Lifting the baby to his shoulder, he patted his lap. "C'mere."

She went.

His hand went to her hair, tangling his fingers in it. "Is that what you want? For me to touch you?"

"That's not why I was asking."

"You didn't answer my question."

"Maybe," she whispered.

"See, Linn, that's why I haven't." He planted a kiss on her forehead. "I need an enthusiastic yes. I need to know I'm not pushing you too soon, that you really want *me*...like you wanted me that day.

"Believe me when I say this, there's nothing I want to do more than touch every part of you with every part of me. Fall asleep beside you every night. Wake up next to you each morning." His lips softly touched hers. "I love you. I will always love you. And I can wait until I know you're ready to let go and commit yourself to me."

"Let go of what?"

On an exhale, Dillon squeezed her hand in his. "My brother."

Tears rushed to her eyes and she blinked.

"I'm sorry, I didn't mean for it to come out like that." He combed his fingers through her hair. "Kyan will always be a part of us, baby. Always and forever. But I need you to let go of being his widow so that one day you can be my wife. Understand?"

Sniffling, she nodded. "I do." Gazing into his summer-blue eyes, her fingers skimmed his cheek. "I don't know if this helps, but most of me—ninety-nine percent of me—wants to feel you inside of me." She pressed her lips together. "But that other one percent is clinging to...anyway, sometimes she can be very loud."

Dillon lowered his forehead to hers. "I love you and I'm not going anywhere."

"I love you too." Linnea wrapped her arms around Dillon holding their daughter. "I want you to touch me, okay?"

He kissed her.

Dillon glanced at Linnea in the passenger seat as he drove the familiar route up to the lake house. He took her hand, and lacing their fingers together, rested it on his thigh. The five-carat rock he and Chloe helped Kyan pick out at Tiffany's shined at him like a beacon, a glaring reminder she was still married to Kyan. In her mind anyway. At least that's how he interpreted it.

He couldn't say why he was so stuck on that ring, but he was. It was symbolic of their marriage, wasn't it? Maybe he should just give her a ring of his own. But anytime Dillon imagined doing that, he slipped the ring he'd chosen for her onto a bare finger. He shouldn't have to take his brother's ring off first.

Maybe he should just get over the stupid fucking ring. Ignore it. But he couldn't. A niggling voice in his head wouldn't let him. Dillon wanted to make love to *his* future, not his brother's past.

Linnea, Chloe, and Katie wrangled toddlers and unpacked a weekend's worth of groceries while he, Brendan, Jesse, and Taylor unloaded the cars.

"Why is it every time we come up here there's more shit we have to carry into the house?" Jesse complained.

Brendan smirked. "Babies."

Dillon brought their bags up to his room—well, their room now. The girls, namely Chloe, decided to give Kyan's old room to the kids until they were big enough to sleep in the bunkbeds downstairs. Four portable cribs were lined up along the walls. Baby monitors. His cousins and their spouses would have some privacy. Linnea would share his bed with him. He made a mental note to send Chloe flowers or something to thank her.

After dinner out on the deck, Dillon grabbed a beer for himself out of the cooler. "Anyone need one while I'm up?"

"I'll have one. Thanks, mate," Taylor replied with a sleeping almost three-year-old draped across his lap.

"Sure thing, man." He chuckled. "Chandan is down for the count."

"Give him to me, sweetie." Chloe stood. "I'll take him upstairs."

"Leave him be, love." Taylor stroked his son's long curls. "He's fine where he is and we wouldn't want him to wake up now, would we?" He winked.

Declan and Ireland were already fast asleep upstairs in their beds. It took a bit longer to wear Chandan out. The kid had a lot of energy.

Dillon handed Taylor his beer and sat down with his next to Linnea. Charlotte was happy and content in her mother's lap. Katie looked happy in Brendan's too. Chloe sat between Jesse's thighs while he played with her hair. For the first time in a long time, they all talked and laughed while the fireflies danced in the air across the lawn. No one was sad, at least not today. He'd forgotten just how fucking good that felt.

Charlotte began to fuss and Linnea put her to her breast, then reached for his hair like she always did. It had become their thing. While she fed the baby, she massaged his head. He sure wasn't going to complain about it.

Chloe tugged on the ends of Jesse's hair. "Awe, that makes me want to have another one."

"I'm all for practicing." He waggled his brows.

"We have two." Taylor side-eyed them. "My God, how many more do you want, cherry cake?"

Yeah, Chandan had a *lot* of energy.

"Um, I don't know." She giggled. "A couple maybe."

"Fuck," he muttered under his breath.

"Want to make another baby with me, sweet girl?" Brendan winked at his wife.

"Yeah." She grinned. "One day."

"Now."

"Oh, well…I guess we're saying goodnight then." She got up from his lap.

"We are." Brendan stood too, and nodded. "Night."

Taylor rose with his sleeping son in his arms. "Come on then, let's put him to bed. We've got some practicing to do, don't we?"

Not too long after, once the baby was fed and asleep for the night in her crib in the room next door, Dillon lay in their bed while Linnea took a shower. *Their* bed. They hadn't slept together in the same bed since the night Kyan died. Nope, he was not going to think about that right now. His brother's birthday was tomorrow and that was going to be hard enough.

She came out of the en suite in one of those cropped bralette tops of hers and matching boy shorts. Long hair loose. Smelling all sexy and sweet. His cock was half hard already.

Jesus. I'm so fucked.

"You're killing me, gorgeous."

Linnea softly laughed and tsked, shaking her head. Then she got under the covers and laid her head on his shoulder. He stroked her just-washed hair.

"All that baby talk got me thinking," she said. "We've never talked about it."

"What?"

She gazed up at him. "Do you want one?"

He did. One day. But if Linnea didn't, or couldn't, then that was okay too.

"We have Charlotte."

"I know, but later on." She was looking at his chest now. "Do you want more children?"

He tipped her chin up. "Do you?"

"If I can have another baby, yeah, I'd like to." She smiled.

Dillon smiled too. "Then we will."

One day.

Maybe in a few years. Once they got past all the firsts and the sadness, when they were married and settled. He wasn't sure why they were even talking about this now, except that his cousins must have baby fever or something. They hadn't even had sex yet, for chrissakes, and Charlotte was still nursing.

He chuckled. "I have a confession to make."

"You do?" Still smiling, Linnea arched a brow.

"Yeah."

"What is it?" she prompted him.

Fuck it.

Dillon stared at the ceiling as he said it, "Sometimes…I get turned on watching you feed the baby."

Linnea snickered behind her hand.

He turned his head with a grin to look at her. "You think I'm a freak, don't you?"

She shook her head, still giggling. "Well, if you're a freak then so are your cousins—Taylor too."

Get the fuck out!

"You girls actually talk about this shit?"

"Not usually." She shrugged. "It came up in conversation one day because Brendan—"

"No, don't tell me." Shaking his head on the pillow, he covered her mouth with his hand. "There are some things I'd rather just not know."

She laughed again and then it faded. Linnea put his hand on her breast. "It's okay to touch them."

He squeezed. "Fuck, you're killing me."

"You keep saying that."

Dillon placed both hands on her breasts and squeezed. "I'll want to touch other places and not just with my hands."

"Ninety-nine percent, Dillon."

I want one hundred, baby.

He pulled that little top she wore down, exposing those luscious breasts that taunted him.

He kissed her nipple.

In the room next door, Charlotte began to cry.

Linnea went to get the baby and he glanced at the clock.

Midnight.

Happy birthday, brother.

Twenty-Three

S unlight filtered into the room through the curtains that fluttered with the morning breeze. Dillon blinked his eyes open to Charlotte's baby blues staring at him from her co-sleeper. He picked her up and laid her on his chest.

"Good morning, sweet pea." Stroking her downy-soft hair, he kissed her little head. "Didn't like bunking in with your cousins, huh?"

The baby lifted her head from his chest, drool dripping down her chin, and gave him a gummy smile. Linnea said she'd be getting her first tooth soon. Chuckling to himself, he smiled back. Teething, playdates, and birthday parties. It all made sense to him now. This little girl and her mother were his entire world.

He glanced around the room and into the en suite. She wasn't there. "Where's Mommy?"

Dillon carried Charlotte downstairs with him into the kitchen. It wasn't quite six thirty in the morning, the rest of the house still in their beds, but Linnea and Chloe already had breakfast in the works. "What are you girls doing up so early?"

"If you want to eat, we have to get started before the hellion awakens." Chloe looked up and muttered with a smirk, "Jesus, Dillon, it should be illegal for you to walk around without a shirt on."

Linnea giggled and put down the bowl she was whisking eggs in. She reached up to kiss his cheek and Charlotte. "Morning. You two looked so darn sweet asleep."

"Morning, gorgeous."

She seemed to be in good spirits considering. Maybe Linnea

forgot what today was. The only thing on his agenda was to do his best to keep her mind—and his—off the birthday they wouldn't be celebrating.

"There's a craft fair or something going on in town," he said, stealing a grape off a platter and popping it into his mouth. "I thought we could go check it out later."

"Yeah, okay." Smiling, she returned to her whisking. "That'd be nice."

"I can watch Charlotte if you want," Chloe offered, winking at him.

He made a mental note to send Chloe flowers *and* chocolate.

After breakfast, they drove into town. Dillon parked on Main Street, close to the square. Local farmers, crafters, and artists had erected tents and booths to display their goods. Sweet corn roasting. Funnel cakes. A band was playing an old Bee Gees' song under the gazebo. Linnea loved this kind of thing.

They strolled hand in hand to the square. "This feels so weird."

"What?"

She glanced up at him. "Not having to push a stroller."

"Enjoy it while you can, gorgeous." He chuckled, wrapping his arm around her shoulder.

"Oh, Dillon." Linnea stopped to admire a display of black-and-white paintings. "Look at these. They're incredible."

Devoid of color, they were stark. Simplistic, yet detailed. Maybe that's what made them so beautiful.

She pointed to a canvas. "Is that our lake?"

"Yeah." He grinned. "From the other side. See? That's our dock right there."

"It looks so different."

While Linnea moved on to look at some of the other paintings on display, Dillon whispered with the artist.

Hooking his arm in hers, he caught up to her a few minutes later. "C'mon, let's get a lemonade and go for a ride."

"Where are we going?" Linnea asked when he turned down a narrow dirt road.

"You'll see."

The road ended at a small dirt and gravel lot. Dillon took her by the hand and led her along the well-traversed path to the old fishing pier. They sat down at the end of it on a timeworn plank and let their feet dangle over the water.

"It always looks different from the other side." He pointed to the house across the lake.

She rested her head on his shoulder.

He was relaxing on the deck after dinner, Charlotte napping contentedly on his chest. His gaze was drawn to the water. In the twilight, he could barely make out the old fishing pier across the lake. When they were kids, they used to paddle the boat over there to fish. Didn't matter they had a dock of their own right here. His brother always insisted the fishing was better on the other side.

As much as Dillon tried to distract himself today, it was impossible. So many of Kyan's birthdays had been celebrated here at the lake house. The memory of each and every one of them now a gift. Kyan would never grow another year older, but today still belonged to him.

Brendan came outside, holding onto Declan's hand, and plopping down across from him, pulled the toddler up into his lap. "We were kindly asked to leave the kitchen." He chuckled as Chandan tore through the open slider, Taylor chasing after him.

Jesse followed, balancing Ireland on his hip.

Then the girls appeared. Chloe carried a tray with a chocolate cake on it. The frosting was chocolate anyway. It was Kyan's favorite.

She set it down on the low table between the two sofas. The top of the cake was covered with messy globs of candy sprinkles,

212 | DYAN LAYNE

Ireland's handiwork if he were to guess, and written on it, in white icing, '*We miss you*'.

Katie added a sparkler.

Linnea lit it.

What were they supposed to do now? Sing "Happy Birthday"? He wasn't sure. Holding the baby to his chest, Dillon sat up and glanced to his cousins. Chandan clapped for cake in Taylor's lap. Declan did the same from Brendan's. Ireland was just mesmerized by the light of the sparkler.

It was Chloe who began to sing. One by one, they all joined her. Except him. He couldn't find his voice. Blinking her eyes open on his chest, Charlotte looked up at him and smiled. Kyan didn't get to see that beautiful face. He didn't get to hold her. Or tuck her in bed at night. Dillon's vision blurred and he closed his eyes.

Her arms came around him. Linnea perched herself on the arm of the sofa at his side and leaned her head to rest on his. Opening his eyes, he kissed her cheek. "I need a minute."

Taking Charlotte with him, Dillon went down to the lake. He stood at the edge of the water, the last vestiges of the sun slipping from the sky, and rubbed his cheek against the baby's silky soft hair. Warm liquid seeped from his eyes and a strangled sob escaped his lips.

Big boys don't cry.

But he couldn't stop the tears from coming.

After almost nine months, making it through all those firsts, and a cake fucked him up? Overwhelming sorrow, fresh and new, rushed at him out of nowhere. Rocking with Charlotte on his shoulder, he inhaled a lungful of desperately needed air.

A sibling relationship, the bond between brothers, is one of the closest there is, and he and Kyan were closer than most. When he died, a huge part of who Dillon was died with him. No one else in the world knew what that felt like. Not Brendan. Not Jesse. Not even Linnea.

It was soul crushing if he thought about it, so he didn't allow himself to. Instead, Dillon focused on Linnea and Charlotte. Kyan's wife and daughter. The family his brother entrusted him to care for. *His* family now.

And he felt guilty.

Because he was here to love Linnea. He was there for Charlotte's birth. Why didn't Fate send him to the warehouse that day? Why was he here and his brother not?

It isn't fucking fair!

But then life seldom is, is it?

The baby made noises, sucking on her hand. He held her up so they were face to face. "Sorry, I took you away from the cake, Char. You're too little to eat it anyway, yeah?" He planted a kiss on her forehead. "I'll sneak you a taste of frosting later, okay? Just don't tell Mommy."

Charlotte grinned and the world felt all right again.

Brendan came up behind him, his hand heavy on his shoulder. "You good, bro?"

"Yeah." He nodded.

Then Jesse was at his side. No words needed to be spoken. The three cousins stood together looking out at the water.

Sounds of childish laughter and little feet trampling over the grass could be heard in the distance behind them. Dillon halfway turned to see Chandan and Declan scampering across the lawn with little toy flashlights, Taylor on their heels. Linnea, Chloe, and Katie followed in their wake.

Jesse squeezed his shoulder. "We wanted to do something for Kyan."

The girls, each one carrying an unlit paper lantern, approached them. Taking Charlotte in exchange, Linnea handed him the one she held. Chloe gave hers to Jesse and Brendan took his from Katie.

One for each of them.

One for each decade they'd been given to share with him on this Earth.

Beautiful and precious, Dillon knew better than most how

life can change in the blink of an eye. He lit the fuel and let it heat, as the tears he'd never shared with anyone streamed down his face. Then he gazed at Linnea holding Charlotte, vowing to himself he'd love them even more fiercely than he already did, freely and without guilt or fear, because life can be so very fucking short.

Everything loved is eventually lost.

Then he let it go.

"Look up, Dill." Linnea and Charlotte stood in the shelter of his arms.

The moon shined down upon them.

A thousand stars flickered in the sky.

He watched the lanterns float away to meet them.

I've got them, brother. I love you.

And he smiled.

Twenty-Four

Linnea sat on her bed, finger-combing her just-dried hair, as she thought of all the summer festivals that came before this one. So many happy memories. Smiling, she pulled a light cotton boho minidress off the hanger. It was cool and loose, so she'd be comfortable. More important, it had a V-neck and spaghetti straps, so it would be easy to feed Charlotte wearing it.

She gazed at her reflection in the full-length mirror.

Yeah, and Dillon would like it too.

He was downstairs with the baby, waiting on Chloe and Jesse. And her. Leaving most of it down and loose, she pulled her thick hair back at the crown, and wove it into a braid. After one last glance in the mirror, festival ready, she left her room to join him.

Dillon was on the floor playing with the baby. One week shy of six months old, Charlotte could sit up fairly well on her own, but he was down there with her anyway, stacking blocks and making sure she didn't topple over. Watching them together, her heart was so full it could burst.

He glanced up and that dazzling smile of his that she loved lit up his face. "Look, Char." He pointed to her. "There's Mommy."

Linnea smiled back, and scooping up Charlotte, Dillon crossed the room. He cupped her cheek in his free hand. "Gorgeous." And sliding his fingers into her hair, he lowered his lips to hers. Slipping his tongue inside. Stealing her breath.

She heard the soft whimper that escaped her. God, what this man could do to her with nothing more than a kiss. A tingle ignited between her thighs. Goosebumps rose on her skin. Her body craved to have him inside her, and that hunger grew stronger with every passing day.

A throat cleared behind her. "Sorry to interrupt." Jesse stood there sporting a grin, gathering his hair into a man bun. "Chloe and the kids are out front."

"Be right there." Dillon winked at his cousin.

Heading back out the door, securing the hair on his head, Jesse muttered, "Damn, that was hot."

They pushed the strollers at a leisurely pace along the paved trail, bypassing the midway and cutting through Coventry Park, to get to First Avenue. No reason to rush such a picture-perfect day and it was cooler beneath the shade of the old oaks. Charlotte had already fallen asleep. Dillon had his arm around her, his fingers trailing up and down her hip, as they walked. Even that small touch was making her crazy.

'You two are playing house without the sleepovers.'

Maybe it was time to change that.

Linnea had the feeling they were in for a hot summer as they stepped out onto the avenue and into the sun. Not that she was going to complain about it after the frigid winter they'd had this year. She didn't mind the heat, in fact, she preferred it. A thought popped into her head and without meaning to she blurted it out.

"I think I want to put a hot tub in on the patio."

"Where'd that come from?" Dillon arched a brow. He was smirking at her, though.

Why did I say that?

She felt the blood flow to her cheeks and she shrugged. "Just a thought."

"Yeah? Well, I like the way you think." His hand on her hip squeezed.

Just ahead of them, Jesse and Chloe stopped at the doublewide booth in front of Rossi's. Directly across the street from Beanie's, they had two side-by-side storefronts on the avenue. One for the pizzeria and the other their Italian bakery. Best damn cannolis on the planet as far as she was concerned. The girl helping Mrs. Rossi on the bakery side looked familiar.

Linnea pushed the stroller faster. "Isn't that Gina?"

"Who?"

"My nurse," she said. Dillon looked at her like she had ten heads. "When Charlotte was born."

Seeing Linnea coming, Gina came out from inside the booth and peered into the stroller. "Oh, wow! She's gotten so big." Then she hugged her. "You look fantastic! How are you?"

"Good." Linnea nodded with a smile. "I'm good. You remember Dillon?"

"Yeah."

But Dillon wasn't paying them any mind. He nodded to a guy working the pizza side of the booth that Jesse was talking to. "Hey, Nick. How's it goin', man?"

Gina's eyes widened. "You know my brother?"

"Nick's your brother?"

"Yeah." She pointed to Mrs. Rossi. "That's our mom right there."

"I went to school with Nick. Tony too." Now it was his turn. Dillon dropped his jaw. "Wait a minute. You're little Gina Rossi?"

Biting her lip, she nodded. "That would be me."

"Well, damn. You couldn't have been more than six or seven when we were in high school," Dillon said, nodding along with her.

"Sounds about right."

"I never got a chance to thank you for taking such good care of my girls." With his arm circling Linnea's waist again, Dillon kissed her crown. "So, thank you. I owe you one."

Gina glanced at the baby and smiled. "She's beautiful. Congrats, again."

Linnea waved goodbye and they continued down the avenue, taking in the colorful sights, the magical sounds, and the delicious smells. The annual event was woven into so many happy occasions that to her it represented joy. "I love festival time."

"I remember when you didn't like it so much." He smirked, tickling her side.

She giggled. "Because you made us wear those godawful crop tops and booty shorts."

"And you looked so damn hot in them too." His hand skimmed her outer thigh.

"It was hot as Hades that year, Dillon. I was cursing you every damn minute for making me work the patio."

"Yeah, I remember." He cocked his head in thought and grinned. "You were all sweaty."

"Oh. My. God." They were in front of Charley's. Two college girls wearing crop tops and booty shorts worked the tables outside. "They're still wearing them."

He winked. "Lunch?"

Marcus gave them a table in the corner of the patio so the strollers wouldn't be in the way. "Are you sure you don't want to sit inside?"

"Positive." Dillon grinned as he took his seat beside her. "Linn's feeling nostalgic."

Chloe's gaze flitted from Dillon, to her, to her husband, and she grinned. "He's baaack."

He was, wasn't he?

Charming, flirty, and funny. He'd reverted to the man she'd always known him to be, the man who'd been her friend long before he was anything else. Linnea hadn't seen Dillon like this since…well, since before Kyan died even.

"What?" he asked Jesse and Chloe, both of them looking at him with knowing grins on their faces.

"Nothing." Chloe giggled.

An hour of laughs, two pitchers of beer, and an ungodly number of chicken wings later, they were back on the avenue. Their plan was to grab an iced latte from Katie, stop for a breather in the park so she could feed the baby, then hit the midway before Venery's show.

But Charlotte wasn't having it.

"We'll meet you at the beer garden in an hour." Linnea hugged Chloe, waving to Katie and Kevin in Beanie's booth as they walked past.

Dillon spread the blanket beneath a tree while she got a very hungry and unhappy Charlotte out of the stroller. He leaned up against the trunk and patted the space between his legs. She rested against his chest and slipping the strap from her shoulder, put the baby to her breast.

He played with her hair. Combing his fingers through it, Dillon pushed the strands over to one side. He kissed her crown.

"Enjoying the view," she softly spoke.

"I never should have told you that." Dillon squeezed her shoulders and ran his fingers lightly down her arms. He dipped his head to kiss the spot beneath her ear and whispered, "Fuck yeah, I am."

"Good." She smiled.

"You're killing me, gorgeous."

I know.

Charlotte was not about to go back into the stroller. She protested, and loudly, every time Dillon or Linnea tried. In fact, the only thing that soothed her was when he held her. So, he wore the baby on his chest and they pushed an empty stroller to the beer garden.

"Happy now, sweet pea?" She played with the chain on his neck and showed off her single tooth.

The beer garden was at the entrance to the midway in the front of the park, and the concert stage, where bands played all day and Venery would headline later, was just beyond that. Chloe and Jesse waited for them at a table on the edge of the garden area. Chandan ran around on the grass. Jesse held Ireland on his lap, a pitcher of beer and one of those large souvenir mugs in front of him.

He pushed the mug toward Linnea when they reached the table. "For you." Jesse winked.

"Champagne slushy," Linnea exclaimed, smiling.

"I remember how much you liked them."

"I do, thank you." Her smile fell. "But I can't."

"Yes, you can." Chloe chimed in. "You have bottles at home. Pump and dump. Enjoy yourself a little, sweetie!"

Linnea glanced at Dillon as if seeking permission or reassurance—not that she needed it. He nodded. "You just fed her and I can give her a bottle when we get home."

With a beatific smile on her face, Linnea closed her eyes as she took that first long suck on the straw. She swallowed and slowly licked her lips.

Jesus.

"Ah, so good."

Dillon never thought he'd be as jealous of a straw as he was right then.

"C'mon, let's kill off this pitcher." Jesse poured beer into plastic cups for the three of them. "We promised Chandan a ride on the merry-go-round."

"Carousel." Chloe winked.

"Same shite," Jesse retorted, imitating their British husband, and they both laughed.

Linnea polished off her frozen champagne as they parked the stroller. They got in line for the merry-go-round. With his arm around her waist, Dillon drew her into his side. Patting her back, Charlotte yawned on his chest. He kissed the top of her head and smiled.

Happier than he had a right to be. Everything he'd ever wanted was right here in his hands. Waiting to get on a kiddie ride, Dillon had never experienced such contentment as he did at that moment.

She mounted a white horse, a peek of pink lace flashing him from beneath her dress. Dillon stood at the horse's mane, grasping the brass pole with one hand and cradling Charlotte's head on his chest with the other. The band organ cranked up and they began to move. Slowly at first. Her hand lightly gripped the pole just below his, their fingers touching. A gentle breeze softly blew through her hair, lifting it from her neck and sweeping it behind her.

Faster now, with her feet in the stirrups, knees gripping the wooden flanks, she rode. The horse moved up and down the hanger, her plush bottom lifting from the saddle with every turn. Linnea gazed down at him, lips parted in a smile. There was no mistaking the light in her pretty green eyes. The pure, unadulterated joy on her face at such a simple thing. A ride on a carousel.

And Dillon found joy just watching her.

As the ride slowed, he grasped her nape and pulling her to his mouth, he rasped, "I love you." He kissed her. With everything he had, right there on the merry-go-round, with Charlotte asleep on his chest, he kissed her. "I fucking love you."

They walked the midway, and as they neared the Ferris wheel she stopped. Linnea glanced up to the top and smiled. Then turning to him, she stood on her tiptoes and with his face in her hands she kissed him. "I love you too."

Joy.

Dillon was smiling so big his face hurt. Linnea was smiling too, leaning against him, pushing the stroller, as they followed Jesse and Chloe toward the commissary tent set up for the band behind the stage. If Chloe hadn't stopped to get his attention, he would have never even noticed her standing there.

Kelsey stood at the barricade to the right of the stage. Dillon recognized the man who was with her as one of the attorneys from her office—the managing partner if he wasn't mistaken. Married too. At least he was. He was one of the suits she got off the elevator with the night she left him on the sidewalk like an asshole. A big diamond flashed from her ring finger, and suddenly it all made sense.

How did that saying go? Once a cheater, always a cheater?

Good luck, sweetheart. Karma can be such a bitch.

He walked right past her and kept on walking.

Chandan ran straight into Taylor's lap the second they reached the tent. Dillon was able to lay a sleeping Charlotte back down in her stroller. He glanced around. Plush sofas. Portable air conditioning. A bar and buffet table with attendants. "Rock stars got it pretty good."

"Yeah, they do," Brendan answered from behind him, chuckling. "And they can thank your girl there. We just sponsor them, but she arranges it all."

'...*your girl...*'

God, he could happily get used to hearing that.

Dillon grinned. "Well, if I'm paying for it, then I might as well eat."

"Help yourself, man." Bo, sans shirt as usual, play-slapped him on the back. "I'm going to talk to Linnea, if that's okay. I need her help with something."

Piling shrimp scampi on a plate, he glanced back at Bo. "She doesn't need my permission."

"In private."

Oh.

"She still doesn't need my permission," he repeated, wondering what on Earth he could possibly need Linnea for.

"Don't worry." Bo grinned. "It's nothing bad and I promise to behave."

"Just so you do, drummer boy." Dillon smirked, adding a slab of prime rib to go with his shrimp.

Jesse delivered another slushy into her hand and Linnea went with Bo to a sofa in the corner. He minded the baby in her stroller and tucked into his food. Brendan sat down with a bottle of whiskey beside him.

"Yeah, time has a way of taking care of things." He stole a shrimp off his plate and tossed it in the air. Catching it in his teeth, Brendan winked.

"Showoff."

"It makes me happy to see you and Linnea happy." His cousin squeezed his shoulder. "It's about time."

"Yeah." Dillon smiled. "It is."

It *was* time.

And he was ready for it.

Twenty-Five

"She do okay with the bottle?"

They didn't stay for the concert. Dillon was flipping through the channels in the family room when Linnea came down from upstairs. Fresh out of the shower in one of those little bralette tops that drove him mad and a pair of pajama pants, she sat beside him smelling sweet and delicious. Edible.

"Yeah, baby. She's asleep." Automatically, his fingers went to the hair piled on top of her head, combing through the strands.

She laid her head on his shoulder. "Why did I drink all those slushies?"

"Two." He chuckled. "You're allowed."

"It's been so long."

"Since you had champagne?"

She glanced up at him. "Since you kissed me."

"I kissed you on the merry-go-round."

"Kiss me again." Linnea straddled his lap. "Kiss me like you did on my birthday."

Fuck.

It might be the champagne talking, but he didn't care. Dillon was so done with taking it slow. He released her hair from its tie and watched it fall. His fingers slid through the caramel tresses to grasp her nape, bringing her mouth to his. Their lips met softly. Slowly kissing her, one hand slid from her neck, gliding over the warm, bare skin on her back to squeeze her fleshy bottom. He kneaded it, pushing her against the hardness in his pants that ached to be inside her.

She gasped into his mouth.

He deepened their kiss.

Linnea held onto his shoulders and pulled herself into him, silk sliding over denim, lace grazing his bare chest. And he didn't want to hold back anymore. He wanted her. Dillon wanted so badly to just let go. To make love to her, fuck her senseless, and make love to her again. To set her free and watch her fly.

To make her truly and completely his.

It was time.

Sliding his thumbs beneath the edge of the lace, Dillon lifted the bralette up over her breasts, brushing her nipples. Linnea sucked the air in through her teeth as he peeled the little top from her body and tossed it to the floor. He gazed at her, awestruck, licking his lips as he took her warm, supple flesh in his hands and squeezed. Her back arched, pushing out her chest, and those breasts, those succulent nipples, so tantalizingly close to where he wanted them to be.

Fucking hell.

He leaned forward that fraction of an inch and took that tempting morsel in his mouth. His cock lurched in his jeans. She exhaled a moan. Then he sucked on that nipple, licking it and grazing it with his teeth while he rolled the other between his fingers. More sensitive than Dillon remembered, Linnea clutched his shoulders, digging her fingers into his muscled flesh. Teeth pressed into her bottom lip.

"Ah, Dillon," she mewled.

And if that didn't tell him she wanted this, wanted him as much as he wanted her, then what would? His mouth never left her breast as he lowered her to the turquoise sofa. Her fingertips skimmed his chest, stopping to rub his nipples. He groaned, kissing and licking his way from her breast, up her chest and along her collarbone, to the gentle curve of her neck, sucking on the delicate skin there.

Linnea moved her hands from his chest to his back. Her fingertips skated up his spine and swept across his shoulder blades before skimming down his sides to his ass. She clenched her fingers into him, but couldn't find purchase through the denim, pressing his erection into her.

Lifting his head from her neck, Dillon growled and knelt

between her thighs. With nimble fingers, he untied the silky pajama pants and pulled them off her legs. She laid there, naked and beautiful. Panting. Palms on her stomach. Her pretty green eyes glazed, pupils dilated.

"Let me see you," she breathed.

Dillon stood to the side of her and let his jeans drop to the floor. Linnea raised herself up onto her elbows. His eyes bore into hers as she looked her fill and glanced up at him. "You're so beautiful," she whispered, swallowing. "Even more beautiful than I remembered."

Did she think of that day on her kitchen floor? He did. As much as he'd tried to forget the one and only time he felt her from the inside, Dillon thought of it often. The memory haunting him for almost four years now.

Linnea reached for him, the tips of her fingers brushing along his cock from the base to the tip at his navel. She smeared precum around the head with her thumb, then brought it to her lips, her tongue peeking out to taste him.

His dick twitched at the sight.

"I'll eat you alive," he rasped.

Taking back his place between her legs, Dillon took her calf in his hands and placed it on his shoulder, opening her wide. Swiping his finger slowly through the wet lips of her pussy, he gazed into her pretty green eyes and sucked it into his mouth. Like a kid getting his first taste of cotton candy, he closed his eyes, relishing the delicate sweetness that was uniquely her.

She was the flavor he'd love for the rest of his life.

Dillon kissed the tender skin along her inner thigh on the way to his destination. He couldn't wait to get there, but at the same time he wanted to savor every inch of the journey. Firsts only happen once, and this was one first he never wanted to forget.

The scent of her arousal beckoned him. Parting her with his thumbs, Dillon breathed Linnea deep into his lungs. He kissed her clit, cushioning his lips in her wet softness, licking and suckling until her whimpers reached his ears, her head began to thrash, and her thighs began to quiver.

He glanced at her from his position between her legs. Linnea was looking down at him, her eyes black saucers, rolling her nipples in her fingers. She subtly lifted her hips, spreading her legs wider in an unspoken invitation.

Taking it, Dillon held her open with his fingers and speared her opening, fucking her with his tongue, dragging it up and down her slit, lapping the copious nectar that flowed from inside her. Sweet ambrosia. He was drowning in her, and it was a high he didn't ever want to come down from. With his lips caressing her clit, he slid two fingers inside her.

"Fuck," she cried out, yanking on her nipples. "Make me come, baby."

Her body told him just what she needed, but then he already knew. All those nights he held her while Kyan got her off. Watching them together at the club. In her row house on Oak Street. But she was his girl now and he wanted to hear her say it.

"How do you want me to make you come, gorgeous girl?" Very slowly, he pushed his fingers in and out of her.

She whimpered.

"Tell me, baby," he teased her clit with a lick. "And I'll do it."

"Fingers." She lifted her hips. "Fuck, please."

He eased a third finger inside, fucking her hard and fast, as he sucked on her clit. At the first sign of a flutter inside her, he stopped. Dillon knew how to get what he wanted, too, and that was her cum.

Fucking her with his tongue, he rubbed her clit fervently, until she screamed his name, filling his mouth with it.

Caressing her hips and thighs, he kissed her pussy as she came down from her orgasm. Then he kissed his way up her body, placing one on each swollen nipple, until he reached her mouth. Dillon kissed her there next. Fingers in her hair, their tongues tangled, messy and sloppy, biting each other's lips. He only stopped to inhale some air.

And that's when the tables turned.

Linnea pushed out from underneath him and straddled his thighs. "My turn."

She cupped his balls, so drawn up and tight against his body, the slightest touch had him groaning. Licking her lips, she teased his dick, tracing the veins with her fingers. Good fucking god, he hadn't had sex in what—eight months now? If she kept playing with him like that he just might blow like a middle schooler going through puberty.

Her hair brushed his abs, tickling his skin, as she lowered her head. Holding the base in her hands, Linnea swirled her tongue around the head and sucked him inside her hot, wet mouth. And as if his cock remembered she was home, a sound rumbled out from somewhere deep within him. Dillon already knew he wasn't going to last.

Holding her head to his dick, he sat up. Shifting her body off the sofa, she knelt on the floor in front of him, jerking his shaft as she sucked on the head. "Baby..."

She glanced up at him without stopping.

He wanted to be making love to her, to be inside her, when he came. Dillon eased her off him. He gazed at her beautiful face. Saliva dribbled from the corner of her mouth. Swollen lips. He brushed the sweat-dampened hair that clung to her cheeks from her face. "...I love how you suck me."

"Let me finish," she crooned, her fingers petting his dick. "Please."

His fingers skimmed her jaw and slid into her hair. Fisting it in his hand, he watched his cock fill her mouth. She gagged and sputtered, gasping for breath, as she looked up at him. Hottest fucking thing in the world was her pretty green eyes on him.

As much as he wanted to, Dillon couldn't hold off another second. Pulling on her hair, he let out a growl, her hand moving between her legs as he came.

She swallowed his gift and the movement ceased.

"Go on." He sat back.

"What?"

With a smirk, he tipped his chin. "I'll watch you finish."

Linnea stood, and placing one knee on either side of his thighs, she knelt over him and spread her pussy with the fingers of one hand so he could see her clit, swollen and glistening. She put two fingers to his lips. He sucked them into his mouth. Then she rubbed her clit with his saliva.

You're so worth the wait.

"My fucking perfect girl."

She was working her clit so hard her back began to bow. He braced her with his arm so she wouldn't fall and watched her fly. So incredibly beautiful.

Leaning forward, she nuzzled into his neck and curled up against him. Stroking her hair, he kissed her crown. "I love you so much, baby."

He was hard again.

She was asleep in his lap.

Maybe it was the champagne.

Dillon had the last of their bags in the trunk when she came out of the house holding Charlotte. He glanced up at her. "All set?"

"Yeah," she answered, smiling, and buckled the baby into her car seat.

Linnea grabbed him by the belt as he passed her to get to the car door and kissed him. "I love you."

"I love you more, gorgeous." He kissed her on the nose. "Let's go."

"I can't wait to get there." She scooted around to the passenger side and got in.

He couldn't wait either.

An entire week at the lake house. Fourth of July was on a Tuesday this year, so rather than an extended weekend they were making a vacation out of it. Chloe, Jesse, and Taylor were already up there. Brendan, Katie, and everyone else would be joining them tomorrow. Floating on the lake with a beer. Dinners on the deck. Fireworks. Summer fun. What was better than that?

A week of having Linnea in his bed, that's what.

And she'd never leave it as long as he had anything to say about it.

She gazed out the window, watching the scenery roll by as he drove. Dillon took her hand and held it on his thigh. Linnea turned her head toward him and smiled, her cheeks turning pink. Something was on her mind.

"You're blushing, gorgeous." He squeezed her hand and winked. "Whatcha thinking about?"

"The one time we...you know." She shrugged, gazing down at her lap.

Linnea did think about it then, or at least she had been. He found her in the kitchen that Thanksgiving Eve morning. It was the same day he negotiated the deal on Park Place. She was baking pumpkin pie, nutmeg and cinnamon in the air, but it was her sweet almond scent that he smelled.

He and his brother had been staying with her—at her little row house on Oak Street—ever since Crossfield, but the thought of having her together began brewing well before then. They'd talked about it. Linnea had actually been having dreams about it.

'Got time for our princess, brother?'

That's what Kyan always called her. Princess. In Dillon's mind, Linnea was the queen he'd foolishly allowed to slip through his fingers. He couldn't say no.

"I think about it all the time," he honestly admitted.

'Two princes inside you.'

"You never touched me again." She glanced back up at him. "Why?"

Had she wanted him to? How did he tell her that being inside her was the most incredible moment of his life? And the worst. Because she was everything he wanted and could never really have—not the way he wanted to anyway. *To himself.*

Dillon kept to the spare bedroom after that and Kyan learned how to soothe her from the nightmares.

"Because I was in love with you." He laced their fingers together. "I still am."

He knew he'd well and truly fucked himself that day. Stuck in a hell of his own making. For eight months the three of them lived together in her cozy row house while they renovated Park Place.

She squeezed his hand, her pretty green eyes filling with tears.

"Kyan knew. We didn't keep secrets from each other. He didn't have a jealous bone in his body and maybe he would have been fine with making the three of us a permanent thing, but...I'm just not built that way, I guess." Raising their joined hands to his lips, he kissed her fingers. "So, I couldn't touch you again, but I never stopped loving you."

Leaning across the console, she rested her head on his shoulder. "I've always loved you, Dillon, but I couldn't be 'in love' with you and with Kyan. I guess I'm not built that way either."

"How about now, Linn? Can you be in love with me now?"

"I already am," she whispered.

"Say it."

"I love you, Dillon." Her lips brushed his cheek. "I'm so in love with you."

"I fell in love with you the day you walked into Charley's." Dillon pulled his brother's BMW into the lake house driveway and parked. "I saw you first, but it didn't matter. You only saw him."

"That isn't true," Linnea implored, taking his face in her hands. "I saw both of you, not that I ever thought I'd be with either one of you back then, but Kyan gave me his heart first, and once that happened..."

He swiped the tears from those shimmering green eyes, and kissed her.

"You've always had my heart."

Twenty-Six

She watched them through the window.

Linnea was in the kitchen with Chloe, cleaning up from dinner and prepping for tomorrow when she happened to look out onto the deck. Three men, each one contentedly holding a child on their lap, talked and laughed together. Chandan, calm and quiet for the moment, played with the ends of Jesse's long hair. Ireland slept on Taylor's chest, her little arms around his neck. Charlotte looked up at Dillon as if he'd hung the moon and stars in the sky just for her.

Watching them together through the glass brought a smile to her face. This wasn't how Linnea pictured her life would look a year ago, but that didn't make it any less beautiful. Sometimes she couldn't help but try to imagine how it would be if Kyan was still here, but he'd been gone so long now it was difficult to bring him into focus. And where would Dillon be then? With that horrid Kelsey? Linnea didn't want to know who she was without him.

Chloe leaned her elbows on the island next to her, tipping her chin toward the glass. "Would you look at that."

"I know." She sighed.

Chloe hooked an arm through hers. "We have the most amazing men on the planet."

"We sure do." Linnea nodded.

"Who knew walking into Charley's seven years ago would lead to all this?"

Dillon would say Fate knew all along.

A sound came from Chloe that wasn't quite a giggle. "Weddings. Babies." She paused for a beat. "Funerals."

Linnea sucked in a breath and glanced at her. Tears pooling in her hazel eyes, Chloe untangled their arms and hugged her. "I see it all so clearly now. It was always supposed to go this way," she choked, turning her head to gaze through the glass. "Kyan was your beginning, but that man out there is your happily ever after."

She hoped so. Except now she knew better than to believe in fairytales.

"I'm still in love with Kyan, Chloe," she whispered, swiping her eye. "I can't just turn it off."

"You're always going to love him, sweetie."

"And what about Dillon?"

Chloe tilted her head. "You're in love with him, aren't you?"

"Yes. So much, yes," she said. "And it messes with my head sometimes…because there's a piece of me that he'll never have. Is that fair to him? And, god, don't get me started on the guilt."

"Listen to me, sister." Chloe grasped her upper arms, speaking in the firm mama voice she usually kept on reserve for Chandan. "And listen to me good. Don't you think a piece of Dillon died with Kyan too? Do you think, for one second, he doesn't understand?" she asked with an arch of her brow. "Trust me, sweetie, he does, and better than anyone else ever could. He loves all your beautiful broken pieces. He always has."

Linnea nodded.

By the time they finished up in the kitchen and went out to the deck, each of the three men held a sleeping child in their arms. Linnea went to take the baby from Dillon. "Here, I'll take her up."

"I've got her." He kissed the baby's forehead. "C'mon, gorgeous. We were about to call it a night out here anyway."

So, while the three men tucked their sleeping children into bed in Kyan's old room, Linnea slipped into the shower. The warm water soothed her like it always did. She would have preferred a long, relaxing soak in a tub, but Dillon's en suite didn't have one.

After she loofahed and lotioned her skin, Linnea shimmied into her usual bedtime attire—a pair of boy shorts and a cropped cami.

Dillon was lying in bed when she stepped out of the en suite, hair messy and damp, hands beneath his head. Linnea slid beneath the covers and his arm immediately encircled her waist, tucking her up against him. Spearmint and sandalwood. She inhaled him. He must've showered downstairs.

His fingers rubbed light circles on her back. "This is what I've been waiting for all day."

"What?" she asked, smiling against his chest, because she was pretty sure she knew.

"Just this." He kissed her hair, rubbing his nose in it. "You."

She tipped her head back, gazing into his pastel eyes. Bathed in moonlight, looking into her own, they smoldered with lust and love. Want. Need. And the only thing she saw was him. Nothing else existed. Every other thought vanished.

Linnea had just one focus, one burning desire, and that was to love this beautiful, selfless man with everything she had left to give him.

He lowered his lips to hers, brushing over them in a whisper, before he kissed her softly and sweetly, slipping his tongue inside. Whiskey and cinnamon. Linnea slid her hand from his side to his back, and turning up the simmer, Dillon pressed her to him closer. It wasn't close enough. It would never be close enough. Pushing her knee between his thighs, she linked their legs, rubbing along his calf with her toes.

His lips traveled to her neck, sucking her skin, as she regained her breath. Dillon rolled her onto her back, his lips at her ear, and whispered, "Do you still dream of me, Linn?"

She did. Often.

"Yes."

His mouth came down on hers, claiming her. That's what it felt like. Dillon taking what was his. She wanted to be taken.

"I need you, Linnea." He fisted her cami, his words vibrating against her lips. "I fucking need you."

The solid cock in his boxers ground into her thigh, and the pulse between her legs hammered. She glanced at her top bunched up in his hand, then flicked her gaze up to meet his, and slipping her hand between them, she gripped his hardness with her fingers and squeezed.

She blinked and the cami she wore was gone.

He held her breasts, one in each hand, and squeezing, pushed them together. Licking and nipping at her nipples. Still holding onto his cock, Linnea whimpered with every breath she took. Then he kissed her again and she let go.

His hand slid beneath the waistband, fingers brushed over her clit that already throbbed to strum through her wetness. Dillon pushed the saturated fabric to the side. "Take them off."

He did and tugging on her nipples, Linnea opened her legs. She thought he'd touch her pussy then, but he didn't. Dillon kissed and nipped her inner thigh. Her belly. Her nipples. He claimed her mouth again, urgent and hungry, before he swooped down between her thighs and ran his tongue deep up her slit.

His satisfied groans as he sucked on her clit mingled with her moans. One hand went to her nipple, the other tugged at his hair. Dillon spread her thighs wider, her foot resting on his shoulder, and his hand reached up her body to pinch the other one.

She exploded and he kissed her.

Dillon sat up beside her, and with her leg still resting on his shoulder, rubbed his entire hand back and forth over her pussy, tapping on her sensitive clit. Maybe he did want to eat her alive, because he leaned over and sucked that swollen nub right back into his mouth. Linnea squirmed and cried out with her second orgasm, but he didn't stop, instead he pushed his finger inside her.

He lifted his head, his finger lodged inside her, and brought his lips to hers. She could taste herself on his tongue. "Do you think I'm done, baby?"

Gasping to get air in her lungs, Linnea couldn't answer.

Another finger slipped inside her. She could hear Chloe, Jesse, and Taylor fucking on the other side of the wall in the room next to theirs. Something about that aroused her.

Dillon must've heard it too. He smirked, slowly stroking in and out of her with two fingers. "I want you loud." He added another finger. "So there's no doubt you're mine when we leave this bed in the morning."

He twisted his hand, spreading his fingers inside her. "Fuck," she mewled, raising her hips.

Lying down beside her, Dillon kissed her as he massaged her wet walls with his fingers. He pressed upward with fervor, faster and faster, her entire body quaking from the mounting pressure. Her eyes rolling back in her head, she screamed and let go, drenching them both in her cum.

Kissing her hot, sweaty skin, with a squelching sound, Dillon withdrew his fingers from inside her. A rush of fluid followed. Feeding them to her, Linnea sucked on them. Then he got up from the bed and pushed his boxers down his legs.

Linnea had only ever been with two men in her life. That Thanksgiving Eve interlude on her kitchen floor, when Kyan and Dillon loved her together, was the only time she'd ever been with anyone else.

He'd only been inside her once, but she never forgot what he felt like.

Dillon knelt between her thighs, his long, thick cock in his hand. He moved over her. Hovering, he kissed up her throat and rasped, "I love you."

"I love you, too."

He notched the bulbous head at her entrance, her eyelids fluttering closed.

"Look at me." Dillon brushed the hair from her face. "Let me see those eyes."

She opened them, gazing into heated pools of vibrant pale blue, and with one thrust he pushed all the way inside her.

So full.

Her lips parted on a silent gasp. It had been so long and he felt so fucking good. Dillon moved his hips, slowly at first, resting her leg on his shoulder, opening her wide to accommodate him. They kissed, caressing each other's bodies, his movements in and out of her coming faster and faster.

A sheen of sweat covered his skin. It rolled in rivulets, dripping from his body onto hers. He stopped. His hand on her breast, he pinched her nipple and pulled out, rolling her over to her tummy.

Sweet baby Jesus.

Ass up. Forearms on the mattress. Thick and delicious, he entered her from behind. Linnea cried out at the exquisite sensation of it. He spread her cheeks and held onto her hips, thrusting hard and deep. So deep, she would swear she was seeing stars. With every movement her nipples brushed the mattress.

His hands moved from her hips. One pushed into the small of her back and with the other he fisted her hair, pulling her head back. He dipped his head to her ear, grunting words she couldn't quite make out as he attempted to breathe. Then he let go of her hair, his hand moving to the front of her throat. He firmly held it, kissing her crown, chanting, "I love you," over and over again as he thrust.

The orgasm blasted through her. She collapsed to the mattress, a boneless, quivering mess, aftershocks rippling in electric waves. Dillon blanketed her with his body, stroking her arms, kissing every inch of her face.

As she drifted to sleep in his arms, there was no doubt in her mind she was his.

And Dillon was hers.

Twenty-Seven

A soft breeze blew in through the open window. The sun hadn't even broken on the horizon yet. Dillon strained to listen for the rustle of babies waking in the next room, but the house was quiet and still. The only sound to be heard was the lake gently lapping at the shore.

Linnea was curled up naked beside him, her back against his chest, hands folded beneath her cheek. He watched her sleep for a while. The subtle rise and fall of her chest. Caramel hair fanned across her cheek. He reached out with his finger, softly tucking it back, so he could see her face.

My gorgeous girl.

"God, I love you," he whispered, tracing the shell of her ear.

Slowly, his finger trailed down the curve of her neck, over the slope of her shoulder. Dillon leaned over and kissed her temple. She sighed.

He should let her sleep.

But he didn't.

Her bottom was nestled up against him. He slipped right inside. A soft puff of air passed her lips. Languid strokes in and out. Hand on her belly, fingers rubbing her skin. It wasn't a quest for an orgasm, even though he knew they'd both come. Dillon just needed to touch her, to feel her, to hold her close. He'd always need to.

Holding onto his forearm, Linnea slid her top foot up along her bottom leg, opening herself for him. Keeping to his unhurried pace, he nuzzled his face in her neck, kissing the tender skin there. She turned her head, falling onto her back, to reach his lips with hers. Dillon held her thigh, thrusting faster as he kissed her.

It was Linnea who reached between her outspread thighs, feeling his cock as it moved in and out of her, before letting her fingers fall to her clit. Squeezing her breast, he watched her rub herself, and pinched her nipple. Her pretty green eyes locked with his and her lips parted, but she didn't make a sound. Dillon felt the first flutters inside her. Sucking her nipple into his mouth, he quickened his pace, going hard and deep until her pussy spasmed on his cock.

The sky outside the window was just beginning to lighten. He wrapped his arms around her, cuddling her. Stroking her skin. Kissing her hair. "Good morning," he whispered in her ear.

Linnea turned over in his arms, and glancing up at him from beneath her lashes, she smiled. "Good morning."

He smiled back. "Best morning ever."

Brendan and Katie were the first to arrive, followed by Monica and Danielle, and finally the rest of the Venery boys. By noon everyone was gathered on the deck of the lake house. Kodiak wasn't coming; he said he already had other plans, but was evasive as to what those were. Dillon didn't question it. Beanie's would remain open for the holiday, so Kevin and Kelly weren't going to be here either.

Oh, darn.

Yeah, the ice queen still rubbed him the wrong way.

They had hot dogs and burgers going on the grill for lunch. Dillon grabbed a couple beers out of the cooler and brought one to Jesse.

"Thanks, man." His cousin wiped the sweat from his brow, and taking a long pull, glanced over his shoulder. "We're going to need a bigger grill—and a bigger deck."

He wasn't mistaken. Their family had grown in the past four years, and it was only going to get bigger. Dillon began counting on his fingers.

"What are you doing?"

"The way I figure it, we could easily have twenty little humans running around here one day."

Jesse dropped his jaw and cocked a brow. "How do you figure?"

"Easy." Dillon took a swig of beer and swallowed. "Let's say two kids each—that's the average. Do the math."

"Shit." His eyes got big. "That's almost two football teams right there."

He chuckled. "It's not a bad idea. Expand the deck. Put in an outdoor kitchen and a fireplace…maybe a hot tub."

"There's a thought." Jesse winked.

"Linn mentioned it."

"I'd ask how things are going, but it sounded like everything was just fine between you two last night." He smirked.

"Yeah, well…" Dillon couldn't keep the wide smile from coming. "…sounded like things were just fine on your side of the wall, too."

"You won't ever hear me complain." Jesse nodded, still smirking, and flipped the burgers. "You should take Linn out in the boat…" He half turned toward him. "…row around the lake—just the two of you. It's romantic, you know?"

He grinned. "Can you watch Charlotte tomorrow?"

Slathered in oil, she was stretched out in a little red bikini, leaning back on her elbows with her feet up on the cooler between his legs. Dillon stared at Linnea as he rowed across the lake. Sunlight reflected off her skin and sweat trickled between her lush breasts, so close to spilling out of the triangles of fabric that covered them.

They were on the other side of the lake, just to the east of the old fishing pier, a minuscule dot on the water to anyone who might be watching them from the house. He pulled the oars in. "Thirsty, gorgeous?"

"Uh, yeah," she murmured, lifting her head and letting her feet slide off the cooler.

"Water, beer, or champagne?"

"You packed champagne?" Smiling, her eyes went wide and she licked her lips.

"I did. Mini bottles." Dillon opened one and handed it to her. "Just for you."

She drank down half of it before coming up for air. Chuckling, he popped the top on a beer for himself.

"What are we celebrating?" she asked, carefully maneuvering to situate herself beside him.

"Us." He grinned, wrapping his arm around her. "The future. All the plans we get to make."

"Hmm." She brought the champagne to her lips and swallowed. "That's my specialty. What shall we plan first?"

"Who's moving in with who…" His fingers traced up and down her arm. "…and what do we do with the other house?"

Linnea pursed her lips to the side in thought. "You're moving and I bet Seth would love to live next door to us. What's next?"

"That was easy. You really are good at this planning thing." He winked and let his finger skim over the little red triangle. "Our wedding."

"You want to get married already?" She giggled and finished off the bottle of champagne.

"Yes." He opened her another. "Is there a reason we should wait? Because I don't want to."

"No, except you haven't even proposed to me yet."

"Don't you worry about that part." He smirked, pointing to his temple. "I have a plan."

His brother's ring was still on her finger, though.

Closing her eyes to the sun, she tipped her head back. "Maybe a destination wedding on a beach somewhere."

"On my birthday." He winked, and picking up an oar, Dillon steered them into a cove. "It's a date."

She smiled. "It's a date."

Dillon dragged the boat onto the shore. Branches from a weeping willow hung over the water. He found a good spot to lay the blanket beneath it. He grabbed towels and the cooler, setting it beside them under the tree.

"It's so hot." Linnea reached into the ice and pulled out two bottles. A beer for him and champagne for her. She held the cold bottle to her heated flesh, ice water dripping between her breasts.

He took the champagne from her hand and leaned forward, licking suntan oil, sweat, and melted ice from her skin. His thumbs traced circles over the scanty red top. Dillon watched the pupils flare in her pretty green eyes.

Linnea untied the strings at her neck. The red triangles fell away, and gazing up at him, she dropped back to her elbows on the blanket. He gazed at her for a moment, then cupping a breast in his palm, he kissed her nipple. Rosy and ripe, like a summer strawberry, he sucked the sweet morsel into his mouth. Flicking it with his tongue. Nipping it with his teeth.

Falling all the way to the blanket, she cradled his head, holding him to her breast. Linnea ran her fingers through his hair and her nails along his scalp as he suckled. Breathy sighs. Contented coos. He brushed the other nipple lightly with his thumb, teasing it to a stiff peak. Her sounds turned into whimpers and he switched sides, twisting and tugging on the nipple, wet with his saliva, while he sucked hard on the other.

"Fuck, Dillon," she simpered on a breath and began to writhe. "I feel you in my clit."

He'd never forgotten how responsive she was. How sensitive her nipples were. It turned him the fuck on how easily she expressed that too. They were alone here, in a secluded spot, where no one could see or hear them, and he intended to take full advantage of it.

Dillon let go of her nipple, and skimming his hand down her oiled skin, dipped inside her bikini. He passed over her clit, teasing it, as he extended his fingers between her slick lips, feeling up and down her slit. She lifted her hips, her movements urging him to penetrate her.

"You want my fingers to fuck you, baby?" He bit her nipple.

"Yes," she whimpered.

He untied her bottoms. "How many?"

"All of them."

She couldn't mean that. Dillon slid two inside her, scissoring and stretching the tight, wet tissue, rubbing circles on her clit with his thumb. Holding her thighs wide, Linnea pushed against his fingers while he drove them in and out of her, hard and fast. Sweetness squished out of her with every deep plunge, covering his hand and coating her thighs.

A bird fluttered its wings, taking to the air at the sound of her cries. Dillon watched her face as she came, lips forming a perfect circle. Then he kissed her. Slowly sliding his hands up her sides. Pulling her in close. His cock, rigid and full, throbbed inside his boardshorts. Dillon ground himself against her hip, seeking some sort of relief, but it didn't provide any.

Linnea reached between them. Pulling at the waistband, she attempted to free him from his clothing. He rolled onto his back and pushed the fabric down his legs, kicking it from his feet. She sat up beside him and picked up the champagne he'd tossed aside. Sweat rolled down the glass bottle. She bit her lip, her gaze flicking to him as she opened it.

"It's so hot."

Her eyes never left his as she wrapped her fingers around the neck of the bottle. Linnea put it to her lips and tipped it into her mouth. Straddling his thighs, she swallowed and let the champagne pour down her body. It splashed over her swollen nipples, down her belly. It spilled onto his abs and his dick, pooling in the space between her pussy and his balls.

Yeah, and it's about to get a helluva lot hotter, gorgeous.

Dillon thrust his hand into the ice. He started at her neck, the cube of frozen water quickly melting against her heated skin. It dripped in a jagged line between her breasts. He grabbed another piece and held it to her nipple. She gasped, but he kept it there. Tracing the circle of her areola, he watched it pucker and licked the melted ice beading at the tip.

She pushed on his chest and scooting down his thighs, wrapped his dick in her fingers. Linnea took him in her mouth, sucking and swirling her tongue around the head. Voraciously, she slurped on him. Cupping his balls. Rubbing the vein that pulsed beneath her thumb.

He fisted the hair at her nape. Thrusting into her hot, little mouth, Dillon held her to his dick until he felt the pull at the base of his spine. He didn't want to come yet, and when he did, it wasn't going to be in her mouth. With a groan, he dragged her up his body, bringing her mouth to his lips.

Linnea reached down and positioning him at her entrance, impaled herself on his dick. She rode him. Knees planted at his sides. Hands behind her head. Chest pushed out. Caramel hair catching in the breeze, her hips swayed along with the willow's weeping branches. Her skin slick with oil and sweat sparkled in the dappled sunlight. Beautiful, wild, and free.

His.

Dillon slid his hands along her thighs, gripping her hips, feeling the movements of her body, the sweetness that dripped from inside her to soak his skin. Her hands dropped to her breasts, fingers pinching and tugging those rosy, ripe berries. Then to her clit. Moaning and writhing on his dick, she rubbed herself.

It took every ounce of restraint Dillon possessed to keep himself from thrusting up inside her. But watching Linnea as she took her own pleasure was everything. Fucking breathtaking.

Her pussy clenched down on his dick and she screamed his name.

Only then did he allow himself to take her. He flipped her over, gripping her shaking thighs, pulling her against his cock, watching as it thrust into her again and again. Hitting the sweet spot deep inside her that kept her screaming.

So perfect.

So beautiful.

He loved her so much it hurt.

You're killing me, gorgeous.

But what a way to go.

Twenty-Eight

Charlotte gazed up at Linnea with her big blue eyes, snuggling and holding onto her breast, as she nursed before the long drive back to the city. Linnea kissed her daughter's forehead. The baby paused briefly to smile at her and returned to her suckling.

Dillon was downstairs, packing up the car. Linnea glanced around the room, doing a final cursory check from her place on the chair in the corner. The only item that remained was her baby bag on the end of the bed. Curled up with him, she hadn't wanted to leave it this morning.

He made love to her before the sun came up. Sweet and slow and tender. There wasn't one square inch of her he hadn't touched and kissed and loved. Dillon made sure her body knew it belonged to him. She could still feel him there in the swollen tissue between her thighs.

The baby's eyes were drifting closed when Dillon tiptoed in. With a smile on his face, he glanced down at Charlotte and lightly kissed her forehead before moving up to kiss her lips. He sat on the arm of the chair. "We're ready to go as soon as sweet pea here finishes her breakfast."

Linnea looked through the window at the lake and sighed. "I'm going to miss this."

His fingers combed through her hair. "Miss what, gorgeous?"

"All this." She angled her head to look up at him. "This week has been so wonderful, waking up with you…"

"Baby, I'm going to wake up with you in my arms every day now." Cupping her cheek, he winked. "Sleepovers for life."

They were half an hour into their drive home. Classical music softly played for Charlotte, who was fast asleep in her car seat. Dillon held her hand on his thigh and brought it to his lips. He kissed her knuckles. "What beach are you thinking?"

Huh?

And then it dawned on her. Their date.

"Hmm…" She smiled, tilting her head from side to side. "…I don't know. What about Mexico? Cabo is supposed to be lovely."

"As long as it's warm."

"It is." She giggled.

He grinned. "Cabo it is then."

Everything was so easy with him. Dillon rarely demanded anything for himself. Except in bed. And even there, he made sure she was more than satisfied before he took what he wanted.

"Just like that?"

"Just like that. You, Charlotte, and warm sand are all I need." He lowered their joined hands back down to his thigh and squeezed her fingers. "We're going to have an incredible life together."

He seemed so sure of it, she almost believed him.

The remainder of the ride was pretty quiet. Linnea thought she might have even dozed off for a bit, because it seemed like she blinked her eyes and he was pulling into the garage. Dillon carried the bags upstairs while she laid the baby down to finish her nap.

Leaning against the island, he was waiting for her in the kitchen when she came back downstairs. Dillon snagged her waist and pulling her close against him, he kissed her. His hands moved over her back and his tongue swept through her mouth, stealing the oxygen from her lungs, igniting her insides like he hadn't already made her come three times this morning. How in the hell did he do that?

She pulled her lips from his to catch her breath.

"You're killing me, gorgeous." He kissed her forehead. "I'm going to take care of some stuff next door, but I'll be back in an hour or so, okay?"

Linnea nodded against his chest. "Okay. I'm going to unpack before Charlotte wakes up."

Dillon kissed her again. "I love you."

"I love you too."

She made her way upstairs and peeked in on the baby in her crib, then went across the hall to her room. Dillon had left the bags next to the bed. She unpacked, separating her things into neat stacks to return to her drawers and hang in the closet, then went into the en suite to put her toiletries away.

On the other side of the double vanity, Kyan's things still sat there, just as he'd left them. His toothbrush remained in its holder, his cologne on the marble counter. Linnea didn't know what to do with it after he died. It seemed wrong to throw it away, so she never did. She supposed she'd have to now—or pack it away at the very least.

Biting her lip, tears came to her eyes, as she reached for his toothbrush and placed it inside an empty box. Before Linnea could dwell on what she was doing, his cologne, shaving gear, and the rest of his things quickly followed. By the time she closed the lid, her tears dripped down her face.

I can do this.

Wiping her cheeks, she sucked in a breath and carried the box to her bed. Linnea put the folded clothes back into their drawers and went to her closet. His shirts were lined up neatly on their hangers. Ties. Jeans. Slacks. Shoes. Why hadn't she let Chloe help her when she offered?

Because in the beginning, it was simply too painful, the wound too fresh. Then later, she found it oddly comforting to see his things there, like he wasn't really gone forever. As Linnea worked toward her new normal, when she didn't have to cry herself to sleep every night, she was afraid she'd reopen the wound. And she was sick to death of all the bleeding. The crying. The sadness. She squeezed her eyes closed.

I can do this.

It would be a year soon. The last thing Kyan would want for her was to be crying in a fucking closet. He'd want her to be happy, right? It was time to make room in her life for Dillon. He loved her. She loved him. Why was it so hard to let go?

She sank to the floor and sobbed.

"Linn?" Dillon's warm hands squeezed her shoulders. He kissed her hair. "Why are you crying, baby? What's wrong?"

"I can't do this."

He must think her a lunatic, sniveling in the closet with a pile of sundresses on her lap. She would have mistaken the wave of grief and sorrow that washed over her for a panic attack, except she didn't have those anymore. God, he deserved someone who wasn't a fucking mess, who wasn't missing a huge piece of her broken heart. Someone who could give him everything she didn't know if she'd ever be able to give him.

"Do what, baby?"

"This." She waved her hand around the closet. "It's too hard."

Dillon got down on the floor with her and held her. "Shh." He wiped her eyes and smoothed her hair. "It's going to be okay."

"I'm sorry. I love you..." She hiccupped. "...so much."

"And I love you." He gently eased her up from the floor. "You don't have to do this now."

Dillon walked her to the bed. He put the box with the toothbrush in it on the floor and they sat down. Linnea flicked her eyes around the room. Kyan was everywhere. From the pillow he no longer laid his head on to his socks paired into balls inside the dresser drawer, he was here.

"How can I? I...I...I can't make a life with you," she sobbed, pulling at the comforter on the bed. "Not when I'm still grieving him. When I feel like I'm married to him."

"Kyan's gone, Linn," he whispered, staring at the diamond on her ring finger. Then he raised his eyes to hers. "I'm right here."

"I know..." She searched for words, but nothing in her head made sense.

"I've always been right here. It was me, Linn. It was me." Dillon pounded his chest. He wasn't whispering anymore. "I'm the one you clung to, the one who could comfort you. I know your past and I am your future." He stroked her hair and his voice softened. "I have always loved you and you can't deny you love me."

She sniffled. "I do love you, but—"

"Don't you dare say but not that way, because you do. You love me and you always have. Your heart knows it. Your body knows it." Dillon pulled her onto his lap and held her in his arms. He tucked a strand of hair behind her ear. "But your mind won't let you admit it because you loved my brother too."

Don't say it like I used to. Present tense. I love him.

Fresh tears rolled down her cheeks and he wiped them away. "I'm so fucking thankful Kyan got to love you and that he was loved by you. I loved him like no other." He kissed her forehead. "But, baby, don't you know? Loving me doesn't mean you loved him any less."

Every word he spoke was the truth. She couldn't deny it or compartmentalize it—she'd been doing that for years. But she wasn't ready to face it yet either.

Once upon a time, there was a girl who loved two brothers. She married one, but then he died, and so she lived happily ever after with the other brother instead...

Now that was some fucked-up, twisted fairytale, wasn't it? Except there was no villain to blame in this story. Only herself.

"I need more time." She inhaled a deep breath through her nose and got up from his lap.

"How much more time do you need—a week? A month? Another year?"

He sounded upset, maybe even angry. And didn't he have every reason to be?

"Can't we just slow down for a little while?" Linnea skimmed her fingers across his cheek.

"What do you mean, slow down? Go backwards? After I spent a week inside you?" He squeezed her pussy, rubbing back and forth along the seam in the crotch of her jeans. "No, we can't."

Charlotte began to cry in the pretty mauve room Dillon had painted for her across the hall. Linnea went to stand, but he was up first. "I'll get her."

The sound of unhappy cries turned into sweet baby giggles. Her daughter was so attached to him. Loved him like no one else. Well, of course she did. He'd been there since before she was born. Dillon didn't father her, but he was *'Daddy'* in Charlotte's eyes. He was all that baby knew.

Family stays together, just like the moon and the stars...

The bracelet on her wrist blurred through her tears.

He came back holding the baby. Charlotte was smiling, but Dillon's blue eyes were glassy. "I love you, but I can't do this. I can't play house with you anymore. When you're ready for the real thing... to have a life with me..." His voice cracked. "...I'll be back."

Squeezing her eyes shut, Linnea pressed both hands against her face.

Hugging Charlotte tight, he kissed her soft curls and placed the baby in her arms. Holding them both, Linnea felt his lips brush her forehead. "Our hearts belong together."

She opened her eyes, but he was gone.

Dillon never asked for anything for himself. Except her.

She glanced down at her daughter. Charlotte looked up at her, blinking her big blue eyes.

Eyes as blue as the summer sky.

Linnea had the feeling she'd just made the biggest mistake of her life.

"What have I done?"

Twenty-Nine

Twenty-four hours later and he still couldn't believe it.

Gutted, that's what he was. Fucking gutted.

They say it's the punch you don't see coming that knocks you out, and Dillon sure didn't see that coming, especially after the idyllic week he and Linnea spent together at the lake house. It'd almost been too perfect. How the fuck did she go from Cabo San Lucas to *'I can't make a life with you'* in the space of an hour?

His timing still sucked, apparently. It didn't matter that he'd taken great care to follow her cues. He didn't rush her. Waited until she was ready, except she obviously wasn't. Kyan's ring was still on her finger, but he'd convinced himself to overlook it. Why didn't he listen to his gut?

In retrospect, maybe he should have known this was coming all along.

And he didn't know what the fuck to do now.

After a bullshit meeting with the neighborhood redevelopment committee, Dillon shrugged out of his blazer and without acknowledging his cousins, went straight to the coffee machine. He'd prefer a finger or two of Glenlivet, but he'd slept like shit—more like he hadn't slept at all—and needed the caffeine. He popped in a pod to brew, tapping his fingers on the wood while he waited.

Brendan cleared his throat and he turned around. "What?"

"Meeting go okay?"

"Same shit," Dillon grunted, grabbing his cup from the machine. He sipped on his coffee and took his seat next to Jesse on the eggplant sofa.

Brendan knitted his brow. "Now, wanna tell me what the hell is wrong with you?"

"Let's see." Dillon leaned back on the sofa, clasping his hands behind his head. "My brother is still dead. Linnea…" He couldn't bring himself to say the words.

"Dillon?"

"You know, I think I'm going to knock off early and head on home." He stood. "I'll catch you later."

But he should have known better than to think he'd be left alone to wallow in his misery. Not too long after he left the office, there was a knock at his door. Dillon didn't bother getting up to answer it. Whoever it was would come right on in anyway.

He downed the whiskey in his glass and glanced up. Brendan, Jesse, and Monica stood there looking at him like a specimen in a petri dish. "Lucky me. I hit the trifecta," he deadpanned, grabbing the bottle to pour himself another shot.

Jesse took the bottle from his hand and sat with Brendan beside him. Monica squeezed his shoulder and sat on the other side. "I'm here as a friend." She took his hand. "I care about you both and I'm sorry that you're hurting."

He stared blankly at the wall, chewing on the inside corner of his lip.

"I don't have to tell you how grief works. Everyone experiences it differently." She squeezed his hand. "This is a temporary setback, Dillon. That's all. And if I may speak frankly…" She looked to him as if seeking permission to continue and he nodded. "…neither one of you have allowed the other to truly come to terms with Kyan's death."

Taken aback, he looked at her with a cock of his brow. "What do you mean?"

"You bonded in your grief. You love each other deeply, so you leaned on one another—that's natural and normal." Her hand moved back to his shoulder. "You threw yourself into taking care of Linnea and Charlotte, without taking the time to tackle your own personal loss. And Linn threw herself into taking care of you."

He rubbed his temple. "What happened to supporting each other is the key to rebuilding life, huh?"

"It is, Dill," Brendan chimed in. "And pain is the agent of change. That's what reshapes us, remember?"

"What the fuck, Bren?" With a shake of his head, he raised his voice. "So, you're saying I haven't suffered enough? Linn hasn't suffered enough?"

"Not exactly."

Jesse nodded. "That's what he's saying, Dill."

Monica cupped his cheek, turning his face back in her direction. "You did everything you could think of to make her feel better, to distract her, to keep her from hurting—am I right?"

"Well, yeah. Of course, I did."

She smiled that warm smile of hers. "And she did the same for you. That's wonderful. There's nothing wrong with that, but at the same time neither one of you were able to fully process your grief. You numbed the pain with each other and now that you've taken your relationship to another level…" She paused. "…Linn is being forced to recognize it. And so are you."

"So what do I do?"

"You have to make peace with the ending to experience the magic of a brand-new beginning. She lost her husband and Charlotte's father. Give Linnea a little time on her own to work through that."

"He was my brother. I watched that baby come into the world." A tear slid down his cheek. "I can't do it."

"Ladies and gentlemen, we have begun our descent into Dublin. Please turn off all portable electronic devices…"

He didn't pay attention to what the flight attendant said after that. Dillon woke up the screen on his phone to check the local time. A photo of Linnea and Charlotte smiled back at him. Pain seared through his gut and clenched in his chest, making it difficult to breathe. He turned it off.

In the evening twilight, the plane descended through a bank of clouds to reveal the dark waters of the Irish Sea. Lights off in the distance. Lush, green land. He closed his eyes and thought of home.

"How long will you be gone?"

A car was picking him up to take him to the airport. Jesse waited with him in his kitchen.

"Don't know."

"Aren't you going to tell her goodbye?" His cousin tipped his head in the direction of Linnea's house next door.

"No, because if I see her I won't go." His throat closed up and he forced himself to swallow. "And I need to."

Dillon missed them all so much already. He couldn't be sure he'd made the right decision to come here, but the one thing he was absolutely certain of was that he couldn't just stand idly by and watch her from next door. If time and space was really what Linnea needed, he couldn't give it to her and remain in his house on Park Place.

Aunt Colleen was there in baggage claim to meet him. "Dillon," she exclaimed, pulling him in for a hug. They rocked together from side to side.

Under the fluorescent lights, strands of silver glinted in her deep chestnut hair. He didn't remember seeing them there at the funeral. His aunt was fifty-six, the same age his mother would be if she were alive. Still young. It was evident in the twinkle of her vibrant blue eyes.

Colleen Byrne Nolan O'Malley was the younger of his father's two sisters. Her first husband, Jesse's dad, his uncle Tommy, committed suicide when he was a senior in college. A year later, after Jesse graduated and went to Baltimore to play for the Ravens, Colleen picked up and went to Ireland, met Tadhg O'Malley, and remarried. That was a decade ago.

Tadhg is an Irish name, pronounced *Tige*—like tiger without the *er* at the end. He never came to the States with his aunt, so Dillon didn't know him very well. A former widower, he never had any children, and owned a tattoo parlor in the Temple Bar District. They lived above it. And that was pretty much all he knew.

Aunt Colleen was quiet for most of the thirty-minute trip from the airport to Dublin City Centre, which was unlike her. Usually she had plenty to say. She'd glance over at him from time to time, as if choosing her words, and pat his hand instead. It made him wonder what Jesse had relayed to his mother. Or Chloe. Dillon knew his aunt spoke with her daughter-in-law often.

The living space, which encompassed both the second and third floors above O'Malley Ink Emporium, was a lot larger than he thought it would be, but then so was the tattoo shop. His aunt showed him around the bi-level apartment. A great room layout, the kitchen, living, and dining area, as well as the master suite and a powder room were here on the first level. Two guest bedrooms shared a Jack-and-Jill bath upstairs.

"Why don't ya get settled while I fix us something to eat, yeah?" she suggested, switching on a lamp. "Tadhg will be up in a bit unless he goes fer a gargle."

The fuck?

"A gargle?"

"A drink at the pub. Course, here it's never just one." Aunt Colleen chuckled. "He'd be happy fer ya to go with him."

"Thanks, *Aintín*, maybe tomorrow. I'm jet-lagged." He pushed his hair out of his eyes and peered out the window. "What time does it get dark here anyway?"

"This time of year…" She chuckled again. "…not until after ten. Come down when yer ready."

Dillon shot off texts to Jesse and Brendan to let them know he'd arrived. As much as he wanted to, he stopped himself from sending one to Linnea. It didn't take him long to unpack. He splashed cold water on his face and looked at himself in the mirror. A tired, worn face looked back at him.

Two places were set at the wood trestle table when he came downstairs. A platter of Irish smoked salmon, brown bread, and horseradish sauce. Cold Guinness to wash it down with.

"This looks good, *Aintín*." He fixed himself a plate.

"I can make some tea, if you'd like."

"No, really, this is great." He raised his pint glass. "*Sláinte*."

They ate without talking. As soon as he swallowed his last bite of bread, she reached for his hand from across the table and squeezed it. "It's all going to work out, ya know."

"Why doesn't it feel like it?" He drained his beer.

"She lost her husband, Dillon."

"Kyan was my brother. I lost him too." His throat constricting, the words came out louder than he intended. "Sometimes it seems like everyone forgets that."

"I know, *nia*..." She cupped his cheek. "...and I know what it feels like to lose both."

Leaning inward, he squeezed her hand in return. "I'm sorry."

"Don't give up on love." Moist, blue eyes locked with his own. "Because once you do you give up on living."

The endless twilight had faded into darkness by the time Dillon returned to his room. He didn't bother switching on the lamp and sat in a chair by the window. Three thousand miles and an ocean separated them. He looked up. The moon looked down at him. Did Linnea see it too? He couldn't imagine ever not loving her.

I'm not giving up on us, baby. Not ever.

Even if it did feel hopeless right then.

Dillon pulled his phone out of his pocket and took a photo of the moon from his window. He captioned the image with two words and sent it to her.

It was already mid-morning when he woke. Dillon knew the hour without even glancing at the clock. Sunlight spilled into the room through the open window. The chatter of passersby could be heard from the sidewalks below. Still groggy, he sat on the side of the bed and adjusted himself in his boxers, chastising himself in his head for sleeping his life away here.

He couldn't use the jet lag excuse anymore. After a week in Dublin, the lie was certainly laughable now. He went through the motions. Showered and dressed, Dillon trudged down the stairs.

Aunt Colleen put a cup of coffee in his hand as he entered the kitchen. "Where ya off to today?"

He'd already walked most of the city, seen all the things tourists flocked here to see. The Guinness Storehouse. The Book of Kells. Trinity College. Grafton Street. Dublin Castle and St. Patrick's Cathedral. While Colleen and Tadhg were down at the shop, he spent his days strolling the River Liffey, crossing the Ha'Penny Bridge, finding a spot to crack open a book on St. Stephen's Green. In the evenings, he made rounds of the local pubs, and they were plentiful. Keeping to himself, he'd sample the whiskeys and have a pint or two or three.

"I don't know." He shrugged, sipping on his coffee.

"I have a couple things to take care of in the office real quick. Come with me." Crow's feet accentuated the outer corners of her eyes with her gentle smile. "You can talk to Tadhg about the ink you want him to do for ya and then we can go to Boxty House for lunch. What do ya say?"

"You had me at boxty." Yeah, his aunt knew he'd never say no to that.

O'Malley Ink Emporium wasn't at all what Dillon expected. Catering to tourists and locals alike, the shop had at least a dozen tattoo and body piercing stations—barbering too. Get inked, pierced, and a haircut all in one stop. Brilliant, yeah?

Old school 90s grunge played on the sound system. Pearl Jam. Nirvana. Alice In Chains. The reminder of Venery's tribute band days brought on a twinge of homesickness. Framed portraits of legendary Hollywood stars like Marilyn Monroe and James Dean graced the brick walls. Hardwood floors. Stained-glass windows. The place was cool with a vintage vibe.

Colleen's husband was up front when they came in. He glanced over, and seeing his wife, patted his client on the back and left him with the receptionist to finish checking out. Tadhg O'Malley wasn't at all what Dillon expected either. Younger than his aunt, though by how many years he couldn't say, the middle-aged guy had a decent physique, a head of thick black hair that he slicked back so it wouldn't hang in his eyes, two silver hoops in his earlobe, and full sleeves on both arms.

If his aunt had purposely set out to find a man the complete opposite of Jesse's father, she had succeeded.

Tadhg kissed his wife and patted her on the behind before she went to the office in the back. Then he turned to Dillon. "Howya?"

Only the Irish said hello by asking a question they weren't expecting an answer to. "Howya?"

"So, yer goin' ta let me ink ye?" The man hooked an arm around his shoulders and led him up front.

"Yeah."

"Know what ye want?"

Kind of. He had an idea anyway.

"Something in remembrance of my brother."

Biting his lip, Tadhg nodded and pointed to a chair. "Here." He placed a thick album of sketches in Dillon's hands. "Look at these ta start off with and then I'll draw up somethin' fierce good fer ye." He turned to the receptionist behind the counter. "Siona, if Boyle doesn't show his arse in the next five minutes someone else has ta do him or he can reschedule."

"Whatever you say, *Uncail*," the blonde answered.

She was young, early twenties if he were to guess, and pretty.

"Tadhg's your uncle?"

"Yeah, by marriage. What's it to ya?" Snippy little thing she was too, apparently.

Chuckling to himself, Dillon shook his head. "Colleen's my aunt."

Perusing the sketches, he didn't pay her any mind after that, and by the time he finished, his aunt was at his side. She glanced at the blonde behind the counter before nudging his shoulder. "Ready, Dillon?"

"Yeah."

Tadhg called out to her as Dillon opened the heavy glass door. "Ask Pádraig ta pack up some coddle fer me, will ye?"

"I will."

"Who's that girl?" he asked his aunt as they walked arm in arm down Fleet Street, in the direction of Temple Bar.

"Trouble, that's who she is." She laughed, but a frown quickly followed. "Siona Dawson. Tadhg's brother is married to her mother—he works at the shop too. She's just helping out for the summer."

He started off with mussels steamed in ale with leeks and lemon. Dillon was already full when the server came out with their lunch, but he made room in his belly, because an Irish boxty is a thing to behold. Tender medallions of fillet beef in a whiskey and mushroom cream sauce wrapped in a traditional Leitrim potato pancake. "Fuck, this is good."

"Dillon," she said his name in a warning tone, buttering a slice of fresh-baked soda bread.

"Sorry." He grinned without shame. "But this is better than delicious, and you all curse like damn sailors here, so."

"Feck isn't exactly the same thing."

"Is too. Change a letter all you want, *Aintín*, that doesn't change its meaning."

She dunked the bread in her stew. "I suppose not."

"So why is she trouble?" Dillon asked and swallowed a mouthful of ale. "Her pleasant personality notwithstanding."

"Siona?"

"Yeah."

"She's just like her mother." Her forehead puckered with a scowl. "Stay far away from that one."

"Don't worry." He scratched the stubble on his chin and finished off his pint. "Wasn't planning on getting anywhere near her."

"It isn't you I'm worried about." Colleen sat back and folded her arms across her chest.

"Oh?"

"It's her."

Oh.

Thirty

*L*ook up.

Linnea read the message he sent her. It was only two words, but she'd looked at them, gazing at the image of a Dublin moon, more times than she could count. She stepped out onto the brick patio and inhaled a deep breath of sweet evening air to keep herself from crying. It already felt like forever since Dillon left her without a word.

She hurt him.

She missed him.

She loved him.

God, she loved him so much. But in her grief for Kyan she'd fucked it all up and now Dillon was gone. Had she lost him too? Happily ever after had been right there in her grasp and she let it slip through her fingertips. Now she'd become the villain of her own story.

Nope. Fuck that. She was going to write herself a new one, because this was not how their story was going to end. Blinking away the tears she'd fought so hard to hold back, Linnea gazed at the half-moon.

I'm looking, Dillon. And I promise, every night until you come home, I'll be looking.

Charlotte was awake in her crib across the hall. She wasn't fussing, but Linnea could hear her movements. The baby missed Dillon too. Any time a door opened, she'd look for him, only to be disappointed when he didn't appear.

With a determined smile affixed to her face, Linnea swooped

into her daughter's pretty mauve room. "Good morning, sweet pea!" The baby beamed hearing the endearment Dillon bestowed on her. She lifted Charlotte out of the crib and held her at eye level. "Mommy has a plan. You want to help me?"

Making a plan, and executing it, whether it was a project, an event, or something as simple as dinner, was the one thing Linnea had always enjoyed doing—and she was good at it. Naturally, she made planning her profession, but it was more for her than that. To have a plan meant taking control. Executing it took methodical focus. It didn't matter that plans often go awry and outcomes aren't always guaranteed. She could roll with it and make a new plan. Isn't that what she'd always done?

Her life was one big event. She knew what needed to be done to live it.

Linnea turned on an old disco station and cranked it up. Charlotte liked it. She opened a new notebook, made her to-do lists, prioritized them. And then she set out to tick off her tasks one by one.

She was on the phone when Chloe came in the front door and flopped on the sofa, making herself at home. With another item crossed off her list, Linnea disconnected the call.

Chloe reached over and tucked her messy hair behind her ear. "Jess and Tay are grilling tonight, so I wanted to see if you felt like having dinner with us." She laid her head on her shoulder, batting her eyelashes up at her. "Katie went to visit her parents so Bren's coming."

"Are you trying to convince me or something?"

"Maybe." She softly giggled. "If I have to."

Linnea wanted to know if Jesse had heard from Dillon, but either way she was afraid to hear the answer, so she didn't ask. "You don't have to talk me into it. Of course, I'll come."

"Good." Chloe kissed her on the cheek, laid her head back down, and softly murmured, "He misses you."

"You spoke to him?" Linnea turned where she sat to face her friend, knocking Chloe off her shoulder in the process.

"No." She pursed her lips and sighed. "Colleen."

"Oh."

"Tadhg gave him some new ink and boxty is his new favorite food."

"Yeah, sounds like he's missing me a lot," she murmured, turning away.

"Linnea, just because he got a new tattoo and discovered potato pancakes doesn't mean he isn't miserable without you. Boxty is fucking delicious, by the way." Chloe gripped her shoulders. "Believe me, he misses you. Colleen told me there's this girl who helps out in the shop—Tadhg's brother's wife's daughter. Something like that. Anyway, she's been trying to get Dillon's attention, but he won't even look her way…" She petted her hair. "…because he's so in love with you."

The buzzer sounded. Someone was at the gate. "Who could that be?"

"Linnea Byrne?" She recognized the old man who stood at her door. He carried two large packages wrapped in brown paper, one under each arm.

"Yes, that's me." Nodding, with Chloe behind her, she stepped back from the door to let him in.

"We met at the Memorial Day fair in town." He bobbed his head, smiling as he spoke. "Where do you want these?"

"Um, what are they?"

"That painting of the lake from the old fishing pier you were looking at. Your husband bought it for you and asked me to paint another one looking at it from your backyard. So you could always see both sides, he said."

She was stunned. Chloe squeezed her shoulder. "I…I didn't know he did that. Thank you."

"Oh, dear." The man scratched his balding head. "Sure hope I didn't spoil a surprise. My wife sent him an email to let him know I was coming."

"No, it's fine. Perfect, actually," Linnea assured him, placing her hand on his forearm. "He's away, so believe me, this couldn't have come at a more perfect time."

"Well, all right then." He grinned. "Where do you want 'em?"

"We've got it." She and Chloe relieved the man of his burden. "Thank you so much. Truly."

With a dip of his chin, he gave her a salute. "I best be going. It's a long drive back."

"See?" Chloe arched a brow and giggled. "Don't ever doubt that man loves you more than potato pancakes."

The days passed quickly. Between Charlotte and her list, there was plenty to fill her hours with. It's the nights that were hard. She'd look up at the sky, then go to bed and think about Dillon. And Kyan. And cry herself to sleep.

Seth waltzed in with two large Americanos and breakfast pastries from Beanie's, same as he did every morning before their run. He set them on the island and scooped his niece out of her playpen, peppering her with kisses until she squealed. After he put the baby down, his smile slowly dissipated, and by the time he sat beside her, Linnea could only describe his expression as grave.

"Are you okay, Seth?"

"Yeah, Linnea, I'm fine," he answered, rubbing his jaw.

But staring out the window, he wouldn't look at her when he said it. "Something's wrong. What is it?"

"I've been debating whether or not I should even tell you." He released a pent-up sigh and took a sip of his coffee. "I got a call last night…" Locking his eyes with hers, he grabbed her hand and squeezed it. "…from Crossfield."

"Oh, I didn't think you still talked to anyone there."

"I don't." He squeezed her hand again. "It was some doctor that called me. I guess I'm still listed as his emergency contact." His gaze returned to the window. "Our father is dying, Linnea."

She didn't know what to say. The man was no father to her. Pastor Jarrid Black was a psychopathic monster and she hated him. Her mother killed herself when Linnea was just a newborn because of him. Her brother had endured hell because of him. Seth still wouldn't talk about it. Harsh as it might seem, Linnea couldn't say she was sorry the man was dying.

"He's in the hospital over in Decatur right now, but they want to transfer him to hospice on Monday." His green eyes, the same shade they both shared with Jarrid, looked into hers. "They need me to sign some papers and I, um, I'm going to the house to clear out his things before the church folk can get in there."

Her sharp intake of breath was audible. "You're going to see him?"

"I don't know." He rubbed the space between his brows. "Maybe."

Without closure, Seth was still suffering at their father's hand. She could see it. Perhaps, with his end, her brother would find peace.

"Will you go with me?"

Her eyes flicked to his. Seth's pain was written on his face in the lines between his brows, the clench of his jaw, his downturned lips. Linnea would do anything she could to ease her brother's suffering. Even if it meant returning to the one place she vowed never to set foot in ever again.

Rising from her seat, Linnea stood between his thighs and wrapped Seth in her arms. She held him against her, stroking his long chocolate hair. "If you need me to, then I will."

His arms came around her waist. He held her tight. "I need you."

Burn in hell, Jarrid Black.

Linnea kissed his hair and laid her head on his. "I love you, Seth."

"And I love you, little one."

After their run, Linnea laid the baby down for her nap and went out into the backyard. She was already sweaty, so she figured she might as well get started on the garden. Another thing to check off her list. The nursery delivered her order yesterday and she'd originally planned to start the landscape project tomorrow, but she was leaving with Seth to go to Crossfield in the morning.

Creating an oasis in her backyard was the one project Linnea never got around to when she lived on Oak Street—probably because she had the courtyard there. She'd always meant to, though. Three years later, and she hadn't gotten around to it yet on Park Place either. Until now, that is. Yeah, she had a plan.

"Dirty and beautiful." Warm fingers pressed into her nape and trailed down her spine. "Makes my dick hard, baby girl."

Sitting on her haunches in the soil, Linnea glanced up at Bo with a snicker. "Breathing air makes your dick hard, drummer boy."

"You aren't wrong." Chuckling, he held out his hand and helped her up. "Kodiak just left my place. Thought I'd come check on you."

"I'm fine," she said, hugging him.

"Where's my kiss?"

Giggling, she kissed his cheek.

"That's better." He grinned.

"You're still incorrigible."

"And you still love it."

Linnea wiped the dirt off her hands on the back of her shorts. She couldn't deny it and grinned back. "I do."

They sat together on the patio. Bo took her hand in his, running his fingers back and forth over the back of it. He tilted his head and his lips quirked slightly as he looked at her. "How are you—for real?"

"I'm okay."

"Don't bullshit me, baby girl. I know a canned answer when I hear one." He winked. "I'm not his cousin and I'm not married to one."

"Most of the time I'm okay," Linnea upheld, her smile shaky. "Really. I'm in a young widow's support group online that Monica suggested. I'm going through and sorting Kyan's things. Remaking my life without him..." Her voice cracked as tears filled her eyes. "...so I can have one with Dillon."

Bo gathered her in his arms, holding her against his hairless chest. "Don't cry."

"I didn't mean to fuck it all up, but I think maybe I did. It's been two weeks."

"You didn't fuck up nothin,'" he assured her, swiping away tears with his thumbs. "If I've learned anything at all, it's that guilt can't change the past, and fretting over shit won't change the future. You both needed this time for yourselves. Dill knows you love him."

"Does he?" She sniffled.

"Yeah, fucking lucky bastard." Bo chuckled, ruffling the mop of hair piled on her head. "And he loves you."

With a gentle smile, Linnea glanced at him through wet lashes. "You ready for tomorrow?"

"Yeah, thanks to you." He smiled wide, his deep blue eyes sparkling. "Now, give me a kiss for luck—a real one and make it good. It's your last shot."

Oh, Bo…

He'd been there with her, through everything, from the beginning. The first larger-than-life penis she ever saw was his—okay, not up close and personal, but it still counted, right? Sandwiched between him and Dillon at the club on more than one occasion. Kyan giving him a taste of her. But she'd never really kissed him.

His skin was as smooth and as soft as luxurious satin, his long blond hair like the finest silk. Linnea clasped her hands around his neck, and touched her lips to his, inhaling clean sweat and spicy sin. Her lips parted and their tongues twirled together. Slow. Sweet. This wasn't a lovers' kiss. It wasn't sexual. It was something else entirely, but she didn't have a word for it.

Spiritual? Yeah, maybe that.

"Goddamn," Bo whispered, pulling away. "I will always regret I never got to have you and Chloe naked together in my bed." He chuckled.

"Goof." She giggled.

"I love you, baby girl."

"I love you too, drummer boy."

Thirty-One

Fifteen minutes into the session, the sensation of the needle injecting ink into his skin was almost pleasant. Tadhg worked in silent concentration, outlining the Byrne family crest over his right shoulder blade. He'd already done a Celtic half-moon for Kyan on his left. Lying prone, with his hands folded beneath his cheek, Dillon zoned out to the steady vibration of the tattoo gun and Chris Cornell singing through the speakers.

How long had he been here now?

Longer than he thought he'd be, that's for sure, and after almost six weeks in Dublin, it didn't seem like Dillon was any closer to figuring out his shit. Nothing had changed, and how could it? So what was he waiting for—some magical epiphany? It was well past time to go home. He couldn't stay here forever.

"Outline's done." With a Puddle of Mudd song playing, the tattoo gun ceased. "Need a break?"

"Nah, I'm good."

"Siona…" Tadhg called out as he got up from the rolling stool. "…will ye bring some water over here, please?" He glanced down at Dillon and winked. "Five minutes."

Looking up from her phone, the blonde behind the counter rolled her eyes at her step-uncle. Dillon chuckled to himself, sat up, and stretched. He didn't know what her problem was, but the insolent girl was in serious need of an attitude adjustment. If she had any redeeming qualities about her, besides a pretty face and a killer body, Siona had yet to show it.

She sauntered over, two bottles of water in hand, hips swaying as she walked. Tight jeans. Cropped top. She plopped a bottle next to Tadhg's workstation and held the other out to him. "Here ya go."

"Thanks." Dillon uncapped the bottle and when he looked up she still stood there. He watched as her gaze slowly traveled over him.

Siona pursed her lips. "Lookin' fine."

"Excuse me?"

"Yer ink, *eejit*." Rolling her eyes, a hint of a smile graced her face. "Yer a finer, all right. Bleedin' massive, but I s'pose yer well aware of that."

With a chuckle he angled his head. "I've no idea what you just said."

"Yer father's needin' ya, Siona." With her arms folded across her chest, Aunt Colleen appeared none too pleased. "Go on now."

Her nostril flared. Curling her lip, Siona lifted her chin and left without another word.

Dillon glanced at his aunt. "What?"

"Would ya ever cop on to yourself?" *Stop acting stupid.* Dillon learned that one the first week he was here. Colleen uncrossed her arms and sat on Tadhg's stool. "She's lookin' to ride ya."

His shoulders shook so hard, Dillon thought he might pee himself. "The fuck, Auntie?" He snorted. "Did you just say what I think you did?"

A smirk replaced her scowl, the crinkles at the corners of her eyes deepening. "I did." Mirth bubbled from deep within her throat. "And what did I say about language, *nia*?"

"Sorry, *aintín*." With a cock of his brow, Dillon pressed his lips together.

"She was flirtin' with ya something fierce," Colleen explained, wiping the evidence of laughter from beneath her eyes. "Ya big sexy, hottie!"

"Is that what she said?"

"More or less." Her expression turned serious. "And don't ya dare fall for it."

A year ago, Dillon wouldn't have thought twice about taking

Siona for a nice, hard ride. Adjust her attitude on his dick. At least he was good for that. Staring at the floor, his gaze went unfocused. Today it was the last thing he wanted.

"It's your life, you don't get another," she spoke in a soft, loving voice, pushing her fingers through his hair. "It's time to start living it, sweetheart."

Looking back up, he blew out a breath. "I know."

Tadhg glanced at his phone resting on the bar, the image of Linnea holding Charlotte displayed on the screen. "Lovely photo. She's a stunner."

"She is."

Even for a Friday evening, the small pub was packed. The Guinness flowed. A trio of musicians covered U2's "With or Without You" as the rowdy patrons sang along. Dillon chuffed out a strangled-sounding breath. The lyrics weren't lost on him.

"It's a helluva way ta get the girl ye love." Inclining his head, Tadhg gnawed at his lip and raised his pint.

Dillon sucked through the cream head, swallowing his lager. "But I don't have her."

"Ah, ye do." Tadhg motioned to the bartender. "Another round and I'll tell ye a story."

Fresh-poured pints in front of them, Tadhg tapped his fingers on the old polished wood bar top. His gaze went vacant for a moment, then with a subtle shake of his head, he lifted his glass and drank. "I was 'bout yer age when I met Colleen."

Dillon did the math in his head. His aunt left for Ireland when Jesse left for Baltimore—ten years ago. So that put Tadhg at around forty-three now.

"Temple Bar of all places." He sniggered. "Fate must've ordained it, 'cause ye know I never go in there."

Dillon chuckled. "It's way overpriced and too many tourists."

"Ah, ye were listenin'." Tadhg grinned. "Anyway, one look at her and I was smitten. Didn't matter none she was older 'n me. Was surprised she gave me the time o'day, though."

"Why?"

His brows pulled together as the smile slipped from his face. "She was cryin' in her Guinness fer Tommy Nolan."

Oh.

"He'd been gone about a year then, but yer *aintín* was still carryin' so much guilt." He took another drink. "Bein' a widower, I understood, and...'twas a sad thing we had in common. I wasn't lookin' ta marry again. Neither was Colleen. Both of us still grievin' and all."

"But you did."

"We did," he affirmed, his brow relaxing. Tadhg set down his glass. "And I love her somethin' fierce."

"She was able to get over Uncle Tommy then?"

"Jaysus, no." With an abrupt shake of his head, ebony hair fell into his eyes. "Will ye ever *get over* yer brother?"

"No."

Never.

Tadhg picked up his glass again. "And yer girl won't neither."

"It's hopeless then."

"Christ, will ye listen ta me?" he implored, his eyes widening as he pushed his hair back with his fingers. "Ye don't stop lovin' a person when they die, but that doesn't mean ye can't love again. Yer *aintín* will love Tommy 'til the day she dies, same as I'll always love Meaghan. And ye never stop grievin' neither. C'mon, ye know that."

He did know that. But Linnea had to let Kyan go. Yes, her story with his brother ended too soon, but the meaningful parts of every story stay with us forever. Cry. Mourn the ending. Then let it go. If she didn't, then she couldn't let him in. There'd be no new beginning. And that's what Dillon feared.

"She told me she couldn't make a life with me..." He chewed on his lip, then inhaled. "...because she still feels married to him."

"Ouch." He actually winced. "Have youse spoken since ye been here?"

"No. Linnea said she needed time, and everyone seemed to agree with her." He shrugged, rubbing the stubble on his chin. "So I left."

"Ran from yer troubles, eh?"

"Not exactly. Maybe. I just…" Is that what he'd done? No. He left to give her the time and space she needed. "…I've been waiting for a sign, or a word…fuck, I'll take anything…to let me know she's ready for me to come home, but I've gotten nothing."

"Maybe she's waiting fer *you* to be ready, *eejit*." His head bobbed when he cocked it. "Are ye?"

He wet his lips and nodded. "Yeah."

"Here's some advice fer ye, Dillon." Looking him straight in the eye, Tadhg clasped his shoulder. "We need ta talk about our people who've died. Tell their stories. I'll wager it felt funny ta talk 'bout Kyan once youse caught feelings."

"Yeah, I guess so."

"Don't ever stop talkin' when ye need ta—both of youse. It's their stories that get ye through the sadness that comes outta nowhere sometimes." He let go of his shoulder and drained the beer from his glass. "I never met Tommy Nolan, but I know him well. And Colleen knows Meaghan. *You* have the advantage of bein' able ta share the stories of a man both of youse knew and loved. That will only bring youse closer together as the years go by—ye get me?"

"Yeah, Tadhg. I get you."

"Well, thank fuck fer that." He slapped him on the back and motioned for the bartender. "A wee sip o' whiskey and then I'm goin' home ta my wife. Ye comin'?"

"Not yet." He had some reflecting to do, didn't he? "Go on, I'll talk to ya."

"Yer gettin' it." With a wink, Tadhg squeezed his shoulder. "I'll be seein' ye."

A glass of whiskey and a fresh pint in front of him, Dillon

glanced around the pub filled with happy, smiling faces. Carousing and carefree. Once, he'd been just like them. Not anymore. He must stick out like a sore thumb.

Home was an ocean away. His heart was an ocean away. Linnea and Charlotte. He missed them so much, words couldn't describe it.

He missed the man he used to be.

He missed his brother. Dillon wished so hard Kyan was here. It made him angry that he wasn't.

The bartender placed another pint in front of him.

Then another.

And another.

Fuck it.

With an elbow planted on the bar, Dillon held his head in his hand, massaging his temple with his fingers. He was going to feel like hell come morning.

Blonde hair swept past him. A flash of bare midriff. Dillon looked to the stool on his left. The very one Tadhg had vacated hours before. Siona sat in it now. "What's the *craic?*"

"The what?" He lifted his glass to his lips, but it was empty. "Speak fucking English."

"Yer bleedin' gargled." She snickered. "C'mon, let's get ya home."

Siona went to help him stand. He brushed her off. "I can do it."

"Suit yerself." Raising her hands, she backed away.

Dillon leaned on her for the walk home, though. With an arm around his waist, and his looped across her shoulders, Siona tethered him to her side. Somehow, she managed to keep him upright. He was glad they didn't have far to go and that she remained silent.

Until she wasn't.

"What got into ya?"

"Huh?" He glanced at her as he swayed along the sidewalk.

"Yer angry. Why?"

He shrugged. "I could ask you the same question."

"I'm not angry." She shook her head with a tsk.

"Could've fooled me."

They reached the back entrance to the shop. Dillon stopped, and looking down at her, he leaned against the old red brick. "Thanks."

She stepped into him and glanced up from beneath her lashes. He reached out to touch her hair and closed his eyes.

Sweet, warm breath fanned his face.

What the fuck am I doing?

Thirty-Two

Her fingertips smoothed over the worn leather cover. Linnea tucked her mother's diary in the back of a drawer. As curious as she was, reading it seemed like an invasion of privacy. Perhaps she would someday, but right now it didn't feel right and she didn't think she was ready to know what was written on those pages.

Seth came across the journal as they sifted through their father's things, packing up the house her brother had grown up in. How Jarrid Black came to be in possession of it, or why he'd kept it, were questions they'd probably never find the answers for. The man had more photos of Grace Martin, and of her, than her grandmother ever did.

Linnea glanced at the photo the hospice nurse had taken during one of Jarrid's more lucid moments. He sat up in his hospital bed, Seth holding a happy, smiling Charlotte on one side of him. She stood on the other. The nurse had it pinned to a board by his bed so he could see it. He held it in his hand when he died. Placing the photo inside the journal, she closed the drawer.

God's promise fulfilled.

It'd been a couple weeks since they'd returned from Crossfield. She and Seth ended up staying longer than they'd planned on or wanted to, but it was over and done with now. The house across from the church sat empty, its walls wearing a coat of fresh paint, and the preacher lie buried in the ground beside her mother. Linnea would never have to go back to that godforsaken place ever again.

Opening the French doors, she stepped out onto the patio.

Linnea almost didn't recognize her own backyard. It was just as she'd always envisioned it. As lovely as she'd made the courtyard on Oak Street, this was even more perfect. The hot tub had been installed. Market lighting strung from a newly built pergola. Full outdoor kitchen. A garden filled with flowers and plants she loved. Cozy seating areas. Space for Charlotte to run and play. Maybe when she was older she and Dillon could get a puppy for her to grow up with.

Was she crazy to imagine her future with him still? He'd been gone well over a month now, and it was her own fault. Had Dillon met someone in Ireland? Is that why he was still there? If he had, there was no one else to blame except herself.

Linnea turned around at the sound of footfalls and Charlotte's delighted giggles behind her. The baby was tugging on Brendan's beard as he carried her outside. She crooned, "Did you have a nice nap?"

"This little sweetheart was standing up and looking at me from her playpen, Linn." Brendan chuckled, though his widened eyes told her he was somewhat surprised her daughter had been able to do such a thing.

She grinned like the proud mama she was. "Yeah, she's been doing that the past week or so. She pulls herself up as soon as she hears a door open."

To look for Dillon.

He lifted the baby over his head and blew raspberries on her tummy. Charlotte squealed. Then, kissing her soft, dark curls, Brendan cradled her against him. "I hope we have a girl."

"Are you pregnant?"

"Nah, not yet. Now that Dec is two we're trying, though." He winked. Eyeing the hot tub, he sat down with Charlotte on his lap. "You've been busy, I see. It looks fantastic back here, Linn. Really nice."

"Thanks, Bren." Linnea took a seat beside him. "I took care of all the things that I've been putting off." Biting her lip, she inclined her head. "Made a list of them."

"Finished them?"

"Every last one." She angled her head up to him. "I set aside some of Ky's things for you that I thought you'd especially like to have. Jesse and Dillon too. There's a box in his office with your name on it."

"Thank you, sweetheart. I'm so proud of you." He wrapped his arm around her shoulders and squeezed her against him. "I know how difficult it had to have been for you to do that."

Determined not to cry, she blinked. "Kyan always seemed so invincible to me, you know?"

"I know. But none of us are." He kissed the top of her head. "It isn't until you lose everything, that you're free to gain anything. Understand?"

Linnea shook her head. "I'm not sure I do."

"It's so easy to get trapped into patterns of thinking. Yes, Kyan's death was tragic and sad. But his death does not define *you*, Linn. You don't have to live as the grieving widow for the rest of your life—none of us want that for you." He tucked an errant strand of hair behind her ear. "It isn't until the pain becomes great enough, though, that the strength and courage necessary to bring about change finally comes."

She blinked again and the tears slipped from her eyes.

"We'll love and miss him dearly for the rest of our lives." Charlotte patted her cheek as Brendan wiped her tears away. "And be grateful that we do miss him, because that means at least we had him once, however short a time it was."

"You sound just like my shrink." It was something Monica would say.

"Maybe after all these years she's finally rubbing off on me, yeah?" Pulling her against his side, he winked. "Katelyn was watching this program on Netflix—some *TED Talk* kind of thing. I wasn't paying attention until I caught the speaker say, '*It takes courage to open ourselves up to joy*.' That speaker was Brené Brown."

She tried to swallow past the lump in her throat.

"You have more courage than almost anyone I know, sweetheart." Brendan placed Charlotte in her arms. "You don't have to miss Dillon. He's still here. Text him. Call him. I want my cousin back, and I have a feeling he's waiting on you."

Linnea pushed Charlotte along in her stroller, not that they were going very far—just to the end of the street. She paused on the sidewalk in front of Dillon's house next door. The front yard was mowed and tidy. Hedges trimmed. She could see a light turn on through the window, and for a moment her heart raced, thinking he'd come home. Then it sank when she remembered his lights were set on a timer. He wasn't there.

Quickly turning away, she crossed the street. Music wafted outside from Kit's open second-story window, but Linnea couldn't identify the tune. Other than that, it was quiet on Park Place, so the creak of Sloan's front door pushing open startled her.

"Hey, Linn."

Sloan stood there on his porch, hand held up in a wave, wearing a pair of ratty jeans he'd probably had since high school, considering how worn they were. Pallid and bleary-eyed, he looked like shit. Linnea had hardly seen him since they were all together for the Fourth, but that wasn't unusual anymore. Something was going on with him. Rarely leaving his house, the voice of Venery kept his own company these days.

"Hey, yourself." Her smile genuine, Linnea stopped at the walkway leading up to his door.

Barefoot, Sloan came down his porch steps and approached her, squatting onto his haunches to see Charlotte. "Hello, pretty girl." Shielding his eyes with his hand, he glanced up at her. "Going to the park?"

"No," she answered, hitching her thumb in the direction of the house next door. "Monica's."

"I saw you coming across the street." Sloan patted Charlotte on the head and stood. "Thought I'd say hello."

Seeming to lose their focus, he cast his blue eyes downward.

Linnea noticed the dark circles beneath them, the pallor of his skin, and it alarmed her. What was he doing in that house all alone?

She reached out and skimmed her fingers across his stubbled cheek. Usually, he was clean-shaven. "Is everything okay, Sloan?"

"Yeah." The corners of his mouth turned up slightly. "I haven't been sleeping too good. That's all."

He pulled her in for a hug. Linnea had the feeling it was so he wouldn't have to look her in the eye. She rubbed circles between the blades of his shoulders. "Will you come over for dinner?"

His muscles tensed beneath her fingers. "Sure."

"Yay," Linnea exclaimed, even though she didn't quite believe him, and kissed him on the cheek.

"See you later." Dismissing her, he went back up the porch steps.

"See you later, Sloan." Linnea watched him go inside, and promising herself she'd check in on him more often, knocked on Monica's door.

They sat at a table in Monica's backyard, beneath an umbrella, sipping iced tea. Danielle lay on her elbow, on a blanket in the grass with Charlotte. Their son, Elliott, rolled his toy trucks through the flower beds. The sun was warm, shining in a cloudless blue sky, but you could smell it in the air, summer was almost over.

"I can't believe he's going to be four already!" It seemed like the first time she walked into Monica's office, shortly before he was born, was just yesterday. And it felt like an entire lifetime ago. "You guys planning on having any more?"

"Nope. He's more than we ever could've hoped for." She smiled warmly, gazing at her little boy.

"I want another baby someday." Sighing, Linnea glanced away. She hadn't really meant to say that.

"Hey," Monica softly spoke, tilting her head to the side. "This isn't about babies, is it?"

"No." She forced herself to inhale a deep breath and stuttered, "It's a year tomorrow. How do I let go? I don't think I can."

"I think you have." Monica gently smiled, squeezing her hand. "Letting go doesn't mean you stop loving or missing or grieving

Kyan, because you always will. It's a part of you now, and it's a part of Dillon—of all of us. Letting go is being grateful for what you had and treasuring those memories. The past is gone and the future isn't here yet. It's loving what is, right now. Being present. Understand?"

She nodded, the tears in the backs of her eyes slowly building. "What if it's too late?"

"For what, sweetheart?"

"Dillon and me."

"A phoenix does not rise from the ashes just one time. A phoenix learns to rise again and again and again. And every time the phoenix rises, she soars higher and higher and higher. No matter what the future holds, you will rise, sweet girl." Monica hugged her tight. "But I have a feeling you and Dillon will be making lots of beautiful babies together."

Sloan never did show for dinner, not that Linnea believed he would. She'd hoped, though. Holding Charlotte up on her hip, she carried her across the street, along with some burgers and sides she'd wrapped up for him. She rang the bell, and knowing he wouldn't answer, left the container on a table he kept plants on by the door.

"We'll just keep on trying, won't we, sweet pea?" She smiled down at her daughter. "It's almost bedtime. Are you ready for your bath?"

Charlotte smiled back at her. She took that as a yes.

Linnea tucked the baby into her crib and sat on her bed in the room across the hall. She glanced around the room, redone in black and white with pops of color. The paintings of the lake that Dillon got for her were hung over the bed. Three framed photos stared at her from atop the dresser. Six-year-old Linnea perched on her brother's shoulder. She, Dillon, and Kyan taken that first Fourth of July at the lake house. Sitting on Dillon's lap, with Charlotte sitting on hers, from this last one.

Look how happy we are.

Memories.

Moments captured through a lens that would remain timeless. It clicked then. They were hers. Moments and memories are what made up her life, each one indelibly etched into her brain, a snapshot in her mind. Nothing could take them away from her, even death, and she was grateful for all of them.

Linnea rose from the bed and went into the en suite Kyan designed to fit in an extra-large clawfoot tub. He knew how much she adored her baths. She turned on the faucet, running her fingers under the stream until the water was comfortably hot. Then she stripped off her clothes.

Naked, she gazed at herself in the mirror. Even though she was fit from running every day, having Charlotte had changed her. Stretch marks were fading. Her breasts were fuller. Fingers brushed over her protruding nipples. Kyan didn't know this body, but Dillon had kissed every jagged pink line that marked it.

She poured sweet-scented bath salts into the running water, watching the bubbles emerge as she stepped into the tub, and reclined against the porcelain. Staring up at the ceiling, fingertips skated over her wet skin. There was a time, before Kyan, when Linnea wouldn't allow herself the simple pleasure of her own touch. He showed her its beauty, giving her the power she'd possessed all along, back to her.

Tears that had been building all day escaped from the corners of her eyes. She pinched her nipples between her fingers, rolling them until the pulse beat between her thighs, until her pussy wept for her touch. The tears dripped past her temples, seeping into her hair. She pulled on them harder, mercilessly tugging and twisting until they throbbed. And the tears kept coming. Sobbing, she thought of how sweetly Dillon had woken her their last morning at the lake house as her fingers found her clit.

His chest was pressed to her back when her eyelids blinked open. Fingers softly stroked between her legs, lips kissed her throat, warm breath fanned her skin. With each pass of his fingers, her clit swelled and she moaned, prompting him to delve deeper within her folds. His lips sought out hers. Dillon kissed her slowly, his tongue dancing with hers in time with his fingers.

He kissed his way down her body, stopping to suckle her nipples along the way. Her clit. Dillon sucked it until she whimpered, writhing on the bed, and hooked two fingers inside her, sliding them over her sweet spot. "Yeah, baby. There. Right there."

But he already knew her body. This body. He'd learned it quickly and he'd learned it well. Watching her responses. Reading every subtle cue. Dillon paid attention to every nuance, mastering her pleasure.

At the precipice, Linnea rubbed herself feverishly.

Dillon.

But she was crying too hard and lacked the air needed to scream.

Wrapping herself in a towel, Linnea stood in front of her bedroom window. And she looked up. So what if she couldn't see the stars. The moon was there.

"Come home," she whispered to it. "Please, come home."

Thirty-Three

He opened his eyes.

The hair between his fingers was the wrong shade of blonde. He let it go.

Dillon took a step back. "Goodnight."

Her hand reached out to touch him. "Dillon?"

Grabbing her by the wrist, he lowered her hand, stopping her before she could. "I'm sorry, Siona. You're a lovely girl, but I won't be kissing you. My heart's already taken."

"Maybe it's not yer heart I'm wantin'." Cheeks flushing pink, she looked up at him through her lashes. "No one has to know."

"I'd know."

Dillon fell into his bed. He didn't even bother getting undressed, not that he could have. The room was spinning, it was doubtful he'd have gotten out of his boots without falling on his face. With one eye open and the other closed, he held onto the mattress, gazing at the ceiling.

He was gargled, all right. In fact, he hadn't been this drunk since Kyan's funeral. Didn't matter how fucked up he got, though, he knew where his heart lie.

He was going home.

Jesus, fuck.

One eye cracked slowly open. Then the other. Dillon blinked a few times, attempting to lick his lips, but there wasn't enough saliva in his mouth. A million tiny hammers pounded nails into his brain. The hangover from hell, his head throbbed like never before, but he didn't care. He'd never felt so alive.

It was well past noon by the time he came close to resembling a functioning human again. He entered the shop through the back. His aunt was in the office. "Morning, *Aintin.*"

"Morning? It's going on two." With a chortle, she rolled her eyes at him. "Ya look like hell, Dillon. Did ya get the tablets I left by yer bed?"

"I did. Thank you." He leaned over and kissed her cheek. "And I know what time it is, but it's morning for me. Tadhg busy?"

"He's finishing up his one o'clock. Why?"

"I'm going home to Linnea, *Aintin.*" Squatting down beside her, Dillon took her hands in his. "And there's something I need to get from him before I go."

September sixth.

The first anniversary of Kyan's death. The last of all the firsts, and the most dreaded first of them all. How could he help but slide down that slippery slope, replaying that horrific day in his head? Dillon closed his eyes and it flashed in front of him. 3:28 *p.m.* The clock on the office wall. The bloodstained sheet on the sidewalk. Holding his brother's hand to his face.

Holding Linnea through the night while she cried.

He had to get to her. Fuck Monica and everybody with their psychobabble bullshit. He couldn't let her face this day alone.

Dillon stared out into the vast darkness through the airplane window. He looked up and smiled. He could see a million stars.

Family stays together...almost there, gorgeous. I love you.

One more hour of this interminable flight. Why did sixty minutes feel so far away?

Jesse was there in baggage claim to meet him. He should have been surprised, and even though he hadn't told anyone he was coming, he wasn't. No doubt his aunt had informed her son of his impending arrival the minute he boarded the plane.

"Hey, man." Jesse hugged him. "Glad you finally got your ass back here. I've missed you."

"Missed you too."

They grabbed his bags off the carousel. He came home with one more than he left with thanks to Aunt Colleen. Dillon happened to glance at the latest crop of disembarking passengers coming down the escalator. Kelsey and the suit, holding the hand of a young boy, were among them. He chuckled to himself.

Yeah, things happen as they're meant to...

"C'mon, the Kennedy is probably a clusterfuck already," his cousin informed him with a chuckle, pushing the door open to the parking garage. "You just had to come in during the morning rush hour, didn't you?"

The Kennedy *was* a clusterfuck.

They moved along at a snail's pace in bumper-to-bumper traffic. A blue line train chugged by. Dillon turned from the window and glanced to his cousin. "How is she?"

"She's good." He nodded, his expression going slack. "You know what today is."

"Yeah."

As if he could ever forget.

It took more than an hour to get home. He was glad he didn't have to drive in that shit every damn day. Didn't folks know the trains go downtown? Dillon dumped his bags in the family room and went straight over to the house next door.

She wasn't there.

Was she out on her morning run? Scratching his head, Dillon turned around on her porch, and looked in the direction of the park. He thought of running after her, but there was something he needed to do first. And he had to do it alone.

He never came back after he stood here in the rain that wretched day after Kyan's funeral. Dillon turned into the cemetery and drove through the wrought-iron gates, slowly traveling the winding drive. His chest tightened as he pulled up and parked. Breathing in so deep his nostrils flared, he got out of the car.

At least today the sun was shining.

Dillon took in the granite landscape, his gaze flitting from stone to stone. One stood out to him from all the others. It hadn't been there the last time he was here. He walked up to the grave beside his mother, where a fresh rose lay atop the stone inscribed with his brother's name.

She's been here.

His fingers traced over the letters etched in granite. Then he sat down, right there on the grass. Dillon stared at Kyan's name until his vision blurred, plucking at the blades. He wasn't sure how to do this. How do you talk to someone who's there, yet isn't?

"Now that I'm here, I don't know what to say to you...I love you, brother. I miss you every moment of every damn day. Fucks me up...you should still be here, you know? So I wouldn't have to miss you."

Dillon glanced around the cemetery from where he sat, thankful it appeared he was alone. He was having a one-sided conversation with a rock, for chrissakes. How ridiculous would he look if anyone saw him?

"You've missed out on so much, Kyan...so, so much. Charlotte is so beautiful. She looks like you...and Mom." His eyes flicked to his mother's stone and his voice cracked, "Are you with her now? And Dad. I hope you are. Maybe I don't need to tell you any of this, huh? Maybe you're watching over us all and you already know."

It gave him comfort to think so. Dillon sat there in reflection for a few moments, still plucking at the blades of grass, the distant sounds of the city out of place in this tranquil setting. Was he waiting for a sign from the grave that his brother was listening? There wouldn't be one. He needed to say what he came here to say.

"I love our Linnea...but then you've always known that. I'm going to marry her, Kyan. And I hope you know I'm not going to replace you, because no one ever could. I know there's room in her heart for us both."

He stood. Brushing remnants of torn grass from his jeans, he pulled the small bottle of Redbreast from his pocket and placed it with the rose on his brother's stone. "Brought you a wee something back from Ireland." Grief poured down his face, yet he smiled. "I love you."

With grass-stained fingers, Dillon touched a kiss to his mother's stone, and his father's, then he walked away.

His phone sat on the console where he'd left it. He started the ignition and woke up the screen. A message.

'Please come home.'

Just three words, but they were the words he'd been waiting for.

Maybe Kyan did hear him. Chuckling to himself, Dillon thumped the steering wheel. He was going home.

She still wasn't there.

But he knew where he'd find her.

Dillon pulled in and parked alongside Kyan's BMW on the gravel drive. It was time for both of them to get something new. Linnea didn't need to be driving around in his brother's old car and the Porsche wasn't exactly practical with a baby. He wasn't sure why the thought came to him now; they could decide what they wanted to do later.

The air was cooler here at the lake. Clean. Fresh. Breathing easy, Dillon inhaled watery ozone and moss deep into his lungs and opened the door.

She wasn't inside the house.

He saw her from the window and swallowed past the lump forming in his throat. Linnea sat on a blanket, Charlotte in her lap, beneath a tree down by the lake. Dillon tore down the wooden steps and raced across the lawn where they'd tossed a football to reach her.

She stood with the baby in her arms, and hurried toward him.

Then, at last, he held her.

Neither one of them spoke. Words could come later. His lips crashed into hers, their tongues twisting together. One taste of her and he was lost.

And, finally, he was home.

This girl had always been the beat of his heart, the sweetness to his soul. And he was never, ever letting her go.

They rocked together, the three of them, where they stood. He breathed in Linnea's almond scent and Charlotte's sweet baby smell, holding them both tight against him, like they would disappear if he didn't.

"You're really here," Linnea murmured softly, nuzzling into his neck.

"I'm here, gorgeous." Grinning up at him, Charlotte pulled on his shirt. He took the baby from Linnea's arms and squeezed her. "Hey, sweet pea."

"She missed you." Linnea sat on the blanket.

"I missed you both so much." Kissing the baby's curls, he sat beside her. "Being apart from you was painful. Please, don't ask me to do it again. I can't."

"Every night I looked up, Dillon." She laid her head on his shoulder. "Every night."

"I did too." He reached for her hand and paused. "You're not wearing your wedding ring."

"This tree has seen so much. We picnicked here. Kyan asked me to marry him here. We made love here." Tears sprang from her pretty green eyes. "So, it seemed only right to say goodbye, to let go of him here." She laced their fingers together and squeezed. "It's time."

His heart skipped a beat. "What are you saying?"

"It's time to turn the page and write a new chapter." She leaned over and kissed him. "Ours."

Driving in two separate cars, the ride back to the city was a long one. After the weeks spent in Dublin, the last thing Dillon wanted was to be apart from her. He took solace in knowing they had the rest of their lives to spend together.

Linnea pulled into her garage just as he came out of his. He got Charlotte out of her car seat. Squishing her little body against his chest, he peppered her face with kisses. Her joyful laughter was the sweetest symphony he'd ever heard.

They entered the backyard and his jaw dropped. Completely transformed, it looked nothing like it had when he left. "Baby, what did you do while I was gone?"

"Hm, checked off my to-do list." Inclining her head, Linnea winked. "I wanted a space where we could look up at the stars."

Dillon followed the direction of her gaze to an in-ground hot tub and grinned. "We are so going to be using that." He leaned over and kissed her. "A lot."

She giggled. "I have some steaks we can throw on the grill if you're hungry."

"I'm starving." He followed her inside. "For dessert. I'll call Rossi's and order us pizza. It's faster."

"Someone's impatient."

Kissing Charlotte on the forehead, he put her down in her playpen. Grabbing ahold of her hips, Dillon pulled Linnea against him and pressed his erection into her. "Fuck, yeah, I am." He kissed her again, plundering her mouth with his tongue. And he kept right on kissing her. He couldn't stop, and he never wanted to.

They scarfed down pizza—a Chicago special with all the toppings, because he knew that was her favorite. Afterward, he got down on the floor to play with Charlotte and read her a story. Dillon turned to the last page of *Goodnight Moon*. "The end."

"Okay, pretty girl." Linnea leaned down and smacking a kiss to his lips, took the baby from his lap. "Bath and bedtime."

He stood and walked over to the French doors, looking out into the darkness. Why wasn't he exhausted? God knows, after being up for well over twenty-four hours and a flight across the Atlantic, he should be. He'd never been more awake.

Hazy moonlight filtered down from the night sky, casting shadows upon the brick pavers. Dillon flipped on the switch and stripped out of his clothes, leaving them there on the floor. He didn't bother turning on the outside lighting, the moon was all they needed. Then he lowered himself into the water and waited.

Linnea called out to him from the open doorway. "Dillon?"

"I'm here." He skimmed his hand across the water.

She stood at the edge of the steaming pool. "What are you—"

"Take off your clothes."

His heated gaze flicked over her, watching as she grasped the hem of her shirt with trembling fingers and lifted it up and over her head. Linnea lowered the zipper and shimmied out of her denim skirt, leaving her in a lace bra and matching panty. She dipped her toes into the water.

He tipped his chin up. "I want you naked."

Obliging him, she reached behind her back. Pale-blue lace fell to the ground. Linnea skimmed her fingertips down the length of her body, over her luscious breasts, hooking them into the waistband of her panties.

He stared, mesmerized at the sight of her.

One heartbeat.

Two.

And the wisp of lace was gone.

He rose, offering her his hand. Linnea caught sight of the ink on his pec and with a surprised gasp, her eyes widened. Dillon helped her descend, halting her on the second step. His eyes level with the junction of her thighs, he grasped her hips, pulling her pussy to his mouth. He kissed her there.

Sweet fucking heaven.

Lifting her into the water, Dillon sat back in the lounger and settled her on his lap. Gazing into her pretty green eyes, he let his fingers slide across every inch of wet skin. He couldn't stop touching her.

Linnea placed her hand on his heart, her fingertips rubbing the ink. "What's this?"

"A rose."

"I can see that," she said, her lips forming a smirk.

"I saw the drawing in Tadhg's sketchbook." His thumb skimmed her soft cheek. "It reminded me of you."

She traced the outline of the burgundy rose he'd wear on his heart for her forever. "Just like the kind you always get me, even the color. It's beautiful, Dillon."

"Did you know a rose is considered a perfect flower?"

"I didn't."

"At the heart of the rose, there in its center, are the pistil and stamen. Male and female together. That's what makes it perfect." He played with a strand of caramel hair. "Look closer."

Tadhg inked their names together. Flawlessly incorporated into the design, you had to know it was there to see it.

Her eyes, pooling with tears, flicked over to his. "Oh, Dillon."

"The first time I got you flowers..." Running his fingers through her hair, a hesitant chuckle escaped. "...I made myself nuts deciding on which color. I didn't want to give you red roses, anything that might remind you of Kyan. I wanted you to think of me."

"Valentine's Day." Her hand rubbed over the rose on his chest.

"Yeah." Lowering his lids, he smiled. "The florist told me burgundy is the deepest, true shade of red and meant feelings that are yet to be revealed—seemed appropriate at the time. Means something else now."

Her hand stopped its movements. "What?"

"My love for you is deeper than red."

To Dillon the color symbolized his enduring passion for her. The deepest desire and truest affection. With his bruised and battered heart flayed open, the love he'd kept locked up inside it for so many years flowed in a torrent through his veins.

Linnea framed his face with her fingers. The tears rolling down her cheeks weren't sad ones. He could see light sparkling in those pretty green eyes he loved.

Lowering her lips to his, she whispered, "I love you, Dillon. In every conceivable way there is, I love you."

She kissed him then. Full, soft lips blanketing his, her tongue dipped inside his mouth. He fisted her hair, relishing the sensation of her naked breasts pressed against his chest.

Skin to skin.

Heart to heart.

Weightless in the water, Dillon effortlessly flipped them over, taking the dominant position. "Open your pretty eyes." Parting her thighs, he gazed into them. "Keep them on me."

She held her hand to the burgundy rose.

He held his to her breast, pushing his pulsing cock inside her.

Linnea bit into her bottom lip with a moan, her eyes remaining on his. Dillon stroked the delicate skin of her neck, gripping it and applying light pressure at the base, as his cock stroked in and out of her. He bent his lips to her ear, rasping into it, "For me, it's always been you."

She breathlessly mewled. Her pussy squeezing on his dick, inciting the primal urge within him to fuck her hard and fast. Dillon focused on her and ignored it. Nibbling on her ear. Stroking the backs of her thighs. Massaging her ass. Placing a leg over his shoulder, she opened wider. He touched every part of her. Inside and out.

He forced himself to slow down his thrusts. Way down. Three times slower. Four. Dillon brought his hands to her beautiful breasts, and squeezing the supple flesh, he pinched her nipples.

Hot nectar gushed on his dick. Her lips parted, the imprints from her teeth remained, and she breathed his name, "Dillon."

"Let go, baby. I've got you." He placed her hands flat on his pecs. "Always. I've got you."

She adjusted herself, both legs over his shoulders now. He kept to the tortuously slow pace. Their hands on each other's hearts.

In. Out. Breathe. In. Out. Breathe.

The tingling started at the base of his spine. Fueled by the love he felt for her, the energy spread further and further, sparking throughout his entire body. His soul.

This transcended the physical.

Joy.

Love.

Bliss.

His chest expanded with it. Healed, whole, and at peace. Love overflowed. It was like nothing he'd ever experienced before.

Staring into his eyes, Linnea lovingly smiled at him. "For a minute there, I thought my heart would explode."

Heart orgasm. Close enough.

Free to love, she let herself go with him. It was beautiful and magical. And this was only the beginning.

He kissed her. "Shall we head upstairs?"

"Sleepover?" She winked.

"Fuck, yeah, gorgeous." Dillon pressed a kiss to her forehead. "This is real. No more playing house."

"Good," Linnea replied with a grin, as he assisted her out of the water. "I saved boxes for you and made room in the closet."

"Oh yeah?"

"Yeah."

"C'mon then." He wrapped her in a towel and they headed into the house. "Did I miss anything while I was gone?"

"Oh, not too much." With a smirk, she pursed her lips to the side. "A wedding. A funeral."

The fuck?

"Whose?"

"I'll tell you all about it…" Taking him by the hand, Linnea pulled him behind her up the stairs. "…later."

Thirty-Four

The crisp air of an early fall morning drifted in through the open window, cooling his heated skin. Predawn light veiled the room in ghostly gray. Dillon held Linnea to his chest, both of them blanketed in sweat, as he rocked himself inside her.

He looked to her long blonde hair splayed out on the pillow beside him, and closing his eyes, he ran his fingers through the strands, gripping them in his palm. The absolute love of his life. Every moment with her was a moment cherished.

Linnea crooned her pleasure with every slap of his balls on her pussy. Completely unabashed, she pulled a nipple and rubbed her clit while he fucked her. Yeah, she knew he enjoyed the visual, and besides, it felt nice, didn't it? He lowered his head, sucking her unclaimed nipple deep inside his mouth.

"Oh, fuck."

Her pussy squeezed his dick. She was close. Dillon increased the power of his thrusts and pushing her fingers aside, replaced them with his own. Then he lifted his lips to hers, swallowing her cries.

Covering them with a blanket, he held her in his arms after. Stroking her soft skin. Kissing her hair. Basking in the afterglow, sunlight crept into the room. Charlotte would be awake soon. He kissed her brow. "I love you."

"And I love you."

Reluctantly, he got out from beneath the blanket and shivered. "Fucking hell." He rubbed his arms. "Remind me to close the window. I keep forgetting your brother's next door and those beautiful noises you make are for my ears only."

She covered her face with a pillow, then threw it at him, giggling. "I'm not that loud."

"Trust me, gorgeous." He winked. "You are."

At the office an hour later, Brendan was already settled in his club chair, a cup of coffee in front him, animatedly talking on the phone. Tipping his chin to acknowledge his cousin, Dillon went to brew himself a cup. Besides waking with Linnea well before sunrise, today was going to be an eventful day. He needed all the caffeine he could get.

Brendan ended his call. "That was Hailey's mom." He took a sip of his coffee. "She'll be finished with her project this weekend, so everything's a go for the opening next week."

He'd still never gone back there. Jesse hadn't either. Brendan saw to the onsite tasks at the warehouse. After the opening shindig, Dillon had no intentions of going anywhere near that place ever again.

"Good." His nod was less than enthusiastic. "How's Katie feeling?"

"She's fine." Expecting their second baby in May, Brendan grinned from ear to ear. "And excited to have Charlotte for the evening. You ready?"

He had the tickets, the ring, and the words. Well, for the most part he did. It's not like he had a speech written out on three-by-five index cards or anything.

"Yeah." Releasing a breath, he smiled at the same time.

"Can I say something?"

"Could I stop you?" Dillon chuckled.

Brendan smirked. "No, probably not." He leaned toward him and exhaled with a bob of his head. "It's your turn, Dillon. Don't feel guilty because you're happy."

"I don't. Well, most of the time I don't, but Kyan—"

"Would tell you the same." Brendan placed an envelope in his hand. "It's time you read this."

He already knew what was inside. Dillon pulled the folded sheets of notebook paper, covered in Hailey's shaky scrawl, from the envelope. *"Take care of them, brother."* He didn't try to stop them. Glancing at Brendan, tears rolled down his face.

"Kyan's destiny was to love her first. Yours is to love her for the rest of her life."

He took her back to the planetarium. The moon. Stargazing. It was their thing after all.

Dillon got tickets to the skywatch event. A chilly October night, he kept Linnea close, their arms linked together, as they strolled the promenade after the show. He stopped so they could take in the amazing skyline view across the water. The city lights reflected on its surface in a myriad of colors. It seemed as if they were shining just for them.

He hugged Linnea closer to him, kissing her crown. "Look up." She did.

Dillon got down on his knee.

Then she gazed at him with those pretty green eyes of hers and the words he had flew right out of his head. All of a sudden, those index cards seemed like they would have been a good idea.

He took her hands in his and squeezed them. "I can still vividly recall the very first glimpse I had of you. Every detail of it. I remember saying to myself, '*One day, you're going to marry that girl—after you're thirty*'."

Tears sprang from the corners of her eyes accompanied by a soft burst of laughter.

"I fell in love with you that day, Linnea, and I never stopped. I tucked it away for a while, but…with you, I never stopped wanting more."

Dillon took the ring he had chosen for her himself from his pocket. He found the five-carat pear-shaped diamond at a jewelers on Grafton Street in Dublin. Set in platinum on a diamond band, as soon as he saw it, he knew that was the ring he was putting on her finger.

"So, I'm asking for more." Heart pounding in his chest, he paused for a beat and looked directly into her pretty green eyes. "Will you marry me?"

"Yes." She sniffled, her chin wobbling. "It's a date."

He slid the ring on her finger and got off his knee. "New Year's in Cabo, gorgeous." Wrapping her in his arms, with the stars and the moon shining down on them, and the backdrop of a sparkling city skyline, he kissed her.

Later, after all the hugs, kisses, and congratulatory toasts that awaited them from everyone gathered at Brendan's when they returned to pick up the baby, Dillon ran the bath while his wife-to-be tucked Charlotte in her crib. Champagne chilled in a bucket of ice. Candles.

"If Tadhg could see me now." He chuckled to himself, pouring bath salts and fresh flower petals into the water. Would they revoke his man card for this? "God, I'm so pussy-whipped."

But he loved Linnea, and she loved her baths. Dillon glanced at the package. He'd endure smelling like calendula and lavender every night of his life if it meant she was happy.

He stripped off his clothes and got in the big clawfoot tub. Then he called out to her, "Linnea."

Her head peeked through the door and her eyes widened. Pushing the door all the way open, she stepped inside. "Baby, what did you do?"

"Made you a bath." He crooked a finger. "Get in."

He held her hand as she stepped inside the tub. Linnea sat between his thighs, her back to his chest. Dillon poured the champagne into glasses. He leaned over her shoulder, and kissing her neck, he handed her one.

His fingers sank into her flesh, massaging the tension from her muscles. She moaned between sips of champagne and tipped her head back onto his shoulder. Dillon took the glass from her hand and set it on the floor.

He pulled her shoulders toward him, so her back rested on his chest, her lush bottom snug against his rock-hard dick, and let his fingers slip downward to squeeze her breasts. Not too big or too small, they fit in his hands just right. He massaged them, brushing circles over her nipples with his thumbs.

"Baby, this feels like heaven." Linnea held onto his thighs and shifted her bottom against him. "You inside me would feel even better."

Fuck, yeah, it would.

She lifted her hips and grasping his cock, Linnea notched him at her entrance. "Oh, fuck," she mewled, slowly impaling herself.

Dillon watched himself disappear inside her. "I fucking love you."

Linnea turned her head on his shoulder and yanked his mouth to hers, their kiss a voracious feeding. Messy and hungry. Feral.

His cock throbbed inside her. He thrust up.

Using his legs for leverage, she pushed down.

Dillon squeezed her nipples.

Linnea took his hand and brought it to her clit.

He rubbed her hard and fast, the way he knew she liked it, until she screamed his name. Then lifting her from his cock, he turned her over, chest to chest, and pushed back inside her. Cradling her head in his hands, he kissed her softly and fucked her slowly.

Lost in their languid rhythm, Dillon dropped his hands. He caressed her shoulders, rubbed her spine, and squeezed the globes of her ass.

"Touch me there," she whispered against his skin.

Dillon glanced to the shelf of bath potions she kept by the tub and reached for a bottle of sweet almond oil. He poured some in his hand, liberally coating his fingers.

"Yes," she purred. Shimmying on his dick, Linnea held her cheeks open for him.

He rubbed up and down her crease, massaging the oil in circles at her puckered entrance. "I want to fuck you here."

"I want you to, baby." She pinched his nipples beneath her. "I want to feel everything with you."

He pushed a finger past the ring of muscle and she moaned. "Tell me all your fantasies. Every secret desire. I'll give them to you."

"You."

Fuck.

He slid a second finger in and scissored it inside her.

"I used to imagine what your cock looked like. Dreamt of it. Of you and Kyan fucking me together. I remember crying when I saw you because you were just so beautiful." She was crying now. "I'd never felt so loved as I did that day."

"I'll never share you, baby. I can't."

"I don't want you to." She kissed him. "The only man I want is you. But God help me, every fantasy I've ever had you were in it. So make me feel everything."

Everything you never even thought to dream of, gorgeous.

"I promise."

With an arm around Linnea, Dillon held Charlotte in the other. The late October breeze tossed dark curls around the burgundy bow in her hair. She gazed up at him with her beaming smile, proudly displaying four baby teeth. So beautiful. He kissed her forehead. Ten months old now, she looked like his mother and brother more and more every day.

They all stood together at the entrance to the old warehouse. Kyan's last project. The place where he died. Dillon refrained from gazing toward the sidewalk where he'd seen him lying in a pool of blood beneath a sheet. The mere thought of revisiting the scene made him physically ill.

One hour.

He'd force himself to get through it. They'd cut the ribbon to the door of the new shopping mall, unveil Hailey's art project, and go home. Piece of cake, right? Thankfully, Linnea never asked for the details of what they'd seen that horrific day. Her last memory of Kyan was kissing him goodbye before he went to the office.

Carrying Ireland, who was itching to get out of her father's hold, Jesse solemnly stood at his side, vacantly gazing down the sidewalk. They exchanged a glance. No words needed to be spoken. Taylor and Chloe were on the other side of his cousin, holding Chandan's hands between them. Brendan, balancing Declan on his hip, and Katie were to Linnea's left. Kodiak, Venery, and everyone else stood directly behind them.

And in the chill of a crisp autumn morning, they waited.

After what felt like forever, Brendan placed his son in the arms of his wife, to greet the members of the neighborhood's redevelopment council. He spoke a few words, but Dillon wasn't listening, then the president cut the ribbon and the doors opened.

He could breathe once they filed inside, where he didn't have to see the sidewalk. The interior was magnificent. Exactly as his brother had drawn it. Kyan would have been pleased.

In the center court, a dozen young girls in plaid pleated skirts stood waiting. Dillon recognized Hailey amongst them. They took their seats in metal folding chairs that had been placed in front of a covered wall.

Brendan shook hands with a woman, Dillon presumed it was Hailey's mother, and a nun in a long habit and veil. Then he, too, took his seat beside Katie. The nun went to the podium, rosary beads clanking at her side.

She cleared her throat. "Good morning. Every year, the graduating class of St. Bartholomew's Parish School participates in a project to beautify our neighborhood. The students come up with a concept on their own. They plan it, design it, and implement it.

"Last spring, one of those students came to me with her vision for this year's project, to which her classmates and I wholeheartedly agreed. We could think of no better way to fulfill the mission of our project than to honor the man who strived to preserve the beauty of our neighborhood…" Going off script, she glanced up from her notecards and smiled. "…he drafted the renovation of this very building."

Dillon squeezed Linnea's hand.

Inhaling deeply, the nun went back to the notes in front of her. "To honor the man who saved the lives of two young students, without giving thought to his own."

The nun dipped her wimpled head.

Hailey and another girl removed the covering from the wall.

He didn't hear one word the nun spoke after that. It was a mosaic. At least twenty feet wide and nearly as tall, irregular pieces of stone, glass, and ceramic had been fitted together, held in place with mortar, to create a stunning mural of the city skyline with the moon and stars shining down from above.

...just like the moon and stars...

"Do you think he's up there watching over us?"

"I don't know."

"I like to think so."

"Maybe he is."

Yeah, maybe. How in the hell did Hailey know? Just a coincidence? Life was full of them, but somehow Dillon didn't think so.

"It's beautiful, isn't it?" Linnea inspected the tesserae up close, her fingertips brushing over the surface.

"It is," Dillon agreed from behind her, a restless Charlotte tugging on his tie.

Hailey approached him then. "Do you like it?"

"It's perfect." Dillon smiled at her. "What made you think of it?"

"I don't know." She shrugged, her cheeks turning pink. "I had a dream."

"You doing okay?"

"Yeah."

"I read your letter." He winked. "Thank you, Hailey."

She glanced from the baby in his arms to Linnea beside him. "Are you two together now?"

"Yes."

"I'm glad." She closed her eyes for a second, her lips curving into a smile. "I think he wanted that."

Family stays together...I love you, brother.

And the odd man out no longer, they were his. Somehow, in the midst of sorrow they'd found joy. In their love for each other. Charlotte. Their family. Carousel rides and champagne slushies. Roasting marshmallows on a fire. Dillon touched his fingers to a star and smiled, a single tear sliding down his cheek. Grief might not have a timeline, but he was so fucking thankful that within a broken heart, sorrow and joy could coexist.

Dillon came inside from the patio later that afternoon. Linnea was in the mood for barbecue, so he had a nice cut of brisket on the smoker. She was curled up in an oversized chair, looking comfy, and yeah, sexy as fuck, wearing one of his old Bears sweatshirts, sniffling as she read on her Kindle.

"Is that the book that makes you cry?"

She looked up, swiping her pretty green eyes. "No, it's the sequel."

He still didn't understand why crying over a fictional character was her idea of a good time, but Linnea obviously enjoyed it. Their house was filled with her books. Dillon sat on the arm of the chair, cuddling her. "So, which guy did she end up with?"

"Neither," she replied and kissed his cheek. "She found her happily ever after with the other brother."

Love.

It rarely goes like you read in the storybooks, Dillon supposed. Sometimes ugly, often messy. But then truth can be stranger than fiction, yeah? Look at their love story. As long and difficult as his journey to Linnea had been, it only taught him to love her even more. Appreciate life more. He'd never take one fucking moment of it for granted.

And that's how he'd honor his brother's legacy.

Later that night, they relaxed together in the hot tub. Steam rose from the water into the chilly air. Dillon lifted Linnea onto his lap. Gazing into the eyes he loved, he brushed her lips with his. "You fill my soul."

Pages of their story were still left to be written, but he already knew how it went.

Linnea was Dillon's, and he was hers.

He looked up.

The moon shined down upon them.

He couldn't see the stars, but they were there.

Epilogue

He should have known better than to go this way. Xander loved to look at the pictures that hung on the wedding wall. He tried slipping past, but his son wasn't having it. Dillon hoisted him up on his hip. "Okay, okay."

The baby pointed to the portrait at the top of the pyramid of photos. "That is your great-grandma and grandpa. They bought this house a long, long time ago—way before any of us were even born."

Xander waved his little hand. Dillon knew the drill and moved on to the next row. "That's your great-aunt, Mo, and Uncle Jimmy," he said, smiling at his son. "And look, there's *Aintín* and Uncle Tommy. Shall we go outside and see her? She and Uncle Tadhg flew all the way across the ocean to be here for your birthday."

Dillon started to turn away. Some photos were still painful for him to look at. But Xander protested. "That's my mom and dad, your grandma and grandpa. And you and me are both named after him. We both look like him too. Look, you even got his hair."

He chuckled. It was true. Charles Alexander Byrne was the spitting image of his father, raven hair and all. Dillon was sure that wherever Charley was, he was tickled over that.

"There's your Uncle B and Aunt Katie."

Xander grinned at the familiar faces. "Li, li, li," he babbled.

"That was before Leah was born. She's not in the picture, but she's outside waiting for you." Dillon kissed his son's cheek. "C'mon, little dude."

But Xander still wasn't having it.

"Okay." He blew out a breath. "There's Uncle Jesse, Aunt Chloe, and Uncle Tay. And next to them is…"

"Ma, ma, ma, ma."

"That's right. Mommy and Uncle Ky." Unshed tears burned in the back of his eyes. Dillon rubbed a curl of his son's dark hair between his fingers. Just like Kyan's. "And last is Mommy, your sister, and me on a beach in Mexico."

"Ma, ma, ma, ma."

"Okay, little guy." He lifted his son in the air over his head and he giggled. "Let's go get us some cake. Trust me, you're going to love it."

Xander didn't protest this time. Maybe it wasn't the photos so much, but the stories that he loved.

Grabbing the pack of baby wipes Linnea asked for, Dillon glanced out the window. Chloe, Katie, and Linnea sat building castles in the sand with the girls. Brendan had the boys together on the lawn taking turns catching a football that Jesse tossed to them.

His cousin was right. Thanks to him, they'd have two football teams here before long. Chandan and Ireland welcomed another sister, London, almost two years ago, and Ashton Michael Thomas Kerrigan Nolan was due to arrive around Thanksgiving. Jesse swore this baby would be their last, but knowing Chloe, Dillon wasn't so sure.

"Good thing we expanded the deck," he muttered as he carried his son out the door, waving to Colleen and Tadhg soaking in the hot tub.

Yeah, they installed a big one—an outdoor kitchen and fireplace too. With all these kids, they'd be remodeling the basement next. They were running out of room and they had to sleep somewhere, didn't they?

Wipes in hand, Dillon passed the boys on the lawn, and walked over to his girls. He let Xander down to toddle in the grass by the sand.

"Daddy, Daddy," Charlotte squealed, jumping up the second she saw he was back, and running into his arms.

"Hey, sweet pea." He hugged Kyan's daughter, *his* daughter, kissing the hair on her head.

Charlotte knew she had two daddies who loved her very much. She was aware that her other daddy was his brother and thought of him as a star in the sky watching over her. At three and a half, she didn't really comprehend what death was yet. He and Linnea told her Kyan's stories, and through them she would come to know what an incredible man her father was.

"Are you going to show Daddy what you made with Mommy?"

Dillon grabbed Xander by the hand and followed Charlotte to the sand.

Linnea glanced up at him with a smirk. "Took you long enough. Let me guess." She giggled. "The wedding wall?"

"You guessed right." He leaned down and kissed her.

"Here." Standing up, she thrust Xander's twin sister into his arms. "She missed you."

His little sunbeam. Madison Margaret Grace, named after their mothers, favored his wife. Her hair was the palest blonde and her eyes the bluest blue—same as they all had. Those Byrne genes must be strong.

"I'm going to take Charlotte for a quick dip with the older ones. We won't be long, and then we can have cake." She kissed him. "I love you, handsome."

"I love you too, gorgeous."

God, he loved her. And his children. His family. He loved his life. Every day of it.

Seven years had gone by since that first Fourth of July. Sitting in the sand with his twins on their first birthday, Dillon glanced around him, taking it all in. He looked in awe at this big, beautiful family they'd created. His greatest strength and his only weakness. His joy. Together, their love shined brighter than all the stars in the sky.

"Dillon?" Linnea called out from the shore.

She stood there, pointing to their daughter. Stunned.

"Dill, do you think my turtle will be okay?"

"Sure, Ky. He just missed playing with the other turtles, that's all."

Charlotte crouched in front of a big, old turtle, petting its time-worn shell.

Grabbing the twins, Dillon scampered to the shore. His cousins, having heard Linnea shout with alarm, came up behind him.

Jesse reached Charlotte and the turtle first. He glanced back to him and Brendan. "No way. It can't be Kyan's turtle after all these years, can it?"

"They can live a long time." Brendan shrugged. "It's possible."

But Dillon knew in his gut that it was.

See, Kyan? Told you he'd be fine.

"Take care of them, brother." He heard his voice clear as day, as if he were right there behind him. Dillon turned around, but no one was there.

"Always, Kyan," he spoke out loud, not caring who heard him. A single tear rolled down his face. "Always."

I love you.

Epilogue

Matthew "Matt" McCready

She came back. He knew that she would. "Wanna fuck?"

"What?" She cocked her head, indignant.

But then, why else would she be here? That's all any of them ever wanted.

"You heard me. Do you wanna fuck?"

"Wow!" She slowly shook her head. "You're bold."

He didn't have time for bullshit. "The answer to an unasked question is always no." Taking a step closer, Matt saw she wasn't just pretty. Long, dark hair. Hazel eyes. No, she was beautiful. And she didn't back away from him, even though he wished she would.

Run, rabbit, run.

"Why should I?"

"Because you want to." He smirked. "I've seen you looking. You've been imagining this big dick inside that pretty little cunt of yours for weeks." He nuzzled his nose in her neck, smelling her, and softly growled. "Know what, bunny? I've been thinking about it too."

"I don't even like you."

"Yes, you do."

"No, I don't."

He took her hand and placed it on the hard bulge in his jeans. She whimpered. "You do."

"I don't."

Matt slid his hand inside her pants and felt between her legs. "See?" He held up his finger, coated with her sweetness. "You like me," he informed her, licking the taste of her from his finger. "I'd say you like me a helluva lot."

The End
...until *Drummer Boy*

Acknowledgments

It isn't often that I'm at a loss for words, but as I sit here writing this, not quite a week after typing 'The *End*' to Dillon's story, the last of the Byrne cousins, I have none—none that are adequate anyway. Any and every emotion you felt reading this book, I experienced tenfold writing it—and I still am. But Kyan would be the first to tell you, as he told me, "This is always how their story was meant to go."

As you can imagine, this book was extremely difficult to write—it was so, so hard. I had to painstakingly pry every single word out to get them onto the screen. I felt Dillon's pain, his hesitancy, his healing, and in the end, his joy. Linnea was the only woman he could ever truly love. The Pinterest board and the playlist for *The Other Brother* on Spotify and YouTube are open. Bo's story, *Drummer Boy*, is next in the *Red Door Series*, coming in 2022, as well as a twisty stepbrother romance, *Don't Speak*. As always, I've included sneak peeks following these acknowledgments.

I know I say this every time, and I'm sure I'll continue to say it—this is so surreal. Book 4. *Serenity* released less than two years ago. I couldn't have imagined then that this is where we'd be now. I have so many people to thank for being on this journey with me, supporting me, and loving me. These people are my family. My tribe. My heart.

Thank you to my babies—**Michael** and **Raj, Charlie, Christian, Josie Lynn** and **Josh, Zach** and **Sam, Jaide, Julian, Olivia,** and **Jocelyn,** who is due to make her debut into the world *very* soon! Never stop looking up. I love you more than all the stars in the sky.

My healthcare family, most especially **my fellow nurses** who are still on the frontlines of COVID. I know how hard you work and how much you sacrifice. I know you're tired. *You* are the true heroes of the world. I am humbled, and so honored, to work among you. Thank you for everything you do.

My editor extraordinaire, **Michelle Morgan.** Gif wars weren't nearly as fun with this one, were they? Lots of crying and hugs. While this story was painful, thanks to her, editing it was painless. It remains my favorite part of the writing process. I truly, truly, truly couldn't do this without her. I love you, beautiful!!! xoxo

Linda Russell and her fantastic team at **Foreword PR.** Where do I even start? I don't know what other publicists do, and I'll never know, because I hit the jackpot with mine—and she's stuck with me! Linda alpha reads each chapter as I write them (she's been crying since March, folks). She listens to me vent, my plans and ideas, while she tirelessly works behind the scenes for me and all of her authors. My selfless, loyal, trustworthy friend—all my love and thanks go to you. It seems like forever ago we had that first conversation…I listened to every wise thing you told me, and that won't ever change. A Foreword girl from day one, and I *always* will be. I love you hard!!! xoxo

The amazing, beautiful, and brilliantly talented, **Michelle Lancaster,** my cover queen of hearts. She captured this exquisite and captivating image of **Tommy Pearce**—it's a true work of art. I knew it was the cover of this book the second I saw it. I teared up, that's how perfect it was. Every conceivable emotion Dillon experienced is right there in Tommy's eyes. I often wonder what he was thinking of at that moment. On a side note, Michelle and I have more gorgeousness coming your way, don't we? I'm such a tease, I know. My deepest thanks to both of these beautiful humans. I love you from the bottom of my heart!!! xoxo

Lori Jackson took that hauntingly beautiful image of Tommy and created this masterpiece of a cover—it's absolute perfection and I can never thank her enough for the magic she makes. She's such a joy to work with and I'm looking forward to all the future covers we have planned. Yeah, I'm teasing you again. I love you, Lori!!! xoxo

Ashlee O'Brien is a dear and special person to me. Together from the beginning. Not only is she the design goddess behind *Ashes*

and Vellichor, trusted and loyal, she's my book daughter, and in so many ways my right hand. Together with Linda, she is the only other person who reads each chapter as I write them. She likes to make me cry—it's her goal. Overachiever that she is, Ashlee knocked it wayyyy out of the park this time. I get teary-eyed every time she sends me a file, but I sobbed out loud (ugly cried) when I saw the cover reveal trailer. Her gift, her ability to visually nail a story, always astounds me. No idea how she does it. Ashlee tells me she has an idea and I don't question it. I just tell her, do your thing, girlie. The trust goes both ways. Now, as I'm writing this, I haven't seen the full pre-release trailer yet. But I'm going to have a full box of Puffs at the ready. Oh, and Dillon is hers. I love you to the moon and the stars, Ashlee!!! xoxo

Stacey Blake of *Champagne Book Design* is the queen of formatting. As I write this, *The Other Brother* is still with my editor and beta readers, but I already know the pages behind the cover are going to be beautiful. She's just that good at what she does. I love you, neighbor—so close and yet so far, right? I'll meet you at the mouse house one of these days! xoxo

Hilary Robinson for proofreading through blurry eyes I appreciate you. xoxo

My beta team—**Jessica Biggs, Jennifer Bishop, Kim DiPeiro, Heather Hahn, Charbee Lightfield, Marjorie Lord, Melinda Parker, Sabrena Simpson, Rebecca Vazquez,** and **Lindsey Ward,** together with my **ARC team**—I'm sorry for tearing your hearts to shreds and making you cry. Thank you for knowing me well enough and trusting that I'd put it back together. I'm glad, though, that Dillon's story touched your heart. Thank you for loving it through all the tears. I love and appreciate you so very much.

Bloggers and Bookstagrammers—It would be remiss of me not to recognize your continued support of the *Red Door Series*. I'm beyond grateful every time one of you likes a post or shares a graphic. All the beautiful edits. You blow me away!!! I appreciate every single thing you do, big or small, to support me and share my books with readers. There isn't one indie author that would be anywhere without you, your love of books, and your dedication to us—so thank you, thank you, thank you!!!

The beautiful **Redlings** in my Facebook group, *Behind the Red Door*. They hold a special place in my heart, always. Knowing these wonderful humans, they already have a support thread going should you need it. Join them—you'll never meet a more welcoming group of people.

And as always, my lovely **readers**—thank you for still being here and loving the *Red Door* world. I know how real these characters become to us, and how heartbreaking it can be to say goodbye. Kyan will always be with us—he lives in our hearts and on the pages forever. I can't thank you enough for loving him, Dillon and Linnea, Chloe, Jesse, and Taylor, Brendan and Katie, Bo, Kodiak, Matt, Kit, and Sloan. Good things are coming…I promise!

Until *Drummer Boy*…

Much love,
Dyan xoxo

Sneak Peek of *Drummer Boy*—Red Door #5

Three years ago…Tampa, Florida

"What's your name?" Bo asked the girl.

She was young, pretty, with long blonde hair and soulful blue eyes. Just his type. Not that he had a particular type—did he? Bo had to admit he was attracted to her, though. There was something about her that set her apart from all the other fans waiting backstage to meet them.

"Shelley."

"Short for Michelle?"

"No. Just Shelley."

"Well, it's nice to meet you Shelley, not short for Michelle."

But she'd already moved down the line.

"I love you, Taylor!" the girl gushed, hugging his bandmate.

Too bad she didn't know the lead guitarist of Venery hated that shit. Bo liked it, though. A lot. He was a hugger. A toucher. A kisser. A lover.

You put your money on the wrong horse, stupid girl.

Yeah, there was something about her. Bo couldn't put his finger on it, but as he watched her fangirl all over Taylor, blood rushed to fill his cock. Deliciously fuckable. Soft and warm. Craving some pussy tonight, he licked his lips as if he could already taste her.

If Bo couldn't have her, then surely another groupie would be more than happy to accommodate him. He wanted to fuck *her*, though. Shelley, not short for Michelle.

One of the radio station people put a big plastic cup in his hand. Their logo, the band's logo, and the tour sponsor's branding for a new alcoholic beverage were plastered all over it. A beer and whiskey kind of guy, Bo took a tentative sip of the carbonated Kool-Aid. It wasn't half bad.

"Don't taste like anything's in here. I can get a buzz off this shit?" He downed half the contents in one swallow.

"Yeah, man." The radio station dude bobbed his head, a dopey grin on his face. He reminded Bo of Sean Penn in that old 80s movie his mom liked. Surfer dude. Spicoli. What was the name of it? "Fourteen percent alcohol by volume. Trust me, you'll be feelin' it."

"Well, all right." Bo drained his cup and the Spicoli look-alike put another one in his hand.

These meet and greets grew tedious. He figured he might as well get something out of it. Get drunk. Get laid. Get back on the motherfucking bus. Then tomorrow he'd get to do it all over again.

"Might as well enjoy it," he muttered to himself. Just a few more weeks and they'd be back home in Chicago.

"Enjoy what?" Taylor leaned into him, a plastic tour cup dangling in his hand.

Like the deviant he was, Bo grinned. "Debauchery."

"What's it to be tonight, mate?" His bandmate chuckled. "See a bird or bloke that you fancy?"

He homed in on the girl with long blonde hair. Shelley, not short for Michelle, stood with her nondescript friend at the portable bar drinking carbonated Kool-Aid. Fingers rubbing over his bare chest, his thumb grazed a nipple. Bo's dick twitched in his tight leather pants.

"Yeah." He pointed to her. "I want that one."

"Aidan, baby."

His mother took him by the hand and pulled him along behind her as she hurried out of the kitchen. He'd only eaten half of his grilled cheese sandwich and some grapes when the banging started. It startled him and he knocked over his juice. By the time she went to the front door to see who it was, the banging noise was coming from the other side of the house.

"You can't keep me out, bitch."

It was a man. He was yelling. He sounded angry. Aidan didn't recognize his voice.

His mother seemed to, though. Her eyes got real big and she covered her mouth with her hand. It was shaking.

There was a hutch in the living room that the television sat on. It had doors on the bottom. He hid in there sometimes. His mother opened one of the doors, and tossing the toys that were inside it to the floor, she kissed him on his head and urged him to crawl inside.

"We're going to play a game of hide and seek from the loud man outside, okay, baby?" his mother whispered.

Aidan nodded.

The banging got louder.

"You have to be very, very quiet so he doesn't know you're here." It sounded like she was choking and tears leaked out of her eyes, but she smiled at him.

"Like at story time?"

Aidan's mother took him to story time at the library every Saturday, and afterward if he'd been a good boy, she would let him get an ice cream.

"Yes, baby. Just like that." She nodded with tears running down her face. "Now stay very still and don't speak a word until I tell you to—no matter what, okay?"

He nodded again. "Okay, Mommy."

"I love you, Aidan."

"I love you, Mommy."

* * *

Everyone said the place was haunted. The kids at school. The people in town. It didn't look scary, but nobody ever went anywhere near the two-story white clapboard house that was set off by itself on the cove.

It was to be her home now.

Molly stood at the wrought-iron gate with her mother, holding onto her hand. She clutched her *Bear in the Big Blue House* backpack, that she'd had since she was four, with the other. A boy with sandy-blond hair sat on the porch steps. Aidan Fischer. He didn't pay them, or his father unloading their belongings from the U-Haul, any mind. He had a notebook in his lap and a pencil between his fingers. It looked like he was drawing.

The boy chewed on his lip as he moved the pencil over the paper. Even though he was in the fifth grade, and three years older than her, Molly knew who he was. Everybody did. He was the boy who didn't talk. And six days from today, when her mother married his father, that boy was going to be her brother.

Books by
DYAN LAYNE

The Red Door Series
Serenity
Affinity
Maelstrom
The Other Brother
Drummer Boy (coming soon)

Standalones
Don't Speak (coming soon)

About the Author

Dyan Layne is a nurse boss by day and the writer of edgy sensual tales by night—and on weekends. She's never without her Kindle, and can usually be found tapping away at her keyboard with a hot latte *and* a cold Dasani Lime—and sometimes champagne. She can't sing a note, but often answers in song because isn't there a song for just about everything? Born and raised a Chicago girl, she currently lives in Tampa, Florida, and is the mother of four handsome sons and a beautiful daughter, who are all grown up now, but can still make her crazy—and she loves it that way! Because normal is just so boring.

One

I'm going to fuck you. You may not know it yet, but I do. It's only a matter of time. I've been watching you. I swear that you've been watching me too, but maybe it's all in my head. No matter. Because I've seen you, I've talked to you and I've come to a conclusion: You are fucking beautiful. And I will make you lust me.

The words danced on crisp white paper. Her fingers trembled and her feet became unsteady, so she leaned against the wall of exposed brick to right herself, clutching the typewritten note in her hand. She read it again. A powerful longing surged through her body and her thighs clenched.

Who could have written it? She couldn't fathom a single soul who might be inspired to write such things to her. Maybe those words weren't meant for her? Maybe whoever had written the note slid it beneath the wrong doormat in his haste to deliver it undetected?

Linnea Martin, beautiful? Someone had to be pulling a prank. *Yeah. That's more likely.*

She sighed as she turned and closed the solid wood front door. She glanced up at the mirror that hung in the entry hall and eyes the color of moss blinked back at her. Long straight hair, the color of which she had never been able to put into a category—a dirty-blonde maybe—hung past her shoulders, resting close to where her nipples protruded against the fitted cotton shirt she wore. Her skin was fair, but not overly pale. She supposed some people might describe her as pretty, in an average sort of way, but not beautiful.

Not anything but ordinary.

Linnea slowly crumpled up the note in her hand. She clenched it tight and held it to her breast before tossing it into the wastebasket.

Deflated, she threw her tote bag on the coffee table and plopped down on the pale-turquoise-colored sofa that she'd purchased at that quaint secondhand store on First Avenue. She often stopped in there on her way home from the restaurant, carefully eyeing the eclectic array of items artfully displayed throughout the shop. Sometimes, on a good day when tips had been plentiful, she bought herself something nice. Something pretty. Like the pale-turquoise sofa.

Linnea grabbed the current novel she was engrossed in from the coffee table and adjusted herself into a comfortable position, attempting to read. But after she read the same page three times she knew she couldn't concentrate, one sentence blurred into the next, so she set it back down. She clicked on the television and scrolled through the channels, but there was nothing on that could hold her interest. The words replayed in her head.

I'm going to fuck you.

Damn him! Damn that fucker to hell for being so cruel to leave that note at her door, for making her feel…things. The words had thrilled her for a fleeting moment, but then the excitement quickly faded, replaced by a loneliness deep in her chest. Love may never be in the cards for her, or lust for that matter, as much as she might want it to be.

Once upon a time she had believed in fairy tales and dreamt of knights on white stallions and handsome princes, of castle turrets shrouded in mist, of strong yet gentle hands weaving wildflowers in her long honeyed locks—just like the alpha heroes in the tattered paperbacks she had kept hidden under her bed as a teenager. She thought if she was patient long enough, her happily-ever-after would come. She thought that one day, when she was all grown up, that a brave knight, a handsome prince, would rescue her from her grandmother's prison and make all her dreams come true.

Stupid girl.

Her dreams turned into nightmares, and 'one day' never came. She doubted it ever would now. It was her own fault anyway. She closed her eyelids tight, trying to stop the tears that threatened to escape, to keep the memories from flooding back. Linnea had spent years pushing them into an unused corner, a vacant place where they could be hidden away and never be thought of again.

It was dark. She must have been sitting there for quite a while, transfixed in her thoughts. The small living room was void of illumination, except for the blue luminescence that radiated from the unwatched television. Linnea dragged herself over to it and clicked it off. She stood there for a moment waiting for her eyes to adjust to the absence of light and went upstairs.

Steaming water flowed in a torrent from the brushed-nickel faucet, filling the old clawfoot tub. She poured a splash of almond oil into the swirling liquid. As the fragrance released, she bent over the tub to breathe in the sweet vapor that rose from the water and wafted through the room. Slipping the sleeves from her shoulders, the silky robe gave way and fell to a puddle on the floor.

Timorously, she tested the water with her toes, and finding it comfortably hot, she eased her body all the way in. For a time serenity could be found in the soothing water that enveloped her.

You may not know it yet, but I do. It's only a matter of time.

At once her pulse quickened, and without conscious thought her slick fingertips skimmed across her rosy nipples. They hardened at her touch. And a yearning flourished between the folds of flesh down below. Linnea clenched her thighs together, trying to make it go away, but with her attempt to squelch the pulsing there, she only exacerbated her budding desire. And she ached.

Ever so slowly, her hands eased across her flat belly to rest at the junction between her quivering thighs. She wanted so badly to touch herself there and alleviate the agony she found herself in. But as badly as she wanted to, needed to, Linnea would not allow herself the pleasure of her own touch. She sat up instead, the now-tepid water sloshing forward with the sudden movement, and reaching out in front of her she turned the water back on.

She knew it was wicked. Lying there with her legs spread wide and her feet propped on the edge of the tub, she allowed the violent stream of water to pound upon her swollen bud. It throbbed under the assault and her muscles quaked. She'd be tempted to pull on her nipples if she wasn't forced to brace her hands against the porcelain walls of the clawfoot tub for leverage.

Any second now. She was so close.

I'm going to fuck you.

And he did. With just his words, he did.

Her head tipped back as the sensations jolted through her body. The sounds of her own keening cries were muffled by the downpour from the faucet. Spent, she let the water drain from the tub and rested her cheek upon the cold porcelain.

Prologue

C hloe looked around the frilly pink bedroom.

Where to start?

What do you take with you and what parts of your girlhood do you leave behind? She wasn't sure. She didn't feel any different today than she did yesterday, but today was different.

Today her life as a real adult began. She had her acceptance letter into the marketing and graphic design program at the college she wanted. In the city. She had a little apartment just waiting for her to move into. She only had to pack up her life and go.

Armed with empty boxes and tape, Chloe sifted through drawers and emptied her closet. She was surprised at the lack of nostalgia as she sorted her things. She had expected to feel some. She didn't. Her fingertips rubbed at a spot on the bright-pink satin comforter where she sat upon the white canopy bed, memorizing the familiar feel of it, as she scanned the posters and pictures that adorned the walls.

She smiled.

Taylor Kerrigan smiled back at her. Well, sort of. It was more like a smirk. A smoldering bad-boy smirk. He had long lustrous black hair with caramel highlights that flowed over broad shoulders. His bare chest was chiseled and a myriad of tattoos accentuated his perfect olive skin. How could any man be that beautiful?

Photoshop, that's how.

The lead guitarist of Venery had been her fantasy man, her celebrity crush, ever since their first album came out. He was there when she cried her eyes out over that douchebag Danny Damiani when he broke up with her just a week before junior prom last year. She'd wiped the tears from her eyes and there was Taylor with that sexy grin. If that asshole quarterback thought she was going to miss her prom because of him, he'd best think again. Danny took Brittany McCall instead, who apparently drank one too many glasses of spiked punch and yakked up the contents of her stomach in front of the entire junior class in the middle of the dancefloor. Chloe had gone stag with her friends, had a blast and giggled at the sight of Mr. Popular futilely attempting to clean off the vomit that dripped down his tux.

Karma's such a bitch, isn't she?

Chloe carefully removed the poster from the wall and thought of the many nights she'd lain beneath the canopy and touched herself fantasizing it was him, imagining what his guitar-callused fingers would feel like on her petal-soft skin. She thought of all the times he'd watched over her while her father was away on business yet again. He traveled and left her alone a lot. She was used to it.

It was time to throw away her schoolgirl fantasies. Chloe was all grown up now and real life adventures awaited her in the city. Secretly, she still wished that one day she would meet her rock-star crush. He'd fall hopelessly in love with her and she'd be the envy of every girl at school when they saw her face gracing the covers of magazines in the grocery store check-out line on the arm of Taylor Kerrigan.

She scoffed to herself. *Yeah, right. Like that could ever really happen.*

The sound of the squeaky hinges on the front door brought her back to her ordinary reality. "Chloe, are you about finished up there?"

"Yeah, Dad. Five minutes."

He sounded impatient. He was probably in a hurry to get her to the city so he could take off again and not feel so guilty about it.

Hmm. Keep him or toss him?

"Chloe, honey." Michael Bennett stepped inside his only child's bedroom. "I'm going to start taking these boxes down. I've got the U-Haul in the driveway."

She decided to keep him. What was the harm in wishing? Chloe rolled up the poster of the smoldering bad boy and snatched the bright-pink satin blanket from her bed. "I've got everything I need. I'm ready."

And she was. She was ready for whatever awaited her in the big beautiful city—for the people she'd meet, the new friends she'd make. For her real life to start.

They do say be careful what you wish for because you just might get it.

If only she had known.

Prologue

Fuck this.

His head was pounding. One hundred and twenty decibels pumping out of the amplifiers wasn't helping. Brendan gulped his whiskey down in one easy swallow and tossed the plastic cup into the trash. That probably wasn't helping either. Maybe he just needed to get away from the concert for a bit. Take a walk.

He glanced at his cousin who sat at the VIP table with him near the stage, then he got up from his seat. "I'll be back."

"Where you going?" Dillon shouted over the music, looking up at him with a perplexed tilt of his head. "You okay?"

"Yeah, man." He patted Dillon on the shoulder. "Just need some air to clear my head."

"Bren, we're sitting outside." He gestured around the table. "There's plenty of air," and he chuckled.

Brendan pointed toward the path that meandered through Coventry Park behind them. "I won't be too long."

"Whatever, man." Dillon shrugged with a smirk on his face, then his voice took on an Irish brogue. "Be mindful, the fair folk are about tonight."

Litha. Midsummer.

When they were young boys, their parents, aunts, and uncles often recounted Celtic folklore that had been passed down from one generation to the next. He smiled at the reminder of their fond childhood memories. Tonight was the eve of the summer solstice. A night for faeries, magic, and dreams of your true love—not that he actually believed any of that.

"Sure, Dill." Shaking his head, he left the blaring music behind him, walked past the commissary tent and Venery's bus, in the direction of the old oak trees along the path.

He just needed to let it all go for a few minutes. The tension. The worries. The load he carried. It was a weight Brendan took upon himself gladly. No one asked him to, but he felt responsible for them all. His family. And the shit coming down on them was his fault anyway. He should have listened to Taylor and Jesse the night they met that fucking viper. Why hadn't he?

'Did you love her or something?'

Brendan told Taylor he didn't, and that was true. Hell, most of the time he didn't even like her. He tried to once. He'd tried to love her or like her—to feel something for her. To feel anything at all. He felt nothing. He did like fucking her, though. And as it turned out, that was his first mistake.

He'd made a lot of fucking mistakes.

He'd think of a way to fix them.

His head was down, both hands stuffed in his pockets, as he walked the paved trail that wound through the century-old oaks at the back of the park. He inhaled a deep breath of city air, the first breaths of summer, and thought he should turn around and go back before Venery finished their set or Dillon came looking for him.

She ran smack dab into him the instant he turned around.

Hands clutched onto his shirt and his arms instinctively wrapped themselves around her so she wouldn't fall. She was probably average height—maybe five and a half feet. But next to him she was a little wisp of a thing. Her long hair gently fluttered in the breeze. The beautiful face of an angel looked up at him. Full lips. Flushed cheeks. Eyes a shade of blue he couldn't quite make out in the dark.

Her breathing was uncontrolled, ragged pants that passed through parted lips. Why was she running? Brendan gazed out along the path but he didn't see anything. They were alone. She wasn't in danger of falling anymore. He should let her go. But she wasn't letting go of him either. She still held onto his shirt, looking up at him with those enchanting eyes of hers.

A pink tongue peeked past her lips to wet them. Brendan didn't even stop to think about it. He lowered his head and brushed those lips with his. Her hands unclenched to rest flat on his pecs. He pressed her closer against him and softly took her mouth. Sweet spun sugar. Her hands slid up to his shoulders and he deepened the kiss, tracing her lips with his tongue.

Open up for me, sweet girl.

And she did.

His hands reached around her thighs as his tongue slipped inside and he lifted her up. She wrapped her legs around his waist, her arms around his neck. He inhaled deeply through his nose. Sunshine. White chocolate. Jasmine. She kissed him back with those full soft lips. His cock throbbed beneath his jeans in time to her sweet tongue dancing with his.

Her tits pressed into his chest. He could feel her nipples harden and wondered how they'd fit in his hands. How they'd feel between his teeth. He held her with one hand splayed between her shoulders and slid the other up her thigh, past her belly, to cup her breast over the cotton sundress she wore. He squeezed. She fit perfectly in his palm.

What the fuck was he doing, kissing some random girl in the middle of the park? And who the fuck was she letting him? But he kept on. She smelled so good, and she tasted so good, and she felt so good. He hadn't felt anything in a long, long time.

He should let her go.

Slowly, he lifted his lips from hers and lowered her back down. She smiled up at him, but never spoke a word. He kissed the crown of her head and watched her walk away from him for a moment before he turned to walk in the opposite direction. His dick ached. He rubbed it over the denim. He could hear the faint strains of Venery up ahead in the distance. He didn't even know her name. He should've asked her. Why didn't he ask her?

He turned around, but she was gone.

That night in his bed, he dreamt of a girl with long hair streaked in gold by the sun. It gently fluttered in the breeze. The beautiful face of an angel. Lips swollen from his kisses. Cheeks flushed pink. Her eyes were neither blue nor green, but the color of a stormy tropical sea. He asked her for her name, but she just smiled and turned away. She took the light with her.

Brendan sat up in the dark, alone in the middle of his big bed. For a moment he could have sworn he smelled the sweet scent of jasmine. He shook the cobwebs of the dream from his mind, laid back down, and closed his eyes.

Take the light with you, sweet girl.

I'm used to the darkness anyway.

Cast of Characters

In alphabetical order by first name

Aggie—owner of gift shop on Maple Street

Angelica—vamp (blood fetish) girl at masquerade ball

Ashton Michael Thomas Kerrigan Nolan—youngest child and son of Chloe, Jesse, and Taylor

Ava Liane Harris—Katie's college classmate and friend, babysitter

Axel—head of security for the Red Door

Becky Brinderman—Taylor's date to senior prom

Bethany—former high school sweetheart to Jesse

Elizabeth "Betsy" Bennett—mother to Michael, grandmother to Chloe

Billings—Kyan's friend from high school, now with the state attorney's office

Robert "Bo" Robertson Jr.—drummer of Venery

Brendan James Murray—eldest of the Byrne cousins, runs the Red Door/CPA, husband to Katie

Brigitta Thurner—wife/submissive to Hans, hostess at the Red Door

Brittany McCall—high school classmate of Chloe, former fiancée to Danny

Cameron Mayhew—Katie's college classmate/former boyfriend

Catherine Lucille Martin (*deceased*)—grandmother to Linnea

Chandan William Arthur Kerrigan Nolan—eldest child and son of Chloe, Jesse, and Taylor

Charles Alexander "Xander" Byrne—son of Dillon and Linnea, twin to Madison, brother to Charlotte

Charles Dillon Byrne—brother to Kyan, cousin to Brendan and Jesse, second husband to Linnea

Charles Patrick Byrne (*deceased*)—father to Dillon and Kyan, uncle to Brendan and Jesse

Charlotte Kyann Byrne—daughter of Kyan (*deceased*) and Linnea

Chloe Elizabeth Bennett Kerrigan Nolan—wife to Jesse and Taylor

Colleen Byrne Nolan O'Malley—mother to Jesse, sister to Charley and Mo, aunt to Brendan, Dillon, and Kyan, second wife to Tadhg

Courtney—Kit's ex-wife

Curtis "CJ" James—Venery's manager

Danielle Peters—photographer, wife to Monica

Danny Damiani—Chloe's high school classmate and former boyfriend

Declan Byrne (*deceased*)—father to Charley, Mo, and Colleen, grandfather to Brendan, Dillon, Jesse, and Kyan

Declan James Murray—son of Brendan and Katie

Andrew "Drew" Copeland—Katie's dad

Elliott Peters—son of Danielle and Monica

Eric Brantley (*deceased*)—son to Hugh Brantley

Gillian—bartender at the Red Door (resigned)

Gina Rossi—labor and delivery nurse, family owns Rossi's Pizza and Italian Bakery

Grace Martin (*deceased*)—mother to Linnea

Hailey—girl at warehouse accident

Hans Thurner—husband/Dominant to Brigitta, host/manager at the Red Door

Hazel—Tommy's mother, waitress at diner in Crossfield

Hugh Brantley—real estate investor

Ireland Aislinn Kerrigan Nolan—second-eldest child and daughter of Chloe, Jesse, and Taylor

James Murray (*deceased*)—father to Brendan, uncle to Dillon, Jesse, and Kyan

Pastor Jarrid Black (*deceased*)—father to Seth and Linnea

Jason—kitchen boy at Charley's

Jenkins—construction/warehouse project manager

Jesse Thomas Nolan—cousin to Brendan, Dillon, and Kyan, husband to Chloe and Taylor

Jonathan Reynolds (*deceased*)—childhood best friend to Seth

Kara Matthews—aunt to Katie and Kevin

Katelyn "Katie" Copeland Murray—wife to Brendan, barista at Beanie's/college student

Kelly Matthews—aunt to Katie and Kevin, owner of Beanie's

Kelsey Miller—girlfriend (former) to Dillon

Kevin Copeland—younger brother to Katie

Kim Matthews—aunt to Katie and Kevin

Christopher "Kit" King—bassist of Venery

Seth "Kodiak" Black—half-brother to Linnea

Kristie Matthews Copeland—Katie's mother

Kyan Patrick Byrne *(deceased)*—brother to Dillon, husband to Linnea, father to Charlotte, cousin to Brendan and Jesse

Leah Brianne Murray—daughter of Brendan and Katie

Leena Patel Kerrigan—mother to Taylor

Leonardo "Leo" Hill—baker/Kelly's assistant at Beanie's

Linnea Grace Martin Byrne—half-sister to Kodiak Black, widow to Kyan, wife to Dillon

London Elizabeth Kerrigan Nolan—3rd child and daughter of Chloe, Jesse, and Taylor

Lucifer—friend of Brendan's, devil-masked member at the Red Door

Madison Margaret Grace Byrne—daughter of Dillon and Linnea, twin to Xander, sister to Charlotte

Marcus—manager at Charley's

Matthew "Matt" McCready—rhythm guitarist of Venery

Michael Bennett—father to Chloe

Milo—Angelica's partner

Mitch Rollins—State Senator, member of the Red Door

Monica Peters—clinical psychologist, wife to Danielle

Margaret "Peggy" Byrne (*deceased*)—mother to Dillon and Kyan, aunt to Brendan and Jesse

Maureen "Mo" Byrne Murray (*deceased*)—mother to Brendan, sister to Charley and Colleen, aunt to Dillon, Jesse, and Kyan

Meaghan O'Malley (*deceased*)—first wife to Tadhg O'Malley

Murphy—Brendan's childhood friend, detective with the police department

Nick Rossi—second-eldest Rossi brother, same class as Jesse, family owns Rossi's Pizza and Italian Bakery

Payton Brantley—son to Eric and grandson to Hugh Brantley

Phil Beecham—Brendan's attorney

Roberta Torres—obstetrician

Roman—Jesse's Bernese mountain dog

Rourke—alias of arrested priest and former Red Door member

Roy Francis Martin (*deceased*)—grandfather to Linnea

Salena Dara (*deceased*)—former hostess at the Red Door

Shelley Tompkins—groupie who instigated "baby mama drama"

Siona Dawson (pronounced *Show-na*)—receptionist at O'Malley Ink Emporium, step-niece to Tadhg O'Malley

Sloan Michaels—lead vocalist/lyricist of Venery

Stacy—former girlfriend to Kelly Matthews

Tadhg O'Malley (pronounced *Tige*)—Colleen's second husband

Taylor Chandan Kerrigan—husband to Chloe and Jesse, lead guitarist of Venery

Thomas Nolan *(deceased)*—father to Jesse

Timo—Chloe's Bernese mountain dog (Roman's son)

Tommy—classmate of Linnea's, cook at diner in Crossfield

Anthony "Tony" Rossi—eldest Rossi brother, same class as Brendan/Venery, family owns Rossi's Pizza and Italian Bakery

William Arthur Kerrigan—father to Taylor

Made in the USA
Monee, IL
21 April 2023

31880025R00215